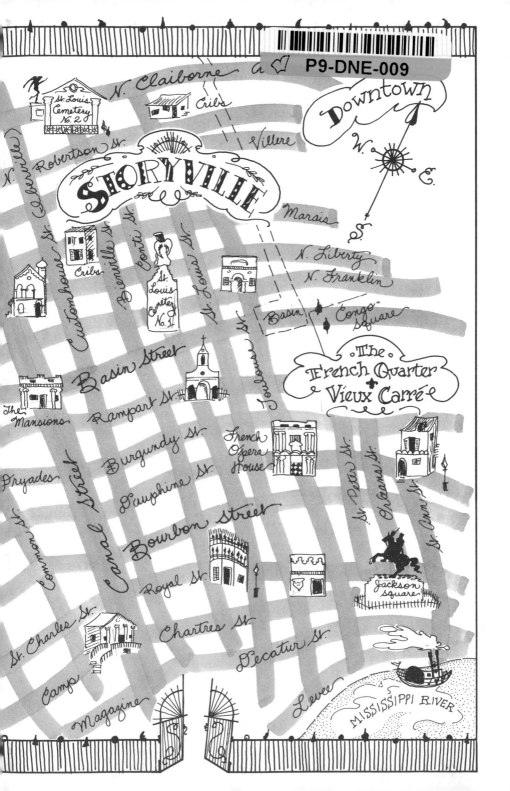

Storyville

Also by Lois Battle

✦

The Past Is Another Country
A Habit of the Blood
Southern Women
War Brides
Season of Change

Storyville

Lois Battle

Viking

VIKING
Published by the Penguin Group
Penguin Books USA Inc., 375 Hudson Street,
New York, New York 10014, U.S.A.
Penguin Books Ltd, 27 Wrights Lane, London W8 5TZ, England
Penguin Books Australia Ltd, Ringwood, Victoria, Australia
Penguin Books Canada Ltd, 10 Alcorn Avenue,
Toronto, Ontario, Canada M4V 3B2
Penguin Books (N.Z.) Ltd, 182–190 Wairau Road,
Auckland 10, New Zealand

Penguin Books Ltd, Registered Offices:
Harmondsworth, Middlesex, England

First published in 1993 by Viking Penguin,
a division of Penguin Books USA Inc.

Grateful acknowledgment is made for permission to reprint excerpts
from the following copyrighted works:
The Nineties, by Heywood Hale Broun. By permission of the
author.
"St. James Infirmary," by Joe Primrose. Copyright © 1929 by
Mills Music, Inc. Copyright renewed 1957. All rights reserved. Used
by permission.

ISBN 0-670-83867-5

Printed in the United States of America
Set in Garamond No. 3 · Designed by Francesca Belanger
Photograph by Bellocq from the collection of Lee Friedlander
Map by Virginia Norey

*To Ernest Bellocq, photographer,
through whose eyes I first saw
the girls and women
of Storyville.*

Acknowledgments

For their generous advice and support, I wish to thank
Hy Darer, Meg Ruley, District historian Al Rose and his wife,
Diana—and especially Gene Jones, a Lu'siana music lover
who's always tried to bring harmony to my life.

Storyville

1943

*H*e wasn't just a taxi driver, he told himself. He was a student of human nature. He'd invented a game, a kind of psychological solitaire, to make the day go faster. He sized up his fares, guessing age, profession, place of birth, and reason for being in the city, and by the time he dropped them off he'd verified his guesses. If he was on target he gave himself a dime, if he was off, he put the dime into the piggy bank stashed under the seat and gave it to his old lady on Saturday night. He never cheated because he didn't have to: nine out of ten times he collected. But this time his old lady might win. He couldn't get a handle on this one.

He'd noticed her right off at the train station. She was the kind of woman you noticed. Tall, dressed all in white, not much meat on her bones but a nice curve to her slacks, blondish hair piled high, bright red lipstick. She stood there like a queen bee while the crowd, mostly men in uniforms, swarmed around her. Not lost and not young. Mid-forties, he guessed, real sure of herself. Maybe one of those professional women, though she was too jazzy-looking for that, so maybe a former showgirl or a singer. As she followed the redcap who'd loaded her bags onto a cart to the taxi stand, he saw her slouchy, determined walk, as though she were coming off a country club golf course, and thought, No, not an entertainer, probably some navy officer's wife come to meet him while he was on leave. But when she reached into her purse for the tip, he saw age spots on her hands but no wedding ring, and her hair wasn't blond but chestnut streaked with silver, and there were lines around her eyes and mouth. Older than forties, but how old? It was always hard to guess when the dame had money, and despite the fact that the only jewelry she wore was a little gold heart that could've come from Woolworth's, he was sure she had money. She confirmed that by telling him, "The St. Charles Hotel," in a cigarette-ravaged voice that had just a trace of a New Orleans accent. But if she was a native, she'd been long gone. The tan and the slacks said Florida or maybe California. As he pulled out from the curb, a few drops of rain spattered the windshield, and he tried the usual opening gambit about the weather, but she wouldn't bite. He tried talking about the war—even the most taciturn passengers had something to say about the Japanese overrunning the Philippines—but she just said, "Yes, I've read the papers," so that put an end to that.

As they drove along, she glanced at the vacant lot on the corner and said, almost to herself, that there used to be a department store there. "Yes, ma'am," he jumped in. "That come down 'bout eleven years ago, back in thirty-two. Guess it's been a while since you've been in town?" She made a dismissive "Mmmm," and he knew he might jeopardize his tip if he persisted in trying to draw her out, so he shut up and checked her in the rearview mirror. She stared straight ahead, smoothing the back of her neck as though her hair were coming down, which it wasn't. It was a habitual, self-comforting gesture, but not in the least nervous. Looking at her big amber eyes he thought, Hell, we could be in a wreck and those eyes wouldn't blink.

They had almost reached the hotel when she leaned forward. "Driver, I've changed my mind. Take me by the Metairie Cemetery."

He made the turn and had driven about a half mile when she shook her head as though agreeing with an inner voice and said, "No. Take me to 1730 Poydras Street. Do you know where that is?"

Sure, he told her, he'd been born in the Quarter and knew every neighborhood in town. The one she'd mentioned had been fashionable at the turn of the century, but now most of the grand old mansions were falling down, nothing but trouble for the police and fire departments. "Some folks say those old houses are haunted," he told her.

The right side of her mouth turned up and she said, "I sometimes believe in reincarnation, but I don't believe in ghosts, or is it the other way round?"

They don't build 'em like that anymore, he thought as they reached the house. It took up the better part of a block, and unlike its neighbors, it had been newly painted and its tall columns and many windows fairly blazed in the sun. Freshly planted shrubbery and banks of flowers edged lawns that surrounded the circular drive.

"Shall I go up the drive, ma'am?"

She stared out the window and seemed not to hear him. He waited, then asked again, his voice almost lost in a clap of thunder.

"No," she told him, "just pull up to the curb."

As he did so, the skies opened as though the bottom had come out of a paper bag full of water. She rolled up the window, took out a gold case, and extracted a cigarette. He reached in his pocket for a lighter and turned around to face her. "Do you want one, too?" she asked, and when he told her "No thanks," she nudged the case close to his shoulder as though she knew he was just being polite. He took one, thinking, I'll bet she had a lotta men after her. Any woman who can tell that fast what you really want must've had a lotta men. He said thanks, and to his surprise, she leaned closer and lit his cigarette. A whiff of her perfume mingled with the smoke. He had never had a lady like her light his cigarette. A shower of hail tattooed the roof and he raised his voice.

"We get these rains 'most every afternoon this time of year. They come down hard, they drench you, then they're over before you know it."

"Like life," she said with the same half-smile.

He opened his mouth to speak, but she'd already forgotten him. She took a long drag on her cigarette, let her head loll on the seat back, and shut her eyes. After a while he turned off the motor.

She didn't have to look at the house to see it. It was all in her mind's eye as clearly as if it had been filmed, but she hadn't known until recently, when the early years of her life had started to come back unbidden, just how much of it she'd recorded— the winding staircase in the entrance hall, the fireplace big enough for a man to stand in, the fountain in the garden, the pink-veined marble bathroom with the massive tub and brass fixtures, the ballroom in which she'd never danced. And the hoards of treasure—all that furniture, well padded, ornate, just as the women had been—the silver and crystal, the paintings, clocks, tapestries, and statues. Julia had always said it was more a museum than a home, and now it was one. She was too far away to read the gold plaque near the front door, but she knew what it said because last month, when it had been put into place, Miss Ashburton had sent her a photo of it. "Museum of the Women of New Orleans," and below that, "Randsome House. Built in 1870." Ah, Julia, she thought, only you would appreciate the irony. And wouldn't you be shocked to know that I'm the one who helped you get the last laugh?

The tip of her nose tingled and water came to her eyes, but

she knew she wouldn't cry. The only thing that let her cry was music, and not the highbrow stuff, no *Tristan and Isolde* for her, but a good low-down blues would turn on her waterworks. She snuffed out the cigarette and raised her hand to stroke the back of her neck. The year before she'd come to New Orleans, when she'd turned fourteen, her mother had told her that it was time to pin up her hair. As a child she'd longed for that outward sign of womanhood, but when her mother had piled her hair high and secured it to the top of her head, she'd cried, knowing it wasn't just a change of style; it was the beginning of all the prohibitions. She would never be able to run in the woods again or go fishing or swimming with her brothers, and she must never let any man see her hair down or touch it until she was married. People would laugh at such things now. They'd say inhibition, silly Victorian morals. Yet there had been extraordinary sexual energy in the days when an exposed ankle could excite desire and a stray lock of hair was an invitation. Just being alone in a room with a man had caused a palpable tingling tension. After all, if you didn't pin your hair up, how could you really ever let it down? Years later, when she'd left New Orleans, and before it was even fashionable, she'd bobbed her hair in a daringly short, boyish cut. But it was never really her. Even now, when she was getting old and her hair was not as luxuriant as it had once been, she had to have it long. It had been her crowning glory. They'd all said so. Lawrence had said so.

The downpour stopped as suddenly as it had started, and she opened her eyes, rolled down the window, and breathed in the moist, heavy smells of honeysuckle, jasmine, clematis. She was about to tell the driver to go on to the hotel when a young woman came out of the front doors. She wore a tailored dress and had a kerchief on her dark, shoulder-length hair, and after looking up at the sky, she tucked an umbrella into a string bag full of books and came down the drive with a brisk, purposeful walk that reminded her of Julia. She leaned from the taxi window. "Miss Ashburton?"

"Why, yes." The young woman stepped closer, a quizzical look on her narrow face. "And you must be . . . ?"

"Mrs. Cavanaugh. Yes. But please call me Katherine."

"And please call me Abigail. What a surprise. It's a pleasure to finally meet you."

"I just swung by on my way to the hotel. Could I give you a lift?"

"I was about to walk to the streetcar."

"Do hop in. If you have the time, you might come by the hotel and have a cocktail with me."

"That would be delightful. That is, if you're not too tired."

"Not at all. You must be the one who's tired, what with all the preparations."

"I think I have everything under control," Abigail said as though she were a first sergeant reporting to the captain. "But one can't help but be nervous. Tomorrow's the big day. Oh, would you care to come in and see the house? The caterers were by this afternoon for the preliminary setup, so the dining room and the kitchen are rather chaotic."

"The luncheon tomorrow will be time enough. Do get in. Driver, the St. Charles, please."

So, he thought as he shifted the car into gear, her name is Katherine Cavanaugh, and she can shift gears pretty fast herself. The woman who'd just ordered him to the hotel in a society drawl and was now chatting about a ladies' luncheon didn't bear much resemblance to the one who'd lit his cigarette. He figured the small talk would soon be over and then he'd pick up some real clues, but to his disappointment it was the younger woman, encouraged by Katherine Cavanaugh's polite questions, who talked about herself. Abigail Ashburton was from Connecticut, but that was no big news. Her getup and her hurried walk had tipped him off that she was a Yankee even before she'd opened her mouth. She said she was a graduate of Smith College. Her grandmother, who was an old friend of one of the women on the society's board, had recommended her for the job, but until six months ago, when she'd come down to take charge of the restoration of the house and the establishment of the museum, she'd never been farther south than Richmond. She rambled on about her interest in antebellum architecture and Creole cuisine. They were getting closer to the hotel and he was about to give up hope of learning any more about Katherine Cavanaugh when, finally, Abigail tried to draw her out. But Mrs. Cavanaugh wasn't forthcoming about either her history or her geography. Asked about Mr. Cavanaugh, she said, deftly closing the door on the subject, "He's dead." After an appropriately regretful pause, Miss Ashburton asked how long it had been since she'd been in the city. A vague "Many years" was the reply.

"So you no longer have any family here?"

"I never had family here. I lived here in my youth, but only for a brief time."

"Oh. Since the women on the steering committee speak of you as the guiding force behind the museum, I'd just assumed you were a native."

"I've traveled so much that I don't consider myself a native to anything but my own skin. My interest in creating the museum is primarily because of Julia Randsome."

"So you knew her?" Mrs. Cavanaugh nodded. "Wasn't she a remarkable woman?" Miss Ashburton said. "It seems she was in the forefront of every reform movement of her time. And she knew so many fascinating people. Susan B. Anthony, Elizabeth Cady Stanton, Edith Wharton! But I suppose you know all that."

"Some of it."

"But reading her diaries, I get the impression that she was never really accepted in New Orleans society."

"No, she never was."

"I can understand what that's like, being an outsider down here, I mean." Apparently feeling that it would be inappropriate to discuss her difficulties, Abigail shifted to the more neutral role of tour guide. "I certainly hope you'll be here long enough for me to show you around, Mrs. Cavanaugh. It's such a fascinating city. Even after a long day at the Randsome house, I put on my walking shoes and wander all over the place. And I've learned so much. This street, for example"—she gestured out the window—"it used to be called Basin Street, but they changed the name to North Saratoga. You see, many years ago this part of town . . ." She lowered her voice.

The driver caught "red light" and "houses of ill repute" and smiled. There was no need to be coy about it. Everyone knew about Storyville, or "the District." Out-of-towners always wanted to hear about "the cradle of jazz," but some of them didn't realize that the sex business came before the music business and the hands that rocked the cradle belonged to saloonkeepers and madams. He earned fat tips by telling stories about Jelly Roll Morton, King Oliver, and Louis Armstrong, and if the passengers were men, he threw in anecdotes about Lulu White and Josie Arlington and other famous madams and watched them get nostalgic about the good old days. He got even bigger tips by directing them to the underground spots where commercial passion still bloomed, albeit in less grand and open style.

"So it was legal all those years, until the Department of the Navy shut it down in 1917," the Yankee babe was whispering like a school kid showing dirty pictures. But Katherine Cavanaugh's face was as blank as a poker player's at a predawn game. And that's when it hit him like a light going on above the head of a cartoon character, and he almost laughed out loud. Why hadn't he figured it out before? She wasn't an entertainer or a society lady or any officer's wife. She'd been "in the life."

"I feel so lucky that you came by this afternoon," Abigail Ashburton said. They sat at a corner table in the St. Charles supper club. It was after six, but a "tea dance" was still going on, though judging by the closeness of the couples swaying to the band's rendition of "I'll Be Seeing You," tea was not the drink of choice. Abigail herself was on her second martini and feeling its effects.

The waiter, who'd been hovering, stepped forward and asked if they'd like another round. Over Abigail's objections, Katherine told him they would and said they'd be going into the dining room as soon as they'd finished their drinks.

Abigail put her elbows on the table, cupped her chin in her hands, and stared at Katherine, who was tapping her long red nails in time to the music. "Please tell me what you remember about Julia," she begged. "Tell me what she was really like."

Katherine laced her fingers together and looked down at them. "I can't tell you much. I was very young when I knew her."

"Yes, you must've been very young." This was no idle compliment. Ever since she'd met her, Abigail had been trying to figure out how old Katherine Cavanaugh was, but the martinis kept scrambling her calculations. "And Julia's husband, did you know Charles Randsome, too?"

Katherine stared at her as though deciding whether or not to answer, but the band struck up "In the Mood" and the floor was suddenly crowded with jitterbugging couples. A sailor and a girl with peroxided hair were putting on a real show, and the other dancers fell back into a clapping semicircle. The girl wore a cheap blue-and-white-striped blouse and a bright red skirt, and as the sailor twirled her around, her skirts sailed out, exposing her legs above the tops of her stockings, and she tossed her head and bumped her hips with exhibitionistic zest. "They call them 'victory girls,' " Abigail said with a mixture of amusement and disdain. "They work in the local factories and they hang around the hotels and clubs, supporting the war effort with a rather free distribution of their charms."

Katherine smoothed the back of her neck. "If they had any sense, they'd be getting paid for it."

Abigail covered her shock with a laugh and raised her voice above the din, but it was no use. The music had reached a blaring crescendo, and the crowd was shouting "Hubba hubba!" and "Go, go, go," whistling and clapping to urge on the sailor and the blonde. The sailor grabbed her waist, lifted her off the floor, bounced her on one hip and then the other. The glimpse of her garters and panties brought whoops of delight and a chorus of wolf whistles. He set her on her feet, spun her out, lost her hand, caught it, reeled her back in, and dipped her to the floor in a back-bending kiss timed exactly to the final note. There was wild, foot-stomping applause. The bandleader tucked his baton under his arm, turned, and said, "How 'bout that!" into the mike while the girl, chest heaving to burst her buttons, wiped the sweat from the sailor's forehead and hugged him. "How 'bout that!" the bandleader asked again as they staggered from the floor. He waited for the applause to die, then said softly, "And now, in a more mellow tone, a ballad written by one of our most famous jazzmen of the early days. Louis Guérin, ladies and gentlemen, better known as Monkey, who, sad to say, died just a few weeks ago in Chicago. Here's Monkey's 'Your Eyes Have Told Me.' "

The waiter was placing their drinks on the table, but Katherine Cavanaugh was rising from her chair. Abigail looked up, expecting Katherine to excuse herself to go to the powder room, but Katherine was talking to the waiter. "I'm Mrs. Cavanaugh, in room . . . I seem to have forgotten the room number, but please put this on my bill." She gathered up her cigarette case and lighter. Her hand was not steady. "Abigail, I'll have to ask you to excuse me. The noise and . . ." She made a vague gesture. "I'm sorry, but I don't feel well. No, no," she went on when Abigail started to rise. "Don't get up—that is, unless you want to leave, in which case, I'll walk you to the lobby."

"I am sorry you're not feeling well. Let me come up to the room with you."

"No. I'm fine, really." She glanced over her shoulder, and her mouth shaped a welcoming smile. "I see a young man heading this way. I expect he's going to ask you to dance. Why don't you, the night's younger than I am."

Abigail couldn't help but feel rejected by this abrupt departure. "If you're sure you're all right," she began, and when she got a decisive nod, "Well, perhaps I will stay for one dance."

The chest pains that had seized her in the supper club had stopped soon after she'd come up to the room, and she'd thought with a calm, almost vicarious interest, Nothing serious, Kate old girl. You're not going to die tonight.

But Monkey was dead. She wondered why the news had hit her so hard, because when she thought of him, which was rarely, she assumed the booze, dope, and one-night stands had long since claimed him. The last time she'd heard him had been on a radio broadcast from the Chicagoland Music Festival at least ten years ago, when his fame had already peaked. She hoped he hadn't died poor. He would've hated that. He loved his gold watches and diamond rings and fancy cars almost as much as he loved his music, certainly more than he'd loved any woman.

She ordered whiskey and cigarettes and lay down on the bed. The noises from the hallway seemed intrusive, and she wished she were home in Key West. During the last years she'd slipped into a jealously guarded reclusiveness. She'd had a high wall built around her property, she seldom went out, and she wouldn't keep a live-in staff.

After her order was delivered, she took a long, hot bath, then stood before the mirror. The years when she would have snatched on a robe because she couldn't bear to see the changes in her once famous body were past. Now that she knew that no one but a masseuse and, ultimately, an undertaker would see her naked, she liked being au naturel.

A breeze billowed the curtains at the window near the bed. Dusk had fallen, illuminated by a faint moon and many streetlamps. She could smell the river and hear the distant strains of a Dixieland band. As she sat on the chair near the window and sipped her drink, a deep sense of calm came over her, so that even the noises from the hall—a door slamming, the rattle of the room service cart, a tipsy couple singing a love song—were as comforting as the sound of rain on a tin roof. How many nights had she sat, naked, behind a locked door, surrounded by strangers? The only difference was that now she wasn't waiting for a man. Images, snatches of conversation, even memories of smells began to float up—she saw the mermaid tattoo on Judas's bicep, heard Billy Shakespeare quote, "I would walk barefoot from here to Arabia for a touch of his nether lip," smelled Sophronia's cinnamon buns. And there was Mollie Q. and the Spider, and Banjo Annie, and . . .

She was still sitting there when the sun came up. She heard the soft thump of newspapers being set by the guests' doors, and the sound of a tired solo clarinet rose high into the cool dawn air.

CHAPTER

I

There are no secrets better kept than the secrets everybody guesses.

G. B. Shaw, *Mrs. Warren's Profession*

1898

*T*claim only one hour of the day as my own, Julia Randsome thought bitterly, but that hour I must have. It was her custom, between the hours of two and three, to put aside her always pressing obligations—committee meetings, household management, letter writing, visits to the sick and elderly—and retreat to the privacy of her room; but her mother-in-law, Carlotta, had insisted that they lunch together because she had something of the utmost importance to discuss. Julia glanced across the dining-room table to the clock on the mantel. A gold, recumbent Neptune, surrounded by nymphs, pointed his trident at the dial: fourteen minutes after two. They had now been at table for well over an hour, and Carlotta had mentioned nothing more important than the cut of Yvette Liscomb's latest evening dress. Julia understood that she was being punished but didn't know why.

She had cut short the meeting of the Widows and Orphans Fund and hurried back to the house on Poydras Street. Though she had lived in it and been its ostensible mistress for some twenty years, ever since Charles Randsome had brought her to the city as his bride, she still thought of it as "the house on Poydras Street," never as home. How could anyone consider a structure as massive as a museum, chockablock full of objects whose sole function was to impress, a home? This afternoon as her carriage had rounded the corner, the little park across the street had looked inviting, but she had never been one to put personal whims above obligations, however unpleasant.

Entering the hallway, she had removed her hat, gloves, and jacket and announced her presence in a voice she knew would carry. On her way to the dining room, she had paused at the French doors leading to the inner courtyard. The courtyard was the only part of the house she liked. Its airy colonnades and arches, reminiscent of Spanish architecture, were not only pleasing to the eye but practical in a tropical climate, and Julia put a high value on practicality. Moving to the dining room, she had seen Maggie, the new girl, arranging serving dishes on the sideboard. Julia had called, "Carlotta, I'm home," but Carlotta had not responded. Julia knew she could be heard because, through the partially opened door to the adjoining room, she could hear Carlotta talking to her parrot, Robespierre.

Several years ago Carlotta had claimed that the stairs were too much for her and, in violation of all propriety, had appropriated what had been a drawing room as her bedroom. She had furnished it with yellow silk draperies, gilt furniture and mirrors, paintings of gods and goddesses in various states of undress, and a huge low-slung bed that might have belonged to some Zola courtesan. The door was usually left ajar to facilitate eavesdropping. Once a great beauty of the Creole ruling class, Carlotta now boasted that she dressed only for the bishop and the opera. It was her habit, if such an undisciplined woman could be said to have habits, to get up around noon, at which time Marie, a mulatto maid almost as old as Carlotta herself, laced her into her stays, arranged her thinning hair, and helped her into one of her many dressing gowns. While taking coffee laced with brandy, Carlotta put on her jewels and powdered her face. Weather permitting, she took breakfast in the courtyard, then ambled back into her room. Though she was rarely ill, she had been known to receive guests while propped up in bed.

Julia ordered a pot of tea and asked that the mail be brought to her. She had hoped for a letter from Charles, who had gone abroad to inspect the family's shipping companies in London and Marseilles. Instead, amid the invitations, thank-you notes, and requests, there was a letter from their son, Lawrence. She supposed all couples hoped for an ideal child who would inherit the best of each parent, but in Lawrence that impossible wish seemed to have come true. Lawrence had Charles's looks and easy manner, but he'd inherited her idealism and sense of purpose. He could easily have adopted the leisurely life of other young men of his class and gone into the family business, but he had chosen to go to MIT and study engineering. He wrote often and at length—warm, intelligent letters about his studies and his future plans. This letter was full of concern for the Cuban *insurgentes* who had been fighting to throw off Spanish domination. It was Lawrence's nature to feel sympathy for the underdog, but, like most mothers, Julia was not so patriotic that the thought of impending war did not terrify her.

She had finished her second cup of tea and was rereading the letter when Marie shuffled out of Carlotta's room, carrying Robespierre on his perch. Though Marie's eyes were doleful and her mouth was shrunken where some teeth were missing, one could tell that she had once been a beautiful woman. After placing Robespierre's stand next to Carlotta's chair, she asked Julia to send Mr. Lawrence her regards and went off to the garden to smoke her pipe. Moments later Carlotta emerged, perfumed, powdered, coiffed, and feigning surprise at having kept Julia waiting. She chatted, first to Robespierre, then to Julia. She complained about the turtle soup and the weather. She discussed various women's wardrobes in exhaustive detail. She asked Julia to read her Lawrence's letter but lost interest halfway through.

Nineteen minutes after two. As Julia watched the minute hand tick down, the pain behind her left eye intensified. She looked across the table and felt an almost physical revulsion. Carlotta, pearls dangling, one cuff stained by the soup, was stripping a morsel of jellied hare from the bone and offering it to Robespierre, who rejected it with a horrible squawk. "I claim only one hour of the day as my own," Julia began, giving voice to her thought, "but that hour . . ."

"Why, surely, dear Julia. I hadn't realized. It's past your nap time."

"I don't nap." She daydreamed. She wrote. She escaped.

"Whatever it is you do, please feel free to do it. How can a woman get through life if she doesn't please herself?" Carlotta said in a purposefully sugary voice and, seeing Julia about to rise, asked, "And what do we have for dessert?"

Manners kept Julia on her chair. "I believe there's some pear tart left from last evening's supper."

"You and your leftovers! One would think we were paupers." Carlotta had not acknowledged Maggie with so much as a thank-you throughout the meal, but now her eyes twinkled seductively in their network of wrinkles. "I'll bet this little girl has a sweet tooth, now, don't you? Of course you do. You may have the tart. Just bring us a bowl of fruit."

The girl's eyes were respectfully downcast as she removed the plates, but Julia knew Maggie had taken in the tug-of-war, would think her a cheapskate, and would gossip about her in the kitchen. Carlotta made no attempt to control her behavior with the servants. She yelled at them and had even been known to hit them, but, like a bad parent, she alternated abuse with indulgence, overlooking their slovenliness, giving them presents, letting them wander from the house. Much to Julia's chagrin, her own evenhanded dignity failed to secure their loyalty. Worse, her ten-year-old daughter, Angelique, had started to imitate Carlotta's high-handed ways. Undermining Julia's authority was as typical of Carlotta as financial extravagance, tippling in the afternoons, and being in a constant state of semidress, but pointing out these indiscretions, however subtly, was useless. They were Carlotta's "little ways." Once, driven beyond endurance, Julia had allowed her disgust and anger to overflow. Carlotta, with the utmost condescension, had said that being great-great-granddaughter of the marquis Pierre de Vaudreuil, the governor who had introduced the lavish style of the French court to the colony, she did not propose to have the daughter of a Yankee who made pots and pans tell her how to live.

In a voice that was sharper than she'd intended, Julia repeated the order to bring a bowl of fruit, then softened her tone to add, "If you will, Maggie." She folded her napkin, laced her fingers together, and looked at Robespierre, who returned her gaze with a dull, malevolent eye. She stared back, implacable. Her own notions of correct conduct had also been bred in the bone. Her family, the Ridgeways, had a place in Boston society that was at least comparable to that of the Landrommes in New Orleans. The Ridgeways traced their ancestry to yeoman farmers who'd fought in the Revolutionary War, men and women who despised titles, inherited wealth, papists—anything that smacked of the Old World order. Over the course of time they had acquired great stretches of Massachusetts farmland, but when her grandfather had patented a cherry pitter, they'd abandoned farming for commerce. By midcentury they owned two textile mills and an iron foundry that manufactured the cherry pitter, other kitchen utensils, and stoves. Shortly before the Civil War, when Julia was just an infant, her father, Joshua, had converted the foundry to the manufacture of cannon. Social conscience (the Ridgeways were fierce abolitionists) had united with business interest to create phenomenal profits, so much so that the doors of society from Newport to Philadelphia had been opened to them. The Ridgeways had not deigned to enter. Their wealth was Providence's reward for right thinking and hard work; displaying or squandering it was, if not sinful, at least bad form. Joshua had gone into politics—not, as Carlotta's ancestors had done, so that he could get his hands on the public purse, but out of a sense of civic responsibility. Her mother, Emily, was known for her good works, literary teas, and leadership in the National Woman Suffrage Association. In her youth Emily had been bold enough to wear the scandalous pantaloons and loose coat of the Bloomer costume. She held the radical belief that stays were harmful to the female reproductive organs and did not wear them until she was past childbearing age. Emily was friends with Susan B. Anthony and Elizabeth Cady Stanton. When the Ridgeways entertained, conversation and debate replaced the more frivolous pleasures of dancing and drinking. Their table was set with inherited plate and silver, but the fare was simple, and except for holidays, second helpings were not offered. Guests were given a glass of decent after-dinner port, but the Ridgeways would never have thought of housing a wine cellar.

It was, Julia believed, this simple style of living, progressive thinking, and independence that had attracted Charles to her. He had told her soon after they'd met that he was disgusted with debutante balls and marriage-minded mothers who displayed their daughters as though they were in a marketplace. He was coolly resistant to coyness and coquetry (after having met Carlotta, Julia understood why), but he'd been bold enough to tell her, the first time they were alone, that he admired the line of her cheek and (she still warmed at the thought of it) the turn of her ankle. After a mere month of courtship, he'd proposed.

Her father was against the match. To Joshua, all Southerners were suspect, Southern aristocrats doubly so. Aristocrats were people with abominable habits who didn't pay their bills on time. Emily liked Charles personally but feared that Julia could no more survive transplantation to New Orleans society than a lily of the valley could thrive in a tropical climate. But true to her principles, she'd said that the choice was Julia's. At the time Julia had felt that she was making the decision. In retrospect she understood that choice had nothing to do with it.

At twenty-five she'd had her share of proposals, mostly from friends of the family, progressive men who echoed her stated ideal of a partnership based on mutual respect and shared beliefs, men who would willingly expunge the word *obey* from the woman's usual marriage vow. But in her secret heart she longed for a passionate love, an ecstatic union of spirit and flesh, such as Elizabeth Barrett and Robert Browning had known. She knew great loves existed only in literature and the imagination, so she'd already accepted the fact that she might never marry. Then she'd met Charles Randsome. No man had ever evoked such a powerful physical response in her. When she was with him, she was so acutely aware of his hands, his mouth, his thick dark hair, the forthright but seductive look in his eyes, that she often lost her thought in midsentence. Away from him, it was even worse. She remembered his deep, softly accented voice, the relaxed, confident way he held his body. But it wasn't just his looks, she told herself. He was fine in every way. He was intelligent, serious-minded, compassionate. He listened to her with undivided attention, discussing the most important topics without ever losing that gleam in his eyes. Where she was stiff and shy, he was easygoing and charming. Life, everything about him seemed to say, was a serious business, but it was also full of fun, surprises, pleasures great and small. The first time he'd kissed her, she'd known what one of life's greatest pleasures might be. She would have followed him anywhere.

But her mother had been right. She had never adjusted to the corrupt and indulgent society of which her marriage had made her a part. Her relations with Carlotta were as chafing as an unseen and incurable rash. But Charles had not disappointed her. He had proved to be both friend and confidant and a robust and gentle lover. She was one of the few women she knew who had a marriage that was passionate and totally honest. Duty alone would never have kept her in this house. No doubt her present irritability and her persistent headaches were caused by his absence. How she missed him! Thinking of him, she softened and made another try.

"*Maman,*" she began, but this affectionate term of address drew up her mouth like the taste of vinegar. "Carlotta," she amended, "you said you had something important to discuss."

"Did I?" Carlotta studied the stain on her cuff, then put her chin in her hand and studied Julia. Since she'd never felt the need to analyze or hide her dislikes, her antipathy for her daughter-in-law was even more virulent than Julia's for her. How she despised that humorless Yankee earnestness! She had known even before she'd met Julia that the marriage was a mistake.

Shortly before Charles's twenty-ninth birthday, Carlotta had begun a serious search for the right girl. For over a decade Charles had enjoyed the sexual prerogatives of any healthy male of his class; indeed, she would have taken it amiss if her only son had not been something of a rake. Naturally, most of his liaisons had been with women of a lower order, though gossip had it that he'd managed to seduce a few younger matrons of their own set, but since he was almost thirty, it was time for him to settle down and produce an heir. Carlotta had encouraged the choice of

Yvette Damille, and it had seemed that Charles was on the verge
of accepting her advice when he'd taken a trip north. He'd met
the Ridgeways through an associate in the shipping business and
had sent a photo of himself with Miss Julia Ridgeway. Carlotta
had never expected trouble from that quarter, Julia being far
from any popular standard of beauty. She was almost as tall as
Charles, with dark hair drawn back severely and a challenging
look in her eye. Her figure, dressed in one of the new tennis
costumes, looked boyishly angular. Two weeks later Charles
wrote that he had fallen in love with Julia, with whom he shared
"a life of the mind." Though quick-witted, Charles was by no
means an intellectual, so Carlotta supposed that the Ridgeways
were even richer than reported and that Julia's father had made
a generous offer. She had no objection to marriages based on
money. Love, as she'd discovered over the course of three marriages and several affairs, was at best ephemeral; assets were
tangible. But there were girls from better families, who had both
fortunes and beauty, closer to home, and Charles had the pick
of the crop. She'd written as much and had received an aston-
ishing reply: arranged marriages were a thing of the past, money
was not a consideration—indeed, a lawyer was drafting docu-
ments that would allow Julia some control over her inheritance.
He had already proposed and been accepted. Carlotta wrote back
that, owing to ill health, she would not be able to attend the
wedding. That Charles, who usually honored her wishes, had
gone against her in so crucial a matter both enraged and humil-
iated her, because she had already told the Damille family that
a match was all but guaranteed.

The battle lines were drawn at her first meeting with Julia. The
couple had forgone the usual European honeymoon to go hiking
in the Adirondacks. Julia had forwarded her trunks, and Carlotta
had succeeded in picking the locks. Three trunks contained expensive but dowdy clothes, two were packed with books. She

also found a packet of love letters that had nothing to do with "a life of the mind"—in fact, they were so full of erotic yearning that she supposed the athletic Julia would, at least for a year or so, have ample exercise in bed. She understood the to-each-his-own peculiarities of sex—some men liked them dark, some plump, some liked to tie them to the bedpost. Apparently Charles was so jaded that only the conquest of an overeducated near spinster could whet his appetite.

During their first conversation, after Charles had carried a flustered Julia over the threshold, Julia had asked what organizations might best benefit from her services. The Randsomes, Carlotta informed her, sometimes donated buildings to the city, but they had never been, and never would be, part of any do-good organizations. Charles, seemingly oblivious of the friction, patted Julia's hand and said perhaps all that should change. Julia smiled. But later, when she came downstairs for supper, her mouth was set in a tight expression that over the years had etched a permanent parenthesis of disapproval on either side. Julia had made no more than a passing remark about one of the trunk's locks having been broken in transit, but Carlotta understood that despite her pains to leave everything as she'd found it, Julia knew she'd been into her things.

"You were saying?" Julia prompted when Maggie left the room.

"Ah yes, I was thinking that since Charles has been away and we've missed so much of the season, it would be fun to give him a really fine welcoming-home party."

"Charles doesn't mind missing the season."

"You mean *you* don't mind. Ever since he was a child, Charles loved it. When he was no more'n six or seven, he had a little devil costume for the Mardi Gras, an' he was a fine little devil." Carlotta chuckled, then added, "I thought we could open up the ballroom. Angelique would love it."

"I hardly think so," Julia said. The ballroom had been closed for years. Reopening and renovating it would require a tremendous expenditure of money and energy, mostly hers, and Angelique was far too young to attend adult parties. Besides, she had already planned that they would avoid society, at least for a week or so, when Charles returned.

The clock struck the half hour. Julia put both palms against the edge of the table and pushed back her chair. "We can discuss it some other time. Just now, if you'll excuse me, I have to write a letter."

She had almost reached the door when Carlotta said, "Are you going to write to the city council? I've heard that one of your women's groups is planning to protest the new ruling about the District." Her voice was so low that Julia knew instantly this was the topic Carlotta wanted to discuss. Though no one in the state, let alone the city, was unaware of the District, respectable women generally pretended that it did not exist. This pose of ignorance had become more difficult to maintain since City Alderman Sidney Story had proposed an ordinance to legalize it.

Without turning, Julia said, "That's right. Now, if you'll excuse me . . ."

"I must say, Julia, that I don't think that would be wise."

"I see no reason," Julia said, her eyes focused on the clock, "why we should be the only city in the nation to legalize"—she wanted to say "vice," but plain speaking was best, even when it caused embarrassment—"prostitution."

Carlotta played with her pearls and sucked in her cheeks. "It doesn't actually legalize it. It merely confines such women to a segregated district."

"You are speaking with Jesuitical casuistry."

"If you don't speak more plainly, I don't see how anyone can know what you mean."

"I mean," Julia said evenly, "that you are twisting the argument in order to hide the truth. Whatever the legal convolutions of the ruling, the effect will be to legalize prostitution. Why should we be the only city in the nation to parade our shame?"

Carlotta sighed. "My dear Julia, there have been women like that since the beginning of time."

Julia turned. "Or certainly since the beginning of this city."

"In any port city . . ."

"I am not aware of the existence of such establishments in Boston."

Carlotta's laugh was throaty. "If such places exist in Boston— and I'm sure they do—you must admit that you'd be the last to be aware of them."

"I am not a stranger to human misery. I have seen—"

"Yes, yes. I'm sure you have." Carlotta knew Julia's work for the Widows and Orphans Fund had taken her into neighborhoods that would make the flesh crawl, and it was genuinely beyond her imagination to understand why anyone would voluntarily expose herself to such unpleasantness. "But you shouldn't assume that inhabitants of the District are all miserable. Some of those houses are quite opulent, I hear. They have Mardi Gras parties that put ours to shame." Was Julia so abysmally naive that she didn't know that men who dined in this very room frequented the better houses?

"The shame is that we should even consider legalizing such places. If there were a woman on the city council—"

"A woman on the city council! Any woman who'd want to be on the city council should have her head examined. I hear their meetings are very dull, and they have no real power."

"Apparently they have enough power to adopt this ordinance." Julia's head was pounding. Why was she bothering to argue? And with Carlotta of all people?

Carlotta sighed. "Julia, Julia, people were arguing about this a hundred years ago, and they'll be arguing about it a hundred years from now. Anyone who can't accept that simply doesn't understand human nature."

"It isn't human nature. It's the nature of dissolute, indulgent men who prey on girls who . . ." She couldn't complete the sentence, for though she'd given considerable thought to the matter, understanding such women was beyond her. She believed that women had, by nature, a finer sensibility, that once they'd gained their rights, they would uplift the morality of the entire nation. How could any woman be so debased that she could perform the most intimate act with a total stranger? "Saying that we shouldn't try to put a stop to it is like saying that doctors shouldn't seek a cure for cholera or diphtheria. Human nature is always the argument of those who want to excuse society's evils." As Maggie came in with the fruit, Julia said what she hoped would be the last word: "I've promised to draft the petition, and I will honor my promise," and again turned to leave.

"Only a fool like your friend Alcesta Davenport would associate herself with such a position."

Julia reached out to the mantelpiece to steady herself and told Maggie to leave. Now she understood: Carlotta knew about the petition because yesterday, when Alcesta had come to tea, she had spied on them. Julia's mind raced back to the conversation. Surely Carlotta couldn't have heard Alcesta's more intimate disclosures, because when Alcesta had started to sob and said that they must not only overturn the city council ruling, but close down the District, Julia had gotten up, closed the door, and lowered her voice to a whisper, encouraging Alcesta to do the same.

But Alcesta had been oblivious. "We must shut down the District!" she'd insisted, hitting the table so hard that the teacups had rattled. "Please promise me, Julia. Promise that you'll help me."

Still trying to calm her, Julia had whispered, "Of course."

She was shocked and embarrassed by the outburst. In all the years they'd known one another, Alcesta had never displayed emotion unless she was talking about God and the afterlife. She pitied Alcesta's poor health and childless state and appreciated her work with charitable committees, but she found it very taxing to be in her company. Alcesta alternated between agonized rigidity and fluttering nervousness; her features, though potentially pretty, were drained of attractiveness by her morbid inner life; in conversation her eyes seldom made contact but darted about, then fixed disapprovingly on various objects, so that one turned, trying to discover what she found unpleasant about a painting or a flower arrangement. On the other hand, Julia liked Alcesta's husband, Abraham Davenport, more than any man in their set. Like her, he was an outsider, a Kentuckian who'd gone west as a young man to work on the railroads. Now he owned a railroad, but the rough-hewn mountain boy still showed through. He drank hard and had a booming voice. His clothes were from the best tailor but never seemed to fit. He was easy with men but acutely self-conscious with women. He had no talent for polite conversation, and flirtatiousness undid him completely—she had once seen him spill wine on his vest when Yvette Damille Liscomb had leaned toward him offering her dimpled smile and risky décolletage. The other reason Julia liked him was all too human: she knew that he liked her. At parties he would often draw her aside to talk, and upon occasion he sent her books he thought she might enjoy. So when Alcesta had sobbed, "You don't understand. Prostitution has ruined my life," then cried, "Abraham, oh, Abraham!" with a hateful vehemence, Julia had not wanted to hear any more.

In an attempt to end the conversation, she'd promised to draft a petition, but Alcesta's confession had come as freely as her tears. "I didn't know about it when I married him. How could I? What good woman would know about such things?" Alcesta had demanded. "But those who do know can tell just by looking at him. Haven't you noticed the way he covers his mouth when he laughs? Haven't you noticed his teeth?"

Julia had bowed her head. The grayish color of Abraham's teeth was as obvious as his bowed legs.

"And do you know what that's from?" Alcesta rushed on. "Of course you don't. But I can tell you. It's from a mercury treatment that was supposed to have cured the infection he contracted when he was a young man. But of course it didn't work. As soon as I married him, my health began to fail. But it wasn't until I'd had my second miscarriage that the doctor told me that I was infected. Can you imagine my humiliation, having a doctor tell me that! I wanted to die. I have never shared Abraham's bed since the day I found out. I tell you," she said in a strangulated voice, "it is only my belief that God will finally judge him that has kept me going."

Julia could think of nothing to say. She sank beside Alcesta's chair and put her arms around her. "I'm so sorry, Alcesta. So terribly sorry."

Alcesta pushed her away and stood up. Her tears stopped as abruptly as they had started. She smoothed her skirts, pulled on her gloves, and said, "Don't bother to get up. I'll show myself out." At the door she turned and, before lowering the veil of her hat, glanced back at Julia. Her red-rimmed eyes pleaded, "Don't tell," then hardened into a look of accusation, so that Julia knew Alcesta not only regretted the confession, but somehow blamed her for it.

"Alcesta . . ." she began. But Alcesta was already out the door.

Julia got up and stared at the tea table, desperately wishing that Charles was home so that she could talk to him. Could she tell Charles without betraying Alcesta's trust? But what if Charles already knew? Did men tell each other such things? As for Abraham . . . She couldn't help it, her fondness for him was now tinged with disgust, just as her feelings toward Alcesta were now colored with compassion and—who could forget that parting look?—apprehension.

Robespierre squawked, and Julia recovered herself. "Alcesta was not well yesterday," was all she could get out.

"Oh, that woman," Carlotta said dismissively, examining a bunch of grapes. "She's always sickly."

Relieved that Carlotta seemed not to have overheard the worst of the conversation, Julia said, almost to herself, "If Charles were here, I'm sure he'd agree with the petition."

"Do you suppose the city council took this action, or would take any action, without Charles knowing and approving?"

The truth of the statement hit Julia as swiftly as a dart. Though Charles teased that he left all civic responsibilities to her, nothing important took place in the city without his advice and consent. But it was impossible to think that he'd approve of . . .

"The ordinance," Carlotta told her as patiently as if she were talking to a child, "will stabilize property values in the District."

"That's no concern of mine."

"Oh, but it is. You must know that we own a good deal of property in the District." She tossed off the remark, popping a grape into her mouth, but her eyes glittered with satisfaction as she watched Julia trying to control her reaction. "That information will undoubtedly come out if you insist on this silly petition. People will think you either ill-informed or hypocritical." She spat the grape pits into a silver salver. Robespierre shrieked and fluttered his wings.

Julia wanted to grab the bird and throttle him. "If we have property in the District, then we must dispose of it."

"You'd best wait until Charles comes home to discuss it with him." Though Charles still went to great pains to please Julia, Carlotta was sure that he wouldn't bend to her wishes in this.

The District properties were among the family's most lucrative investments, and since the tenants were hardly in a position to complain or to move, rents could be raised without any obligation to maintain, let alone improve, the houses. "But I've kept you from your nap. I do apologize, my dear. I'm sure you'll reconsider all of this. Turn it over in your mind while you're resting." With that, Carlotta turned her attention to Robespierre, who bent his head to take a grape from her outstretched palm.

As she strode past the French doors, Julia looked out into the courtyard. Marie and her daughter, Sophronia, who often came to visit, sat under the oleander while Angelique, dressed in one of Carlotta's cast-off gowns, minced around the fountain, carrying the cat, Boodles, in her arms. Boodles, trussed in a doll dress and bonnet, struggled to free herself. "Angelique! Why aren't you upstairs doing your lessons with Miss Branioner?"

"I have a fever, Mama," Angelique whined. "I'm too sick to do lessons."

"If you're sick, you should be resting," Julia reasoned irritably.

"It's too hot in the schoolroom."

"It is awful hot up there," Marie said.

"Since it's so hot, imagine how Boodles feels with a dress on top of her fur coat. Take it off her immediately. Then go up and see to your lessons."

A flicker of resentment sharpened Angelique's face before she arranged it into the sweetly compliant expression that was Carlotta's stock-in-trade. "If you say so, Mama." Still, she didn't move. Julia, ready to scream with frustration, hurried to the stairs.

In her bedroom she paced between bed and dresser, unbuttoning her blouse and throwing it onto the bed. Needles of pain made her left eye twitch. She raised her fists to her forehead, squeezed her eyes shut, and achieved a moment of complete denial. Charles would never have approved of the ordinance; certainly he would never accept profits even remotely connected with vice. And yet . . . what did she really know about their property holdings? No more than Angelique would know. That Charles's father had made a great deal of money during the Civil War by smuggling quinine through the Union blockade, that he'd bought several houses, that their rental made up a good part of the family income. Why had Charles never discussed it with her? More important, why had she never asked? She felt childish and stupid, yet somehow betrayed. Surely Charles must know everything about the disposition of their properties. Though he affected a gentlemanly disregard of business, he had such a keen eye that he picked up minor errors in her household accounts. She had met the agent who managed their properties once or twice, but she could hardly go to him for information. She must write to Charles and demand the truth. She sat down at her desk, uncorked the inkwell, dipped the pen, almost began with her usual "Dearest Husband," then amended it to "Dear Charles," before realizing that the letter would have no chance of reaching him before he sailed from Marseilles to London. And how could she address such a problem in a letter? As she stood up, she brushed a recent letter from her mother, Emily, onto the floor. Picking it up, she caught sight of the final line: "I now accept that I shall not live long enough to see the vote, or any other great changes in the lives of women."

But Julia would see changes. She would help to bring them about. She would write the petition. She had promised to do so, and she always honored her promises. She remembered Alcesta's brimming eyes and Carlotta's smug smile, and she caught the reflection of her own face, flushed, eyes narrowed with pain, in the mirror.

Stepping out of her skirt, she went to the window. The garden looked overgrown, and the cloying smell of tea olive and honeysuckle was suffocating. How was it possible to think clearly in such a climate? She closed her eyes again, imagining the landscape of her childhood—pristine blue-gray skies, trees stripped to the essential beauty of bare limbs, air so bracing that it stimulated both body and mind. She went into the bathroom, splashed her face with tepid water, blotted it, and turned toward the door to Charles's bedroom.

When she'd first come to the house on Poydras Street, she'd disliked the idea of separate bedrooms, but over the years she'd come to see the wisdom of it. Most often she and Charles slept in her room, but when one of them was sick or when Charles had a late night out with his men friends and didn't want to disturb her, they slept in separate beds. And when Charles was in an amorous mood, they played a sort of game. He would go into his own room, wait until she was in bed, then knock on her door. "Yes?" she would say, but there was never a question in her voice. And he would, without question, say "Yes" when she asked him to dispose of these properties in the District. Because he hadn't chosen them, he had merely inherited them, just as, inevitably, he'd inherited a few of Carlotta's characteristics. He would dispose of the properties. He was an honorable man, and he loved her.

She went into his room, touched the brandy decanter, the humidor, picked up one of his brushes and sniffed the hair tonic and perspiration. Her eyes fell on a photograph he'd begged from Emily shortly after they'd met. He'd always said it was his favorite because it showed the face of the girl he'd fallen in love with, though she was only eleven when it had been taken. In it she stood near a snowbank, one gloved hand holding the rope to the sled she'd been given that Christmas morning, so bundled against the cold as to appear chunky, and flashing a smile more broadly confident than was her wont even as a child because, finally, she'd managed to sled down the hill without a spill. She'd come atumble on her first tries. Her mother had scolded her brother for laughing at her, but no one had helped her out of the snowbank. In voices that insisted pluck could overcome any obstacle, her parents had told her to keep on trying, and try she had, until her face stung and her nose ran, and she'd fought back tears. But she had conquered the hill.

Now she remembered something that had happened later that Christmas Day. She had gone into the woods with her cousins and, hearing the sound of a rushing stream, had wandered off from them. After a time she could no longer hear their voices, and looking around, she'd realized that she was lost in the gathering dark. She'd called but no one had come. She'd run through the trees, and the trees had all looked the same. She had no recollection of who finally had found her, but she had the same panicky realization now that she'd had then: that no amount of pluck or perseverance or cheerfulness could save her.

CHAPTER

II

The New Orleans red-light district, "Storyville," in the period from 1898 through 1917, was unique among them all in being the only one that was legally established.

Al Rose, *Storyville, New Orleans*

*O*ld William Truhame, better known as Billy Shakespeare, stirred into wakefulness as the first light came through the French doors and fell onto the strip of grimy carpet. Half registering the familiar sound of teacup rattling against saucer, he chased a dream in which he'd been brandishing a sword and shielding a girl from a band of bullies, then reached to the foot of the bed for the purple velvet cape that served as his dressing gown. For the stiff price of a dollar fifty a week he'd persuaded his landlady to bring up his morning tea. It was a luxury he could ill afford, but he'd decided years ago that little luxuries made it possible to overlook the fact that he lacked the necessities. He opened the door, muttered "Thank you" without looking the landlady in the eye, and quickly closed it. The last thing he wanted in the morning was conversation.

He carried the tray to the dusty bedside table and wrapped his hands around the pot, partly to warm them, partly in ritual blessing. "How often I feel how hard it is to live up to my blue china," Oscar Wilde once said. Hearing the quote, Billy had bought this set for six, also blue. He'd carried it with him through the hotels and boardinghouses of at least sixteen states. Only the pot with the chipped spout and a single cup and saucer remained, but that was all he needed now. He lit a cigar, coughed, and wheezed. The sulfurous smell of the match, the first hit of nicotine, and the initial scalding sip of Mandarin tea—another luxury he couldn't afford—caused his dream to flow back. He saw the girl's breast through her torn dress, felt his panic as the attackers advanced, and . . . his sword turned into a flower stalk. Impotent, even in dreams!

With an unconsciously regal gesture, he tossed the cape over his shoulder, went to the French doors, tried the handle, cursed when it wouldn't give, and with gestures that were anything but regal, shoved his cigar between his teeth, planted one foot against the base of the swollen wood, flattened his palm high on the jamb, and gave it a violent jerk. Recovering himself, he retrieved his cup of tea and stepped out onto the little balcony. By standing at its extreme right corner, he could see, above the rooftops of the French Quarter, that great brown aorta, the Mississippi. Against the still-dark sky, it seemed as incapable of pumping life into the city as his own heart was of pumping blood into his cold hands and feet.

He pulled a handkerchief from the cuff of his nightshirt, honked his nose, and muttered, "Holy Mother!" That had always been a favorite exclamation, but recently it had brought memories of his own mother to mind. She was long since dead, he supposed. A few years after he'd run away from their Kansas farm to join a troupe of actors, he'd sent her a glowing review from a Philadelphia paper, the address of the St. Louis theater in which he was scheduled to appear, and a twenty-dollar bill. But he'd never made it to St. Louis, and he'd never again had the extra twenty dollars with which to demonstrate his success, so he'd blocked all thoughts of her. But lately, when he was going to sleep or waking up, she'd been an almost palpable presence. Wouldn't she be surprised that he, who'd been a slugabed child and had turned night into day for most of his adult life, now got up with the dawn? He took another sip of tea and blew his nose again. The New Orleans climate tortured his sinuses, but in most other respects the Crescent City suited him fine. Some ten years ago (when he'd still had to glue on a white beard to play Polonius), the company manager had nicked off with the box office receipts and left the company stranded, so Billy had taken stock of his fallen arches and ambitions and decided that New Orleans was a better place than most to settle down. It was the most European of American cities, fond of the gallant gesture and all indulgences of the flesh, with a live-and-let-live ambiance that was kind, or at least indifferent, to adventurers and drifters. It patronized the arts; the architecture was graceful; the food was the best in the country; and the Versailles Hotel, where he'd found employment as a desk clerk, satisfied his need for drama—if not as actor, then as spectator.

As he leaned against the railing, the "Get thee to a nunnery" speech from *Hamlet* came into his head. It pleased him that his memory, so frayed that he had to look at a calendar to remind himself what day it was, had delivered the speech in its entirety. It, like his dream, must have been triggered by that girl, Kate. He was sure to see her today. Hunger or desperation would surely drive her down from the rooms at the Versailles where Frank Staughton had left her. Anticipating that scene, he drained the teacup and padded back into the room to begin his toilette.

He pulled off the velvet cape and poured water from the pitcher into the washbowl, shivering as he rinsed his face and made a soapy pass at his armpits, then threw the scummy water into the street. Back at the bureau, he brought his face close to the pitted mirror and patted it with rosewater, then combed his beard, waxed his mustache, and slicked back his hair with pomade. He sniffed at his long johns, decided they would do for another day, took a clean shirt from the wardrobe, and lifted the mattress to retrieve the trousers he'd pressed there overnight. He pulled up his suspenders, tied his cravat, brushed off his coat, snapped the head from the last carnation in the vase and put it into his buttonhole, drew on his chamois gloves (frowning at the unmendable hole in the left thumb), and stood back to look at himself. He knew people took his fastidious grooming as a sign of vanity, but the opposite was true. Careful grooming was just an attempt to make the best of a bad job. Though he'd once had the soul of a lover, he'd never had the looks to match it. He was of less than average height and slightly built—though, he had to admit, smiling at the irony, now that he was a mere desk clerk he looked more impressive than he ever had. His beard and mustache, formerly a motley combination of red and brown, were now snowy and wiry enough to disguise his less-than-impressive jaw. His receding hairline gave an added breadth to his brow, and his shock of remaining hair, also white, formed an elegant crest. His nose—well, there was no improvement there—still had an unfinished look, as though a sculptor had just begun to shape the clay when he'd been called away from his work. His eyes, large and gray, had always been his best feature. They had once looked out at the world with an intense but defensive curiosity; now they had the sometimes amused, sometimes sad, but always tolerant look of the experienced observer. But weren't all artists observers, perhaps voyeurs of a sort? And wasn't he still an artist? He picked up his hat and his ivory-handled cane and left the room.

The sky was pewter-colored, and the air smelled of rain, smoke, flowers, and seafood. At the corner he saw a huddle of Italian children warming their hands over a charcoal fire while their mothers arranged flowers on carts. What traffic there was, moved in the opposite direction, toward the French market. A Negro, humming to himself, carried a catch of fresh fish, each strung through its mouth with a bit of palmetto leaf; another wheeled a barrow full of crabs, their claws still waving, and, looking up at the sky, predicted, "We be wet as these fellahs 'fore the day be out."

Billy nodded and moved on. It was his habit to take the long way round to the Versailles, strolling through the District. Strange, he thought as he passed another hawker, that he, who, as a boy, had valued the Bible more than the Bard, now began each day by walking through the largest and most famous red-light district in the country.

As he turned onto Rampart Street, two nighthawks, their feathers drooping and their eyes sightless as newborns, bumped into him. "Go steady, Jack," one said to the other, taking his companion by the elbow. They had come out of one of the rows of modest-looking houses, small operations involving only a "landlady" and two or three girls. But the District was literally a demimonde, a small world unto itself, accommodating every taste and income, from the squalid cribs, where service was performed for as little as a dollar, to the mansions of the famous madams, where a man could tarry on credit and champagne went for seventy-five dollars a bottle. No one knew the exact number of women in the District, though estimates went as high as four thousand. Girls of every color, nationality, and description, from haggard waifs to great beauties, and the army of barkeeps, musicians, laundresses, cooks, shopkeepers, doctors, druggists, pimps, and dope dealers who serviced and often exploited them. A few blocks farther, on Customhouse Street, the houses were larger. Billy saw a heavyset man, still buttoning up his fly, hurry down the steps of Mabel Kranz's place. He turned on Bienville and through an open window heard a cracked tenor singing, "Oh, the moonlight's fair tonight along the Wabash, / From the fields there comes a breath of new-mown hay. . . ." He smiled at the bucolic fantasy, knowing that the room must be heavy with stale tobacco, perfume, and liquor. As he approached the next block, a mouth-watering smell of coffee and sausage came out of Jessie Brown's open kitchen door. Madam Jessie billed herself as "the workingman's friend" and did a volume business that included a breakfast special served between six and nine, except Mondays.

Cutting over to Basin Street, he saw that lights still burned in the dormitory where Minnie White put the customers who had to sleep it off. Minnie's was known as an entertainment house, where bawdy songs were sung and boozing was the principal attraction. No doubt several of last night's celebrants were raising Minnie's surefire cure for the jimjams to trembling lips.

A Negro in livery was still standing guard at the door of Mahogany Hall, where Lulu White employed thirty mixed-blood beauties. He waved a greeting, and Billy doffed his hat. Three doors down, Queen Mollie Q. opened her door and ushered out two young men. She brushed off one man's collar, then, like a mother getting her children off to school, darted back into the hallway and reappeared with a forgotten hat.

"Billy," she called when the men had walked off, "have you time for a cup of coffee?"

Billy shook his head but said he would drop by that evening on the way home. Often at the end of his workday, when the District was beginning to come to life and the prospect of his room was too oppressive, he would settle onto one of Mollie's leather chairs by the piano while Mollie's "professor," Silt Simmons, warmed up and the girls, curried and combed, drifted downstairs. He was a great favorite in the house, being generous in his praise of the girls' usually bungled attempts to look like society ladies. He never failed to notice a new hairdo or compliment an artful application of rice powder and cochineal, and

since the girls were occupationally required to be listeners instead
of talkers, they were glad of the chance to unburden themselves.

"Ah, I'm done in, I tell ya." Mollie pushed a hank of red hair
beneath her skew-whiff tiara and leaned against the door. Sometimes, when she took a holiday with the bottle, her bright blue
eyes were bloodshot and the broken capillaries stood out on her
cheeks; but this morning she just looked tired. "Had a slew of
young-'uns last night, and they don't know the rules yet and get
a bit boisterous. And Agnes is down with the flu and y'know
she's one of the most popular girls. And one of Vinnie's grand-
children is sick, so we've had no decent cooking for two days,
and the ceiling in the third-floor bathroom is leaking *and* the
little back parlor needs a paint job. I've told the rotten agent
about it, and he promises to talk to the owner as soon as he gets
back in town, but y'know that Charles Randsome is such a rich
bastard he wouldn't give a fig if the entire building went up in
flames. I tell y', if I ever see Charles Randsome face to face, I'll
put a bullet in his heart an' not bother to go to confession. Christ,
I hate landlords."

" 'When troubles come, they come not as single spies, but in
battalions,' " Billy commiserated. It was no small challenge to
run a house as large as the one Mollie rented and was trying to
buy. She had to keep her girls, eighteen in all, her household
staff, the clients, and the law happy.

"I was dumb enough to think things might improve once Mr.
Story made us legal," she complained, "but nothin's really
changed."

Billy nodded. Mollie had been the first to tell him that one of
the city aldermen, Sidney Story, had proposed an ordinance that
would confine the trade to a specific area, thereby rendering it,
for all intents and purposes, legal, though the girls could still be
arrested if they ventured beyond its boundaries. Rumor had it
that the idea for the ordinance had come about in Mollie's dining

room, where many of the city fathers conducted unofficial business. Another rumor claimed that Mrs. Alcesta Davenport, a society lady who had appointed herself moral guardian of the city, had interrupted the meeting and been dragged kicking and screaming from the house. He could readily believe that the meeting had taken place at Mollie's (he had often seen the city fathers there and had drunk schnapps in the kitchen with the chief of police when the chief had come by to collect his payoff), but the presence of Mrs. Davenport was a myth. If Alcesta Davenport had been intrepid enough to venture into the District, she would have been stopped at the door by Judas, Mollie's houseman.

Mollie covered a yawn with pudgy, bejeweled fingers. "Ah, I can't wait to do the accounts and put m' feet up. I swear it's the only bit of privacy I get. See y'tonight, Billy." She waved goodbye and closed the door. A pale sun shone momentarily, then disappeared behind threatening clouds as Billy quickened his step.

The Versailles Hotel was situated on the edge of the District. The awning read "A Grand Hotel," but it was now grand in name only. The chandeliers had been removed, the draperies were faded, the overhead fans had dust on their wings, and the potted palms drooped. Ladies of the night plied their trade several blocks away but were easily smuggled upstairs. No liquor was served on the premises, but most guests kept it in their rooms. The clientele was, depending on your perspective, either one-third up or two-thirds down the great pyramid of success—Caribbean adventurers on to the hot deal, touring thespians, traveling salesmen, the occasional farmer, railroad and seafaring men, and old Confederates who polluted the air with cigar smoke and stories of battles they might have won.

As Billy crossed the lobby, one such old war-horse raised his head from the newspaper and, nostrils flaring, told him, "Things are finally moving in Congress. That lily-livered President McKinley will have to declare war soon. Then we'll blast those Spanish bastards off the face of the earth!" Jingoistic editorials and lurid stories of Spanish atrocities had been firing the general clamor for war even before the battleship *Maine* had blown up in the Havana harbor the previous month. New Orleanians took the ship's destruction as a personal affront since the city was to have been its next port of call, and the ubiquitous madness that normally abated after Mardi Gras had been kept going with rallies, parades, and cries of "Remember the *Maine!*" Billy dared not point out that no one had determined whether the "Spanish bastards" were actually responsible for blowing up the *Maine.* Anyone who wasn't yelling for war was considered a crank whose patriotism might be restored by a bloody nose, so he nodded politely, walked to the desk, and focused his attention on the cubbyholes behind it.

The envelope Frank Staughton had left for the girl was still there. After he'd removed his gloves, smoothed his hair, and said good-bye to the night clerk, he touched it. What could that blackguard Staughton possibly have written to her? "Your breasts are like the hawthorn buds that op' in the month of May, but I've got a wife already? Go home to your mother, I'll see you next time through?" He'd thought of carrying the envelope to the hotel kitchen and steaming it open but decided that he, at least, would play an honorable role.

He had always mistrusted Staughton. The man was handsome in a vulgar sort of way, quick with compliments and easy with the tips he tossed to the boys who carried the suitcases full of frippery he sold at exorbitant prices to the girls in the District, yet Billy had seen a ruthlessness behind his salesman's bonhomie. Staughton came through town three or four times a year, but when he'd come in last week, he'd pretended not to know Billy and had asked for a suite instead of his usual single room. The reason for that had sat a few feet away, looking around as though this were the real Versailles. Naturally, she was pretty—honey-colored eyes that slanted at the ends and a full mouth—but most girls in the first bloom were pretty. This one had that patent but difficult-to-define quality of sexual allure. Her country-girl dress hung loosely on a body that had yet to develop real curves. The black lace parasol and feathered hat she wore might have been borrowed from her mother's closet but were more likely gifts from Staughton. When Staughton said she was his wife, the color rose to the roots of her thick chestnut hair. It had been a long time since Billy had seen anyone blush. She might have been fourteen or sixteen. Holy Mother! Billy had thought, there oughta be a law. Well, there were laws, but he wasn't in the business of enforcing them any more than were the local police. Still, he'd felt a surge of disgust and indignation as he'd handed over the key for a third-floor suite and watched Staughton lead her up the stairs.

He'd seen her only a few times since, when Staughton had brought her down to the dining room. Her inexperience was apparent—she didn't know what silver to use or what to do with her napkin ring. Staughton, aware of the predatory glances of the other men, had played a brotherly role, but the girl was so obviously infatuated that no one would have taken her to be Staughton's sister. The day after they'd registered, Staughton had come through the lobby with books under his arm and said with a leer, "Gotta keep the little lady's mind occupied," then he'd left her in the rooms while he'd gone about his business. Then, yesterday afternoon, saying he was flush, Staughton had paid in advance for another week. When Billy had noticed his suitcases, Staughton had said he was going to show some merchandise and, almost as an afterthought, had taken the envelope from his pocket, asked for a pen, marked it "Kate," and put it on the counter. When Billy's expression had let him know that he wasn't putting anything over on him, Staughton had winked and slid a dollar bill across the counter. Billy'd raised his head so high his neck stretched. A sheepish look had flitted across Staughton's face, then he'd laughed, pocketed the dollar, picked up his suitcases, and walked off.

Billy attended to his duties, read the newspapers, chatted with the regulars, wondered if there would be a war, but at all times kept one eye on the stairs. At ten he sent a tray of biscuits and coffee up to the girl's room. The charwoman reported that the girl had taken it but immediately closed the door.

It was almost noon when she finally appeared, and to his surprise, he turned away. He'd seen a lot at the Versailles—seen a drunken sailor argue ineffectually with his captain, lurch to the exit, then turn back and drive a knife into the captain's belly. He'd seen a regular, who paid by the week but was so nondescript Billy had never known his name, carried out, his slashed wrists dripping onto the carpet while the manager bewailed the difficulty of removing the stains. He'd seen an impromptu duel—had it been over money or a woman?—not ten feet from this desk. The combatants had stood back to back, then started to mark off their paces. One hit his foot against a brass spittoon, spun round, and shot into the air, and his adversary whirled and finished him off with a single shot through the forehead. The victim touched the tiny hole with a look of offended surprise, said, "I'll be damned," and toppled to the floor. The crowd moved in for a better look, and a policeman, in the process of inspecting the body, pocketed the victim's gold watch. Yes, he'd seen a lot. But he couldn't bear to look this girl in the eye.

She stood with one hand on the banister, her spine straight but her head slightly bowed, with that expression of inward-looking concentration actors had while waiting in the wings. Then she lifted her head and came toward him, holding a steady and direct gaze. She had some grit.

"Excuse me . . ." she began. She smoothed her parasol, and Billy noticed that she'd turned the stone of the gimcrack ring toward her palm, hoping to make it look like a wedding band. "I thought I might go for a walk. It's such a pretty day." It had already rained twice.

"You might want to stroll over to Jackson Square," he suggested, making his face as bland as custard. "But mind the direction you go. There're some rough places here'bouts if you take the wrong turn. Why don't you go over to the d'Orleans Theatre? If you tell the caretaker Shakespeare sent you, he'll more than likely show you around." He reached for a piece of paper and began to sketch a map. She studied it and, without raising her eyes, whispered, "Have you any messages from . . ." She couldn't bring off "my husband." ". . . Mr. Staughton?"

He reached into the cubbyhole. As she accepted the envelope, her face showed both relief and anticipation. Holy Mother, Billy thought, to be so young! To expect everything and understand nothing. He said, "If you turn right as you leave the hotel, then . . ." But her pretense of a walk was over. She remembered her manners, turned back to thank him, then hurried to the stairs.

As Kate mounted the stairs, she felt no part of her body except the hand that clutched the envelope. Frank had told her that he had to go to a neighboring town on business, but he'd be back by nightfall, so surely the letter would explain why he hadn't come. She'd been so frightened last night that she'd put a chair against the door, but every time she'd heard a noise in the hallway, she'd started awake, petrified that someone would break in. Surely the letter would explain. . . . As she approached the door, the charwoman who'd brought her breakfast leaned on her broom, a look of open curiosity on her sallow face. Kate shut the door and leaned against it. A wave of panic hit her so forcibly that she felt light-headed. What if he didn't come back? Who could she turn to? What would she do for money? "Don't you love me?" he'd asked over and over again, then, "Don't you trust me?" She did love him and trust him. She did. She sat on the bed, knees and hands together, the envelope at her side. She could hear the clop of horses' hooves and a voice hawking vegetables in a singsong patois. She went to the partly opened window and pressed her forehead against the pane. As far back as she could remember, she'd heard stories of this great port. It was only three hundred miles from the landing where she was born, but it had seemed as far away and mythical as Atlantis. And he'd brought her here. And no one had guessed their secret except that sharp-eyed little man at the desk, and that was only because she hadn't been able to hide her surprise when Frank had asked for a single suite and said they were already man and wife. It was wrong of Frank not to have told her that he was going to do that. On their trip downriver they'd had separate cabins, and he'd told her he wouldn't touch her until they were married, but as soon as he'd closed the door to the rooms, he'd changed so much that even his face had looked different and his voice had a timbre she hadn't heard before. They'd stood at the window, she leaning out, trying to get a look at the sidewalk. Not sidewalk, he'd told her, here it was called a banquette. The buildings at home were clapboard and got a single coat of whitewash when they were first put up, but here the buildings were grand, painted pink, yellow, and blue, with ironwork as delicate as her little sister's curls. She had never been in such a grand place or so high up. The whole world was before her, and the man she loved was standing behind her, nuzzling her neck, taking the pins from her hair. She'd felt a downward pounding of blood and a weakness in her legs. Didn't she love him? Didn't she trust him? Then he'd slipped off her jacket as gently as he'd skin a peach. Then he'd said other things: Keep quiet or they'll hear you, and Be still, and, later, when she was crying and he'd moved onto her again, "Nobody will miss a slice off a cut loaf."

The hawker's voice rose in a wail of surprise as a flash of lightning split the sky. Spurts of warm rain blew into the window and onto her face and hands. In the sudden darkness the envelope glowed white on the bed. She had never seen his handwriting before, and she traced the scrawl of her name with her fingertip. There was a rap on the door. She ran to it—it must be Frank.

The charwoman held a plate of rice and beans. Her scalp showed through her hair as she inclined her head to the coffeepot and dishes on the table. "I see you finished yer breakfast, so I come to pick up the dishes and give you this." When Kate didn't move, she stepped past her, put the plate on the table, and pulled up a chair. "You've still got yer hat on."

"I'll pay you later," Kate said. But with what? Frank had pocketed the money he'd put on the bureau.

"Compliments of the house. From Billy Shakespeare. You know, that natty li'l one at the desk. Go on and eat."

"I'm not hungry just now. I have a headache," Kate said, wishing her gone.

"I get headaches m'self. An' I get the neuralgia something fierce, an' all the stoopin' and bendin' don't help." A further list of complaints gave her a chance to look Kate over. "You know what it's like. Ever done any cleanin' work?"

"Only at home."

"It's a donkey's life and that's fer sure, but there's not much else available unless you go into service, but then your life's not yer own. I hear they're lookin' fer a girl down at the fish market," she went on, casual-like, "an' Madame Destault hires a lot of young girls. Got a millinery establishment. Makes hats for all the rich ladies, and some who ain't ladies but have got the price. I hear she's a terror, but if you're betwixt and between . . ." The girl was looking into her face, frightened as a jackrabbit. "I mean," she added more gently, "until yer husband gets back." That Shakespeare was a gloomy one, always looking on the dark side; his artistic nature, she guessed. But he was right about this one: seduced and abandoned sure as God made little apples. "Go on and eat," she said, gathering up the dirty plate and the coffeepot. "Things is always brighter on a full stomach." Because any directive was welcome, Kate forked the rice and beans into her mouth. "Finish it up, that way I won't have to come back fer the plate." Kate did as she was told and wolfed it down.

As soon as the woman had gone, she went to the bed. She picked up the envelope, tore it open, and touched not paper but bills. She shut her eyes and swallowed the saliva that poured into her mouth. She mustn't move, mustn't move. If she didn't move . . . The money scattered as she ran. She made it to the bathroom door before a great arc of vomit spewed out.

When she came back into the bedroom, she picked up the scattered bills. Thirty dollars.

III

There are now fallen women who have been led astray while employed by milliners and dressmakers who make a speciality of just such a class of customers. There is hardly a single dressmaker or milliner in New Orleans who does not pursue such practices.

New Orleans Mascot, 1898

"*Madame* Destault" was etched on the shop window in gold and beneath it, in smaller script, "Latest Parisian Fashions." Kate stared at the black leghorn hat with the gossamer spotted veil, then reached for the doorknob. A bell tinkled her entrance. The shop was narrow but deep, with brocade wall panels, a purple velvet settee, and three gilt chairs facing mirrored dressing tables on which combs, brushes, hand mirrors, and hatpins had been arranged. A heavy curtain masked the rear door. A hat of such fine materials and workmanship that the cabbage roses decorating its brim actually seemed to exude a fragrance was displayed on a stand. In contrast, she saw the hat Frank had bought her when the boat had docked in Baton Rouge for the cheaply pathetic thing it was. She raised her hand to touch it, saw the grubby cuff of her dress, and was about to run out when the curtain parted. A midget-size woman bustled toward her. Her hair was a dead shade of black sculpted into such stiff curls that Kate knew it must be a wig. Her smile exposed large, yellowish teeth, but after the briefest glance she determined that Kate wasn't a customer, and the smile vanished.

"Are you Madame Destault?" The woman's close-set, currant-colored eyes demanded "Who else?" and Kate, sensing that she was about to be dismissed, rushed on, "I heard that you might be looking for some help."

"You have training in millinery?"

"No, but I'm good with my hands. I've decorated hats and . . ." She had redone her mother's straws with scraps from the sewing basket and feathers she'd collected in the woods. Madame smiled as condescendingly as if she'd actually witnessed these meager efforts, then took a step back and looked her over. "This hat you wear," she demanded, "where did you get it?"

"In Baton Rouge."

"You are from that place?"

"Near there."

"So you are new here?"

"Yes, but . . ."

"Where do you stay?"

"Just now at the Versailles Hotel."

"Ah-ha." Madame pursed her lips and gestured for Kate to turn around. Kate wondered what her appearance had to do with her chances of employment. Perhaps Madame needed a girl to serve in the shop. "You are a pretty little thing," Madame said at last. "A bit undernourished, perhaps, but this is why you seek work, *n'est-ce pas*? To put some meat on the bones and"—the tombstone teeth were bared again—"and perhaps to buy a dress to complement this hat some gentleman give to you. You are how old?"

"Fifteen."

Madame raised her eyebrows. "Or perhaps a little less? But no matter. Your parents?"

"Both dead," Kate lied. Her mother was; her father might as well have been. In fact, she wished he were.

"And there is no other family," Madame said, as though this were a foregone conclusion.

Kate swallowed. "No."

"*Pauvre jeune fille!* It was just so with me." She took Kate's chin in her hand, turned it to study her profile, then tutted. "Already you have the sadness in the eye that is so appealing. But you can be a merry girl, I think? Pretty things, dancing, the attention of some gentleman, would that make you merry?" Kate nodded at this unexpected gush of concern. "Your name is?"

"Kate."

"K-K-K-Kate," Madame affected to stutter and began to laugh. Thinking a show of good humor would help, Kate laughed, too. "Yes," Madame said, her laughter breaking off abruptly, "I think I find something for you. Come." She turned and pulled back the brocade curtain, gesturing for Kate to follow.

They went down a narrow hallway that opened onto a neglected courtyard. Conversation could be heard coming from a large shed, but as they approached its open door, the talk stopped. Four girls, sleeves rolled up, collars open, bent over a long table. After the bright elegance of the shop, Kate felt as though she'd been taken to the reverse side of a tapestry. The only light and ventilation came from the open door. There were feathers everywhere—in boxes, pegged to the walls, hanging from the low ceiling. The place even smelled like an aviary. Masks, ribbons, pelts of fur, and swatches of fabric were scattered about; the table was littered with mounds of beads, spangles, spools of thread, scissors, pins, a half-eaten sandwich. A pile of featureless display heads, looking as ominous as the harvest of the guillotine, lay in a corner next to a stack of hatboxes. "Emma," Madame said peremptorily, "get up." She took a dark-haired girl by the arm, nodded for Kate to take her vacated chair, then held up a mask. "See what she does? Sewing the spangles all around the eyeholes? Just so. You can do this? I think a sheep can do this." Kate took Emma's needle, put a spangle on the felt mask, and speared it. "Just so, yes. In a smooth line," Madame instructed, leaning over her shoulder. A bell, apparently connected to the one in the shop, jangled overhead. Madame said, "*Merde!*" then, "Keep working!" and hurried back across the courtyard before Kate realized that she hadn't asked about the salary or the hours.

The girls hunched over their work, looking at her from the corners of their eyes until the one sitting opposite, a girl of about twenty with a thin, pockmarked face, said, "My tag's Gertie, what's yours?"

"Kate."

"Hello to you, Kate. This is Anna. . . ." She nodded to a haggard-looking older woman who was fashioning satin rosettes. "And this is Emma."

Emma acknowledged her with a gap-toothed smile. "Pleased to meet ya. Take off yer hat and stay a while." Gertie and Anna laughed, but the plump girl at the end of the table remained expressionless. "Don't mind her," Emma explained. "That's Cabbagehead. She's German. Just off the boat, so she don't get the jokes."

As Kate took off her hat, Anna said, "Mind you don't get it mixed up with the others or the Spider will sell it out from under you."

"Oh, no"—Emma laughed and imitated Madame's accent— "'ve sell only ze latest styles from Paree." At this even Cabbagehead joined in the laughter.

"Almost done," Anna said, holding the hat with the satin rosettes at arm's length. "Ain't it a shame to think this'll go to a
prune like that Mrs. Davenport."

Seeing Kate's expression, Gertie said, "You shouldn't talk like
that. Besides, Mrs. Davenport ain't half as bad as Mrs. Dewitt.
She's changed her mind twice about the binding on this brim,
and it was perfectly all right the first time."

"Oh, that bitch Mrs. Dewitt." Emma pulled a face. "If you
squeezed her, you'd get pickle juice. And that stuck-up little
daughter of hers is even worse. Do ya know they have a long
red carpet, and when they give parties, they roll it all the way
out to where the carriages come?"

"Well, I heard . . ." Anna began.

The trickle of gossip became a free-running stream. The girls
seemed to know even the most intimate details of the customers'
lives—where they traveled, what they owned, who got along with
their husbands. They chatted about upcoming balls and dinner
parties as though they had been invited to attend. At first Kate
listened, fascinated, but then she began to feel sad and a little
contemptuous. It was like listening to her mother talk about
Christmas turkey when they were eating squirrel meat. She finished sewing on the spangles, but when she held up her handi-
work, Emma reached behind her, pulled another half-dozen
masks out of a box, dumped them in front of her, and said, "You'll
have to work a damned sight faster than that," then started talking
about a party Judge Asbury's wife was giving the following week.

After some time Madame Destault came back, complaining
about their lack of industry before she even came through the
door. She picked up one of Kate's masks. "I said a sheep could
do this? A sheep could do it better." She ripped off the spangles,
tossed the mask down, said, "Again!" and told them she was
closing the shop for lunch. Kate kept her head down and stiffened
herself to stop from crying.

By midafternoon the air was so heavy you could punch a hole in it, and the conversation had dwindled to complaints about the heat, sighs, and an occasional curse. Cabbagehead straddled her chair and pulled up her petticoats to fan her legs. Anna undid her bodice, rolled down her stockings, and put her feet up on a chair. Kate heard a tune, and a skinny barefoot boy with light brown skin and simian features came to the door, knocked the spit from his harmonica, looked at her, and asked, "So who's the new piece of calico?" Emma told him to hush up, took some money out of her shoe, and said he should run around to the druggist's and get her some headache powders.

"And if the Spider's still out," Anna told him, tossing some coins onto the table, "sneak by the saloon and get us a bucket of suds."

"That's Monkey," Gertie told her when the boy had run off. "He can get you anything you need."

Kate took up another mask. Her back ached, her eyes were gritty, and her fingers were as punctured as the pincushion. "How much longer do we work?"

"It's from cain't see to cain't see, just like the slaves," Gertie told her, biting off a strand of thread.

Around sunset Anna lit two lamps and put them on the table, but it was soon too dark to work. Madame came to let them out through a back gate into an alleyway. Anna stretched and said good night. Cabbagehead made a dumb show of farewell and humped off after her. Emma licked the last of her second packet of headache powder from the paper and said she was going off to a dance.

"It's those headache powders keeps her hopped up," Gertie whispered after Emma had run off. "Just wait'll you see her in the morning." Kate looked around uncertainly. The alley was dark, and she wasn't sure which direction to go. "You hungry? You must be 'cause you didn't bring no lunch," Gertie said, sensing her unease. "Why doncha come along to my place? They'll set an extra place for fifteen cents. Where y'from, anyways?"

"A little town upriver." Kate weighed the prospect of unwanted questions against the misery of being alone. "I am real hungry, so . . ."

"Sure, come on along." Gertie was by nature generous but had few opportunities to demonstrate it. "We'd best get a move on before the others snatch it all."

Kate mopped the remains of the fish soup with a piece of bread. The other boarders, all girls, had wolfed down their portions, gabbling in the same overlapping, coarse conversation Kate had heard in the shed, then disappeared. "You are hungry," Gertie said, pushing her bowl of applesauce to Kate and refilling her cup with oily coffee. "Don't they feed you where you stay? Where do you stay?"

Spooning into the applesauce, Kate muttered, "Just now, at the Versailles Hotel."

Gertie sucked in her breath. "The Versailles! How did you come to be there? No decent girl is safe there. It's right on the edge of the District."

"What's the District?"

"Oh, you are green! The District is . . . well, it's full of saloons and dance halls and"—she lowered her voice—"brothels. It's a terrible dangerous place. The women there are all lost souls who've given up their virtue, so's no decent man will have 'em. All they care about is sin and money. And some of 'em make plenty of it, let me tell you. I know all about it 'cause my fiancé, Herbie, is on the police force. He's told me some of them places are regular palaces of sin, with carpets and crystal chandeliers an' all, and those girls that live there, they can make as much in a night as a decent girl can earn in a month." A flush of indignation colored Gertie's pitted face.

"How much would that be?" Kate asked, but Gertie rushed on.

"Just a few weeks ago Herbie went on a raid on North Franklin. Now that used to be a decent neighborhood, but these houses are spreading like a contagion. Some family from out of town had moved in next door and they were kept awake all night with the shouting and music and the devil knows what else. They complained to the mayor, y'see, so the police went in and"—she lowered her voice as the Negro cook began to stack up the dirty dishes—"there were women sittin' around in, well, they didn't so much as cover themselves. They're beyond shame, y'see. So," she concluded, "you'll have to get away from the Versailles. Besides, it must be expensive. How'd y' come to go there?"

"I was supposed to stay with my aunt, but she's moved." The ease with which she was able to lie surprised and comforted her.

Gertie's face lit up. "Why don't you share with me? There's two beds in the room, and you won't be able to afford much else working for the Spider. At least stay tonight. I can sneak you upstairs with no one the wiser. It's too late to be walking back to the Versailles. You mean to say your aunt moved away without letting you know?"

"I would be grateful if I could stay," Kate said, ignoring the question, "just for tonight."

She followed Gertie up three flights to the room. Two iron bedsteads stood on either side of a narrow window, a wardrobe and a chair were shoved against dun-colored wallpaper that had started to peel. Gertie put the lantern on the floor and, catching Kate's look, said, "It ain't half bad for the price. There's a bath down the hall you can sign up for. I'll be getting married soon as Herbie gets his promotion, and you could have it for yourself."

She put her hands in the small of her back and stretched. "Oh, I'm done in. I've only the one nightdress. Well, really I have another, but I'm saving it for my honeymoon. You can take that bed." She nodded to the one on the right. "Watch out you don't step on that trap. We've got rats here. Landlord sez they're mice, if you can believe a mouse could be as big as a kitten."

Kate sank onto the bed and began to unlace her boots. Gertie took off her dress, pulled the nightdress over her head, and removed petticoat, camisole, and bloomers without showing another inch of flesh, all the while describing her honeymoon nightdress and saying how glad she'd be when she didn't have to work anymore. "Aren't you gonna take off your dress?" she asked.

Kate shook her head. "I'm too tired." She lay back and stared at the fly-specked picture on the wall. It was titled *Hope* and showed a woman, garments blown by the storm, her hair streaming, clinging to a huge stone cross. Gertie braided her hair and talked about how lucky she was to have found a steady man like Herbie. She's older than I am, Kate thought, but I already know more than she does. She doesn't know if her Herbie's good and steady, not yet she doesn't. Her mind had never completely left Frank throughout the dismal day, and now, fatigue sharpening memory, she fought a sob.

"There, there." Gertie sat on the bed and patted her hand. "I can't understand how your aunt could go off like that without letting you know. Have you any other family here? Can't you go back home?" Kate wiped her eyes with the back of her hand but remained adamantly silent. "We've all got our troubles. . . ." Gertie sighed, knowing that at least for the time being, she wouldn't get any further information. She suspected that Kate had run away from home, and that, young as Kate was, it must involve a man. She'd noticed the attention Kate had gotten as they'd walked to the boardinghouse. She couldn't wait to tell

Herbie how she'd rescued her. "If we just say our prayers to Almighty God, He'll take care of us," she added, getting up.

Slipping into her own bed, she thought that even though she'd tell Herbie about Kate, she might not introduce them. Not that she didn't trust Herbie, but, after all, he was a man and, she supposed, though he had too much respect for her to have given evidence of it, prey to the temptations of his sex. She thought about the honeymoon nightdress she'd saved so long to buy, the pretty ruffles at the neck and wrists. Herbie had told her that he was disgusted with those prostitutes displaying themselves, but it made her angry and suspicious and—she couldn't deny it— jealous. Her wedding night was spoiled. Herbie had already seen other women in their bloomers.

"So, Kate," Madame Destault instructed, "take down your hair and brush it smooth, like so. And when you hear the bell, come straight into the shop." She gave Kate's cheek a pinch. "Ah, you have become so pasty, the complexion is like bread dough," she said irritably, as though Kate's pallor were deliberate rather than the result of dawn-to-dusk sedentary work. She turned at the door of the shed, eyes narrowing. "Emma, wipe the hands. You sweat on the ribbons, you pay for the ribbons."

"Go piss yourself," Emma muttered as soon as she was out of earshot.

Anna slapped at her armpit, dug inside her dress, found a flea, and crushed it between thumb and forefinger. "I wonder why she wants Kate in the shop."

"Because she's the prettiest," Emma explained. She had already had a packet of headache powders, and her eyes were brightly derisive.

"Yar, ay," Cabbagehead agreed, "that why." Only partially comprehending, she'd found it best to agree with everything.

"Well, at least you'll be out of here for a while," Gertie said encouragingly. Madame had been unusually brutal with Kate, so much so that it seemed she was consciously trying to break her spirit. She criticized everything Kate did, told her she was incapable of learning, and threatened constantly to let her go.

"Yes," Kate agreed. Even a few minutes' break from the drudgery would be welcome. She was no better than a farm animal plowing the same furrow day after day. She got up at dawn, trudged to the shop, worked until it was too dark to see, trudged back to the boardinghouse, swallowed whatever was put in front of her, and fell into bed. All but five dollars of the money Frank had left was gone, settling up the bill at the Versailles, paying for her room and board, buying a dress and another pair of drawers. And she couldn't stop herself from what Gertie said was needless extravagance—new combs for her hair, a book of poems, a box of strawberries. Without those indulgences, she thought, she might throw herself into the river. Sunday was their only day off, and for the first three she'd stayed in bed and slept most of the day; but last Sunday, not wanting to risk Gertie's disapproval, she'd gone along to church with Gertie and Herbie. The minister had worked himself up into a fit, taking as his text "The Whore of Babylon." The women in the congregation seemed to share his condemnation, but she'd noticed an appreciable lack of fervor in the men; in fact, the man to her right had looked at her through most of the sermon. Could he see that she was already a "daughter of Eve"? And how was it that all sin was blamed on the temptation of women? The men, even the ones who pretended to be respectable, must have something to do with it. Her mood became even more resentful when, after church, Herbie rented a carriage and took them for a ride through the fashionable neighborhoods. Gertie oohed and aahed, grateful for just a glimpse, but Kate felt a keen, inchoate sense of injustice. When Gertie started to act cool toward her, because Herbie was showing her too much attention, she supposed, she said she had a headache and went back to the room. Though she had no idea where to send it, she wrote a letter to Frank, first telling him how he would be punished, then begging him to come back. Then she tore it up, crawled into bed, and tried to imagine her future. She could see nothing but a blank wall.

After making sure that Gertie wasn't watching, Kate took the stopper from the little bottle of Golden Tonic Emma had given her and took a quick and guilty swig. Gertie said the tonic had dope in it, but she didn't care. She'd felt tired and sick to her stomach for weeks, and the tonic seemed to help. She stared down at a devil mask. It had a protuberant nose, and sequins glittered around the eyeholes. She tried it on, giggled, and started to brush out her hair. Wearing her hair down was another of Madame's improbable demands. It made her look like a child and was hot on her neck. Emma looked across at her and winked.

The bell jangled. "So go, you lamb to the slaughter," Emma said.

"Yeah," Anna added, "and whoever the rich bitch is, drive a hatpin into her scalp for me."

When Kate drew back the curtain to the shop, Madame took her hand, then brought her forward as though to introduce her. "And this," she said with surprising pride, "is Kate. Kate, this is Mrs. Lefevre."

Two women sat on the settee. Because of the difference in their ages and the fact that the older woman held the younger's hand in her lap, Kate assumed they were mother and daughter, though they were not at all similar in appearance. The older one wore a tailored suit, and her blond hair was drawn tightly back beneath a black Persian lamb toque that peaked over her wide forehead. She had a sharp nose and chin, and her eyes were so unnaturally pale as to appear sightless. The young one was dark-complexioned, with a full, pouty mouth. Her green dress, in the latest hourglass fashion, was topped with a tiered cape of darker green, and her hat was a veritable jungle of birds and foliage. But it was her shoes that captured Kate—the softest tan kid with tiny mother-of-pearl buttons. What wouldn't she give to have a pair of shoes like that! One of her boots had split down the back seam, and the long walks to and from work had worn a blister on her heel. The younger woman, a girl really, not much older than she, stared at her belligerently, yawned without covering her mouth, and complained about being up so early, though it was after eleven.

"Then, my dear Bertha," Mrs. Lefevre said, "let's get on with it."

Bertha pulled off her gloves, moved languidly to one of the dressing tables, and looked up at Kate, ordering her to remove her hat. Taking out the largest hatpin, Kate remembered what Anna had said and one side of her mouth quivered with a repressed smile. Madame Destault picked up the new hat, put it on Bertha's head with all the solemnity of a coronation, then stepped back, pursing her lips. She liked to get the jump on possible complaints by displaying an initial skepticism, and in those rare instances when the customer was satisfied, she often invented a minor problem in order to correct it and thereby convince the client of specialized service. "Ze bow . . ." Madame shook her head slightly and ran a doubtful tongue over her teeth. "I am not sure about ze bow at the back."

Bertha demanded a mirror that was well within her reach, and after Kate had handed it to her, she turned this way and that, lowering the veil, raising it, touching her fingers to her temples. "You're right. The bow is too stiff. It should be satin instead of taffeta, don't you think?" She turned to the settee, but Mrs.

Lefevre's attention was not on the hat. Her gaze, bland and inscrutable, rested on Kate.

"M'mselle, you are right," Madame assented. "On the block it was perfection, but now I see it on you, yes, a softer look. Definitely satin. And perhaps a brighter hue, to accent the color of your eyes."

"I'm not sure," Bertha said, miffed at Mrs. Lefevre's inattention, "That I like it at all. No, it simply won't do."

Madame looked pained but resigned. "Ah, *tant pis*. It is very similar to the one that Madame Dewitt purchased for her daughter to wear to the Amonsetts' wedding. Not the same. No, no, no! No two are alike. And, of course such a hat, with such a wide brim, requires a graceful neck and, *entre nous,* little Mademoiselle Dewitt, she . . . ." She shrugged off the sad reality of the debutante's inferior neck. "No, no, she cannot support such a brim. I advised her so, but her mother, Madame Dewitt, always has the final word."

Mrs. Lefevre allowed herself a tight smile. "So I have heard from Mr. Dewitt."

Madame was amused. "I think"—she wagged her finger—"that you see Mr. Dewitt very often."

"When the stock market goes up, his . . . how shall I put it?" Mrs. Lefevre sought the word. "His *spirits* are inclined to rise, and he is such an unhappy man that he sometimes has trouble raising his spirits." The older women laughed.

"He's disgusting," Bertha hissed.

"By the way," Mrs. Lefevre said quickly, "he gave me a tip on some railway stock. Perhaps I could share it with you." Madame went to the settee, and they put their heads together.

Kate was out of her depth in these subtle and swift-moving conversational currents. She touched the hat's ribbon and mimicked Madame's concern. "I agree that satin, and perhaps in a brighter shade . . . but it is very becoming, and as Madame said, the full brim requires a graceful neck." There was nothing graceful about Bertha's neck; in fact, now that Kate studied her, she thought she looked coarse.

Bertha shot her a suspicious look and asked, sotto voce, if Miss Dewitt had indeed bought a similar hat. Kate had no idea but said yes, but in fuchsia. Bertha turned to Madame Destault. "Then make the changes and I'll take it. And . . ." Her eyes flitted to a brown crushed velvet decked with violet and lavender pansies that Kate had secretly tried on some days before. "Let me see that one."

Mrs. Lefevre took a gold watch from her waistband, and Madame Desault pretended not to hear Bertha's request. She clapped her hands and said, "*Très bien,* so you take this one. You will not be sorry. You have made the right choice. We will have it finished within the hour." She reached up to the crown of Kate's head, let her hand slide down to gather up her hair, and held it out as though it were the mane of a prize filly. "Such a pretty one, isn't she? And so unfortunate that she is an orphan and does not know a soul in the city. Shall I send her around with the hat?"

Mrs. Lefevre nodded once, slowly.

"Not while I'm taking my nap," Bertha snapped.

Mrs. Lefevre got up. "Madame, your taste is, as usual, impeccable. And I shall send payment in the usual manner. Send her around." She looked at Kate, then led the way out. Bertha, gathering up her things, followed.

Madame winked, put her finger to the side of her nose, then reached up, dislodging her wig as she drew a key from under it. She unlocked the cabinet where she kept the cash and her bottle of absinthe, straightened her wig, poured herself a glass, and knocked it back in one gulp. "To your health, *ma belle,*" she toasted, and filled the glass again. "Who knows, perhaps one day you, too, will buy hats from poor Madame Destault. Ah, little girl, if God had given me your hair or your fine teeth, who knows where I would be now? Never believe the fools who tell you that beauty is a curse. They speak with envy only." She settled on the settee, her feet not touching the floor. "And you are also intelligent. I watch you. I see you know how to make the client feel important." Kate smiled at the unexpected praise. Madame touched her forehead and whispered, "Yes, God give you the gray matter *and* a fine derriere. What more can a woman want? And since the derriere is all the man wants, the brain she must use for herself." She chuckled again. "One day you will thank me. Now what does this Bertha want done with the hat?"

"The bow changed to satin, and of a brighter color."

"From the provinces." Madame sighed. "If she lived within the sight of the Arc de Triomphe, she would always be from the provinces. But you . . . the first day you come, I see you know already that your *chapeau* from Baton Rouge is not so fine. Maybe you already know that the gentleman who give it was not so fine either?" It made the hair on Kate's arms stand up to think that she had been so acutely observed. Madame wagged her finger. "Before you are taking anything from a gentleman, you must first see what it is worth, *n'est-ce pas?* Your mother never teach you such things?"

Kate pictured her mother—eyes lakelike and trusting as a cow's, shoulder blades showing through her cheap calico dress, teeth gone, her belly swollen with yet another pregnancy. She felt sick again and thought it must be the Golden Tonic.

"Now go," Madame ordered. "Go on with the rest of your life. Tell Anna to make the changes on the hat. Monkey I will send around to take you to Mrs. Lefevre."

IV

No written law has ever been more binding than unwritten custom supported by public opinion.

Carrie Chapman Catt (1859–1947)

*I*t was Mrs. Lucretia Asbury's turn to host the Society for the Beautification of the City, and she'd spent the morning in such an agony of indecision and preparation that she'd had to take a glass of sherry to calm her nerves. First she'd had to decide how many chairs should be set up. Before "the season" began, women were desperate for any excuse to get out of the house, and as many as forty might show up, but once the round of balls and parties started, the ranks could wither to as few as a dozen. She fretted, decided on thirty, and told the servants to set up the chairs in the solarium. They had almost finished doing so when she'd gone in, found the solarium had a disconcertingly earthy smell, and instructed that the chairs be moved to the library, a room so rarely used that it required a complete dusting. While moving the library furniture, Samuel had dropped the statue of the Dying Gladiator on his foot. The Gladiator was, thank heavens, unharmed, but Samuel seemed to have broken his toe, so she'd had to see to that.

After the lectern had been put in place and potted palms arranged on either side, she rushed to the kitchen to see to the refreshments. The meeting was called for eleven, but it went without saying that it wouldn't start on time and with that ditherer, Lucy Grainton, in the chair it was bound to drag on. She couldn't be expected to provide luncheon, but perhaps a seed cake should supplement the cucumber-and-watercress sandwiches. Underneath these taxing decisions lay an even greater anxiety: Julia Randsome had asked to be given a few moments at the end of the meeting to discuss "a subject of the utmost importance," and there was no denying her. She was Mrs. Charles Randsome, after all, and though her involvement with beautification was desultory at best, she never forgot her annual contribution and could always be counted on in an emergency. And the fact that Julia had to put up with that witch, Carlotta, elicited a certain amount of sympathy. But Julia was such an odd fish. One could never predict what she would do or say. She had formed the Equal Rights Association but left it because the members wouldn't include Negro women. She had two carriages at her disposal but rode around on a bicycle like a nineteen-year-old shopgirl. At dinner parties she either fell silent or embarrassed everyone by discussing politics and books. One could only hope that she wouldn't spoil the meeting with some harangue about sweatshops or women's property rights or try to enlighten them about what a pack of wild-eyed radicals, whom Julia referred to as "our sisters," might be doing in London or New York. Mrs. Asbury fortified herself with a second glass of sherry and went upstairs to put on her new morning dress.

Despite the changeable weather, Julia rode her bicycle to the meeting and was one of the first to arrive. Only Sophie Besquith, old Beatrice Ravenal, and her companion, Grace, were in the foyer, and Julia was annoyed with herself for having rushed. She knew these club meetings never started on time, and though she had long ago abandoned the hope that her punctuality would set an example, she had never been able to wean herself from the habit of promptness. Surely eleven o'clock could mean nothing but eleven o'clock, even in New Orleans. She exchanged greetings with Beatrice and Grace, tucked her striped blue shirtwaist into the belt of her navy linen skirt, removed her gloves, and went into the library. A volume of Dante caught her eye, and she almost picked it up before remembering that she had once taken a book from these shelves and found it full of silverfish. In the Asbury home, as in so many others, books were merely part of the decor. She smiled, thinking that if Lucretia used her bath as little as she used her books, she would look like the most wretched street urchin. She saw that Clara Parkes was sitting at the desk, her ledger open, her little cash box at her side. Clara's husband was so tight-fisted that he wouldn't even allow her to manage the household accounts, so she often volunteered as treasurer, handling money with as much caution and pleasure as if it had been her own. Julia was asking her if she could find the time to take over purchasing for the children's milk fund when Lucretia Asbury bustled toward them.

"Oh, Julia, don't you look pretty today!" Julia nodded. One could be red-eyed and covered with spots and still receive this standard greeting. "And, mercy, I neglected to ask what it is you're going to speak to us about."

"I have drafted a petition that—"

"A petition?" Mrs. Asbury couldn't stop herself from interrupting, nor could she keep the alarm out of her voice. "What sort of a petition?"

"As you must know," Julia began, but Beatrice Ravenal's companion, Grace, who had helped that lady to the front row but was having difficulty easing her bulk onto a chair, signaled for assistance. As Julia moved to help, Lucy Grainton came through the doors, and Mrs. Asbury hurried to greet her.

Beatrice Ravenal was a very old woman, as corpulent as she was affluent. Cursed with gout, she moved slowly and only with the help of a cane, but her eyes were sharp and her mind was quick. "Thank you, Julia," she said as Julia arranged her footstool and handed back her cane, "you are always so kind."

Beatrice smoked in private, and her breath smelled of nicotine and violet pastilles. She had lost a husband and two sons in the war and had worn nothing but black for over thirty years. She and Julia had been friends from their first meeting—a torturous affair when Carlotta had put Julia on display and Beatrice, sensing the situation, had whispered, "Don't feel you are the only animal of its kind in the zoo." Since then it had become their standing joke. When she sent notes to Julia, Beatrice addressed her as "Dear Aardvark" and signed herself "Your Hippo." Beatrice opened her tin of violet pastilles, offered them to Julia, and asked about Lawrence's progress at college.

As the room began to fill, Lucy Grainton went to the lectern, saw that it was too tall for her, and looked around in confusion. "I'm sure the only solution that occurs to Lucy is to have the butler saw off the legs," Beatrice whispered. "Give her my footstool to stand on, or we'll never get started." Julia said she would ask a servant for one, accepted Lucy's thanks for that ingenious suggestion, and went into the adjoining room, where a girl was arranging teacups. After sending the girl off for a stool, Julia opened her haversack, took out the petition, a bottle of ink, and a pen, and set them on the table near the windows. She was rereading the petition and wondering if she couldn't have phrased it more forcefully when Alcesta Davenport came in. Seeing Julia, she turned as if to leave. Julia noticed the movement, attributed it to Alcesta's general nervousness, and went to her. "Alcesta, how are you?"

Alcesta looked at the carpet, the portrait of Judge Asbury, the teacups. "I really must have a cup of tea."

"But how are you?"

"Very well, thank you," Alcesta answered as if they'd just been introduced.

"I drafted the petition. But then, you already know that." She had sent Alcesta a note as soon as she'd finished writing it, but weeks had gone by and she hadn't received a reply. "I thought you might be ill," she said. Alcesta had the contained and distracted look of someone who was a little hard of hearing. She looked past Julia to the table near the windows. "Yes," Julia confirmed, "that's it. I thought we should take advantage of this meeting to get some signatures."

"I really must have a cup of tea before the meeting starts. Surely someone . . ." The girl came in with the footstool. "I see that you haven't prepared the tea yet," Alcesta said, "but I'm quite parched. Do you suppose . . ." She took the girl by the elbow and led her off.

Julia had expected that Alcesta would show some embarrassment when they met, but she had not anticipated an outright snub. The rejection stung her cheeks as though she'd actually had her face slapped. She went to the table and bent over it, biting her lip as she stared at the petition, then uncorked the ink, picked up the pen, and signed her name.

The library was almost full when she reentered. She gave Lucy the footstool, took one of the chairs behind the lectern, and looked out at the sea of faces. She knew so much about these women—knew that Alice Bessant broke out in a rash if she ate oysters; that Thea Custom's frequent bruises came not from her clumsiness, as Thea claimed, but from her bullying husband; that Emily St. Gervais planned to cut her relatives out of her will; that Edith Gailyard had tried to kill herself—and yet, with the exception of Beatrice, she could not count one of them as a real friend. Was she such a hypocrite that she cared for the rights of women in the abstract yet found their actual company oppressive?

Or was it only this particular group of women? Mrs. Dewitt, who was sitting toward the back with her daughter, Adeline, caught Julia's eye, smiled broadly, and with a subtle movement of her elbow encouraged Adeline to do the same. Adeline, always a model of pliancy, put down the novel she was reading and obliged. Adeline had come out last season, and Lawrence Randsome was on her list of possibilities. Miss Evelyn Bardaron, a spinster whose single status and limited income kept her on the lowest rung of society, sat in the second row, her face as blank as a plate, ready to receive any tidbits Mrs. Duncan, that master chef of warmed-over gossip, might dish out. Phillipa Cotrane was turning her head this way and that to show off her new hat. A divorcée with a less than savory reputation, Phillipa provided a social link for newcomers with more money than pedigree. Carrie Bonisett stood up to get Julia's attention, waved, and sat back down. She was one of the youngest matrons in the group and a talented singer. Before she'd married, she'd given concerts as far away as Philadelphia; now she gave parties for visiting opera stars. But surely Carrie could be counted on. She was young, intelligent, and kindhearted. Unlike most of the others, she did not merely affect an attitude of social concern as a way of ignoring personal problems or promoting self-esteem. Of course, she and Julia had never talked about prostitution, but they had discussed the importance of a single standard of conduct for men and women, and Carrie's husband, Walter, supported the vote for women. Remembering how touched she'd been by the sight of Carrie and Walter at the altar, Julia thought of other husbands, fathers, and sons of the women present. How many of them frequented the District? Until recently that question, like Bluebeard's chamber, had been sealed off in her mind. And if she, who believed that facing facts was an unmitigated good, had done this unconsciously, then surely the other women present, who were far more accustomed to denial, had done the same. For how could any woman see her son across the breakfast table or offer her face to her husband to be kissed if she let herself know that . . .

"Shouldn't we get started?" Lucy Grainton asked, and Julia said yes before realizing that the question had been addressed to Lucretia Asbury. The audience was now so restive that there would be no hope of regaining it if they didn't start soon. Still, Mrs. Asbury hesitated, her brow furrowed with the weight of another decision. "Perhaps a few more minutes," she said. "Yvette Liscomb said she was coming, and with the weather being so changeable . . ."

"Rain or shine, we can always count on Yvette for the disruptive drama of a late entrance."

"Why, Julia!" Mrs. Asbury pretended to be shocked. She attributed Julia's remark to jealousy. Decades past, when Yvette Damille had lost the matrimonial sweepstakes for Charles Randsome, she'd married Vincent Liscomb, a man with a long, sallow face who was old enough to be her father. This Beauty and the Beast alliance had so upset romantic souls that Liscomb's wealth (the obvious reason for the match) was ignored in favor of the myth that Yvette and Charles had been lovers and that he had cruelly deserted her for Julia. Lucretia Asbury was sure that it was true. One had only to see Yvette and Charles together to believe that the attraction still survived.

"I really think . . ." Lucy persisted.

Mrs. Asbury sighed, got up, and opened her pale, plump hands for order. The room calmed, but only because the collective attention had turned to the doors. Yvette had finally arrived, carrying her little bull terrier. She was a petite but full-bosomed woman with dark curls and dark, exaggerated eyes. She prolonged her entrance by handing over the dog and giving instruction as to its care, then moved down the aisle, one hand raised in languid greeting, an expression of polite boredom on her face.

Yvette often played the visiting monarch when in the company of women; her behavior with the opposite sex was so different as to suggest another personality. With men she became animated, listened with undivided concentration, laughed at the lamest jokes, called attention to herself with artful movements of her shoulders and hands. Now she gathered up the train of her lavender dress and perched on the edge of a chair as though she might have to leave at any minute.

But as Lucy brought the meeting to order, Julia's attention was caught by an actual departure: Alcesta Davenport was in the hall waiting for the butler, who was struggling with Yvette's bull terrier, to find her umbrella. Alcesta pretended not to notice Julia's stare by fixing her gaze on Mrs. Asbury. When she finally caught her hostess's attention, she put her hand to her forehead in a pantomime of headache, accepted her umbrella, and left.

As Lucy began her singsong reading of the last meeting's minutes, Julia stared straight ahead. She wanted to go into the other room and retrieve the petition, but that was as impossible as it was cowardly. She would honor her commitment even if it meant standing alone, but she felt her confidence leaking away. Her fear of public speaking was as strong as some people's fear of heights or snakes. Her mother had told her that this, like any other weakness, would be conquered if only she would confront it. After years of public speaking, she had succeeded in hiding her fear, so much so that she was often complimented on her confidence, but she had never conquered it. Even when she had a sympathetic audience, the apprehension was still there, and as she listened to Clara Parkes give the treasurer's report, her hands began to sweat. She smoothed the notes in her lap and mentally rehearsed her opening remarks.

By the time Mrs. Asbury had taken the lectern, Julia was flexing her left foot, trying to get rid of the pins and needles, and her mind had drifted off to Charles's homecoming. The audience members had become as restless as schoolgirls waiting for the bell on a summer afternoon. Adeline Dewitt had gone back to reading her novel; Vernette Stillerton had taken out a mirror and was examining her chin; Phillipa Cotrane mouthed "Luncheon engagement" to her neighbors and crept toward the exit with such exaggerated furtiveness that she succeeded only in calling attention to herself; and even a sharp look from Mrs. Asbury couldn't quiet Mrs. Dunlop's whispers. After soliciting volunteers to serve tea at the benefit to be given in Sophie Besquith's rose garden, Mrs. Asbury asked, "Any other business?" There was a general rustle as purses were opened, gloves were put on, and chairs were pushed back. "But before we adjourn for refreshments," Mrs. Asbury said, halting them, "Julia Randsome has requested permission to discuss . . ." She looked at Julia quizzically, turned her hands one inside the other as though washing them, and finally said, in a dying fall, "A topic of the utmost importance."

As Julia got up, she felt as queasy as if she were on the deck of a pitching ship. She smoothed out her notes and gripped the sides of the lectern. "Thank you. I appreciate this opportunity to speak to you, though what I have to say has nothing to do with the beautification of the city except in the moral sense." She had thought to expand this opening remark by talking about the relation of beauty to truth but decided against it. "As you probably know," she plunged in, "an ordinance sponsored by Mr. Sidney Story has been passed by the city council. This ordinance . . ." There was a general stiffening of spines and lowering of heads. Only old Beatrice Ravenal lifted her chins and gave an encouraging nod. Julia read the ordinance, then said, "As you see, its stated purpose is to protect us from vice by confining 'women abandoned to lewdness' to a designated area. But if we examine what the real results will be . . ." She went on to describe the inevitable growth of crime and the exploitation of women in the District. When she mentioned the threat of disease, the thought flashed through her mind that perhaps it was best that Alcesta had left. She lost her place, looked down at her notes, and, when she raised her head, caught Yvette Liscomb's eye. Yvette had the smugly patient look of someone listening to a foreigner try to speak English. Julia pressed on but felt as though she were in an echo chamber. When she spoke of the violation of the single standard, her combination of fervor and nervousness gave her voice a strident tone, and when she tried to modulate it, she felt as though she were whispering into a gale. She had intended to encourage the women by telling them about British women's successful campaign to combat prostitution, but their eyes were so glazed they reminded her of a shop window full of dolls. She cut to the end, told them that the petition was on the table in the other room, and began to thank them for their attention.

"And thank you, Julia," Mrs. Asbury put in hurriedly. "Now, ladies, the refreshments will be served. Thank you for coming, and don't forget the . . ." The room emptied as quickly as if a conductor had announced the departure of a delayed train.

Beatrice Ravenal motioned for Julia to come to her. "You do know how to stir things up. I'm glad I made the effort to come today."

"I'm afraid I wasn't very articulate. I was nervous."

"You succeeded admirably in concealing it."

"Then it was well argued?" Julia was ashamed to ask for reassurance but was very much in need of it.

"You were most articulate. Far too articulate."

"Very well argued," agreed Beatrice's companion, Grace.

"Though reasonable arguments don't always win the day," Beatrice warned. "Don't be disappointed if you don't get many signatures. Most won't sign anything without permission from their husbands, and this is obviously a topic they won't be eager to discuss. Some will automatically bow to the wisdom of the city council because it will secure property values. And some don't much care what their menfolk do so long as they do it discreetly and the money keeps flowing." Noticing that Grace was looking around to see if anyone could hear them, Beatrice assured her, "Don't worry, Grace. I'm so old that anything I say can be dismissed by claiming I've gone soft in the head. Since I have neither father, husband, nor son to answer to, I shall sign it. There's only my brother, who, by the way, is on the city council, and he's such a pompous ass that it always gives me pleasure to go against him." She would sign out of loyalty to Julia, though she didn't expect the petition would accomplish anything.

Julia said, "I hope you are wrong about the women not caring what their men do so long as they are provided for. That would make them little better than those in the District."

Beatrice chuckled. "Certainly not in the eyes of society." Julia's idealism sometimes clouded her common sense. "And not many marriages," she continued, "are founded on the mutual affection you so happily enjoy. And how is your dear husband? I haven't had the pleasure of his company in a long time."

"He's abroad, in Marseilles. He'll be home in another twenty-three days."

"Twenty-three days. And how many hours?" Beatrice teased, but Julia, whose attention was focused on the archway to the other room, didn't catch her tone.

"I don't know," Julia said.

"I only meant that a less devoted wife would have said he'd be home in a few weeks. So, Charles will barely have time to take off his traveling clothes before he puts on evening dress for your party."

"What party?"

"The homecoming party you're giving for him. I received Car-

lotta's invitation just this morning." Julia's expression changed
so quickly that Beatrice knew she had blundered. She turned to
her companion. "Grace, do go in and enjoy a cup of tea. Don't
bother to bring me anything. All I want is a cigarette, and I shall
have that as soon as I'm in the carriage." When Grace had excused
herself, Beatrice turned back to Julia. "I see I've put my foot in
it. You didn't know about the party?"

"No. Carlotta suggested it, but I wasn't in favor of it. It seems
she's gone ahead without letting me know. When's it to be?"

"On the eighteenth."

"Thank you for telling me. I should have been very embarrassed to have heard it from anyone else."

"I imagine it's a very large guest list. Why else would it include
a fossil like me who will take up two chairs? I shall, of course,
plead a prior engagement. I never thought it would happen, but
I have reached the stage where I had rather sit on my gallery
with my feet up than attend the most glittering party." She saw
that Julia's face was being held together by a profound exercise
of the will. She wanted to console her but knew better. It was
the seemingly self-possessed ones, not the whiners, who came
apart when offered comfort. "About your petition," Beatrice
went on, "you know that you're battling something that is deeply
rooted in tradition. Prostitutes were pulled out of French jails
and shipped off as colonists at the very beginning of this city.
And the District has been there since I was a girl, though in my
time I don't believe many men of our class frequented it. It was
more the custom for them to have quadroon or octoroon mistresses. It was civilized after a fashion. That is to say," she added,
seeing Julia's look, "some rules and responsibility were involved.
Some men had two families—one with their legal wives, the other
with their concubines. You must've heard about that."

Julia said, "Yes, I've heard about it, but I simply can't understand why the wives accepted it."

"What else could they do? In my day, a well-brought-up girl wasn't even supposed to know she was a virgin until she wasn't anymore. As a wife she had to accept whatever her lord and master did, so what she couldn't accept, she pretended not to see. Ignoring the truth isn't a happy strategy, but often it's the only way one can keep going. But of course the wives hated the mistresses. They called them 'Les Sirènes'—serpent women. Even when I was young, it struck me as wrong to blame them. Oh, I had a great curiosity about them. I remember the first time I met Marie. I knew of her only by reputation. She was a great beauty. There were many men who wanted Marie."

"Marie?" Julia asked.

"Marie Lepelliter. Carlotta's maid," Beatrice explained. "She was Carlotta's first husband's mistress. Carlotta was only a girl when she married him, but even then Carlotta knew how to get what she wanted. She forced him to marry Marie off to a dark-skinned Negro. But such marriages hardly ever worked. The man ran off and left Marie with a little girl to support, so Carlotta took her in. Perhaps Carlotta only did it because she wanted to lord it over Marie, but I've always thought it was one of her few generous impulses."

Julia looked down at the notes in her lap, and her eyes narrowed as though trying to read in a dim light. "How can Marie lace Carlotta into her corsets, pick up Robespierre's droppings, when . . ." She looked up and rearranged her face into a smile, but the smile had a swift and horrible death. "Forgive me, Beatrice, but I have heard so much unexpected and unpleasant information lately that I hardly know how to respond."

Beatrice shifted her bulk and shook her head. "The real reason I seldom go into society anymore is that I've lost the habit of censoring myself. Perhaps I *have* gone soft in the head. I should have realized that Carlotta would never discuss anything like this with you."

"But Charles might have. Though he hasn't." Since Carlotta's revelations, the suspicion that Charles was part of a conspiracy to keep her in ignorance was always lurking.

"Very likely Charles knows nothing about it. It was well before his time. Ancient history. Every family has its secrets."

"But from its own members?"

"Especially from its own members, dear aardvark. I was twenty years old before I found out that I was not my mother's child, but her younger sister's who had run off. My husband had to die before I found out anything about our finances, and that was far more shocking and, surprisingly, far more upsetting than my discovery of his dalliances. My tongue-lashings about them had become disgracefully mechanical, but I was young then and couldn't control myself. And I was fifty before I found out that my brother, who was supposed to be protecting my interests, was robbing me blind. But by then . . ." She sighed and folded her arms beneath her massive bosom. "By then I'd developed a protective armor."

Grace came toward them. "Are you sure you wouldn't like some tea, or perhaps a sandwich?" she asked.

"No, no. But I'm longing for a cigarette. Yes," Beatrice said as she planted her cane and motioned to be hoisted up, "a cigarette, and when I get home, a roast chicken and some chocolate cake. So, Julia, if you will be so kind as to fetch the petition . . . You can put it back for other signatures as soon as I've signed."

How could a woman as bright as Beatrice have allowed food to become her only solace? How could she comfort moral indignation with a chocolate cake? "I should imagine that anyone who was going to sign has done so by now," Julia said crisply.

The other women did not ignore her as she moved among them, but she had a sense of being greeted without being acknowledged. As she walked back into the library, she looked at the petition. The signatures: Grace's and Carrie Bonisett's she had expected, and Clara Parkes' and Vernette Stillerton's did not really surprise, but Adeline Dewitt's was a bit of a shock. That young lady had appeared to be reading her novel throughout her speech, so either she was willing to go to unusual lengths to please Julia because of Lawrence or she was glad for an opportunity to displease her domineering mother. Still, five. Only five. She had a flash of the they-get-what-they-deserve contempt that all but the most saintly reformers feel from time to time.

After Beatrice had signed, Julia helped her to the front door. Beatrice took Julia's chin in her hand, said, "I do wish . . ." then shook her head and said good-bye.

As Julia packed the ink bottle into her haversack, Yvette Liscomb and Lucy Grainton entered the hall. Yvette took her bull terrier from the servant, sent him out to get her carriage, and began to coo to the animal in baby talk. Lucy held back, her eyes flitting from Yvette to Julia. "I'll see you at Charles's welcoming-home party," Yvette said to Julia as she swept past. "It will be so nice to have him back again."

"Yes," Julia agreed. Not wanting to leave with Yvette, she loitered, going to the mirror to secure the pins in her straw hat and adjust the haversack over her shoulder.

"Do you think the meeting went well?" Lucy asked. "I always get the jitters when I have to—"

Julia was curt. "Yes, I know."

Lucy lowered her voice. "If we could just . . ."

"Just what?" Julia demanded, not bothering to hide her impatience. She wanted to be off before the others straggled out, wanted to escape their simperings and posturings and unnaturally girlish voices, their endless fussing over purses and gloves and umbrellas and hats, needed to get on her bicycle, grip the handlebars, and pedal so furiously that she created a movement of air, needed to push up a hill, though there were no hills, until she felt the comforting exhaustion of strained muscles—and here was this ditherer, this mouse who was afraid of her own shadow . . .

"If we could just step into the alcove," Lucy whispered, "I'd like to sign."

CHAPTER

V

For the lips of a strange woman drop as a honeycomb, and her mouth is smoother than oil; but her end is bitter as wormwood, sharp as a two-edged sword. Her feet go down to death; her steps take hold on hell.

Proverbs 5:3–5

onkey sat on his haunches outside the shed and played his harmonica while Anna redid the hat. When it was finished, Madame herself placed it in the box and handed it to him, told Kate to brush her hair again, and led them through the courtyard and out the front door.

"C'mon, let's get crackin'," Monkey said, and darted ahead of her.

"How far is it?"

"What you care, you're out of the shed, ain't you?"

She was. It was an unusually breezy day, and despite the blister on her heel, her step was light. The street was full of wonderful sights and delicious smells. In the baker's window trays of golden croissants, glazed tarts of apricot, apple, and blueberry, and tiny cakes iced in pastel colors were on display. Through the side door of a restaurant she could see a verdant courtyard with tables set under canvas umbrellas. The aromas of coffee, spices, and roasting meat, so enticing after the cabbage and fish smells that hung about the boardinghouse, made her mouth water so much that she had to keep swallowing. They passed an apothecary with amber, red, and green jars shining in the window, then a cobbler's and a cabinetmaker's. Kate turned her head and looked up at the balcony above a jewelry shop. A woman sat there, combing the hair of her little dog. She was such a pretty sight that Kate continued to look at her over her shoulder till Monkey's arm hit her in the midsection as she stepped off the curb.

"Watch where you be goin'. You 'bout walked into that horse." She recovered herself and hurried after him, but he nimbled along ahead of her, proud of the recognition he got from various shop owners and street people. "I'm takin' you the long way 'round. We're in the Quarter now," he announced after several more blocks. "Figured you're such a hayseed I'd give y' the tour."

"How old are you?" Kate asked.

"Old as you," Monkey snapped back.

"You sure don't look it."

"I'm fourteen."

"I would've guessed twelve." If he called her "hayseed," she could be rude, too. "I guess you were born small. I guess that's why they call you Monkey. What's your real name?"

"I do all right," he said over his shoulder. "I make mor'n you do."

"Just by runnin' li'l errands?"

"I only do that in the day. Nights I'm steerin'."

She wouldn't compromise herself by asking what that was, but he volunteered, "That's standin' on corners handin' out callin' cards an' tellin' gentlemens where to find what they're lookin' for. And I make good tips playin' with the Razzy Tazzy. That's my band. Willie Joe an' Warm Gravy an' Lagniappe an' me."

"If you're so rich, how come you don't have shoes?"

"Feels better goin' without. 'Sides, I'm savin' to buy me a piano."

"You'll have to make a lot of tips to buy that."

"You ain't heard us, have you? So's you don't have no legitimate opinion. I 'specially don't like uppity girls havin' 'pinions 'bout things they don't know nothin' 'bout."

He shoved on ahead, but she made no further effort to keep up with him. She understood why he'd been so surly with her. He was like her brother Newland's friends, who'd told her she couldn't go fishing with them because she was a girl but had really tried to cut her down because they were sweet on her. And she knew this little pipsqueak, ugly as a gibbon, had eyes for her, too. She didn't care. In fact, she thought it was funny. She held her head higher and felt her hair bounce against her back as she picked up her step. A man raised his hat to her. She didn't acknowledge him outright but put more of a sway in her hips, causing another man to stop and look. She was pretty, that she knew. Grown men, even boys like this Monkey, acted foolish when they saw a pretty girl. If she had the right clothes, she knew even important men would look at her. She felt both excited and frightened at the possibility, but just now she didn't want to think about men, or even boys. She thought how fine it would be to go fishing on a day like this, to sit on the landing and bait the hook and daydream. Last week a Cajun girl who delivered her family's catch to the boardinghouse had talked with her, and afterward Kate's imagination had billowed. She would run away again, this time from the horrible shed and the dingy boardinghouse, and she would live in the bayous, take what she needed from the land, set traps, and sleep all she wanted. One thing was sure: if you were poor, it was better to be poor in the country. But she didn't know how to set traps, and here in the city . . . The street they were now on was still shuttered. A faint melody, as though someone were picking out notes of a new tune on a piano, tickled her ears. This was the sort of neighborhood that came to life only after dark, and it intrigued her. A Negro swept the banquette with slow, even strokes. Another, bare-chested, suspenders looping down over the sides of his trousers, opened the doors of a saloon to release the night's accumulation of sour beer and cigar smoke. Everything seemed slow and easy. Another melody—was it just coming from her own head?—floated on the air. A woman of indeterminate age and color sat in a doorway, bent, motherlike, over a banjo, telling it "Yes, yes" and plucking it with thick-as-tortoiseshell fingernails. Wasn't it a mystery how a sad little tune could ease your heart at the same time it grabbed your throat and made you want to cry? Kate wasn't aware that she'd stopped until Monkey backtracked and stood beside her. "That's Banjo Annie," he told her. "She so far gone she don't even care 'bout money no more. Buy her a drink, she'll play for an hour. Hey, Annie!" He leaned over. "Have a good night?" The woman seemed completely unaware of them.

Kate thought it was mean for Monkey to jeer at such an unfortunate. She wanted to sink down beside her and listen to her sad little tune, but she would never sit down in the street, and certainly not one like this. "How come she doesn't go somewhere else?" she asked.

"I told you. She don't care no more. 'Sides, once you live in the District, it's like bein' stuck on flypaper—you pull an' you pull, but you never get free. Old queer name of Shakespeare said that." She was about to tell him that she too had met Mr. Shakespeare, but he swung the hatbox over his head and bounced off. She stopped at the curb and lifted her skirts to avoid a pile of garbage. The silence of a side street caused her to turn her head, and she saw a scene of such pitiful desolation that it rooted her to the spot. Past a shuttered saloon with a faded BEER AND DANCING sign stood row upon row of tightly packed shacks, each no more than ten feet across and with a single door and window. A mulatto woman wearing nothing but a shift tossed a bucket of slops into the street, then stood flamingolike on one leg, hand to head, scratching her calf with her big toe and squinting at the sun. An infant, gummy with dirt and naked except for a little shirt, smacked an empty bottle in the dirt.

Monkey darted back and jerked her by the elbow. "Hey, you don't wanna go that way. That's Conti Street, where the cribs are." But she still didn't move until three blasts from a bugle startled her. "It's the waffle man. C'mon. I'll race you."

Monkey took off at full tilt, and she grabbed up her skirts and tore after him, released by the sheer joy of running. Down the street, around a corner, up another street, until she stood panting by a mule-drawn wagon with "Genuine Hot Waffles—5¢" painted on the side.

"Beat ya!" Monkey crowed. Then, "We'll take two, Sam. My treat."

A man in shirtsleeves stood in the bed of the wagon and poured batter into a cast-iron waffle maker. Rivulets of sweat from the coal fire slid down his face and into the batter. Kate looked around. This street, too, was eerily quiet but lined with fine houses, many with gaily painted doors, fanlight windows, and wide stoops. Monkey demanded an extra dusting of powdered sugar and handed one of the waffles to Kate. She said thank you, first to Sam, then to Monkey.

"Glad to see you got some manners," Monkey said with his mouth full.

The waffle was crisp and buttery sweet. She could have eaten a half dozen. When they'd finished eating, he took her hands and wiped them down the front of his shirt "so's you won't get yer dress dirty." Walking to the middle of the block, he told her, "This is it." She followed him up the stairs to a mahogany door with a lion's-head knocker. Monkey did a little dance step, banged twice, and handed over the hatbox. "Don't be a rube and you'll be okay."

The door opened and a tall woman in a striped cotton dress, her head tied with a *tignon,* looked down at them from beautifully shaped, slightly bulging eyes. A long, puckered scar ran from her right ear down into her collar, disfiguring her coffee-colored skin. "Sophronia, I brung this girl. Name's Kate," Monkey said. "I'm goin' next door. See you later." And he was down the steps.

Sophronia looked at her impassively. "She's upstairs. She's expectin' you." The tone of "she" gave Kate to understand that Sophronia didn't much like her mistress.

She followed Sophronia into a high-ceilinged entrance hall. The draperies were tightly drawn, but she made out, to her right, some tall white pillars fronted by statues of bare-breasted women and, beyond them, what seemed to be a parlor. To her left there was a larger open room with chairs ranged in a semicircle around a raised platform with Oriental screens. The floors were carpeted, and their steps made no sound as they mounted the stairs. A caw of high-pitched laughter, followed by a raucous demand for quiet, floated from an upper floor. "Most sleeps right into the evening 'cause *she* be too cheap to give a regular breakfast," Sophronia muttered. She stopped at the first door at the head of the stairs and rapped.

"Come," Mrs. Lefevre's voice rang out. The sweat around Kate's hairline and in her armpits turned cold. She wanted to bolt and run.

It was a bedroom-*cum*-office. Mrs. Lefevre sat near the window at a desk, pen in hand, account book open. Bertha, her hair loose, stripped to chemise and bloomers covered with a kimono, was sprawled on a canopied bed, fanning herself. Mrs. Lefevre put down the pen and turned to Kate. "I've brought the hat" was all Kate could get out.

"Of course you have. Perhaps you would like some coffee."

Kate shook her head. "Coffee," Mrs. Lefevre ordered.

As Sophronia turned to go, Bertha added, "And cinnamon rolls for me."

"Come, sit over here near the window so I can see you." Mrs. Lefevre motioned to a chair. Bertha rolled over, cupped her chin in her hands, and looked at Kate with undisguised hostility as Kate felt her way into the chair. "So, Kate," Mrs. Lefevre began, "you've been working for Madame Destault. Madame tells me that, though you're a willing girl, you have no skill or talent as a milliner. In fact, Madame has told me that she will have to let you go. It would be a great pity if you waited until that happened and found yourself out on the streets. A great pity." She looked away, as though it pained her to be the bearer of such sad news; then her pale eyes returned to Kate's.

"She don't need a sales pitch. She knows she's broke," Bertha scoffed.

"You could find a home here, Kate," Mrs. Lefevre went on. "A comfortable home with a room of your very own that would be so much nicer than your present accommodations. A place where you would be protected. And you could also earn a great deal of money."

"Fifty percent minus board," Bertha put in.

"One more peep out of you and you'll go to your room," Mrs. Lefevre said without losing her composure. Bertha turned her attention to the hatbox. "Yes, there's a great deal of money to be made, Kate. More than you've ever seen. Money for pretty clothes and sweets and whatever you"—Kate missed some of the words, hearing Bertha tearing at the tissue paper—"and you would, of course, be free to leave. But by then you'd have your-self a nest egg. You'd have other choices. That's how we should plan our lives, isn't it? To have enough money to have choices. Without money . . ." Mrs. Lefevre got up and stood behind her, placing her hands on Kate's shoulders. Her fingernails sent

needlelike shocks straight to Kate's scalp. She was only periph-
erally aware of Bertha posing in front of the mirror and Sophronia
coming in with a tray.

"... and the only thing for you to do under the circumstances.
Do you understand what I'm saying to you?"

Bertha muttered, "No, draw her a picture. You know, this
bow at the back . . . ."

"Certain gentlemen are particularly attracted to a girl of your
age and condition, and they are willing to pay a great deal of
money for what amounts to only minutes of your time. So will
you come and live with us, Kate?"

Kate started to get up but found she couldn't. Her stomach
turned and bile flowed into her mouth. She closed her eyes,
grasped the arms of the chair, and with monumental effort tried
again to rise, then toppled over sideways onto the floor.

Sophronia put down the tray, grabbed the fan from the bed,
and knelt over her, fanning her face. Mrs. Lefevre said, "Oh,
shit!" put her fist to her mouth, and walked to the window.

Bertha smeared butter onto a cinnamon roll and edged closer,
staring down at Kate's body. "Fainted dead away when you even
talked about it." She laughed, then took a bite of the roll.
"Whadda you think she'd be like if she saw one of the shows or
some joker put a special request to her?"

Sophronia felt Kate's forehead, unbuttoned her dress, and
slipped her hand in next to her heart. She leaned back on her
haunches, looked over at Mrs. Lefevre, and asked, "Think she
might be in the family way?"

Mrs. Lefevre was rigid with anger. "She goddamned better
not be. That Frenchie midget swore to me that the girl was a
virgin."

"She sure is a pretty one," Sophronia said. "An' young enough
so's you'd think . . . Could be I'm wrong, but looks like, feels
like, maybe . . ."

"Get her out of here. Take her down to the kitchen and give her some water and find out what's what."

Sophronia laced Kate's arm around her waist and began to drag her to the door.

"So what if she ain't a virgin? She sure acts like one," Bertha said.

"Go up to your room."

"This is my room, too."

As Sophronia half lifted, half dragged Kate down the stairs, the squabble between Bertha and Mrs. Lefevre reached screeching proportions, and one of the girls stuck her head out of her door and yelled, "Cain't a body get any sleep around this joint?"

Kate came to, sitting at the kitchen table. A batch of cinnamon rolls protected with a little mesh tent was before her, an enamel bowl was between her legs. Sophronia held a wet cloth that had a peppermint smell against her forehead. "Keep yer head low. Jes' keep yer head low an' take long, slow breaths. Y' be all right any minute."

A woman in a pink wrapper and shiny slippers came to the door whining for coffee. Sophronia told Kate to keep the cloth in place and went to the stove. Mug in hand, the woman left, and Sophronia came back, offering a glass of water. She knelt in front of Kate, took the cloth to wipe the sweat from her neck, and made shushing sounds.

Kate took a sip of the water. "Oh, God, Oh, dear God." She wiped her mouth with the back of her hand.

"You already been with a man?" Sophronia asked. Kate shook her head violently from side to side, then slowly moved it up and down. "How long since your last flux? You remember? Can you remember?"

The enamel basin, her knees, the floor, swam before her. "Maybe four weeks, no, five, no . . ." She forced her mind back and could see her own hands, dunking the soiled rags into the washtub—that was when she'd heard the whistle of Frank's steamer as it was about to dock. "Oh no oh no oh no."

"Hush now. No need to work yo'self up. Y' only a month or so gone, we fix you up with a good dose of herbs. Make you sick, but not so much sicker than you be now. I'm gonna give you some bread an' a pinch of salt now. Take it even if yo' stomach say you don't want it. I don't want you throwin' up on this floor I just washed this mornin'." Sophronia got to her feet. Kate straightened, and the room came into sharp focus. She had never seen anything so plain—everything seemed to be outlined with black edges, even the fly that buzzed against the mesh tent protecting the rolls. Then it all went fuzzy.

She was still in the chair, arms dangling, head thrown back, staring at the pea-green ceiling, when she came to again. Monkey was saying, "So do I take her back to the Spider's?" The oven door opened, releasing a blast of heat. The smell of hot cinnamon both nauseated her and flooded her mouth with juice.

"No," Sophronia said. "You gonna help me take her up to Josie's old room on the top floor."

"I never seen anyone faint before. You think she's jest pretendin'? How come she—"

"For a boy goes 'round tellin' everyone how smart he is, you be dumb as a post sometime," Sophronia said tiredly.

"Damn. I thought she was on the level. She sure's hell acted like it."

"Don't be railin' 'gainst a girl in trouble when you been hanging out next door lettin' them nasty mens buy you drinks. You know that a bad house, Monkey. They's inverts over there, just lookin' fer a boy like you to be doin' strange things with."

"I was only playin' the piano."

"Oh, shut yo' mouth, and if you can't do it natural, stuff a roll into it an' help me with this girl. Then you go on 'bout yo' business. There's this note you s'pose to carry back to that woman." She gave him an envelope and turned her attention to Kate. "C'mon now. Up. Help yo'self up." She took Kate by the arms and lifted her into a standing position. "Good, now one arm round my waist, other one round Monkey's shoulder." The disparity in their heights caused her to wobble.

Monkey copped a feel of Kate's breast as he steadied her, and felt a tremor of excitement. He wasn't going to let no queer get ahold of him, leastways not until a nice piece of change was involved. He pushed open the door, and they steered her to the stairs.

Kate tried to walk, but her feet trailed behind, useless as fins. Reaching the landing and stopping for breath, Monkey asked, "What the note say?"

Sophronia could no more read than could Monkey, but she'd witnessed the resolution of Mrs. Lefevre's tantrum. "That hat woman's gonna have her commission cut. She ain't gonna get no two-hundred-dollar fee 'cause this girl's no virgin, now are you, honey?" she added, as though this would urge Kate on. "But she's gonna keep her. Girl look this good, 'course she gonna keep her. An' the shape this girl's in, where else she gonna go?"

The drapes were drawn against the afternoon heat. Kate raised herself on one elbow, gasped as she saw a moving figure, then realized it was her own, reflected in a full-length mirror opposite the bed. She wore only her bloomers. Her skin felt poached as she crossed her arms over her breasts. The room looked as though it had been vacated in a hurry. Clothes and an odd shoe spilled from an open wardrobe, bureau drawers were pulled out, her dress was thrown onto a chaise longue piled with rumpled sheets, towels, and pillows embroidered with "Daisies Won't Tell" and "Come with Me, Honey." On the wall there was a poster advertising a Mardi Gras ball, a calendar from "Howard's Canning Company, Joplin, Missouri," showing a rosy-cheeked child and

mother in matching aprons, and a group of photos. She got to
her feet and stepped closer to examine them: a naked man and
woman in contortionists' positions. Backing up, she bumped into
the dressing table. The empty bottle of Raleigh rye clattered
against the mirror. There was a box of powder, a few scent bottles,
a note printed in a childishly shaky hand—"VIVIAN YOU WILL
ROT IN HELL." The sound of high heels approaching sent her
scurrying back to the bed. There were no sheets on it, and even
in the dim light she could see that the ticking was badly stained.
She grabbed up her dress to cover herself, lay down, and closed
her eyes.

Bertha bumped the door closed with her hip. "You awake? I
bet you're just playing 'possum. You awake?" It was an accusation.

She put the tray on the nightstand near the window and yanked
back the drapes. Kate's hand shot up to cover her eyes from the
glare. "See that li'l ol' black pill?" Bertha nodded to the tray,
which held teapot, cup, a small bottle of brandy, and a black
pellet. "Take that black pill, then drink that whole pot of tea.
Vivian says the pill will work by itself, but Sophronia don't trust
it, so she brewed up some mess of voodoo weeds. One or the
t'other's got to work. Me," she bragged while pouring the tea,
"I grew up knowing what to do so's I don't get pregnant, and
now I mostly do French stuff, so there's not the risk. This tea
tastes like swamp water an' pee, so I brung you the brandy to
wash it down with." When Kate drew up her legs and rolled over
onto her side, Bertha prodded her gratitude with, "I took the
key to the liquor cabinet while Vivian was takin' her nap."

"Thank you."

Bertha shrugged. "You're welcome. Just remember you owe
me one." She uncorked the brandy, took a long pull, and looked
around. "Josie sure did leave this place a mess." She went to the
dresser, examined the perfume bottles, and slipped one into her

pocket. "Go on, take that pill," she urged. "I seen it work for some girls. 'Course sometimes it makes some of your hair fall out. Then drink down that tea. Two of 'em together should have you cramping up by morning, then you'll cat up anything you've eaten, and then you should start. And you better pray you do, 'cause elseways we'll have to get the midwife, an' that'll cost you *beaucoup* dollars, and you'll be in the hole even 'fore you start workin'."

Kate took a sip of the tea. It was so foul-tasting that it puckered her mouth. She picked up the pill, but the prospect of taking something that would make her vomit or, worse yet, make her hair fall out so frightened her that she stalled and asked, "Why did Josie leave?"

"Some fight with a customer. She oughta know Vivian always stands up for the customers. She told Sophronia she was runnin' off to get married, but if you believe that, you'd believe pigs could fly. That Josie's a real peckerhead. She's prob'ly draggin' her tail all over the streets, and the police'll prob'ly pick her up, and I know she don't have no protection money, so she'll land up in jail."

Bertha flopped onto the chaise longue and began to trace the embroidery on one of the pillows. Kate pretended to swallow the pill but slipped it under her backside. "Bet she's sorry she couldn't carry these pillows with her," Bertha went on. "She was always doing embroidery or knitting. When she first come here, she wanted to carry it into the parlor and work on it while she was waitin' for the customers." She gave a little barking laugh. "You take that pill?" Kate nodded. "You sure do look bad," Bertha said with satisfaction. Something akin to pity stirred in her, but she could express it only as exasperation. "You sure got yourself into a fine mess, didn't you? Go on and have a pull on that brandy."

Kate did as she was told, but the liquor started to come up as soon as she'd swallowed. "Where are you from?" she asked.

"From my mother, same as you," Bertha drawled.

"I meant—"

"I know what you meant. I come from right here."

"New Orleans?"

"Right here. The District. I was makin' a good livin' by the time I was thirteen."

"Where's your mother now?"

"She's croaked. Where's yours?"

"She's croaked, too," Kate said, adopting the lingo.

"What she die of?"

"Puerperal fever."

"Say what?"

"That fever you get when you have a baby." She could see her mother lying in the coffin, the stillborn baby next to her. She had vowed that she would never let herself become what her mother had been—a bag of bones, teeth missing, belly always swollen with another baby.

"Well, my old lady died of the gleet. Don't matter how careful you be. You're in the life, you might catch it. But I give her a fine funeral."

Kate had never heard of gleet but didn't have to ask what it was. She turned her face to the wall.

"You want for Monkey to go round to where you were staying and pick up your things?"

Kate shook her head.

"I figured you didn't have nothin'." Bertha looked around to see if there was anything else she could scavenge. "Guess I'll take these pillows. Sort of a memento of Josie. Hide that brandy if anyone comes in."

As the sun set, the house began to come to life. Kate heard

footsteps, the sound of running water, a girl singing "In the Sweet By and By," another demanding to know who the hell had stolen her hairbrush. She got up and poured the tea out of the window. Sophronia came in with another pot, lit the lamp, and asked how she was feeling. "Just keep drinking that tea down," she said.

"What's in it?"

"Pennyrile, false unicorn, and a mess of other herbs. You don't need to worry your mind. Just rest now. She'll be in soon."

When Sophronia had gone, Kate lay very still. All she could think to do was wait for her heart to stop beating hysterically so she could think what to do next. But no thoughts came. It was like a nightmare wherein she was being attacked but could not move. The noises from the street and downstairs whirled around her—horses' hooves, men's voices raised in song, shouts of expectation and anger, a thrumping banjo, a piano pounding out a rollicking beat.

"Are you all right now?" Vivian Lefevre's voice was as soft as a bedtime story. She stood near the bed touching the diamond star that caught her upswept hair. "In a little while I want you to get up and take a bath and brush your hair, then put this on." She held a child's white nightie. "I've contacted a gentleman who wants very much to meet you. He'll be coming by later this evening, but you won't have to come downstairs. He'll come up to the room to visit. There's no need to be frightened. He's very fond of innocent girls, you see."

Kate's tongue had swollen to twice its size. "I don't feel good."

"I have taken you in, Kate. You appreciate that, don't you? I'm going to fix you up, and when you feel better, you can leave if you like, just as I told you this afternoon. But you'll be leaving with money. Just think about that, and it will be over very, very soon."

A skein of calm, heavy as a trance, was woven over Kate's

mind. Sophronia helped her to the bathroom, and while she brushed her hair and put on the nightie, Sophronia made up the bed, grumbling that it was the maid's job. When she found the bottle of brandy Kate had tucked under the mattress, she handed it over. "Go on, finish it up. You'll be fine. Man that old not gonna bother you much."

Kate upended the bottle, then lay back down to wait.

"She's a little scared," Vivian said softly, holding back the door as the man entered. "Only natural."

"Only natural," he echoed.

In the light of the lamp his eyelids were wrinkled and yellow and his face had a dull red-orange glow. His hand, reaching out for her shoulder, looked like a bird's claw. When she shrank back, he said, "How you doing, little girl?" and Vivian closed the door.

CHAPTER

VI

It's no disgrace to be poor, but it might as well be.

Frank McKinney Hubbard

Queen Mollie Q. stood fully dressed but barefoot at the sideboard in her Turkish parlor, arranging bottles of her best liquor so that the labels would show. It was her turn to host the meeting of the Society of Venus and Bacchus, and she'd planned to have her cook, Vinnie, make some dainty cakes she'd seen in *Godey's Lady's Book*. But Vinnie had sent Monkey 'round to say she couldn't come in, so Mollie decided to make up for the lack of food with high-class liquor. She usually served cheaper grades funneled into cut-glass decanters to all but her best customers, but, since most of the madams did the same, they'd notice the difference. Never let it be said that Mollie Q. didn't put out the best.

She knew that she would have to let Vinnie go, and it made her sad. Vinnie had been with her for five years, was a good churchgoing woman, never padded the grocery bill, and made the best shrimp soufflé in the District. But a madam needed a reliable cook almost as much as she needed police protection, a good laundress, or a tough houseman, and since Vinnie's daughter had run off up north and left her with the care of four grand-children, Vinnie was, understandably, less than reliable. Mollie liked to give her girls a healthy feed, and she made a tidy profit on the late suppers for customers, so she was desperate to find another cook. Last Sunday, when they were closed as usual and Vinnie hadn't come in, she'd put on the apron herself. As a girl she'd learned nothing beyond boiling potatoes or porridge, but during the brief time she'd been married, she'd tried, as any good wife would, to master a decent meal. But that had been thirty years ago. Last Sunday she'd forgotten to truss the turkey, so it had come out a splayed, dry thing, more cremated than baked, and she'd burned the arse out of the pan trying to make gravy, and the mashed potatoes had so many lumps in them that the girls had picked them out and thrown them at each other. It wasn't a performance she would repeat.

And then there was the problem of Agnes. Agnes was a hard-working, popular girl who could put the sag in the mattress springs, but she'd been sick on and off for over a month. At first Mollie had thought it was the flu, but now she knew it was consumption. She'd been up and down with the girl all night, putting mustard plasters on her chest and ladling hot tea with honey and brandy down her throat. Around four in the morning, when things were quieting down, she'd stuffed a pillow over Agnes's mouth to muffle the sound of her coughing. No man wanted to hear a sick whore in a sporting house. She was going to have to pack Agnes off to a sanatorium, and Agnes was a flibbertigibbet who hadn't saved a dime. The money for the sanatorium and the cash she'd give to Vinnie to tide her over would be quite a chunk of foliage. And there couldn't be a worse time to be understaffed.

There was war fever in the air, and nothing, not even the Mardi Gras or a sudden bull market, increased business as much as war fever. The boys were gearing up to fight, and even the old coots who'd never seen more than domestic battles had caught the fever and wanted to get their licks in. "Remember the *Maine!*" had replaced toasts to beauty and good times; some fool had stuffed little American flags in her potted plants; and her professor, Silt Simmons, had earned over a hundred and fifty dollars in tips the other night by playing patriotic anthems. When war was declared against Spain—and she had it on good authority that it would be a matter of weeks, if not days—she'd probably have to bar the door. She'd written to an old friend in St. Louis asking if she could spare a couple of extra girls, but it was risky to take on girls she didn't know. She didn't like to board girls who turned their money over to fancy men or had let their drinking or drug habits get so out of hand as to interfere with their work. And she had certain standards of attractiveness to maintain.

"Damn it to hell!" she muttered. Her feet were killing her, and the prospect of missing out on volume business made her sour. She uncorked a bottle of Clos de Chapit white burgundy, poured herself a glass, picked up a copy of the recent edition of the *Blue Book,* in which the madams advertised their establishments, and went to sit on one of the divans.

A few moments alone with her possessions usually had a calming effect, but this afternoon not even the sight of the painting she'd just bought from the Ringrose Emporium made her feel better. It showed some joker with his head wrapped in a towel lounging on a carpet, surrounded by his wives, smoking a hookah and eyeing a dancing girl who was about to drop her last veil. She knew every man who saw it would put himself in the place of the pasha or raja or whatever he was, and when she'd bought it, she'd thought it had just the right tone (stimulating but not vulgar); but now she suspected she'd paid too much for it. She'd learned to spot shoddy clothes, jewelry, furniture, and booze, but she couldn't trust herself when it came to art. She should've asked Shakespeare's opinion. Shakespeare understood the fine points. She'd always thought a painting was vulgar only if it actually showed quiff, but he'd told her that anything ugly, coarse, or too easily available was vulgar. When he'd said that, she'd said she'd have to count most of her early life as vulgar. Liquor, thank God, had erased much of her memory, but at times like these, when she was worried about juggling things, memories of those years when she'd first come out floated back. She'd been just fifteen when she'd serviced General Hooker's Union troops in a tent city outside Washington. In the summer you never wore more than a shift, the gnats and fleas bit you raw, you couldn't get rid of the flies, and the smells . . . ! But the winter was worse. You never took your boots off, let alone your clothes, and neither did the men. You put a bit of oilcloth at the foot of your cot so they wouldn't get mud on your blanket, and hoisted your skirts, the hems of which were always muddy. Your hands and feet ached with cold, your lips chapped and cracked, you had to break the ice on the water tank and heat the water over campfires to wash up.

But now she sat in a make-believe tent—yards of paisley damask with gold threads draped above the divans to create a Turkish effect. Now she had—she didn't have to open the *Blue Book* to read the advertisement Shakespeare had helped to write— "one of the most opulent mansions in the Crescent City, complete with hot and cold running water and furnishings imported by Vantine of New York, offering a bevy of beautiful, well-mannered, and companionable young ladies." She had four stories chockablock full of real walnut and oak, none of that cheap lacquered stuff, and canopied beds, Chinese vases, tapestries, statues of Greek goddesses and English shepherdesses, cut-glass decanters, a solid-gold salt and pepper set, good napery for the table . . . and soap. She could never get enough soap. She had an entire bureau filled with soap. But at times like this, when she was worried, the taste of poverty came into her mouth, strong as raw onions.

She took a swallow of wine and let her mind drift to her retirement dream: she would go back to Ireland and pass herself off as a widow. She would live modestly but comfortably near the sea, in a little stone house with a garden. That would be her heaven on earth until she had to go to the other place. She knew St. Peter wouldn't let her pass through the pearly gates right away, but if she gave to the poor and did good works and prayed to the Virgin to intercede for her, she could cut down her time in purgatory. But she didn't have enough money to do that. Not quite yet. She had some money in the stock market, but that was as unreliable as gambling. And since that bastard landlord, Charles Randsome, didn't maintain the house, she was always doling out for repairs. What if she surprised herself and lived to be an old woman, and her nest egg ran out? She wanted to give to the Sisters of Charity, but she didn't think it would be much fun to be dependent on them.

"God help us all," she muttered. She had promised herself that she would be out of the life by the time she was fifty. And she had passed her forty-ninth birthday last October.

The front doorbell rang. Judas, her houseman, was still sleeping in his back room; Mamie, her housekeeper, was in the kitchen with one of the maids; and she'd sent the other one around to the bakery to get some rolls for the girls' breakfast. So she got up to answer it herself. "You silly cow," she cursed herself, "why are y' moonin' about the past and the future when you should be plannin' a strategy for the meeting!" Now that the District was legal, it seemed to her that madams should have the same rights as any other tenants, and she hoped to organize the others to stand up for those rights.

Without looking through the keyhole, she opened the door. Jessie Brown, "the workingman's friend," was on the stoop. In her straw hat and high-buttoned dress, she looked as though she might be going to a church picnic. She even carried a covered dish.

"Good afternoon, Mollie. Don't you look grand?" Jessie admired Mollie's fuchsia-colored dress decorated with jet beads, then, seeing Mollie was barefoot, added, "Your feet botherin' you again?"

Mollie nodded. "Who woulda thought a woman who'd spent most of her life on her back would end up with lousy feet?"

"It don't have nothin' to do with standin'. It's a family weakness."

"From what I remember, they had every other weakness, why not feet, too?"

Jessie handed over the dish. "It's not for the meeting. Since you said Vinnie wasn't comin' in, I brought some hash for your girls."

"You're a treasure, Jessie. Will you carry it to the kitchen, then show yourself into the Turkish parlor while I get m' shoes on?" She looked out at the weather, then called over her shoulder, "And have Mamie bring an extra can to put the umbrellas in. It looks like rain."

She was about to close the door when she saw Lady Caroline swanning along the banquette, umbrella already unfurled. Lady Caroline was not a lady—in fact, not even a woman, though he got himself up in such a mess of padding and paint that, unless you looked at the hands or came close enough to see the bluish tinge beneath the face powder, you couldn't have guessed. Some of the madams wanted to draw the line at Lady Caroline, but Mollie stuck up for him. The flesh trade was the flesh trade, and a madam was a madam, and if you wanted to get particular, there were a few others Mollie would exclude, Vivian Lefevre topping her list.

"What a night!" Lady Caroline dabbed at the sweat on his upper lip with a lawn hanky. "You know that carpet in my vestibule? Stiff with beer! And I've got a bruise the size of a plate on my backside." He collapsed his umbrella and rolled his eyes. "Coupla sailors started to break up the place. Reggie tried to stop it, and one of them knocked him out cold. I tried to tackle 'em, but they ran off before I could collect for breakage. And when we tried to wash out the carpet, the colors ran. I paid four hundred dollars for that carpet not six weeks ago."

"Well, you know the merchants always rook us."

"I'll have to get my lawyer on to it."

"I am sorry. Why don't you go on into the parlor, dearie? Pour yourself a drink, or better yet"—she remembered that Jessie didn't approve of Lady Caroline—"come into my bedroom while I get m' shoes on."

She went to the dining room, yelled for Mamie to take care of the front door, and hurried back. Lady Caroline followed her into her bedroom, still bewailing his ruined carpet. After adjusting the tilt of his hat in front of the mirror, he moved to the window. "I don't expect we'll have much of a turnout this afternoon. It looks like rain, and business has been so heavy I wouldn't have come myself, but I thought I'd lose my marbles if I didn't get out for a while. I said to Reggie, 'Goin' to Mollie's is like goin' home.' That's why you've got customers who come by regular even when they don't take a girl upstairs."

Mollie grunted as she bent forward to roll on her black stockings, "Sure, I think some of 'em, at least the older gents, wouldn't bother mussin' the sheets if they weren't afraid of what their friends would think. They mostly want to smoke and play cards and talk free." She forced her foot into a shoe. "Ah, I used to have such pretty little feet, but now it's like pushing sausage meat into a casing. Every time I put on a shoe I feel like a Chinese concubine."

"You shouldn't complain. It takes the side of a cow to make

me a pair of heels, an' I have to order 'em special." Lady Caroline
lifted the lace panel in the center of the velvet drapes to get a
better look at the street. "Well, I'll be damned. Here comes
Violet Johnson wearin' the same dress I saw on that society bitch
Phillipa Cotrane when I was in Krauss's Department Store. She
musta had it copied special, but she's built like a tugboat, and all
them flounces . . . She's with Lena Friedman. I thought those
two were on the outs."

"Ah, someone's always on the outs with someone else. It's like
a shebeen at closing time," Mollie said tiredly, pulling down her
skirts. Rivalries, vendettas, shifting allegiances were the woof
and warp of life in the District. "I suppose we'd better get this
show started."

Violet Johnson called Mollie *"ma chérie"* and kissed her on
both cheeks. In the *Blue Book,* Violet billed her place as "the
House of All Nations," and she had *"Aquí se habla español"* and
"Ici on parle français" printed on her calling cards. She claimed
to be from Paris, but her accent flattened to a midwestern twang
when she got riled up. Lena Friedman was from Poland, had
flaming red hair, and was more clever than a sack of cats. She'd
started a craze for redheaded Jewish girls, claiming they were
more passionate, and half the girls in her house came out of the
same bottle.

Lena got right down to business by asking if Mollie had negotiated a percentage with the new fellow who was hawking
earrings from house to house. Then Mini Haha came up the
stairs. Mulatto madams, such as Lulu White and Countess Willie
Piazza, did the lion's share of the District business but never
mixed with the white madams. Mini, a light-skinned Negress,
claimed to be Indian and had a huge portrait of her alleged
parents, Mr. and Mrs. Hiawatha, hung in her front hall to prove
it. Everyone knew Mini's Indian-princess story was bunkum, but
nobody said so because both madams and girls made up equally

tall tales about their pasts, and some were so far gone that they'd actually come to believe them. Predictably, because no man wanted to think he was buying cheap goods, the stories ran to aristocratic births or having come from good families. A girl who'd run away from a barren Arkansas farm said she was the illegitimate daughter of Prince Albert; another who'd quit sewing shirtwaists in a New York factory upped her stock by saying Andrew Carnegie was her father. Mollie had known only one girl who came from money, and she was so sick in the head that she thought it was fun to go to bed with strangers and didn't watch the clock. Her unprofessional lust and frequent crying jags had forced Mollie to let her go.

Beyond the individual myths there were the collective ones. There was the one about the man who'd deserted his family and years later met his abandoned daughter in a cathouse; the one about the madam who was giving a bum a handout when she recognized him as the man who'd first led her up the path of sin; or the one about the planter who wouldn't pay his bill, so the madam told him his mother had been a Negress and he shot himself.

Mollie complimented Violet on her dress (thinking that all those flounces *did* make her look like a tugboat masquerading as a yacht) and turned to greet Lillie Dupree when she heard the familiar racking cough. Agnes was on the landing, gripping the banister with one hand and holding the neck of Mollie's old white nightdress closed with the other. Her hair was lank, and red patches like some old, nearsighted woman's rouge stood out on her cheeks.

"I can't sleep and I want some food," she whined.

"Go on up. I'll be right there," Mollie told her, equally cranky. "She's got the flu," Mollie explained, knowing that Lena would like nothing better than to blab it around that one of Mollie's girls had something catching. She ushered them into the Turkish parlor, told Mamie to take over the door, then went to the kitchen for some rolls, tea, and brandy. As she carried the tray upstairs, she cursed with every step.

It took her another twenty minutes to pat Agnes down from a coughing fit and rouse one of the girls to sit with her. When she came back downstairs, the entrance hall was empty and the cacophony from the parlor indicated that the meeting was about to start. The front door had been left ajar, and as she went to close it, she glanced in at the parlor. From a distance the assemblage might be taken for any group of well-heeled, civic-minded women, but if you looked closer, you could see the differences —a gold tooth here, a scar there, brighter hair and darker skin tones (Mini and a lone Italian), more jewelry than proper women would show in the afternoon—and you could hear the difference, too—unrestrained laughter, foreign accents, a peppering of four-letter words no good woman would know, let alone utter. One day, Mollie told herself, she would belong to a club for real ladies. She'd serve tea, not booze, and little cakes, and she'd hear what genteel women had to say about their husbands and never let on that she'd spent her whole life listening to the other side.

There was a clap of thunder. She stepped out onto the stoop and saw Vivian Lefevre hurrying along the banquette, running a head of steam to bust the livers. The sky opened as Mollie stepped back in. It was all she could do to stop herself from slamming the door in Vivian's face. How she hated that face, with its taut cheekbones, icy eyes, and little pointy chin. It was so resistant to any appeal to common humanity that she wanted to cross herself whenever she saw it. She knew Vivian was dangerous. Not because she made her girls perform in "circuses" to whet the customers' appetites or catered to "special tastes" that put the girls in physical danger, or made them pay back loans at exorbitant interest, or even because she dabbled in voodoo, but because, Mollie had it on good authority, Vivian had stooped to blackmail. A blackmailer was as bad as an informer. A blackmailer spawned fear and mistrust with customers, and that threatened the entire profession. "Are you comin' or are you not?" Mollie shouted. "The meeting is about to start."

Vivian crossed the threshold, collapsed her umbrella, and looked around as though she were in a shop but couldn't see anything worth buying.

"You're drippin'," Mollie told her, indicating the growing puddle from Vivian's umbrella with her toe.

Vivian ignored her and took a step back to the open door. "Hurry up! Hurry up, can't you!" she yelled.

Her pet, Bertha, ignoring the downpour, dawdled up the front stairs as though she were picking wildflowers. Her face had the tense but perversely expectant look of a child who wants to see how far she can go before she gets slapped. "Your umbrella," Mollie said again.

"Yes," Vivian replied, and handed it over as though Mollie were a mere attendant. She then told Bertha to come, as though she were ordering a dog to heel, and headed for the parlor. Mollie's heart thumped with indignation as she bent and moved a hooked rug to absorb the puddle. As she straightened, she came level with Bertha's pouty face. She didn't like it much more than she liked Vivian's, but she tried to be charitable because she knew that Bertha was a "trick baby" who'd been born a few blocks away. The girl had never known any life but the District, so she couldn't be expected to have normal feelings.

"Hello, Mollie."

"Hello to you, Bertha. Just put your umbrella in that can and get on in there."

"We got a new girl at the house," Bertha whispered.

"And what's that got to do with me?"

"She's real unhappy."

"Show me a happy whore, I'll show you a dead whore. The

meeting's starting." She was about to move, but Bertha's sly I've-got-a-secret look stopped her. "What are you after tellin' me? Out with it."

"I thought maybe you'd like to meet her. I could have Sophronia bring her by."

Mollie stepped closer. "What's she like?"

"She's just been hatched. The Spider tried to pass her off as a virgin, and Vivian's hot as hell's hinges about that. She's—"

"Is she pretty?"

"There's some who'd say so," Bertha said grudgingly.

Just then Lady Caroline put his head around the jamb of the parlor door. "Mollie, it's getting out of hand. Let's start."

"Well?" Bertha demanded.

"I'll talk to you before you leave. C'mon now."

There were perhaps twenty-five madams sitting or lounging on the divans, most with drinks in their hands and talking a mile a minute. With a quick look round the room, Mollie saw that Alma Heflin was coke-frisky and Lady Caroline had already worried down two or three whiskeys. Gertrude Hauser, a big blonde with skin the color of biscuit dough, came up to Mollie and in guttural, accented English said, "I sink ve should talk about zis first," waving the *Blue Book* under her nose.

"Well, go on and talk about it," Violet Johnson told her.

"You are not going to chair zis meeting?" Gertrude asked. Mollie told her no and took a seat near the sideboard, where she wasn't the focus of attention but had a good view of the room.

Lena Friedman stood up. "Let's get on with it."

"Oh, Lena, you always try to do things too fast," Alma Heflin drawled, falling back among the pillows with exaggerated languor. Alma had once been an actress and still knew how to get attention. Her place was next door to Lena's, and until recently Lena had done the more lively business, but Alma had recruited an imitation Little Egypt who'd been doing the hootchy-kootchy at stag parties in Chicago and billed her as "an artist straight from the Sultan of Egypt's harem." Her business had picked up, and she wanted to let the women know that the pecking order had changed. "Lena pushes customers out her door while they're still buttoning up their trousers."

This caused a general round of laughter that rose higher when Lillie Dupree said, "Let's let Gertrude talk first, since she's the oldest."

"Ze hell I am," Gertrude protested.

Flora de Chalmette probably was the oldest, but no one could determine what her age was. Flora only dealt with customers in a room lit with candles, and she never appeared in public without a veil. Just now she sat on a high-backed chair, an *éminence grise* swathed in purple silk, though no skin was visible except an age-betraying hand.

"But before ve have chaos, I vill go first," Gertrude went on. "I vonder if next year ve shouldn't go outside the District to print ze *Blue Book*. To get some bids before ve decide."

"No printer outside the District would take it," Violet reasoned. "Besides, you get what you pay for."

"Except at Lena's," Alma put in.

Lena raised a chuckle when she countered with, "Oh, Alma, you'd probably like to hang out the old red lantern like you did on your papa's shack."

Gertrude pounded the sideboard and made the bottles rattle. "Ve are talking about ze *Blue Book*."

"Ladies, ladies!" Mollie clapped her hands, then spread them in a pleading gesture. She got up, reminded them that Gertrude had the floor, and, as soon as Gertrude got a run on what she wanted to say, poured herself another glass of wine, sat back down, and turned her attention to Bertha.

Bertha sat on an ottoman, pigeon-toed, rolling a strand of wet hair around her finger, eyes on the carpet. Sipping her wine,

Mollie turned Bertha's proposition over in her mind. She didn't want to get the reputation of being a raider, and there was a possibility that she was being set up. Perhaps this new girl was a dud and Vivian was using Bertha to palm her off. But intuition told her that Bertha was acting alone, getting her own back for past injustices—or driven by jealousy and fear that the new girl would replace her in Vivian's affections. Though "affections" could hardly be the word for anything Vivian might feel.

As she looked out the window at the now steady drizzle, Mollie's thoughts turned gloomy. What real affections did she have? Hadn't she almost smothered Agnes last night because she was afraid the girl would wake the overnighters? And didn't she think of that poor child's illness only in terms of what it would cost her? But how else could a woman live when she had no one but herself to depend on, knew the world thought she was scum, and had had an army of men wipe themselves on her? Thank God she didn't have to worry about servicing men anymore. She hadn't worried about a man in decades, unless she counted Sean Hanratty.

Ten years ago she had broken the rule she'd adopted after her brief marriage and had given Sean Hanratty money. She hadn't done it because she had the itch for him. He was only of middling height and average looks, though he had a fine tenor voice and powerful arms and thighs. She'd given him money because he'd been born in the city's Irish Channel, had been everything from newspaper boy to bricklayer, and since he'd had enough blarney to talk her into a loan, she'd figured he'd make a success of the saloon he wanted to open. The night he'd paid her back and told her he was going to open a second saloon, they'd gotten sentimental with homesick songs and too much champagne and ended up in bed. In terms of commercial desirability she was already past it, because men liked them young. She was much happier administering the house than servicing men. But Sean was an entirely different matter. As they'd thrashed about, she'd used every technique she'd learned for their mutual pleasure. She'd thought it would be a one-time shot, but it had gone on for years, and even now, though far less frequently, when they got sentimental about their friendship or were pleasantly tiddly, they still had a roll in the hay. Sometimes she thought she loved him. He had three saloons now and was the unofficial mayor of the District. He also had a house, a wife, and four children, but she couldn't begrudge him that.

Returning her attention to the room, Mollie realized that the talk had gone from the *Blue Book* to the probability of war, through a discussion of a wholesale liquor manufacturer who was said to be watering the product, and was now settling on how the ordinance would affect protection payments. It had been the custom for the police to make weekly collections based on a certain price per head for every girl in a house.

"But if we're legal, why should we have to pay now?" Lillie Dupree, who had a face sweet as a custard pie and a mind no firmer than its filling, wanted to know.

"You always need protection," Clarise Russell told her.

"Sure you do," Alma Heflin seconded. "What if one of your girls goes shopping outside the District and gets picked up for something, or one of your customers gets so rough you can't handle it alone?"

"Remember what happened to Nell Kimball," Flora de Chalmette warned.

"What happened to Nell Kimball?" Nora Easton asked. Nora hadn't come up through the ranks. A trolley car manufacturer from Cleveland had sent her down to run a house in which he had a controlling interest.

"Some local scion by the name of—" Alma stopped when she saw Flora put her finger to her lips. "This rich little bastard," she amended, remembering that the young man's family was prominent, "got violent with one of Nell's girls. She was only fighting back in self-defense. . . ."

"If she vas properly trained, it vould never have happened," Gertrude said.

Jessie Brown's eyes blazed. "You mean a whore doesn't have the right to defend herself?"

"If she vas properly trained . . ."

"*And*"—Alma leaned on the word and got everyone's attention—"the girl hit him with a poker and accidentally killed him. Nell woulda been in awful trouble if the police hadn't been behind her. They took the body out to the river and made like he'd drowned."

"Weren't they afraid the kid's family—"

"They got permission from the family first. Then they took him out and . . ."

Mollie had heard it all before and went back to considering Bertha's offer. As though she could read Mollie's thoughts, Bertha slid her eyes over in a quick conspiratorial glance.

". . . and that's a true story," Alma concluded, and looked as if she wanted to take a bow. "I swear by my mother's eyes. But even so, Nell had to leave town 'cause the boy's family made that a condition. She's out in San Francisco on the Barbary Coast now."

"Those poor Chinese bitches out there. I hear they only get ten cents for a 'feelee' and seventy-five cents for a 'dooee.' They really get a raw time of it," Jessie, who was a bit of a radical, put in. "They don't even have any madams to protect them. Men are runnin' the show."

"Nell wouldn't be around *them*," Alma said with pride. "Nell's white, she's got a high-class trade."

"I hate all coppers," Lady Caroline told his drink. "No matter how much I pay 'em, they're always on my tail." He looked around as though someone had disputed him, then repeated, loudly and angrily, "I hate coppers."

That stopped the room for a second, and Mollie, sensing a further degeneration of the discussion, laughed. "Sure, they've been skinning us alive before and they'll keep on doin' it now. But Alma's right, Lillie, you've got to keep 'em on the payroll. But I've been wonderin' if we can't take advantage of the ordinance to squeeze the landlords for repairs."

"That wouldn't concern some of us," Vivian said.

Jessie flared up again. "It concerns most of us. Just because you own and you've got something on the tax assessor so you only pay enough taxes for a chicken coop doesn't mean—"

"I suggest you call a separate meeting if you want to talk about your problems as tenants," Vivian persisted.

The discussion deteriorated into overlapping protests and complaints. Shakespeare had warned Mollie that she wouldn't get too far with her organizing efforts. The madams, he said, were like all artists, so competitive and wedded to thinking they were special that they preferred to be screwed individually.

"That new painting you got is very elegant," Mini Haha told Mollie above the din.

That seals it, Mollie thought, now I know it's vulgar enough to tree a wolf. She realized it was getting on to four and the girls would be coming down for breakfast, and since she was hostess, she decided to close the meeting on a more positive note and told Mamie to break out the champagne so they could toast the ordinance. Mollie raised her glass and said, "Here's to being legal." Glasses were clinked and drained. Jessie asked for a hand up from the low divan. Women said their good-byes and started to leave. Mollie refilled her glass and said, "Respectable at last. Thank sweet Jesus."

Lena Friedman cleaned her top teeth with her tongue. "Why

do whores, especially mick whores, always have to bring Jesus into it?"

"Mollie's very religious," Jessie said to no one in particular.

Mollie took that as a compliment and began to smile, then she heard Vivian Lefevre say, "That's because she likes the idea of a naked man nailed to a cross."

Anger cracked through Mollie like lightning. She lunged forward, sloshing the champagne. "There'll be no blasphemy in this house, Vivian Lefevre. You have brought your smirking face and your evil ways in here, but you will not blaspheme!"

"Let it go." Lady Caroline put his hand on Mollie's chest and pushed her back. "Everyone knows Vivian's a worthless cunt."

"And aren't you jealous, you pathetic thing?" Vivian said calmly.

"Stop it! Stop it!" Alma cried in a voice that could reach the top balcony. Her dose had worn off, and she was raw and jittery. "I declare, I can't take this. I have to go home."

Mini took Alma by the arm. "Come on. I'll walk you."

Vivian stood as still as if she were having her picture taken, but the left side of her mouth twitched. "Come," she said to Bertha, and swept out.

Bertha hesitated, then started after her, but Mollie grabbed her arm. "You send that girl around as soon as you can," she whispered furiously. "And you send Sophronia with her."

She turned back into the room, panting. Only Lady Caroline remained on the floor, mopping up the champagne with his handkerchief, muttering, "I hate that bitch almost as much as I hate the coppers."

"I'm going to take one of her girls," Mollie said softly. "If she's pigeon-chested and cross-eyed, I'll have her work in the kitchen. And if I have to offer her twenty dollars a week to be my cook, I'm going to take Sophronia, too."

Two days later, as Kate lay torpid in the afternoon heat, Bertha slid into the room quiet as a shadow and hissed, "Wake up! Get up! Vivian's gone out. Y' gotta run now, an' fast."

Kate jerked up, feeling sick and muzzy. "Where'd she go?"

"To the bank. C'mon, will ya!" Bertha yanked her to her feet, gave her face a little slap, and handed her her dress. "I swear I never seen a body sleep so much. Look alive, will ya? Sophronia's waitin'."

"I thought you said tomorrow," Kate said dully, pulling the dress over her head. She didn't really know what day it was. She slept sometimes fourteen hours straight. At night men did things to her. "I was supposed to get paid today."

"You know Vivian'd find an excuse not to pay you. She's still deductin' for that medicine and those days you had the flux and couldn't work. Button up yer tits, will ya?" She pushed Kate's hands aside and began doing up the front of her dress.

"Bertha . . ." Now that she was leaving, Kate was tempted to tell that she hadn't taken the herbs or the pill, that she'd gotten out of five days' work by pretending she was bleeding.

"Stop jawin', get yer shoes. No, dummy, don't put 'em on, just carry 'em."

"What's this Mollie like?"

"I told you, she's okay. Ya got everything?"

Kate stared around. There was nothing to get. "My hair," she said, feeling the matted mess and reaching for the brush.

"Screw your hair, get your hat. An' come quiet so's you don't wake the others."

Sophronia was sitting at the kitchen table, carpetbag on her lap. "You sure Mollie wants both of us?" she asked.

Bertha was wild with excitement. This intrigue was better than a good brawl. "I already tolt you. Get a move on, will ya!"

Sophronia mumbled, "Vivian'll get her voodoo woman an' put a hex on us for sure."

"Well, 'fore she does, y'all'll be livin' in hog heaven, won't ya? I oughta be gettin' a commission."

Sophronia looked around. "S'pose it can't be any worse than it is 'round here." She opened a drawer, took out a boning knife, and slipped it into her bag. "No, rabbit," she told Kate, "I'm not gonna be cuttin' anyone. Cook needs a good sharp knife. You ready?"

Kate finished buttoning up her boots and nodded. She was more afraid than she'd been when she'd run away from her father's house.

"It's only three blocks," Sophronia told her. "An' we'll walk slow an' regular, like we're going to the store." She opened the back door.

Bertha laughed. "Vivian'll bust a gut when she sees y're gone. So, 'bye, Kate. See y' around."

" 'Bye, Bertha," Kate said. "Thank you."

Bertha was magnanimous. "It's nothin'. Jest remember you owe me."

Mollie couldn't believe her luck. She'd been ready to take anything, but this was the sort of girl you recruited once in a lifetime. After showing Sophronia around the kitchen and introducing them to the staff, she took Kate's hand and led her upstairs to her room. "There's nothin' to be scared of now," she assured her, seeing that Kate was still shaken. "If Vivian Lefevre wants revenge, she'll come after me, not you, an' I'll be ready for her. So, dearie, sit down and tell Mollie all about yerself."

The kid was too upset to say much, but how much could her story vary from the usual? Her father had probably knocked her about, she'd run away with some joker who'd popped her cherry and left her flat, she had no one, she was broke—the details would all come out later. Right now Mollie was interested in fixing her up so she didn't look like a scarecrow, and to that end she sent the housemaid around to the dressmaker's to tell her to come as soon as possible.

She took Kate into the bathroom, told her to undress, and ran a tub for her. Turning around after scattering a generous amount of bath salts into the water, she saw Kate sitting naked on the chair and exclaimed, "Oh, dearie, you're sittin' on a gold mine!" The girl's body was as beautiful as her face. Once she was dolled up, she'd be the toast of the District.

While Kate bathed and washed her hair, Mollie gave her usual lecture, explaining the cost of "board" and the cut she'd take on the customers. She opened the cabinet and showed her the douches and preventatives. Kate listened with wide-eyed concentration, wishing she'd known such things before.

"I'm glad y're not a virgin," Mollie told her while toweling her hair. "It's against m' principles to take a virgin. But I don't s'pose Vivian gave you any proper training."

There were certain positions, squeezes, and feigned cries of pleasure that could bring a man off fast. You shouldn't take off your clothes unless the customer was an overnighter. There were ways of protecting your breasts and face if it looked as though the customer were going to get rough. "I got a high-class clientele," Mollie bragged, "and I expect my girls to act like ladies. You gotta handle the customers firm but gentle, like a farm girl handles the animals or," she amended, giving a more genteel example, "like a lady handles party guests. Upstairs they all want more or less the same thing; it's downstairs where you can raise the price. You gotta move to show off yer equipment to the best advantage. Y' listen an' act interested no matter what balderdash the man's tellin' y'. You always compliment 'em. Tell the ugly ones they're handsome and the handsome they're smart. Well, any girl knows that, even if she's the governor's daughter. Y' encourage them to eat and drink. For the time bein' you won't have to take any heavy traffic. For the time bein' y're a novelty an' y' can actually make more by doin' it less. I'm gonna treat y' exclusive-like. I'll give y' the high-rollin' out-of-towners, that way word'll get 'round, then the locals 'll be lining up. You're only a new girl in town once, Kate, but if you play yer cards right, every one of 'em will think he's the first."

She gave Kate some drawers and a camisole she'd grown too fat for, and when the housemaid came to say the dressmaker had arrived, she took her down to her own bedroom.

"Leave a half inch or so," Mollie ordered the woman who was taking Kate's measurements. "I'm gonna fatten her up some."

Kate thought of Hansel and Gretel being fattened up so they could be eaten, but she smiled. She felt good enough to eat, sweet-smelling, cared for.

"Uh-oh, there's the door," Mollie said, and rushed out.

With a deft and gentle touch the dressmaker measured her waist, and Kate felt a frisson of pleasure. She couldn't remember how long it had been since anyone had touched her in a gentle, pampering way. But as Mollie appeared at the door with a dapper, silver-haired man, she felt a wave of humiliation.

"Kate, this is my good friend Billy Shakespeare. Billy, this is my new girl, Kate."

It was the desk clerk from the Versailles. He'd recognize her and know how fast she'd given in and become a whore. But his eyes showed only the barest flicker of recognition, and then, like a true gentleman, he took off his hat, bowed, and said, "Pleased to meet you, Kate." Her smile brimmed with gratitude.

"Billy, I'm glad y' come round," Mollie said. "I'm planning Kate's getup. Whatta y' think?" She tapped the pattern book. "How 'bout this in an emerald satin with tassels down the front an' maybe a tiara of diamantés?"

"No. White. All white. Certainly no tassels and not too low-cut." He walked around, studying Kate from every angle. "And perish the thought of a tiara. Perhaps a flower or a ribbon in the hair. And no more than a single string of pearls. She should look like Juliet on the balcony."

"I got no balcony, but I got a hundred Romeos, an' they like a little glitter," Mollie insisted. "She's too pale as it is. She needs some color to brighten her up."

But in the end Mollie gave way to Shakespeare's advice, and a few days later Kate put on an ivory satin corset threaded with pale pink ribbon, white drawers trimmed with ecru lace, and a flounced crepe de chine petticoat. The gown of magnolia satin with a self-belt seeded with pearls was fit for a bride. Champagne-colored dancing slippers and a single string of pearls, on loan from Mollie, completed the ensemble, and a cluster of ribbons attached to a tortoise-shell comb held her upswept hair. The cost, because it was a rush job, was over a thousand dollars, but Mollie assured her that it was a necessary investment and she'd earn it back in the first few weeks.

"Now come downstairs and show it to Shakespeare," Mollie told her, clucking like a mother getting her daughter ready for a debutante ball.

Mollie and Shakespeare stood at the bottom of the stairs as she walked down, nervous about stepping on her train. "Walk slow," Mollie instructed.

"Don't look at your feet," Shakespeare added. "Head up, eyes straight ahead."

"Ah, don't she look grand?" Mollie enthused. "Our little Kate."

"No. Katherine. We'll call her Katherine now."

"Sure, she's lovely. She's lovely." Mollie was almost teary-eyed. "What a piece! She's money in the bank."

CHAPTER

VII

For a marriage to be happy, the husband should be deaf and his wife blind.

Spanish proverb

*A*s he sat in his wife's bedroom smoking a cigar, Charles Randsome seemed the very picture of serenity—handsome in his evening clothes, his large head lolling back on the settee, his eyes half-closed, and his foot, encased in butter-soft patent leather, keeping time to the waltz music that had already started downstairs —but Charles was far from serene. His eyes slid over to his wife, who was sitting at her dressing table arranging her hair. Because they were at odds, he studied her with more than his usual objectivity. The lines around her mouth were deeper than he'd remembered. Her arms were thinner. He hoped that age wasn't going to give her that grim and scrawny look. "The musicians sound fine," he said.

"I don't know them," she replied. "Carlotta engaged them." She turned her attention to a silver hair clasp. Charles shifted his weight and studied the tip of his cigar.

Usually, dressing for some social event was more enjoyable than the event itself. They would move through the rooms handing each other various things while Julia amused him with wry predictions of how the evening would go; if he misplaced a stick-pin or a cuff link, she would automatically join him in the search; she had only to present her back for him to do up her gown. Now the top of her dark blue evening dress was still unbuttoned, but her ramrod-straight back didn't invite assistance.

"Yes, they sound fine," he said again, but got no reply. The silence between them was so unnatural that he had half a mind to pick up the argument they'd left unresolved the night before. But how pick it up? How resolve it? It had been the worst fight they'd had since their early days when Julia had locked horns with Carlotta and threatened to go back to Massachusetts, and it had been doubly upsetting because he'd been expecting the usual homecoming: a supper of his favorite foods, conversation about his trip, and welcoming arms. Over time his lust for his wife had naturally settled into a quieter appreciation, and being away helped to rekindle the flame. Though he always complained about having to go on business trips, he secretly relished traveling alone. It made him feel young, adventurous, and spontaneous and restored his sense of being an active man of the world. But even a man of the world needed the reliable and the familiar, and it was when he returned home after these extended trips that he complimented himself on having achieved an almost perfect balance: he had both freedom and stability, the best of all possible worlds. But he'd known as soon as he'd come down the gangplank that this was not to be a joyful homecoming.

His ship had been two days late in docking, owing to difficulty unloading cargo in Savannah and a storm in the Gulf. Both Carlotta and Julia had come in the carriage to collect him, and that in itself was odd, because Carlotta usually stayed at home. Julia had embraced him with more ardor than she generally showed in public, and Carlotta had made an unkind remark about some women becoming more amorous with age. The undercurrent of tension between the two women was palpable, and the reasons for it were quickly explained. A large party had been planned, and the house was in an uproar of preparation (without being told, he guessed the party was Carlotta's idea but that Julia had fallen in for most of the work). To complicate matters even more, Angelique had come down with the measles.

"And," Carlotta had told him, "we got a letter from Lawrence today. He's leaving college and enlisting. He wants to go to Cuba."

"Perhaps there won't be a war," Julia had said.

"But of course there will be," Carlotta had declared as happily as if she were announcing a picnic. "And it's only natural that Lawrence should want to go. They all want to go. Charles would, too, if he were young enough, wouldn't you, Charles?"

Charles had admitted as to how he would. It was the greatest disappointment of his life that he'd been too young to serve in the War Between the States. He had some memory of the Union navy bombarding the city, but his most vivid recollection was of a respectable woman spitting at a man dressed in the hated Union blue and being hauled off by military police. He thought it only fitting and natural that his son would want to be in the thick of whatever was about to unfold. He said as much, though gently, because he was mindful of Julia's motherly feelings and could see that her feathers were already ruffled.

"Men!" Julia said, and shrank to her side of the carriage, clutching a balled handkerchief and looking out the window. She remained adamantly silent all the way home.

But even after Robert deposited Charles's bags in his room, Julia didn't kiss him or even start unpacking his bags, as she usually did, but took up a place near the window and crossed her arms beneath her breasts. He recognized the posture and went to her, lifting her chin and looking into her eyes.

"I want to kiss these lips, not hear an argument from them," he said.

She said, "Oh, Charles!" clutched him but turned her head away, then quickly disengaged herself and began to pace the room. Had he known that Lawrence was planning to enlist? she demanded. Of course not, he remonstrated. Why should she think that he would know something and keep it from her? Because, she rounded on him, she knew he kept a great many things from her. He didn't know what she was talking about. Well, she would tell him. She launched into a tirade of angry and disjointed accusations for which he was totally unprepared. He could hardly believe that she, who held him in even higher regard than he held himself, should be saying such things. Deceitful? Dishonest? Whatever could she mean? Why, she demanded, had he never told her that they owned properties in the District? It had never come up, he explained, feeling as though he'd been ambushed. He had inherited the houses, had practically nothing to do with them, they were handled by an agent. And who the hell had told her about the properties, anyway? That, she said, was irrelevant. She said she had drafted a petition against the legalization of the District, and that he would have to dispose of the properties. That she should order him how to handle their affairs enraged him. He said, rashly, that the houses were a reliable source of income and he had no intention of giving them up. Her returning volley came so thick and fast that he shot back defensively, thoughtlessly. Suddenly they were fighting about past disagreements that he'd thought were long since buried, and then she flew off entirely, saying that he gave only lip service to the rights of women. The rights of women! What the hell did that have to do with it? He was sick of hearing about the rights of women. "Stiff-necked, meddling Yankee" was thrust; "mindless, hypocritical Southerner" was parried.

Had they really degenerated into such shameful but wounding

clichés? They had. And they kept at it, so much so that when they heard a repeated knock on the door, they stood, facing each other, breathing hard, her eyes swollen, his fists clenched. "Yes, dammit, yes!" he yelled. "Come in!"

It was Marie. She'd come to tell them that Angelique wanted to see her papa, that the staff was assembled and wanted to welcome him home, and that supper was almost ready.

"And then there's Marie. You never told me about Marie," Julia said as soon as the old woman had closed the door.

"What about her?" he demanded, strewing shirts and socks about as he rummaged in his case for the music box he'd bought for Angelique. "No, don't tell me," he ordered as she sank onto his bed and covered her face with her hands.

"Oh, Charles. I had always believed we trusted one another, that there were no secrets between us. I had always believed—"

"Not now, Julia!" he bellowed, then, more quietly, "Please, not now." They were equally shamefaced but still too raw to offer apologies.

"Charles," she said as he went to the door, eager for escape, "we must talk."

"We will talk, but for Christ's sake, *not now*." And seeing she was chastened, he couldn't resist the guilt-producing final word· "What a homecoming!"

Once he'd seen Angelique, he went downstairs to supper and was told that the mistress had taken a tray in her room. He thought of going up to her but was too travel-weary and confused to face another harangue. He heard Carlotta's chatter, which was no more or less annoying than the buzzing of a fly, then pled fatigue and went upstairs.

Their rooms were empty, and one of the servants told him that the mistress had gone up to Angelique's room to read her to sleep. He undressed, bathed, and got into Julia's bed. When she came down, they would talk, but they would talk in bed. You couldn't have a real fight lying down. He would apologize, and they would make love. That would soften everything. That would change the icy burn and return them to a more temperate emotional climate. They would come to some understanding. They always did. His attention was divided between how he might explain himself and the anticipation of sexual release. He had a half erection and what felt like a fever but was probably just wind and sunburn on his face. He promptly fell asleep.

He was only vaguely aware of her getting into bed with him, but later, as the first light came through the windows, dreaming that he was still on the ship and the Gulf squall had turned into a threatening storm, he tossed, rolled over, felt her body, and threw his leg over hers. Semiconscious, thrashing about in sheets and nightclothes as though they were waves, he mounted her. He was well into it before he realized that she was not responding, and for a split second he thought to slow himself, but she was thrusting her hips up, encouraging him in the completion of his desire if not fully participating in it, and it was too late for restraint. Only after the spasm, when he'd moved away from her, did he feel sorry that weeks of wishful longing had come to such an unsatisfactory culmination. He began to stroke the back that was turned to him, hoping that desire would renew itself so that this time he could be attentive to her, but fatigue rolled over him. He felt he was on the ship again, only now it was anchored, rocking him gently back into sleep.

When he woke up, the space next to him was vacant. It was already after ten. He dressed and went downstairs. The foyer was littered with boxes from the florist, and Julia was supervising servants who were braiding garlands onto the banisters. He kissed her on the cheek. "I'll come home early. We'll talk this afternoon," he promised, and hurried off to his office.

He'd intended to make good his promise, but by late afternoon, just as he was putting on his hat, Claiborne Lafitte had dropped by. He'd supported Lafitte for Congress on the usual understanding that Lafitte would return the favor by way of legislation, patronage, or simple commercial advantage. So far he hadn't gotten his money's worth, so he was pleased when Lafitte told him that a government contract for the Randsome shipping lines might be in the offing when war was declared. Lafitte mentioned that he was coming to the party that night but that that was no place to discuss business. Charles knew he was only postponing the inevitable confrontation at home, but he wanted to hear what was going on in Washington, and a possible government contract was not something he could ignore. He took Lafitte to his club and finally arrived home after dark, with barely enough time to look at Angelique's new spots, bathe, and put on his evening clothes.

He finished his cigar. Julia was putting on her pearls. He wanted to say something to put things right, but now was not the time. Not with a hundred guests about to arrive. Julia would appreciate that. She hated scenes almost as much as he did. That was one of the reasons he'd married her. Being the only son of a flamboyant mother and a father who'd worked himself into an early grave trying to restore the riches she'd known as a girl, he'd had more than enough of scenes. As a young man he'd decided that when it came to marriage he would choose character over beauty, constancy and intelligence over charm. Julia's zeal about social causes filled him with both pride and dismay, but better a compassionate, high-minded woman than one who never looked beyond herself or didn't have the backbone to stand up for her beliefs. He'd been cruel to say that he was sick of hearing about the rights of women. He was in agreement with her about their struggle for the vote, though he wasn't sure it would have the uplifting effect on politics that she so naively hoped for. But this business about prostitution . . . Why did it disturb her so deeply? She was not religious in any traditional way; in fact, she'd refused to convert to Catholicism and only under extreme pressure had she allowed the children to be baptized. Like all good women, she idealized sex. "Mere" physical desire had to be transformed by love. Well, it could be. He'd experienced that himself, but he also knew that, at least for a man, the drive didn't wait for ideal conditions. Julia had been brimming with unrecognized desire when he'd first met her. If the right man hadn't come along, she might have turned into one of those tightly wrapped, overly energetic women who jumped when they heard a noise, were either too fat or too thin, and went about straightening pictures and everybody else's lives. Her mother, being progressive, had taught her about reproductive functions, but she knew nothing of orgasms, had never seen a man naked—in Boston she'd never even seen statues—and had never even imagined the sheer fun of it. And he'd been lucky enough to teach her. He'd told her that he'd never loved another woman that way, and that was true enough because he hadn't thought of sharing his life with any of the others. She'd believed their pleasure in bed was the natural right of all happily married couples, never realizing that his considerable experience helped to bring it about. So he'd had what all men wanted: he'd been the tender but masterful teacher of a virtuous but responsive wife.

He watched as she leaned back and studied herself, critically, as she always studied things. A line of dissatisfaction creased her brow, then she bent forward and sniffed at a bouquet of roses. This dissatisfaction with her looks was so familiar that he felt a rush of affection. She didn't realize how handsome she was. She'd once told him that the only time she felt really beautiful was when they made love. "You look lovely," he said now, and meant it. "Blue's your color."

"The dress is old," she said almost to herself, reaching back to do up the top buttons.

He moved to stand behind her, hands poised over her shoulders, smiling at their reflections in the mirror. "Let me."

"No, I can manage."

He seized her hand. "Let me." She dropped her hands into her lap, and he pretended to fumble with the buttons. "Now, let me see . . . it's been so long I'm not sure I remember how to—"

"Charles, hurry up. We should already be downstairs."

She'd said those very words the day of their wedding when, in violation of all propriety, he'd come into her room as the guests were already assembling downstairs in her parents' parlor. He'd taken her in his arms and deftly undone the buttons closest to her heart, sliding in his hand to cup her breast. She'd been so shocked and so aroused that she didn't think she could get through the ceremony.

"Charles!" she said now, remembering. "We haven't time to fool."

Her voice sounded stern, but she bent her head, and he noticed that the tiny hairs on the back of her neck stood up. He finished the buttons and smoothed his thumbs over her shoulder blades. "My angel, I do believe you are sprouting wings."

She smiled in spite of herself. What issue in the larger world, she wondered, could possibly be as important as what happened in this room? His playfulness, his easygoing manner, was the very fulcrum of their marriage. How often had he kidded her out of irritability or melancholy or teased her out of her damnable seriousness? He was the one who put the dip and bounce into the seesaw of daily life. She was ashamed that she'd attacked him the day before. She'd meant to question without accusing, to find out all the facts before she judged, but she'd turned into the worst kind of harpy. And last night in bed, when she could have helped to repair the damage, she'd been too angry and confused to respond. Her body had wanted to, but her mind simply hadn't let it. She'd moved, rhythmically but mechanically, to help him finish it off so she could slip into the oblivion of sleep. She'd hated that feeling—being used, and with her own consent—and hated him when he'd fallen asleep. And this afternoon her irritation had returned. He'd said he'd be home, and she'd rushed about attending to all the last-minute details for the party so they'd have time together. She was used to his promise of four slipping into his apology at seven, but this afternoon, after that terrible fight . . . Why couldn't he have made the effort?

She said, "I'd give anything if we weren't having this party tonight."

"And so would I." He ran his hands down the sides of her dress and took hold of her waist. "Perhaps you could pretend you have a headache and send them all packing."

"I wouldn't have to pretend."

He began to massage her temples. "Then you could faint and I could hint that you're in the family way."

"I'm not the fainting sort, more's the pity." She didn't like jokes about pregnancy. She knew he wanted another child, but she also knew she couldn't face that again. She'd had a friend in Paris send her preventatives for years but had never told him. "Charles," she reminded him, "we must go downstairs."

"We must and we shall." He held out his hand. "Trust me to be the perfect host. I shall balance great courtesy toward my guests with the fond hope that they will soon leave."

She stood and looked him directly in the eye. "And Charles, we must find time to really talk."

"Tomorrow we'll spend the entire day together. I promise. Shall we see to our guests, Mrs. Randsome?"

As they went out onto the landing, Julia noticed a small, ghostly figure on the upper stairs. "Angelique, you should be in bed."

"Come here, young lady," Charles ordered.

Angelique hurried down and stood in front of him, twisting the end of her braid. "You look so handsome, Papa."

"You are justifiably proud," Charles kidded, slipping his arm around Julia's waist. "Your parents are an exemplary and extremely handsome couple."

"Papa, mayn't I sit on the stairs and watch the guests arrive?"

"I'm sorry, dear," Julia said. "You know what the doctor said. When you have the measles, you must stay in a darkened room to protect your eyes. If you weren't sick . . ."

"Mama, you never let me do anything. Please, Papa, just for a little while. Please."

Charles made his voice gruff. "Tonight, me pretty, you are banished to the tower."

He picked her up and carried her up the stairs. Julia smiled as she watched them go, but when Angelique's giggles turned to a wheedling, "Papa, if I go to bed now, will you promise that . . ." she turned away. Strange that she, who had so wanted a daughter, was so disappointed in the one she had.

Both Charles and Carlotta had been overjoyed when Lawrence had been born eleven months after the wedding. She herself had felt that she'd fulfilled some unspoken obligation in producing a son, yet she'd secretly wanted a daughter. With a daughter she could share female secrets and enjoy a physical affection she couldn't have with a son without fear of making him a mama's boy. And she'd had a much clearer picture of how she would raise a daughter. She would foster the girl's independence, see that she had the best education, praise her intelligence as well as her looks, and the girl would blossom into the free-spirited, independent woman she herself had always wanted to be. How could such hopeful and seemingly attainable goals have gone awry?

After the relative ease of Lawrence's birth, she'd had two miscarriages and had developed such a fear of pregnancy that she'd even turned away from Charles in bed. When she'd become pregnant for the fourth time, the doctor had forbidden any exercise, and she'd spent six months confined to bed and couch, maddened by inactivity and the increasing chaos of the house. Lacking her direct supervision, the household had fallen apart—linen cabinets had become messy, flowers had wilted in vases, silver had become tarnished, meals had been served any old time. But then the reward: a perfectly formed girl child, wisps of dark hair already curling on her head.

But Angelique had been indifferent to her from infancy. She was always her daddy's girl—worse yet, her grandmother's. No sooner had Angelique started to lisp than Carlotta had told her about Coco Robicheaux, a naughty little girl in Creole folklore who became responsible for all of Angelique's wrongdoing.

"A sweet little girl like you wouldn't do that," Carlotta would say. "That must've been Coco Robicheaux."

By age four Angelique was vain about her clothes. She hated to read, she didn't want to ride a pony. When she didn't get her way she sulked; when she did, she always pressed her advantage. She told lies and showed no remorse when punished. At ten she was a spoiled, unpleasant child. She would probably grow up to be an equally unpleasant young woman, and Julia secretly blamed herself. But her mother's heart recoiled from such a harsh judgment. How could she predict how Angelique would turn out when the child was still so young? As Charles had told her yesterday, along with his other accusations, she was too quick to judge. Her high standards often brought her to lingering disappointments. She must correct that in herself. And she would start now, by putting their argument and all larger questions out of her mind and enjoying the party.

When Charles came down from Angelique's room, she held out her hand. The scent from the garlanded banisters was sweet, the entrance hall glowed with lights. Robert was rolling a red carpet through the open front doors and down the steps.

"That looks impressive," Charles said, and she nodded, though the carpet had been Carlotta's idea and she thought it pretentious.

As they reached the hall, she started to go into the dining room for a last-minute check, but Charles held on to her hand and led her through the game room and into the ballroom. The mulatto musicians, in evening dress with their almost straight hair slicked back, were playing "After the Ball," and Charles took her in his arms, singing, "Many's the heart that's broken, / If you could read them all; / Many's the hope that has vanished, / After the ball." He was a far better dancer than she, but when she relaxed and followed his lead, she felt light and graceful.

The waltz came to a crescendo. He held her tighter and twirled her round until she was dizzy, lightly kissing her neck, then released her, saying, "Until later, madame," before sauntering off to chat with the musicians.

He still loves me. He still wants me, she thought. The partial reconciliation of the dance and the kiss made her feel she could get through the evening.

As she looked at the dining room, she told herself that what she lacked in social ease she made up for in planning. The crystal and silver glowed in the gaslight, menus rested on each plate, place cards stood near the wineglasses, and banks of orchids ran down the center of the huge mahogany table and were reflected in its surface. Absently she touched the place card next to Charles's chair. Written on it was "Yvette Liscomb," yet she was sure she'd seated Yvette between Senator Togeland and Orson Dewitt. Apparently Carlotta had roused herself from her afternoon nap long enough to rearrange the cards, and, hoping to provoke her jealousy, had placed Yvette next to Charles. Julia picked up the card and walked slowly around the table, realizing with rising irritation that several changes had been made in her original seating plan.

She heard voices from the entrance hall, and simultaneously the door to Carlotta's bedroom opened. Marie, wearing the high-necked maroon dress that was her livery for special occasions and carrying a small gilt chair, came out, and then Carlotta swept into the room. Julia had overheard screeching fights with the dressmaker, but this was the first time she'd seen Carlotta's new gown. It was gold-and-black brocade trimmed with black lace, embarrassingly low-cut for a woman of Carlotta's age. Her hair was padded out to form wings on either side of her heavily powdered face and swirled into a topknot dusted with gold. The overall effect was of a tarnished mannequin, yet Julia could see by the lift of her chin that Carlotta was enormously pleased with herself. What did the woman see when she looked in her mirror? The reflection it gave back must have been like Narcissus' drowning pool. The annoyance Julia had felt just moments before gave way to something like pity at Carlotta's pathetic and unwinnable battle against time.

"Your dress . . ." she began, but couldn't find words.

"Yes," Carlotta said, assuming a compliment. Her attention was focused on the entrance hall. Like an actress who has heard her cue, she muttered, "The guests have begun to arrive," and sailed off.

Julia started after her, then realized she had the place card in her hand. There was no time to rearrange the seating now.

As she moved to replace the card, she felt Marie looking at her. Ever since Beatrice had told her about Marie's life, she'd been acutely aware of Marie, and it seemed—though perhaps it was just her imagination—that Marie sensed her interest. No conversation other than the usual household banalities had passed between them, yet sometimes, when their eyes met, it seemed that, like schoolchildren or prisoners who were condemned to silence, they shared an unspoken understanding. Just now Marie's eyes, luminous in the dim light, told her that she knew about Carlotta changing the place cards. The look also seemed to convey a warning and a compassion that embarrassed her.

"Since you aren't carrying Monsieur Robespierre's perch, I assume he will not be joining us," Julia said. Then she added, "We must be grateful for small blessings."

Marie smiled. "We best be," she said, "since those are all we're likely to get."

Julia motioned toward the entrance hall. "Shall we?"

The Stillertons had arrived. Marie helped Carlotta onto her chair while Julia placed herself next to Charles to form a receiving line. Greetings were exchanged, and Vernette Stillerton, with the universal embarrassment of a first guest, glanced toward the front doors, hoping for reinforcements.

Senator Togeland advanced up the steps, bowed to Carlotta, and said that Mrs. Togeland sent her regrets. She was, he explained, feeling somewhat better, though still not well enough to dine out. There were tuts of surprise, disappointment, and sympathy. The shared fiction was that Mrs. Togeland was the victim of a mysterious illness, but years before, when that unhappy lady had first started sending her regrets, Julia had visited her and realized within minutes that she was drunk.

While Robert removed Vernette Stillerton's cape, Vernette, who changed doctors as often as other women changed shoes, gave Senator Togeland the name of a new physician. He thanked her, but his attention had gone to Charles and Henry Stillerton, who'd dispensed with greetings and were already talking about the war. Distressing though that subject was, Julia thought, it would provide a new topic, or rather a variant on an old one.

Dinner parties often concluded with long-winded stories about the War Between the States. She could never forget that most of the older guests had been slave owners, and she knew they longed to return to that abominable state of affairs, yet she'd lived in the city long enough and heard enough stories from trustworthy sources, such as Beatrice Ravenal, to have some sympathy for the misery that the war and, more particularly, Reconstruction had caused. But she was still a Yankee, an outsider, and any comment she made was met with fish-eyed suspicion. On her rare trips back to Boston, she met with equally rigid prejudice when she attempted to illuminate the Southern case. War, as the beastly General Sherman had said, was hell, but playing the role of peacemaker was purgatory.

The Hunnicotts and their son arrived, followed by the Rousseaus. Then the D'Emilios. The orchestra played a livelier tune, and Julia picked up the pace. It was smile, greet, turn to the next. Smile, greet . . . the Steadmans, the Lafittes. Agnes Lafitte complained of a cold. Oh, surely not! Congressman Lafitte said they would have to leave early because he was journeying to Washington the next day. What was happening in Washington? she asked. But he was already gone, and it was turn to the next. . . . The Dangerfields, just back from Paris. Yes, they must tell her about it over supper. What a charming headdress Anna Dangerfield was wearing . . . smile, greet . . . Ah, the first person she was genuinely glad to see: young Carrie Bonisett, looking lovely in amber satin with full lace sleeves embroidered with butterflies and a cluster of artfully crafted butterflies in her upswept hair.

As Carrie kissed Julia's cheek, she whispered, "Whatever happened with that petition? Do call on me," before her husband, Walter, whisked her off. Mention of the petition brought Alcesta and Abraham Davenport to mind. Julia had thought perhaps Alcesta would send her excuses, but no apologetic note had arrived. She only hoped they would come in the general crush and she would be spared anything more than the most casual exchange. Ah, here were the Dewitts . . . Mr. and Mrs. Dewitt turned their attention to Carlotta while their daughter, Adeline, stared about with bright-eyed anticipation, hoping to find some eligible men. Charles told Adeline how fetching she looked, while Orson Dewitt kissed Carlotta's hand and offered similar, if less sincere, praise. Carlotta, for whom a compliment had the effect of a stimulant, brightened instantly. And then Yvette Liscomb made her entrance, eclipsing everyone else.

She wore a rose-colored gown of glovelike fit and rustling froufrou skirt. Nosegays of tiny satin roses nestled in her dark curls. With the merest shrug of her shoulders she dropped her cape, lined in a deeper rose, into Robert's waiting hands. The glitter of a ruby-and-diamond necklace showed up the whiteness of her bosom, much of which was exposed. Her eyes flitted over Julia, then opened wide as they settled on Charles.

"Oh, you've been gone so long!" she exclaimed. "And we've missed you so!" Without bothering to glance in her husband's direction, she asked, "Haven't we missed Charles, Vincent?"

Vincent nodded his balding head. He was a lean-shanked man, well into his sixties, who carried a bottle of digestive tablets to the most elegant soirees. The delicacy of his stomach and the malarial pallor of his skin had been leading people to predict his death for years.

Yvette offered her hand to Charles, and as he kissed it, she drew in her breath and exhaled a deep sigh of satisfaction. She even breathes with flirtatious intent, Julia thought, seeing Yvette's breasts strain against her décolletage and knowing that Yvette was equally aware of the show. She couldn't help but feel a twinge of jealousy as she watched Charles watch Yvette. She could read his look—it was the expression he had when the curtain was about to go up at the theater or when he was about to buy something. He'd had it most recently when he'd shown her an advertisement for a horseless carriage. He'd never—well, at least not in recent memory—looked at her that way. The posturings of an aging beauty like Carlotta were pathetic, but what a heady feeling to be Yvette, always the object of attention and desire.

Charles said, "I've missed all my friends. It's always good to be home." His look of warm amusement was prompted not by Yvette, but by his private thought: The game would not be worth the candle. Yvette had been a pretty tease when she was eighteen, and she was still a pretty tease. He'd lusted after her then, the sheets of his bed tenting up after parties like this. Sometimes, when the frustration had been too great, he'd gone with his friends to the District. Had Yvette allowed him more than a few furtive kisses, she might have snared him. Now, being a connoisseur of women, he was grateful for his escape. Though Yvette had produced two children in the early years of her marriage, her sensuality was as unformed as little Adeline Dewitt's. Yvette still found pleasure in endless grooming and fine foods (her waist was corseted to the point of suffocation, and her arms were beginning to look fleshy). She collected furs and feathers, rings and baubles, and these Vincent provided in too generous measure. But Charles imagined she'd never been sexually awakened. How could she have been by pathetic old Vincent? Gossip of her love affairs was no more than that, probably fostered by Yvette herself, since she enjoyed the role of femme fatale, but he was sure no man had seen her eyes roll back as she gave way to vigorous penetration or felt her bites or heard her moans. As she squeezed his hand, neither her calculated seductive look nor her bosom, trussed and thrust out, an offering as juicy and unavoidable as a Thanksgiving turkey, excited him. But the knowledge that he now had the experience to force cries and whispers from her, to crack her open, rekindled a flicker of the old interest.

Yvette made him promise to dance with her, and Vincent, who'd been cross-examining Julia about the menu, took her arm and led her off.

Judge Asbury asked Charles about his trip to Marseilles while Lucretia fiddled with an elaborate headdress of pearls and egret feathers that kept slipping over one eye. As the Asburys drifted off, Lucretia still fussing, Charles remembered Julia describing Lucretia as a puffer pigeon in a dust bath and tried to catch her eye, but Julia was looking at Marie, who stood at attention behind Carlotta's chair.

Julia was highly opinionated about Negroes' rights, but since she hadn't been brought up around them, she was usually uncomfortable in their presence; thus the intimacy of the look she exchanged with Marie surprised and somehow irritated him. Then it struck him. Yesterday, during the fight, when Julia was ranting about truth and honesty, she'd demanded, "And what about Marie?" He hadn't known what she was talking about, but now he understood. Somehow she'd found out that Marie had been Carlotta's first husband's mistress before Carlotta had brought Marie to the house to be her maid.

He himself had found out about it when he was fourteen. An older boy had told him during a sniggering conversation about the mysteries of sex. He'd wanted to knock the boy down. Marie, who was still beautiful then, had taken a place in his fantasies, and wanting to rid himself of shameful thoughts, he'd asked Carlotta if the story was true. She'd said, quite casually, that it was. Even at the time he'd sensed an uncomfortable moral ambiguity, but it was easier to accept Carlotta's explanation that Marie's presence in the house was a simple act of kindness. When he and Julia had been in their honeymoon flush and honesty seemed not just desirable but the natural order of things, he'd wanted to tell her about Marie, but Julia was so shocked by life on Poydras Street and so at odds with Carlotta that he knew she would see it as yet another example of Southern decadence. Then, as time went by, he'd convinced himself it was better left buried. His silence was only a sin of omission. But Julia didn't make those subtle differentiations. He'd have a hell of a time explaining it now, and somehow it seemed to be Julia's fault that she'd discovered it. Julia touched his hand, calling his attention to the Glasgows.

The air was heavy with flowers and perfume, and the din of voices made it difficult to hear. Surely, Julia thought as she glanced toward the doors, this must be the last wave, and Alcesta and Abraham were not on it. Remembering Marie's words, she thanked God for that small blessing. The muscles around her mouth were stretched from smiling. What had she just said to Carlotta's second cousin? Something appropriate, she was sure, though for the life of her she couldn't remember what.

Phillipa Cotrane's laughter trumpeted her arrival. She was with a tall stranger wearing a monocle, no doubt one of her endless supply of foreign aristocrats. Because she was a divorcée with a marginal reputation, Phillipa kept her social capital high by introducing "new, but blue" blood into New Orleans society. She hunted them down on her annual trips abroad, and they turned up throughout the year—Count this or Lord that—usually showing the ill effects of inbreeding. On the basis of their titles, many of which Julia suspected of being spurious, they were welcomed into the best homes and often outstayed their welcomes. Last year the Asburys had housed a burly Russian count for so long that one of their servants had turned up pregnant, and even after they'd dismissed the girl, they'd had to close up their house and go on a trip to get rid of him. For reasons Julia couldn't understand, these sordid experiences only increased the appetite for visiting noblemen. Tonight Phillipa, rightly famous for her ability to provide the "extra man," had not only the tall stranger, but Leonce Lambre in tow.

Leonce was Lawrence's age; in fact, they had been childhood friends. Julia had disliked the boy from the time he was five, when he'd willfully destroyed one of Lawrence's little battleships and blamed it on Lawrence. By the time he was seven, Leonce was cheating at games, and she'd got over any guilt she'd had in judging him prematurely. He'd grown up as she'd expected him to: he was a young man about town, living off his inheritance, charming the ladies, who called him "the wild-oat boy." Calling himself a poet, he claimed to be a friend of Baudelaire, which, Julia suspected, meant that they'd once gotten drunk in the same Paris café.

"This," Phillipa announced, "is Lord Arlington, but you may call him Lord Harry."

Sounding as though he had a mouthful of marbles, Lord Harry said he was delighted to visit their charming city.

"And our dear Leonce," Phillipa brayed, exposing her large, crowded teeth, "needs no introduction."

With one of his familiar preening gestures, Leonce tossed his head and pushed back a hank of his dark, untidy hair. He kissed Carlotta's hand, then took Julia's and, bowing low, stared at her with frank sexual appraisal.

"Yes," Julia said, her voice cool, "I know Leonce very well."

"Once, when I was a small boy," Leonce said, his eyes sweeping all women within earshot, "Julia spanked me. Whenever I see her, my flesh tingles in happy remembrance."

There was general laughter. Phillipa batted Leonce's arm with a "naughty boy" flick of her fan. Seeing Julia's look, she cocked her ear to the music, told Lord Harry that the city had the best musicians in the country, and pleaded for a dance.

"Always good to see you," Charles told Leonce.

"And you shall see me again very soon," Leonce said. "Lawrence wrote to tell me that he's coming home before he goes off to Cuba. You may be sure I shall treat him to a glorious farewell."

"Lawrence will only be home for a short time," Julia told him. She wouldn't have to voice her disapproval of Lawrence carousing with Leonce. She knew Lawrence himself would reject the offer.

"Would you be so coldhearted as to send the young hero off to war without an appropriate celebration? I shall be by to see him and"—Leonce turned his attention to Carlotta—"perhaps to coax this lady into an afternoon at the races."

"I so rarely get out," Carlotta lamented. "And why should a handsome young man such as yourself waste his afternoon on me?"

"Because"—Leonce came up with one of his many aphorisms—" 'Both women and melons improve with age. Both are best when ripe.' "

Julia had no recollection of having spanked Leonce but would cheerfully have done so now. She pointedly turned her attention to the door. She wouldn't let her energy flag now. It was just like pedaling up a hill, she told herself, sooner or later you reached the top. Only a few latecomers left. The Trevors with their son and daughter, both of marriageable age; the Lintons; and . . . Alcesta and Abraham Davenport. Her stomach heaved as though she'd just hit a rock and been pitched over the handlebars.

Alcesta wore a bright yellow silk gown. Strange, Julia thought, recovering herself with a trivial observation, how funereal Alcesta looked despite the vivid color. As they came in front of her, Alcesta surprised her by looking directly into her face, her eyes demanding sympathy.

Abraham said, "Julia," made an abortive move to take her hand, then bowed too swiftly. She could tell that he had already been drinking. His face was the color of veal. He had nicked himself while shaving. A tiny blood spot encrusted his chin, and another spot dotted the front of his tuxedo.

"I believe the festivities are about to begin," Carlotta said.

Abraham moved to help her up and apologized for being late. "No need to fret about that," Carlotta drawled. "The only things we have to be on time for are our births and our deaths." She took Marie's arm and walked off.

Charles clapped Abraham on the shoulder and said, sotto voce, "Carlotta claims that I took ten months to come to term. I made her miss a Mardi Gras ball, and she's never forgiven me. Come on, old boy. We'll dance the ladies off their feet. Alcesta, you look like a marigold. You will honor me with the first dance, won't you?"

His sunny charm thawed Alcesta's martyred expression, and as he led her away, Julia nodded for Robert to close the front doors and offered her arm to Abraham.

"Dear Julia," he said, "I am sorry." His voice had a tone not of social apology, but of heartfelt confession, and his watery eyes had such a pleading look that she couldn't meet them. If she hadn't known better, she would have sworn that Alcesta had told him that she'd betrayed his most shameful secrets.

The ballroom was alive with swirling, brightly colored gowns and lilting music. "I'd ask you to dance," Abraham said, "but as you can tell, I'm not too steady on my feet."

"That's all right. I never dance well with anyone but Charles."

"And I never dance well with anyone. When most of these fellows were going to balls, I was out in the territories building railways, trying to get enough money together to start a business. Missed the early training, y' see, so I've always been a rube. Always will be a rube. Can't dance, and I never know how to talk to any of the women but you."

"Doesn't matter." Still unable to meet his eyes, she looked around the room.

"You don't seem in much of a festive mood yourself. I suppose you're worried about Lawrence."

"It seems everyone knows more about my affairs than I do."

Normally she would have been grateful for his concern. It made her sad to think they would never be able to share their former intimacy.

"I wish I was going to war. Not that I'd be much of a fighter, just it would be good to get away from . . ."

"Yes. Ah, I see little Caroline Lavouisseur is without a partner. I'd best do what I can to remedy that." She gave a smile that was completely foreign to her—quick, broad, and patently dismissive.

"You must forgive me if I plead the usual hostess's excuse." Two hours later, seated near the French doors, Julia looked up at Orson Dewitt. "I've spent so much energy on the preparation," she continued, "that I haven't any left for the dancing."

She had already danced with him once, and that was one time too many. He was shorter than she, had neither grace nor rhythm, and had held her too tightly, his pot belly bumping against her and his blubbery lower lip bouncing dangerously close to her collarbone. When she'd tried to release his grip, he'd held her tighter yet, and he'd taken such perverse delight in forcing her to follow his lead that she couldn't help but imagine him forcing a woman in a more intimate situation.

"But your efforts have been rewarded," he said. "Marvelous party."

She nodded her thanks. But it wasn't a marvelous party at all. The men seemed charged up, invigorated by the sniff of war. They danced and chatted with the women because they were obliged to, but then they drifted off into corners or clustered around the punch bowl, where they argued, debated, and toasted the death of Spanish tyranny. Had the women been alone, they too might have formed intimate groups, but being in the men's company prevented them from talking about their own concerns, which, Julia thought, were trivial in comparison. The most mediocre of the men knew about law and business and politics, whereas even those women who read and went to lectures only treated such things as amusements. She would have preferred to talk with the men. The newspapers were bully-ragging for war, full of stories of Spanish atrocities, but they didn't give her any clear picture of what was going on. If she listened to the men, she might be able to find out where Lawrence would train or when the troops were expected to go. Earlier, hearing Congressman Lafitte say that the Spanish government had agreed to release insurgents and was willing to make further concessions, she had joined the group of men to whom he was talking. "So," she reasoned, "if the Spanish have made concessions and are willing to make more, might that not mean that war can be averted?"

"Dear lady," the congressman said, wiping punch from his mustache and looking at her as if she were a child who hadn't yet grasped that two plus two must always equal four, "the fact that they are willing to make concessions means that they are weak. Now is the time to strike a blow for freedom."

Barely concealing their annoyance at her intrusion, the men then shifted the conversation to compliments and trivialities. She resented the fact that her argument had been so swiftly dismissed but felt foolish just the same. As she moved away, they started making bets on which day war would be declared.

Only Carlotta seemed to enjoy the male prerogative. Punch cup in hand, Carlotta strolled from one group of men to the next. Just now she was accepting a little cigar from Senator Togeland.

Julia brought her attention back to Orson Dewitt. All evening long she'd been thinking that he reminded her of someone, but for the life of her she couldn't think who. "Please forgive me, Orson," she said, her eyes sweeping the room. She saw Yvette standing near the bandstand, ostensibly engaged in conversation with Phillipa and Lord Harry, though Yvette's attention was really focused on Charles, who was excusing himself from Carrie Bonisett. By Julia's count Charles had already danced with Yvette

three times, though, since the men were less than usually attentive, she supposed he was only doing his duty as host. "I believe
Yvette is without a partner," she told Orson Dewitt.

He turned to substantiate that unlikely fact, grinned, and swag-
gered off. The grin jolted her memory: he didn't remind her of
a person, but of a painting—a fresco of Bacchus. He had the
same dissolute, blubbery mouth, albeit partly concealed by his
mustache, and the same leering eyes. She and Charles had seen
the fresco while on a trip to Italy shortly after Angelique had
been born. Their guide had drawn Charles aside, and from the
furtive way he'd whispered, she'd thought he must be negotiating
his fee; but when Charles had returned to her side, he'd had such
a sly look that she'd pressed him to find out what had been said.
Apparently there were other paintings. For a price they too could
be seen. But only by men.

She was not surprised that that long-forgotten memory had
surfaced tonight. All evening she'd been obsessed with strange
visions. At one point her imagination stripped the entire assem-
bly. Women whose corseted bodies resembled the figureheads
on ships' prows suddenly had relaxed waists, freely swinging
breasts, pale pink or dark brown nipples, stretch marks, scars,
thatches of pubic hair, dimpled rumps, inviting thighs. Older men
showed hairy chests, middles gone to fat, flaccid scrotums; the
younger ones had powerful legs, muscular arms, penises in various stages of erection. It was not so much arousing as profoundly
shocking, as though she were a four-year-old who'd come upon
her parents naked. While looking at the cornet player, she had
another infantile thought—"He's milk chocolate all over." Perspiration formed on her upper lip, and she squeezed her eyes
shut to rid herself of the vision. When Lucretia Asbury asked if
she was all right, she said the room was stuffy and went to open
the doors to the garden.

Even now, as the orchestra struck up and she watched the

dancers and tapped her foot in time to the music, she couldn't stop herself from speculating about which men went to the District. Orson Dewitt, for instance. Had his wife's obvious frigidity turned him into a leering satyr, or had his grossness turned his wife cold? Whatever the cause of the Dewitts' unhappy union, she was sure he sought release elsewhere. It made her shudder to think that some whore subjected herself to him. How could any woman be so debased?

And what about Senator Togeland? Would a man in his position risk the scandal of discovery? Why not? Open knowledge that he accepted bribes had not stopped him from being reelected, so the conspiracy of silence could just as well extend to other unsavory activities.

And what of the younger men? Leonce Lambre, who had his arm around young George Lavouissier's shoulder and was telling him a joke? How could Leonce, a mere nineteen years old, have such a knowing and subtly contemptuous attitude toward women if he'd had no experience of them? And George Lavouissier? Surely not. He had such an innocent, frank expression. But he was often Leonce's companion, so his expression was no guarantee of innocence.

And what of the outsiders like Lord Harry? She'd heard him say something about the "great sport the city offered. Had he only been talking about gambling and horse racing? And even Walter Bonisett, who was progressive enough to favor the vote for women. Had Walter saved himself for thirty-odd years before he'd married Carrie?

"A penny for your thoughts, Julia."

It was Adeline Dewitt. Julia didn't have to ask Adeline what her thoughts were. She could tell from the girl's tight and slightly bewildered expression that Adeline thought the party was a failure because it had brought her no closer to landing a husband. God help these young girls. They were trained to think no further than the proposal, the purchase of the trousseau, and the social event of the wedding, but on their wedding night . . . if the husband was cruel or clumsy, if the experience shocked or frightened them, they would just have to put up with it. For life. How lucky she had been that Charles had overcome her shyness and ignorance. She couldn't have endured the many compromises of her marriage if they hadn't shared bodily love. Yet men were not born with a superior knowledge of women's anatomy, and Charles's expertise couldn't be just the result of his amorous nature. She had always known he'd had past experience, but, close as they were, he had never told her, and she had never asked.

"I was thinking," Julia said, "that perhaps I should announce the supper."

"Yes. Do. I'm quite famished. And they all," Adeline said, meaning the men, "seem to have their minds on other things."

Julia rose and patted her hand. "Perhaps they'll be more congenial if we bring them together at the table."

Carlotta brought the *café brûlot* to her lips, sniffed the aroma of coffee, citrus peel, and burning brandy, and felt a rare contentment. The last selections of liqueurs and desserts had been served, the conversation was spiced with laughter and sighs of indulgence, the candlelight glowed on a rich assortment of lustrous fabrics, ivory shirtfronts, jeweled shoulders and heads, and it was all reflected and contained in the mirrors. It was better than the opera. And she'd directed it without having to leave home.

Her eyes flitted over the supernumeraries—Leonce Lambre spouting poetry, Orson Dewitt touching Phillipa Cotrane's hand to make a point, then lingering on it, Henry Stillerton whispering a deal into Senator Togeland's ear—and settled on the principals.

Yvette, her eyes *tout gougous,* said, "But, Charles, you must remember! We danced until the dawn came up. Desiree Roene fainted! Surely you remember!" and sniffed an orchid she'd taken from the centerpiece.

It was too bad that Yvette's intelligence didn't equal her looks—a fan might be employed to coquettish advantage even in chilly weather, but playing with flowers was best left to girls under twenty. But Charles had had enough champagne to blunt his critical edge and seemed to be enjoying the reminiscence. Julia was seated opposite them, between Vincent Liscomb and Lord Harry, seemingly giving her attention to the latter. But Vincent was focusing on Yvette and Charles. Julia followed his glance, quickly took a spoonful of the raspberry bombe that had melted in her dish, then turned again to Lord Harry, arranging her features into such an expression of polite passivity that Carlotta knew she was suffering. As well she should be. Since Julia always met things head-on, Carlotta was sure she'd already brought up the question of the District properties with Charles. Since she also knew that Charles never met things head-on, she was reasonably certain that he'd put Julia off. Surely the sight of Charles flirting with an old flame would make Julia realize that her influence was precarious, make her think twice before she stuck her moralistic nose into family business. Charles was loyal, and Julia was the mother of his children, but they were twenty years married and he was clearly the most desirable man in the room. Julia had best not push her luck.

Carlotta again looked at Vincent. His hooded eyes, dark with suspicion, stayed on Yvette and Charles while he rolled little doughballs from the bread that had made up most of his meal. Because he reminded her of her second husband, an equally repulsive man who had made her life miserable with his jealousies (doubly miserable because they'd been justified), she enjoyed his discomfort. Yes, it was far better than the opera. And it was only the second act. She drained her cup, ordered brandy, told a servant to have the musicians start up again. Guests who didn't want to dance would go into the game room. She might be able to win the price of her new gown. Not that money was the object. Really needing the money, as that poor divorcée Phillipa Cotrane did, just made you vulnerable. It was the game she relished, and tonight she knew she was on a winning streak.

"Is that so?" Julia said to Lord Harry, knowing that the slightest verbal nudge would launch him into another chapter of his travel epic.

"Oh, yes," he continued. "If one has not seen India, one can't truly be said to have seen the world. The first time I rode an elephant . . ."

How, Julia wondered, could Yvette be so stupid as to make a show of sniffing an orchid when orchids had no scent? She felt as though she were in a *tableau vivant* of the seven deadly sins: pride, gluttony, envy, and sloth were much in evidence; lust, anger, and covetousness were there in the shadows; and as for lying . . .

"Tamed the whole ruddy herd of the wild beasts, that's when the maharaja gave me the ruby ring," Lord Harry blathered on.

Now the meal was concluded, and everyone seemed to be having a marvelous time. Everyone except herself and Abraham Davenport. He'd tried to catch her eye, but she'd pretended not to notice. Phillipa was next to him, chattering like a magpie, but he'd given up any pretense of listening. His head was down, his hand clutched the stem of his wineglass, and when Alcesta leaned past Judge Asbury and gave him an icy stare, ordering him not to take another drop, he tipped back his head, his jowls expanding like a concertina, and drained the glass.

"What a marvelous idea, Orson." Carlotta raised her voice. "I'd love a game of cards."

"It'll give me a chance to recoup my losses from last time," Orson Dewitt joked.

"But my dear man," Carlotta protested, "you won last time."
"No, no, Carlotta. You won. You always win."

Phillipa said, "Forget the past, let's play again now."

"I must have Robespierre," Carlotta said. "He's my adviser." She ordered that the parrot be brought to her, and got up.

The guests rose to their feet and began to stream out of the room. Congressman Lafitte interrupted Lord Harry's description of the Ganges at sunset and reminded Julia that he and Mrs. Lafitte would have to make an early departure. Vincent Liscomb, looking bilious, suggested to Yvette that they leave, too, but Yvette pretended she didn't hear him and went off on Leonce Lambre's arm. As Julia walked the Lafittes to the front doors, the congressman listed every item on the menu and praised it accordingly—the terrapin was excellent, the oysters delightful, the duck succulent . . . Mrs. Lafitte dabbed at her nose and said her cold had prevented her from tasting anything.

Walter and Carrie Bonisett were also leaving early. Julia bade them good night, thinking how lucky they were to be so newly married that they preferred each other's company to the rest of the world. She climbed the stairs to Angelique's room, made sure the child was sleeping soundly, and came back down.

Passing the ballroom, she saw that the dancing was in full swing and decided she needed to fortify herself with another cup of coffee. As she approached the dining room, she wondered why she didn't hear sounds of the table being cleared, but as she stepped in she saw why: Abraham was still slumped in his chair. Alcesta, ignoring the servants who hovered near the kitchen door, stood over him, demanding, "Why must you humiliate me like this! For God's sake, pull yourself together."

Julia motioned to the servants, who moved, soundless as shadows, into the kitchen. She knew she should intervene in Alcesta and Abraham's argument but didn't know how.

"Pull yourself together!" Alcesta insisted. "Get up and take me home this instant!"

Julia backed into the hallway and stood in the stairwell, wondering what she should do. Moments later Alcesta swept out, calling to Robert to get her carriage.

As she reached the threshold of the ballroom, Charles came up, said he had been waiting for her, and moved her on to the floor. She told him, sotto voce, about the scene in the dining room. He shrugged and smiled. "I wonder that you can be so blithe about a man letting his wife go home unescorted," she said testily.

"My darling," he answered, "we can wine them and dine them, we can't make them love one another."

The response was typical of him. He could say, without malice or pity, as matter-of-factly as he'd mention a change in the weather, that this man had lost his business because of drink or that man had had to leave town because of bad debts. He was neither unkind nor uncaring; he simply saw these things as "life." She both envied and scorned his detachment.

"But Charles," she remonstrated, "Abraham is terribly drunk. He's probably still sitting in the dining room and—"

He pulled her closer. "Relax that backbone," he whispered. He sang, "After . . . the . . . ball," and to the same tune, "Cool . . . moonlit . . . sheets."

She wanted to relax but couldn't.

"It'll soon be over," he said, not bothering to lower his voice.

She knew he was tiddly but would have bitten off her tongue before she'd say so. And it wouldn't soon be over. New Orleanians pursued pleasure as doggedly as her people attended to work.

When the music ended, he bowed with mock formality and handed her over to Senator Togeland. She was next partnered by Etienne Dupree. Then young George Lavouissier made her feel her age by romping her through a vigorous quadrille. The Hunnicotts were leaving. After escorting them out, she looked in on the dining room, saw that the servants had finished clearing and that Abraham was gone. Home, she hoped. Passing the game room, she heard Carlotta shriek a winning hand with the abandon of a street vendor.

She hated women who pleaded frailty in order to get out of things, but back in the ballroom she succumbed to the temptation and told Maurice Rousseau that she had a headache when he asked her to dance. She seated herself near the potted palms. Her left breast was being pinched by her corsets, and she raised and lowered her shoulder, trying to free it. Charles, mindful of his duties, escorted another gaggle of guests out; but she still felt as though she were in a stalled railway carriage and had another thousand miles to go before she reached her destination. Cool, moonlit sheets.

"I've lost the rhinestone buckle from my slipper," whined Lucretia Asbury, looking the worse for wear. Julia, still wriggling her shoulder to release her imprisoned flesh, said she would ask the servants to look for it.

Lucretia sat down next to her, adjusting her headdress and angling for a compliment. "I got this from Madame Destault," she said. "I don't know why you don't patronize her. She's all the rage, and she simply won't let you buy anything that doesn't flatter." Lucretia rambled on about mauve velvet and valenciennes lace, then whispered, with venom, that Adeline Dewitt was too flirtatious and that Phillipa Cotrane was gambling with Orson Dewitt's money.

Would it never end! Could no one say anything kind or intelligent? If she could escape to the garden for a few moments of solitude, she would be able to see it through. On the pretense of telling the servants to wrap leftovers for the musicians, she excused herself. Lucretia pursed her lips in a condescending smile. The musicians were high-yella professionals; they'd take leftovers as an insult. But then, Julia would never learn.

The servants' laughter ebbed as Julia opened the kitchen door, and they made a show of scraping, washing, and wiping. She nodded and moved quickly past them to let herself out the back door.

The moon was full and apricot-colored, the smell of the foliage heavy but fresh. She reached into her bodice to release her pinched flesh, walked to the marble bench beneath the magnolia tree, then sank down, her hand still on her breast, taking deep breaths. Through the French doors she could see the dancers, but the music was muted, no more than an accompaniment to the splash of the fountain. Then she heard another sound, a retching followed by a strangulated groan. Had some overindulged guest actually come into the garden to vomit? She stood up and moved a few steps to her right. Then she saw him, on the other side of the fountain, the bib of his tuxedo white in the moonlight as he heaved up from a bent position, took his hands from his face, and rested his head against the wall.

Abraham.

He wasn't vomiting. He was weeping. His eyes clenched shut, his mouth open, in such a state of naked despair that she moved toward him reflexively, murmuring his name.

Then she spun around and, not caring if she made a noise, for he was plainly beyond noticing, ran back to the kitchen door. Charles would know what to do.

Charles was in the game room, elbow on mantelpiece, pulling on a cigar and nodding at Lord Harry, who was booming, "Have you ever seen a statue of one of those Hindu goddesses? I can tell you, they don't look like ladies. . . ."

The others were so intent on their games that they didn't notice her, but Robespierre stretched his wings and squawked. With a slight nod of her head and shift of her shoulder, she signaled Charles and, drawing him into the hall, told him what she'd seen in the garden.

Her face was pinched with concern, and she looked as though she might burst into tears herself. He smoothed the line between her brows with his thumb, then tugged her earlobe. "Can you see to the rest of the stragglers if I have to take him home?" he asked.

She smiled and nodded. How fine he was, she thought, how much a gentleman. He didn't judge; he simply acted.

Ten minutes later, as Lord Harry, who'd acknowledged the change in his audience with no more than a sodden nod, was continuing his lecture on the mysteries of Hinduism, she glanced into the hall and saw Charles, hat on, negotiating Abraham toward the front doors.

CHAPTER

VIII

For no man tells his son the truth
For fear he speak of sin;
And every man cries "Woe, alas!"
And every man goes in.

Dana Burnet, "Sisters of
the Cross of Shame"

*T*hey had been in the carriage no more than a few minutes
when Abraham declared that he didn't want to go home—"not
tonight, not ever." The desperate mood that had come over him
in the garden changed to one of high good spirits. He began to
hum, bounced on the seat, then heaved the upper part of his
body out of the window and yelled to Robert to take them to
Mollie Q.'s place on Customhouse Street.

"I can't go to the District," Charles told him.

"Whatta you mean you can't go?" Abraham demanded. "You're
free, white, and twenty-one."

Charles felt the carriage slow as Robert awaited his instructions. He was not about to say that he couldn't go because of
Julia, but for perhaps the first time he felt the confinement of
living up to standards that weren't truly his own. He had been
in the District only a handful of times since his marriage and then

only to attend smokers or bachelor parties. Naturally he hadn't told Julia, and naturally he'd been tempted by the girls—if a man didn't feel some increase in circulation when he saw young, available womanflesh, he might as well be dead. He knew there was no risk of scandal (even men who were business rivals or who didn't like each other honored the brotherhood of silence), and he didn't think it morally wrong if an unmarried man, or even a married one whose needs weren't being satisfied at home, took a girl upstairs; but he loved his wife, and his needs were being satisfied, so he'd done no more than drink, play cards, talk politics, and listen to the music.

He told Abraham that it was too late, but Abraham, with a drunk's steamroller determination, declared that if Charles wouldn't take him there, he'd get out and walk. Charles was not in the habit of criticizing or bullying a friend, no matter what state the friend might be in, and he'd had just enough champagne to feel expansive. He smiled at the strange twist of fate that had him going into the District tonight of all nights, told Abraham that he would drop him there but wasn't going in at Mollie Q.'s, and ordered Robert to drive on to Customhouse Street.

He heard the music drifting from the District blocks before they got there. Was there anything more seductive than the sound of distant music? It seemed to pull the carriage like a magnet. The streets had a raucous energy—lamps lit, windows bright, crowds streaming down the streets, cabs pulling up and discharging their passengers. Charles felt buoyed up by the carnival mood and decided that owing to Abraham's state of inebriation, he'd best see him safely deposited before he went home. He called to Robert to drop them on the corner and said he would take a cab back.

"Yessir," Robert said as they got out, his face so purposely blank that Charles would have preferred a wink.

Abraham started down the street as though he were leading a

parade. "This is it," he called over his shoulder, waving in the general direction of one of the brightly painted doors. There was a circle of men on the banquette, listening to a group of ragamuffin boys playing a popular song at frenetic double tempo. One boy, wearing a sandwich board that read "Razzy Tazzy Band," wailed on a harmonica, another pounded a homemade drum, a third crouched, singing and playing the spoons on the sidewalk, while a fourth, eyes bright in his small simian face, danced with wild jerking movements. The sound they made was so original and compelling that even Abraham stopped, swinging his big shoulders to the beat and applauding loudly when they came to a slam-bam finale.

"We're the Razzy Tazzy Band," the monkey-faced boy yelled, passing a hat around the crowd. "What's your pleasure, gents? We play anything old in a new and different way."

Abraham had taken a wad of bills from his wallet and was peeling off a ten. Charles reached over, extracted a one instead, and dropped it into the hat. The boy shot him an ugly look, then grinned mischievously.

"You stay home next time an' let yer friend come by hisself," he told him. Then, raising his voice again, "We're the Razzy Tazzy Band. If y' like the tunes, buy us a drink."

"You're too young to drink," one of the onlookers shouted.

"Does yer mother know ye're out, sport?" the boy yelled back to general amusement. "Okay, y' pikers, y' cheapskates, here we go again . . . And a one, two . . ." He grabbed the harmonica from the other boy, knocked out the spit, put it to his mouth, and pulled a wild, ecstatic groan from it.

Abraham lurched up the steps and rapped loudly on the door. It was opened so quickly that he fell forward, and the slight, nattily dressed silver-haired man who'd opened it caught him and tottered back. "Where's Judas?" Abraham demanded, disengaging himself.

"He's in the back, sir. Mollie's very busy tonight, and I've been pressed into service as porter."

"You sure couldn't be a houseman," Abraham said, then yelled above the piano music coming from the front parlor, "Where's Mollie!"

"Sure, I'm here." Mollie came out of the parlor, perspiring, harried but sweetly polite. "And I see you are, too, Mr. Davenport."

"Ah, here's the face that launched a thousand ships," Abraham said sentimentally, sweeping off his hat.

"It wasn't the face, love," she said, and sent him into a wheezing laugh. "I see you're squiffed and swizzled."

"Damaged bad," he agreed.

" 'And what three things does drink especially provoke? Marry, sire, nose-painting, sleep, and urine,' " the little man said, and seeing Abraham's confused look, added, "That's a quote, sir. I am not an original thinker."

"He's a great actor. He's my friend Billy Shakespeare."

"And this"—Abraham flung back his arm and hit Charles in the chest—"is my friend Charlie Randsome. The best friend any man could have."

"Charles," Charles corrected. No one had ever called him Charlie and never would if he could help it.

Mollie's eyes opened wide. She'd thought she'd recognized him, but since all of her dealings were with his property agent, she hadn't been sure. She put her hand to her breast. She could think of nothing to say but a silly, "Haven't we met before, Mr. Randsome?"

"I think not," Charles said politely.

Seeing that Mollie was having difficulty recovering herself, Shakespeare jumped in with, "Well, gentlemen, what's your pleasure? Mollie has a marvelous new cook if you fancy a late supper, there's a card game going on, she's just redecorated the Turkish parlor, or you could go into the front room and listen to Silt and perhaps make your selection right away, because the girls are very busy tonight."

"Or"—Mollie touched her fingers together and smiled at Charles—"I have a new young lady. And she is a lady. Fresh as a flower and very, very lovely. She'll be downstairs in a short while, if you'd like the pleasure of an introduction. Once you see her, I'm sure you'll—"

"No, thank you," Charles said. "I'm just dropping Mr. Davenport off." But he found himself reluctant to leave. Voices sang a rousing chorus of "Ta-ra-ra-boom-de-ay!" and he watched as a man danced a pretty blonde out of the parlor and over to the stairs, where he bowed, then goosed her as she ran up the stairs.

"You can't go yet," Abraham insisted. "I don't want to go home. I never want to go home."

Mollie said, "And I have no intention of sending you there."

Abraham was weaving on his feet. He wiped his forehead and said, "I don't feel so good. Could you let us have that little back room for a chat, Mollie?"

Mollie raised her voice over the clapping in the front parlor. "Ah, Mr. Davenport, it's a bit of a mess. I'm having it painted, y' see, an' the boys ain't finished it yet." The piano slowed to the more haunting strains of "Salut d'Amour."

"Perhaps," Charles suggested, "you could give us some coffee."

Abraham steadied himself against the umbrella stand. "Where's Agnes? I want to see Agnes."

"She's gone to the country to visit her mother, more's the pity. Come along now. If you gentlemen will excuse the condition of the back room, I'll put you in there and you can have your little chat first." She indicated that Charles and Shakespeare should give Abraham some assistance. They stepped to either side, put his arms around their shoulders, and let Mollie lead the way.

As they passed the dining room, Charles saw a girl, breasts as big as melons, sitting on a man's lap and whispering into his ear. Another girl stood, teasingly holding a shrimp just out of reach of a man who put his hands up like paws and growled and barked, to the general amusement. Though he'd had no appetite at the party, the smell of roast suckling made his mouth water.

As they approached the staircase, a girl in a white satin dress came down, and Charles stopped involuntarily. Here was not beauty, but perfection. Clear amber eyes that had a look of surprise, skin as white and soft as a gardenia, and shoulders that . . .

"Ah, there she is," Mollie said, going to the stairs and taking her hand. "This is Katherine."

Kate lowered her head and looked at Charles from beneath her lashes. Abraham, who was past noticing, lurched on, and Charles tore his eyes from the girl.

"Could you give us some coffee? And perhaps a wet towel," he said again to Mollie.

"No coffee. More champagne," Abraham bellowed.

Mollie patted him. "I'll send in both, and you can argue it out." There was more rapping at the front door. "If you'll excuse me, gentlemen." She hurried away.

Shakespeare nodded to Charles and they moved off, but Charles couldn't resist a backward glance. The girl still stood there, so shyly oblivious of everything around her that she might have been in a garden. Katherine, Charles thought. Her name is Katherine.

"I want Agnes," Abraham muttered as Shakespeare steered them into an ill-lit corridor.

"Just now," Shakespeare said, "I don't think you want anybody. 'Drink, sir, is a great equivocator. It provokes desire, but it takes away performance.' "

A man bumped into them. Shakespeare said, "Excuse *us,*" to remind him of his manners, but the man humped off without apology. Shakespeare propped Abraham against the wall, opened a door, lit a single gas lamp, and motioned for them to come in.

The room smelled of plaster and paint fumes. Furniture had been pushed higgledy-piggledy away from the wall. Shakespeare lifted a rolled-up carpet from a divan. "I'll send in the coffee and champagne," he said quietly, and closed the door.

Charles lowered Abraham to the divan and pulled up a chair for himself. Abraham heaved his left ankle over his right knee and meditatively began to pull off his shoe. His foot slipped off his knee and plopped onto the floor. "You are a fine gentleman and an exemplary friend," he told Charles. "I have taken you away from your party, and I have nothing but profound apologies for my conduct. Where's that damned champagne?"

"It'll be here in a minute. And then I'll have to go."

"Don't go. You can't go." Abraham tore at his collar, struggled unsuccessfully to take off his jacket, gave it up, and leaned forward, elbows on knees, hands supporting his head. "But, of course, you have to go. I've taken you away from your party. Goddamn parties. No offense, but, dammit, I hate those dos. Always feel like I'm at a taxidermist's waiting to have my guts ripped out. But I've taken you away from your party. You shouldn't even be here."

"No," Charles agreed. "I shouldn't."

"I have nothing but the most profound apologies for my conduct," Abraham repeated. "If you could talk to Julia . . . tell her that I'm sorry . . . that I—"

"Julia won't mind. She's very fond of you."

"She used to be fond of me, but not anymore."

"What do you mean?" Charles felt in his pocket for a cigar before realizing that he was in his evening clothes and wasn't carrying any. He desperately wanted a smoke. He also wanted to eat, relieve his bladder, have another glass of champagne, and see Katherine again. Just see her. "Do you have a cigar?"

"Mollie'll give you a cigar. Mollie'll give you anything. I love that woman. I love Julia, too. Do you mind my telling you that I love your wife? I've always loved her—not in that way—wouldn't touch her, and she wouldn't let me—but I love her. Do you mind?" He raised his head and gave Charles a bleary, pleading glance.

"No, I don't mind."

Abraham's features contorted. "But Julia won't love me anymore. Not since Alcesta told her what I'm really like."

There was a tap on the door. Charles was expecting the dapper little in-between with the sharp eyes, but it was she. Katherine. He got up and went to relieve her of the tray she was carrying. It was heavy with coffeepot, cups, a bottle of champagne, and two glasses. She said "Thank you" without looking at him, then moved behind the divan, taking the folded towel she had draped over her arm and telling Abraham to lean back.

Charles looked around for a place to put the tray. The only table was covered with oilcloth, paint cans, brushes, and a jar of turpentine. He put the tray on the floor and, straightening up, saw her bending over, flattening the damp towel on Abraham's forehead. Her shoulders and arms were luminous in the dim light, her breasts so small and firm that they didn't move as she bent forward.

"Ah, the ministering angel," Abraham groaned, grabbing her hand and kissing it. That Abraham should so much as touch her made Charles wince as though he'd heard a singer hit a sour note. He sat back on the chair.

"So you're Katherine," Charles said. She nodded.

Abraham scrunched up the towel and wiped it roughly over his face. "That's better. Where's Agnes? That's what I'd like to know."

"Mollie told you," Charles reminded him, still looking at the girl.

"She's upstairs in her room," Kate said softly. "She's packing. She has consumption and she's packing to go to a sanatorium."

"Well, dammit, I didn't know ol' Agnes was sick," Abraham said. "I'll go up and see her."

"I don't think you should. She's . . . upset."

"Then I want you to give her this." Abraham threw aside the towel and reached for his wallet.

Kate stopped him. "We're not allowed to handle money. Mollie takes care of all the"—she wet her lips and stared at Charles— "arrangements." Her look had none of the usual whore's-leer come-on; it simply told him that she was there for the taking, or rather for the price, and she had no objection to taking him.

And why not me? Charles thought. Better me than some drunken sot or some fool who begs and barks like a dog. What glorious hair she had. And that neck. Was there anything lovelier than a young girl's neck?

"Where are you from?" was all he could get out. His voice was hoarse and impatient, the voice of a young man trying to hide his feelings. And he felt young. Felt his sap rising as fast and urgently as it had when he was eighteen.

She shrugged as though the question were of no importance. "If you want to talk to Mollie . . ." she began.

Was he imagining it, or was there a flicker of real interest in her eyes? He couldn't be imagining it. He knew women. He knew he was attractive. When a woman's eyes locked with yours like that, when you felt that current, it was never one-sided.

"Come on. Come on," Abraham whispered. He was down on all fours, worrying the cork off the bottle. As it popped, the champagne shot up and fizzed onto the floor, and he fell back on his haunches, laughing.

Kate grabbed up the towel and knelt to mop the spill. Charles put his hand over hers. "Leave it." Her hand was soft and wet.

He wanted to lick it finger by finger. He said, "Would you like some?"

She hesitated, looked toward the door. "We're very busy tonight. I have to go back out. If you'd like to talk to Mollie . . ."

Abraham slopped champagne into the glasses. "Yes. Talk to Mollie. Tell her we want some cigars."

Kate took her hand from Charles's and got up. She was so close he could smell her. He wanted to reach out, grasp her buttocks, pull her to him, and smother his face in the folds of her dress. "Yes," he said. His voice had regained authority. "Tell Mollie we want some cigars. And will you bring them yourself?"

She went to the door and opened it. The sound of the music flowed in, a pounding, rhythmic beat, steady and insistent. "I'll try," Kate said, and closed the door.

Charles got up and moved around the room, absently taking the glass Abraham held up to him and finishing it in one long swallow. "I see you're anxious to leave," Abraham said. He finished off one glass and poured himself another. "You have to get back to your party."

"The party's long since over." God, what time was it? Julia would be waiting. He paced until he was stopped by the wall, turned, went back, held out his glass. Abraham was still on the floor, legs sprawled in front of him. He held up the bottle, and Charles took it.

"Julia will be waiting," Charles muttered, but poured another glass. To his amazement, Abraham began to blubber.

"I love Julia, but she won't like me anymore. Not anymore. She won't like me."

Charles barely heard him. What was he doing in the back room of a brothel, giddy from paint fumes and champagne, listening to a miserable drunk? "Of course Julia likes you."

"She *used* to like me." Abraham was emphatic. "She used to like me, but she doesn't anymore. Not since Alcesta told her all about me. She told her I was a whoremonger, she told her that I'd infected her. How could she do that?" Charles stopped and looked down at him, incredulous. "She told her," Abraham insisted, "and she told me she told her. Didn't Julia tell you?"

"Julia told me nothing whatever about you. Or your wife."

"Well, she wouldn't, would she? That's because Julia is fine. She has standards. Her very own standards. But Alcesta told her. How could she do that?" he begged, tears welling in his eyes. "How could she? I know why. I'll tell you why. It wasn't just to get Julia to write that stupid petition. She did it on purpose because she wanted to turn Julia against me, because she doesn't want anyone to love me, not even a little bit. Because she thinks I'm a swine. She called me a swine before she knew I'd infected her, and with God as my witness, I swear I thought I was cured. Would I have married if I hadn't believed that? But what have I done?" he demanded, misery rising to fierce self-righteousness as Charles felt his way to the chair and sat down, amazed. "I haven't done any more than any other man. I promised myself I'd never come into a house again after I got married. I knew a good woman wouldn't really like it, but I thought if she loved you, she'd at least tolerate it. Julia tolerates it, doesn't she? I bet she more than tolerates it. Because she loves you. That's why I like to be around both of you—because I can tell, anyone can tell. . . . But Alcesta called me a swine even before she knew. God as my witness. . . ." He raised his hand as though taking an oath, then crossed his heart. "I didn't know. The way she looks at me! You've seen it. Everyone can see it. No matter how much I give her, no matter how much I do, she looks at me like I'm dirt. That's why everyone thinks I'm a fool. Nothing but hate in her eyes. She begrudges me every breath I breathe. In twenty years of marriage I've never once seen her naked. I think she was glad to find out about me because it gave her the excuse, y' see?"

He pounded his fist on the floor. "I hate good women. Praying for your soul and wishing you dead. Sanctimonious, tight-assed bitches! I hate—" He stopped abruptly and shuddered with guilt and self-loathing. "But I am a whoremonger. I was chasing it and paying for it soon as I came out of knee britches."

His head went down, and his hands fell open, loosing the champagne glass. "I resist it as long as I can," he went on in a low voice. "And when I can't any longer, I come here. I go with Agnes mostly, and she knows the story. She swabs me down— you know that purple disinfectant stuff they use on everyone— and I always wear something. But you know, I never feel satisfied. I don't mean they're cheatin' me. Mollie's a square dealer. But you know the girl wants to get it over with, even when she acts nice. And afterward . . . I dunno, you feel you've been cheated somehow. Because you want . . . *you* know what you want. . . ."
Bewilderment ended in a shivering sigh, and his head fell back against the divan, eyes closed.

Charles got up, straightened his vest, and picked up his hat. "I have to go." There was no response, and he thought that Abraham had probably passed out. He picked up the glass lying next to him, stood for a moment, entirely devoid of thought, placed the glass on the table, and went to the door. In the corridor he saw Shakespeare coming toward him, holding a box of cigars.

"Mr. Davenport is indisposed," Charles said. "If you could see to him, I'd appreciate it."

"Yes, sir. I think Miss Katherine is waiting for you in the front parlor."

"Yes. Well, tell her that . . . I must go home. The bill . . ."

"I believe Mr. Davenport has an account."

"Well, then . . ." He paused, nodded, then strode toward the front door, looking neither left nor right.

Shakespeare looked after him, trying to put it all together, then went in, stared at Abraham's crumpled body, and decided to let him sleep it off. He took a pillow from the divan and stuffed it under his head. "Poor bastard," he muttered, and turned off the light.

What woman hasn't been instructed in the virtues of patience? In one of the first epic stories in recorded history, the faithful Penelope waited for years for the errant Odysseus, rejecting her suitors, weaving her tapestry by day, unpicking it by night. Penelope's anxiety and patience were legend; presumably, she never felt anger. Perhaps, Julia thought as she stared up at the bedroom ceiling, it wasn't such an inspiring story after all.

She had stayed in the game room after Charles had left. Carlotta, shuffling with the finesse of a croupier, hadn't seemed to notice his departure. Lord Harry had told her gleefully he had actually seen an Indian woman fling herself on her husband's funeral pyre. When a card had dropped to the floor and Julia had bent to retrieve it, she'd seen Oscar Dewitt's stockinged foot somewhere between Phillipa Cotrane's skirts.

Julia excused herself and went into the ballroom. Vincent Liscomb, looking so waxy that he truly seemed to be ill, finally persuaded Yvette to leave. She saw them out, then returned to the ballroom.

Mothers sat in corners, sharing desultory conversation while their daughters made last-minute efforts to charm. She saw the Lavouisseurs to the door and returned to the game room. Carlotta had just won a hand. As abruptly as a child who leaves toys that no longer interest it, she scooped up her winnings and said good night. The game went on, but with diminishing enthusiasm. Finally, as though they'd been given a secret signal, the guests began to leave.

Closing the door on the last of them, Julia went through the dining room, which had been restored to such pristine order that the dinner might not have taken place, and into the kitchen, where enough leftovers for a second banquet were piled on the table. The cornet player was gnawing on a duck leg, while Maggie, wearing what must've been Lucretia Asbury's lost rhinestone buckle in her hair, leaned against the sink and stared at him with adoring eyes. She couldn't let the servants get away with appropriating the guests' lost items, but what was a slipper buckle to Lucretia, after all? Finders keepers. She closed the door so quickly that they didn't notice her intrusion.

In the ballroom the musicians were packing up, though the piano player still lingered, picking out a slow, improvised melody with one hand, while servants swept and straightened. They seemed to be having a better time than the guests had had. She told them to leave the garlands until the morning, thanked them, and said good night, then climbed the stairs to Angelique's room, leaning heavily on the banister as she reached the third floor. She pulled down the child's rucked nightdress, covered her, and felt her forehead, but when she bent to kiss her, Angelique flung out her arm and twisted away.

She shut her own bedroom door and leaned against it, sighing in such a parody of relief that she made herself laugh. Struggling with the buttons on the back of her gown, she wished Charles home already. She unclasped her pearls, took down her hair, and catching her reflection in the mirror—what a pinched, tired face—turned down the gas lamp. In the moonlight, as she stepped out of her petticoats, her legs looked lithe and firm. She glanced at the nightdress laid out on the bed and decided not to put it on. She would greet him naked.

She brushed her hair for a long time, listening for the sound of his step, then slipped in between the sheets and stretched. Just lying down was such bliss that she groaned. He would be home any minute now, shutting the bedroom door so carefully that the sound of the lock would be erotic, and she would toss back the sheets and welcome him and . . .

She sat up. But no. The noise that had wakened her was just a floorboard creaking of its own accord. What time must it be? She groped her way to the mantelpiece and brought her face close to the clock dial. Almost four. What could have happened to him? Surely he wouldn't have come in and gone to his own room.

She went through the bathroom and into his room, calling his name softly, though she already knew he wasn't there.

Surely he hadn't let Abraham seduce him into going to one of the men's clubs. Surely he wouldn't have done that tonight. And if he had, the clubs would long since be closed. And if some emergency had occurred, why hadn't he sent Robert to let her know?

She walked slowly back into her own room, wrapping her arms around her breast. It wasn't just the predawn chill that made her shiver, but the picture of herself. She was no nymph anticipating a night of abandoned love. She was a thin, middle-aged woman, ridiculous in her nakedness. She found her nightdress, pulled it roughly over her head, buttoned it to her neck, and, still shivering, got back into bed. As in so many situations when she didn't know what to do, she decided to read, turning up her bedside lamp and picking up the first thing she touched, an article about Impressionist artists sent by a friend who lived in Paris.

As she turned the second page, she realized that she hadn't taken in any of it. If waiting for Charles did this to her, what would it be like when Lawrence was in Cuba and she was waiting for news of him? She bit the inside of her lip until she broke the skin. How could Charles do this to her? Was her love always to be taken for granted, mollified with a kiss, a smile, a promise?

She turned off the lamp and lay back. Of course, she reasoned, he was still angry because she'd challenged him about the District properties. She had overstepped her bounds, and probably without realizing it, he was punishing her. The District . . . The moment the thought occurred to her, it had the force of undeniable truth. He had gone with Abraham to the District. A wave of rage so powerful that it made her nauseated crashed over her. She lay stock still, staring at the ceiling. If she moved, she would surely burst apart.

An immeasurable time later, she heard him on the stairs and bolted from the bed as though she were under siege, locking the hall door, then running to the bathroom door and locking that, too.

He tried the hall door, then went through his bedroom to the bathroom. The faucet was turned on. He was washing his face. She went back to the bed and lay down. As he jiggled the lock to the bathroom door, a little core of satisfaction hardened in her chest. He called her name, softly at first, then more loudly, in a voice half-concerned, half-demanding. I cannot hear you, she told herself, but she was acutely aware when, minutes later, he left the door and went into his own room.

IX

I think I could be a good woman if I had five thousand a year.

W. M. Thackeray, *Vanity Fair*

ollie Q. sat in her bedroom on an emerald-green Regency chair, the skirts of her ruby satin gown hoisted, soaking her feet in a tub of Epsom salts. Billy Shakespeare was hunched over her desk, sipping Pouilly-Fuissé, smoking a cigar one of the customers had given him and totaling up the accounts, while Kate stood at the window, brushing her hair with long slow strokes. Judas, the jug-eared houseman, was asleep in the back room. Sophronia had scoured the last pot and gone home to her children. The house was quiet and dark except for the lights in the entrance hall and the front parlor, where Monkey, who'd wheedled his way into the kitchen with promises to help but had ended up doing impersonations of the customers and wolfing down leftovers, fooled around at the piano.

"You're a darlin' man to help with those accounts, Billy. My eyes cross whenever I have to deal with numbers."

"How else can I express my humble thanks for the bounty of your table and this excellent Pouilly-Fuissé? Besides, tomorrow is my day off at the Versailles."

Kate pressed her forehead against the glass and looked out at the deserted street. It was the no-color of just before dawn. Even the saloon down the street, where the downtown musicians came to play after their society jobs, had shut. The Versailles seemed as far away as her seventh birthday. It was impossible that she'd ever thought it grand, even less real that she'd thought she was in love with Frank Staughton and believed him to be a gentleman. In the few weeks she'd been at Mollie's she'd seen so many like him—quick-talking con men with all-purpose smiles and gold-plated jewelry, "flimflam boys," the girls called them—that Frank seemed more a type than an individual. But sometimes the memory of his betrayal, mixed with a loathing for her own vulnerability, came on her like a sort of fit, and a metallic taste flooded her mouth. She couldn't swallow and her head felt as though it would burst. She'd lied to Sophronia and told her she'd gotten her monthly, but she knew she must be about two months pregnant. She'd gained weight, but Mollie proudly attributed that to improved diet. Her breasts were swollen, but her belly was still flat, and by the time she started to show, she figured she'd have enough money to go away and have the baby. She was going to have it. If she didn't, it would prove she was like the rest of them, nothing but a whore. But part of her was sorry she hadn't taken Sophronia's herbs and Vivian Lefevre's little black pill, because now that Mollie was looking out for her, she might meet a man powerful and rich enough to set her up in her own place. Someone like that Mr. Randsome. How fine he was. Any girl would want to go upstairs with a man like that. And she'd been so sure they were going to when they'd been in the back room with that pathetic Mr. Davenport. She'd felt the pull between them like iron filings stuck to a magnet. She knew he wanted her. Then he'd left without even saying good-bye. Maybe she wasn't as pretty as everyone said she was.

Her head started to ache. How was she going to take care of

a baby? She wanted to break down and confess everything to Mollie, but she was afraid to risk her wrath. Besides, she'd decided that she would never tell anyone the whole truth again. The only way to get by was to trust no one.

But she didn't want to think about any of that now. She was safe now, and happy, in a pretty room where candles flickered on Mollie's little altar with the Virgin statue in the blue-and-gold cape. Her stomach was full of good food, she was fresh from her bath and wearing an almost new dressing gown Mollie had gotten too fat for, with rosebuds embroidered down the front. It was all so cozy. It was like being with your parents before bedtime. Not her real parents, of course—there had never been cozy bedtimes with them. And not even the parents she'd dreamed of, because who could think of a boozy madam and a funny old actor who'd probably never even had a woman as parents? They were more like an aunt and uncle who cared for you and gave you tips about how to get along in the world. She loved it when Mollie and Billy fussed over her.

She'd had only two customers that night—the first an old geezer from New York who'd acted as though he felt sick afterward, and then, after Mr. Randsome had left, a fairly young, corpulent banker from Cleveland, and he hadn't even gotten into bed. As soon as he'd taken her to her room, he'd settled on a chair, unbuttoned himself, asked for a towel, and told her to follow his directions. He'd told her to take off her dress, petticoats, and bloomers. Then he'd had her take her stockings off, then put them on again. He'd told her to touch her breasts. Then he'd told her to touch herself down there and say "I've never done this before" over and over again. She hadn't had to act convincing, because it was true. She'd barely started to do it, thinking that her mother would roll over in her grave if she could see her, when he'd shuddered and ordered her to turn her back.

"He didn't even touch me," she'd marveled when she heard the door slam. She'd taken a bath anyway. The girls weren't supposed to take full baths during business hours, but she could get away with it if she was quiet. She knew Mollie liked her better than any of the other girls, and she couldn't stop herself from taking advantage of it.

"Don't braid your hair, Kate, it'll come out in kinks. Come over here an' I'll brush it for you."

Kate pulled up the footstool and handed Mollie the brush. "And while you're sitting here," Mollie added, "you might as well give my feet a rub. That's the Golden Rule. Do unto others as you would have them do unto you."

"Doing unto others as you would have them do unto you doesn't always please," Shakespeare said dryly. "Tastes vary."

Kate smiled at that and plunged her hands into the little tub. Mollie's feet were pale and lumpy, and the toes curled onto each other like old people's feet, but she didn't mind massaging them, because she was relieved that Mollie wasn't angry with her about Mr. Randsome. Mollie had cross-examined her about what had gone wrong, but she was at a loss to understand it herself.

"Ooh, ah, yes, lovie, that feels good," Mollie moaned. She stopped brushing Kate's hair and let her arms go limp.

"Would you like this last thimbleful of the Pouilly-Fuissé, Kate?" Shakespeare asked.

She shook her head. "It tastes sour."

"It's an acquired taste," Mollie explained. "Acquired taste means you don't like it at first, but you keep forcing yourself to do it and pretty soon you don't mind. Why don't we open another bottle?"

"Dear lady, you're drinking up the profits. I could go and make some cocoa."

Kate said, "I'd like cocoa."

"And I'd like more Pouilly-Fuissé," Mollie insisted.

"I shall have to go soon," Shakespeare reasoned. "Besides, it's almost dawn."

"Then close the damn draperies. If there's one thing I don't need to see, it's the sun comin' up." Mollie had a premonition that she would die at dawn and often turned belligerent when they were closing up shop.

"As you wish, dear lady. As you wish." Billy corked the ink, blotted the accounts, and got up.

"And tell that no-good Monkey to stop pounding my piano. And count the silverware before he leaves. He'd steal the pennies off a dead man's eyes."

"Granted," Billy said, "he is neither a likable nor a trustworthy youngster, but he has the seeds of a great musical talent. Just listen to that. . . ." He shot his cuffs and turned his hand palm up as though offering them the music.

Monkey was playing around with a tune the kids sang when jumping rope, adding a steady throbbing bass and crooning, "I don't want no black woman puttin' sugar in my tea / 'Cause black is evil and I'm skeered she might poison me. . . ."

"Call that music?" Mollie demanded.

It wasn't regular music, Kate thought, but it stopped your heart just the same. It was sad and silly, but it made you think of bodies tussling on a bed. Some men said they came to the District just to hear it, though most customers preferred the more energetic barrelhouse stuff.

"He'll go anywhere to be around music," Kate said. "He follows all the funerals just to hear the bands, and Sophronia told me he was sleeping in the Abyssinian Baptist church and fooling around on the organ before the caretaker kicked him out."

"His father was a light-skinned man who was a master carpenter," Mollie said. "Then he bought a trombone some idiot from the Union army left in a pawnshop, and he never did a day's work once he put it to his lips. Dead now. And the mother works in the kitchen of that café near the docks. Monkey's been running the streets since he was old enough to walk."

"He's a wormy little brat." Kate knew Monkey had a soft spot for her, and it disgusted her.

"He's got no morals. He's selfish to the bone," Mollie said.

"That never stood in the way of being an artist," Billy told her. "I believe Monkey is destined to be a great musician—"

"He'll end up in the gutter," Mollie predicted.

"—in the same way that Kate is destined to be a great courtesan."

"You mean whore," Kate said softly.

"Dear Kate, don't demean yourself. There are lawyers, doctors, clergymen, and politicians who daily sell their talents to the highest bidder. Compared to that, the sin of a woman who sells the use of her person for a few hours is too venial to mention."

Mollie grunted approval. "There's too much hypocrisy in the world."

Kate could see the wisdom of Billy's reasoning, but it was no comfort. No matter what those men did, society didn't look down on them. And they never had to do anything with their bodies that they didn't want to do. "Why will I be a great courtesan?" she asked.

"Because you're beautiful," Mollie told her.

"Beauty is never enough," Shakespeare said. It would have been too cruel to remind Mollie that in her day her looks must have equaled Kate's. "It's because you have learned at an early age to rely on your wits. Because you have an innate good taste. Because you have already learned to trust no one."

"Nonsense! She trusts me." Mollie looked at Kate with motherly pride and took Kate's blush as evidence of her trust. "Now, Billy, stop jawin'. Get Kate her cocoa and fix me a nightcap."

"Your wish is my command." Billy bowed and went into the

hallway. Voices were heard, the front door closed, and Agnes, lower lip hanging, her hair in a tangle, came to the door.

"Was that Mr. Davenport leaving?" Mollie asked.

"Yeah. He's gotta get home before the sun comes up, and I don't think he's gonna make it. I s'pose it's the last time I'll see him, at least for a while."

"Did you ask him about Mr. Randsome like I told you to?"

"Yeah. He said Mr. Randsome wouldn't be coming back. He said he ain't comin' back any more himself." Agnes yawned without covering her mouth. " 'Course he says that every time."

Mollie stamped her foot, sloshing water everywhere, then stepped out of the footbath and began to pace the room. "We almost had him. Almost . . . Monkey! *Stop pounding that damned piano or I'll come in an' slam the cover on yer paws!*"

The piano stopped abruptly, then, like a musical thumbing of the nose, there was a little trill. "That goddamn Monkey! I swear I'll . . ."

Mollie started out of the room, then stopped, laughing at herself, flopping back down on her chair. "I was so sure we had him, Kate. I'm never wrong about these things. I know he'll come back. And he'll come back for *you,* and when he does . . . once he's gotten friendly-like, I'll talk to him about lowering the rent and fixin' up the place. I know he's a decent man. If he knew how that agent of his is gouging me . . ."

Agnes signaled Kate with her eyes that they should leave. "I got a pair of satin heels won't fit in the case. Don't s'pose I'll be doing much dancin' for a while. You can have 'em if they fit."

Kate nodded. She was sorry to see Agnes go. Agnes was grouchy a lot of the time, but that was just because she was sick and because, Kate thought, Agnes had a tragic life. She was an Arkansas farm girl, married at sixteen to a railroad man by the name of Willie, who brought her south. She'd had two babies, but they'd died within a week of each other, of scarlatina. Then Willie had been mashed to death in a train wreck.

Agnes had told her, "I used to walk down the railroad ties and think I'd just hurl myself under 'em, out of loneliness, or just 'cause I wanted a man's arms around me." One afternoon she'd let another lineman, a friend of Willie's, have his way with her. He'd paid her rent for a couple of months, but then he'd beaten her up and told her she wasn't good for anything but bed.

"And he was right. What did I know to do but stir a pot or chop kindling or clean up baby shit? And I did have a taste for men. My husband, Willie, was always a treat in bed, and I'd gotten used to it. I knew I wasn't pretty, but I was healthy, and like I said, I liked it. So I got myself up as best I could and started knockin' on doors in the District. Lucky for me, Mollie's was the first house I come to."

Agnes had been in the life five years now. She had regular customers, but she hadn't saved anything. She still wrote to her folks and told them she was a typewriter girl for the Methodist church, and she sent them most of her money. "Which they would know I couldn't afford if they had a brain, which they don't." She'd told Kate that if you had to do it, you might as well enjoy it. " 'Course you can't with most, but every once in a while you'll get a lively one who can really make you hum."

Kate had never felt that and didn't think she ever would. Doing it always made her feel as though she'd been pushed off a cliff and was hurtling down into raging, lethal waters. She would drown in a minute if she didn't keep her wits about her.

"So," Agnes said now, "I'll fix myself a sweet'nin' water"—this combination of gin and rock candy was her favorite drink—"then we'll go up to my room."

"You keep pourin' sauce down your throat," Mollie told her, "and you'll have the katzenjammers in the morning, and I'll have to get Judas to tie you into the backseat of the cab. Go on into the kitchen and get some cocoa."

"Milk makes me cough."

"Then drink tea." Mollie was exasperated. "You keep on like this, Agnes, and you'll end up in the Saint James Infirmary, and I won't be coming to make the sign of the cross over your slab."

Agnes said, "If you want those shoes, Kate . . ." and started out, bumping into Monkey.

"Someone makin' cocoa?" he asked brightly.

"Not for you. Before you go . . ." Mollie crooked her little finger and beckoned. "Come on over here and tell me . . . You been round to Vivian Lefevre's?"

"I make the rounds," Monkey agreed.

"She's plotting against me, isn't she?"

"She's still plenty mad 'cause you stole Kate an' Sophronia, but what's she gonna do? Go to the coppers?"

"She'll do something. I know her." The thought of Vivian's vengeance plunged Mollie further into gloom. "Ah, it's all too much. Kate, help me with these buttons, will you?"

She sat on the edge of the bed. Kate climbed up next to her and started to undo the "pig tits," as Mollie called them, at the back of her dress. Mollie yawned and slumped over. "You go to bed, Kate. Tomorrow you can come out to the sanatorium with Agnes and me. I know you like to get out."

By law, they weren't supposed to leave the District, but Mollie thought it was a treat to dress up like ladies and take cab rides. Once they'd gone to the Ringrose Emporium to settle up a bill; another time they'd visited the Sisters of Charity. The sister who'd answered the door had been real friendly. Mollie had given her an envelope of cash and asked for her prayers.

"So, go to bed now, dearie. . . ." Seconds later Mollie's face was in the pillow and she was making a soft, wheezing sound.

When Kate tried to lift Mollie's arm, it was such a dead weight that she knew Mollie'd passed out. She rested on her haunches and looked down at her, rubbing her back with slow, circular motions. When she looked up, she saw Monkey staring at her. His eyes were lovesick as a stray dog's, and she talked to him as though he were one. "Get on out of here."

"Bertha sez to tell you hello."

"Tell her I said hello back."

"She's thinkin' of runnin' off, too."

"So ask Mollie if she'll let her have Agnes's room."

"Nope. Mollie don't like Bertha. Which is horrible mean of her, since Vivian give Bertha a black eye 'cause Bertha helped you escape. Besides, Bertha an' me, we're thinkin' of startin' up our own operation."

"Aw, sure," Kate snorted. "You'd make a helluva pimp, Monkey. Bertha's dumb, but she's not that dumb."

"Bertha an' me did it the other afternoon when Vivian was asleep," he bragged. "It was great." At least it had been great for Bertha, or so she'd said. And it was special, because it had been a first for both of them: his first time doing it (which was why she'd wanted him), and Bertha's first time doing it for nothing. It was over fast, but Bertha didn't seem to mind. She'd clung to him, playing with his hair, kissing his ears, telling him that she loved him. He'd wanted to slap her. "You don't know nothin' 'bout love, Kate. Not a thing in the world. You're the meanest piece of dry goods I ever saw."

"Leave me alone. There's nothing you can do for me."

Monkey wiped his hand across his nose and hitched up his trousers. "I'm gone. Don't look for me."

"Till tomorrow night," she said contemptuously.

He wandered off, and she got up to put out the candles. It seemed wrong to have an altar to the Virgin in a madam's bedroom, but in a way she envied Mollie her beliefs. It must be nice to talk, even to a statue, if you believed it could listen. She picked up the candle snuffer but put it down. She pinched the wicks slowly, because the pain burning her fingertips felt strangely satisfying. She went to draw the drapes. The sun was coming up, limning the buildings in pink-and-gold light. There was a ragged cry—someone drunk or being hit on or maybe just being deserted—and then it was quiet. She jumped as Shakespeare came up behind her. He put a mug of cocoa on the sill.

"I have a friend, a Mr. Bellocq. He's an artist, too. He takes photographs. Would you let him take yours?" Her likeness should be captured, he thought, now, before her eyes lost hope and her expression hardened.

"I guess so. Shall we try to undress Mollie?"

He glanced at the bed. "No. Let her be." He got his hat and gloves from the desk and returned to take Kate's chin in his hands and plant a kiss on her forehead. "Off to bed now, blossom."

She nodded, but when he was gone, she still stood at the window, indulging in a full-blown fantasy. She was walking out into the early morning light. Someone grand, like that Mr. Randsome, closed the door behind her and took her gently by the hand and said, "This way."

X

Youth's the season made for joy,
Love is then our duty.

John Gay, *The Beggar's Opera*

"

. . . *A*nd I thought poor little Yvette would faint away when they laid him in the grave," Carlotta said. " 'Course Vincent Liscomb was always sickly, but he sat at this very table not four nights ago, looking no more miserable than usual. Then he went home, took a turn, and"—her bracelets jiggled as she snapped her fingers—"dead the next morning."

Lawrence, who'd arrived home that afternoon, looked around the table. His mother stared straight ahead, maintaining the silence she'd held throughout the meal. His father took a sip of wine, rolled it around his mouth, and closed his eyes as though the classification of the vintage absorbed all his concentration. His little sister, Angelique, stirred her frozen dessert into mush. He was used to tension at family dinners, but rarely of this degree.

"What did the doctor say was the cause of death?" Lawrence asked with the politeness of a stranger, but as soon as Carlotta started to talk, he let his thoughts drift.

Nothing had gone right from the moment he'd stepped off the

train. He'd been expecting his parents, but it was Robert who'd met him, explaining that Vincent Liscomb had died suddenly and the family was attending the funeral. Robert called him "Master Lawrence," which sounded strange to his ears, and looked hurt when he insisted on carrying his own bags. He'd been away less than a year, sharing simple bachelor quarters near MIT, taking trips to New York and visiting the Ridgeways during the holidays; but even that exposure to the wider world made him see the house on Poydras Street with new eyes.

It was hard to believe that he'd grown up here. It was oversize and overdone, garish as an opera set. It struck him for the first time how the house—Carlotta's house, really—must grate on his mother's sensibilities. He knew that his father would be equally at home in a tent or the drawing room of a foreign embassy, but a woman, by her very nature (he'd thought about woman's nature a great deal lately), needed a setting that reflected her personality, because the home was her only real domain.

Remembering that the French doors opening onto the garden were Julia's favorite part of the house, he went to them and found Marie waiting. She took his chin in her hands—had she always been so small, or had she shrunk?—and they kissed and went into the garden. Did he want anything to eat or drink? He wanted nothing but her company.

Soon Robert came out with a tray of coffee, cold meats, pastries, and fruit, and they sat, Marie smoking her pipe and looking at him with moist eyes, Robert shaking his head and saying, "We miss you every day, Master Lawrence." Robert admitted as to how his knees were going and he had trouble getting started in the mornings; they had a new cook who was mean as a snake but made a fine gumbo; Calvin, the old carriage horse, had had to be put away; Marie's daughter, Sophronia, had a new job with a fine lady who treated her good; it had rained too much, and the peach crop was going to be wormy.

Listening to their slow, musical speech and the splash of the fountain, tasting the rich café au lait, Lawrence began to feel relaxed and glad to be home. It was all so lush and warmly indulgent, so different from the Ridgeways', where he'd had to ask for a second glass of port after the Christmas dinner. He told Marie and Robert about his classes at MIT, his trips to New York—the grandeur of the Brooklyn Bridge and Grand Central Station, the concerts at Carnegie Hall, the wonders of Coney Island—and as he spoke, he was aware of how lucky he was. They were on the cusp of the twentieth century, and it would be the American century. The nothing-can-stop-us mood of the country coincided with his own coming-of-age. He was on the verge of great adventure. The tangled plants and warmth of the garden made him eager to be even farther south, in Caribbean jungles. Once the war was over, the free people of Cuba would need roads and bridges and grand new buildings, and he would build them. His father might be disappointed that he wouldn't be going into the family business, but his mother—his dear, idealistic mother—would appreciate the scope of his vision, for hadn't she always said that those born to privilege owed their best to the world?

His expansive mood shriveled as soon as he saw the family. Hearing them come in, he went to the front hallway and sensed immediately that something was amiss. The general tension couldn't be attributed to having come from Vincent Liscomb's funeral, for though Mr. Liscomb had been a longtime acquaintance, no one in the family had any particular affection for him. His father, who usually kissed him on both cheeks in the French manner, slapped him on the back with the too-hearty masculinity of a rowing captain. Angelique, noticeably taller and prettier, danced around and cried, "You're home! I'm so glad you're home!" with more nervousness than delight. Carlotta came to him, raising her black veil decorated with spangles, and offered a cheek as powdery and sweet-tasting as confectioner's sugar. She called him "darlin' boy" and told him how handsome he was, with a sly look in her eye.

But it was his mother who shocked him most. She stood apart, her arms wrapped around her chest as though she were holding herself together, and when his father reached to remove her cape, she stiffened. He had never seen his mother shrink from his father's touch before.

Lawrence had gone to her then, but she'd made no move to embrace him. Her face had a melancholy expression, and when he said "Mother," she nodded as though he'd gotten her name right, then moved to the mirror to remove her hat.

His father tried to cover the awkward silence by saying that though he'd rather stay home, urgent business demanded his attention. "First things first," Charles said. "If you boys are going to be well supplied at the front, there are things we have to attend to. I'll be home for supper. Your mother's ordered all your favorites." He clapped Lawrence on the back again, put on his hat, and moved quickly to the door, still mouthing apologies. Lawrence had the distinct impression that his father was relieved to be leaving. Carlotta said she was going to her room to recover from "the shock." Would Lawrence please come to her as soon as possible? Angelique, over strong objections, was sent upstairs to change her clothes.

As Julia stripped off her gloves, he stood behind her and studied her reflection in the mirror. How could she have aged so much in such a short period of time? Her neck, always long and graceful, looked stringy, the skin of her cheeks and around her hairline was dry and taut, and there was a blister on her lower lip. He wanted to take her in his arms and comfort her, but she asked brusquely if he'd had lunch. He said he'd had plenty, but what about her? She shook her head and said, "Shall we go into the sitting room?"

She closed the door and leaned against it as though listening for sounds from outside, then came to him, pulling him to her with such desperation that he felt her fingernails through his jacket. She moved away quickly, sitting down and folding her hands as though she were going to interview a tradesman, but her words gushed out. "When will you go? Where will you train? Did you say you'd be home for five days or six?"

He took a chair, stretching out his legs and throwing back his arm in the relaxed gesture he'd unconsciously picked up from his father, and when he spoke, it was with his father's gentle, teasing drawl, a tone that, he realized for the first time, was designed to defuse his mother's intensity. "I'll be home for four long days. Long enough to do everything you've planned. Then I'm off to training in Tampa, then . . ." He threw out his arm. "Cuba!"

"And your studies?"

"Going well."

"No, I mean what will happen to your studies?"

"I'll go back to them as soon as the war's over. I have a vision now, Mother. I know I can be a first-rate engineer."

She looked out the window and pressed her handkerchief to her mouth. Tears welled in her eyes. At first he thought the sore on her lip was making her cry, but then her shoulders began to shake. He moved his chair closer to hers. "I can understand that you're worried about my going, but you're the one who's always said that there are things worth fighting for."

She wiped her eyes, blotted her lip, and looked at the blood spot on her handkerchief. "It's a man's war."

He was at a loss to understand what she meant. A man's war? What else would it be?

She said, "I can see you're excited. At the party the other night the men were baying at the moon with excitement, even though most of them are too old to serve. I talked to them, or rather I listened to them."

"In Boston," he said, hoping to placate her, "even the women are talking about it. Everyone agrees that we must fight. Grandmother Emily's pleased that I've enlisted."

"There was a British lord here. When he was leaving he said, 'So our former colony has now grown so great that it begins its own empire.' "

"That's the most ridiculous thing I've ever heard. Only an Englishman would take such a cynical view. The war has nothing to do with establishing an empire. President McKinley has said unequivocally that we have no territorial designs. Once we've helped the rebels establish democracy, we'll get out. The Cubans, the Filipinos, the Puerto Ricans, are all fighting for their freedom. It would be morally reprehensible to ignore their plight."

"The men at the party talked more about shipping lines and fruit plantations. The insurgents were mentioned only in toasts. Increasingly drunken toasts."

He knew what a dim view she took of indulgence of any kind. "Well, at a time like this, at a party, it's only human nature."

"But the men want to fight; they want to conquer."

"I should hope we do conquer, and quickly. The less bloodshed the better." Now he sounded like some platform-thumping politician. "You can't honestly believe," he said more gently, "that we would establish regimes that would in any way resemble the tyranny of Spain."

"No. Our tyranny will be more subtle."

"Mother!" He threw out his arms in exasperation. "When I was in New York, I heard one of Máximo Gómez's comrades speak. If only you could have heard him! He told us about the suffering of his people. Suffering we can barely imagine. They've been rounded up into relocation camps, their homes have been burned, their women violated. Can you honestly think that Americans would ever do such things? Not in a million years! The War Between the States was fought to free the slaves, and the people of Cuba are slaves in everything but name. I should have thought that you, of all people, would not just approve my decision, but applaud it."

"I applaud your sentiment, but—" Julia shook her head. "I don't know, Lawrence, I just don't know."

It was rare that he could best her in any argument, and he felt a momentary satisfaction because it seemed he had done so. But the fact that she, so fair and firm in her beliefs, was uncertain made him feel the faintest shadow of doubt. He listened to the clock tick on the mantel.

"We shouldn't argue," she said. "Besides, it's too late now. You're already on your way." She smiled. "Oh, it's wonderful to see you! You've put on some weight, haven't you?"

"I don't think so. The food in this house has spoiled me for everything else. I'm sure you'll fatten me up in the next few days." She studied him with such maternal pride that he felt self-conscious. He touched his upper lip. "I've been thinking of growing a mustache, though once I'm in the field, I guess that decision will be made for me and I'll naturally go woolly."

"I like you clean-shaven. I suppose it reminds me of your father when he was young."

"How is Father? He seemed very preoccupied. Naturally, I suppose—"

"Your father is a man of the world," she said flatly.

He had heard her say this in the past, but never in such a derogatory tone. He wanted to ask what was wrong between them but knew that was out of bounds. His mother's primary loyalty was to his father; she would never say anything against him.

"Mother," he began, then laughed. "I've said 'Mother' so many times I feel like a parrot. Speaking of parrots, how is dear old Robespierre?"

"Robespierre continues hale and hearty. What is the natural life span of a parrot, Lawrence? Have you ever come across that in your zoological studies?"

He adopted a gloomy, threatening voice. "A hundred and five years to the day."

"Ah, then he'll be here after we're all dead and gone. He'll finally take possession of the entire house, flying from room to room . . ."

"Perching on the mantels and the statues . . ."

"Parrot droppings everywhere . . ."

"Squawking 'Nevermore.' "

He kept her laughing by reminiscing about the time he was six and Robespierre had nipped his finger and he'd yanked out one of his tail feathers in revenge. "That was the only time Carlotta ever raised a hand to me," he said, laughing.

"I still have that feather, Lawrence. I keep it in a box of your playthings and notes you wrote to me when you were a boy."

She asked about her family. He spoke of them with greater affection than he felt, describing her father's health, her mother's suffrage activities, her brother's children.

"You wrote that you went tobogganing last Christmas," she said. "How I envied you. I'll always miss those New England winters."

He agreed, though he was too much of a Southerner to enjoy the rigors that came after the beauty of the first snows.

"I expect you'll remember those winters with some fondness when you're down in Cuba," she said.

He was afraid the conversation would turn to the war again, but Angelique, now changed into her pinafore, came in, saying that Carlotta wanted to see him. He told her that he'd be along later, but Julia got up, straightened her spine, and wrapped her arms around her breasts again.

"Go on," she said. "Carlotta's anxious to see you, and I've missed my solitary hour and have some correspondence to answer." He kissed her forehead, saw her eyes begin to tear, and, knowing that she would be more embarrassed than he if he saw her lose control, closed the door behind him.

Only one set of the long velvet draperies in Carlotta's bedroom was open, admitting a shaft of late afternoon sunlight that slashed across the corner of her littered dressing table, widened on the strip of multicolored Turkish carpet and the yellow satin coverlet that had slipped onto it, then diffused to the flocked wallpaper and a painting where nymphs raised naked arms in a perpetual dance to youth and love. Carlotta, dressed in a peignoir but still wearing much of her jewelry, was propped up in bed feeding a toast crust to Robespierre.

Lawrence almost laughed out loud. Once, after exams, when he and his roommate, George, were in their cups, George had teased him about being a Southerner, and he'd risen to the bait and done an imitation of Carlotta. George had doubled up laughing and told him to stop before he pissed himself. A stab of guilt had sobered him immediately. How could he be so disloyal as to poke fun at his grandmother? He'd told George that he was exaggerating, that Carlotta was no more eccentric than any other old lady. But the evidence was right in front of him. She was a Creole Miss Havisham, a Dixie Marie Antoinette, even more bizarre than he'd remembered.

Angelique let go of his hand and began to talk to Robespierre. Carlotta raised herself from the pillows to offer her cheek. "You'll find your grandfather's pistol in the top drawer of that armoire," she told him. "I want you to have it."

The handle of the pistol was so ornately carved that the weapon seemed a plaything, but when he hefted its weight he wondered how he would feel if actually aiming it with intent to kill.

"He always packed it, though I don't know if he actually fired it," Carlotta went on. "You know, he never went into battle because he was more useful to the cause here at home, and soon's the Yankees occupied us, they put him under house arrest."

He thanked her, put the pistol on the top of the armoire, and pulled up a chair to the bedside. Angelique came and sat on his lap, circling her arms around his neck.

"I suppose," he said, "that Granddaddy Randsome lived through some wild times." He'd heard it all before, but a retelling was better than a round of questions.

"He surely did. We all did." Carlotta began to relate, as he had known she would, how Elisha Randsome had run the Union blockade to smuggle quinine and other vital medicines into the city. Elisha's deeds were described, as always, as heroically selfless acts in the service the Confederacy, but it suddenly occurred to him that the Randsomes, unlike most of their compatriots, had come out of the war with their fortunes not only intact, but miraculously increased.

"But he was back in business right after the war, wasn't he?" he asked. "And it was after the war that he really established the shipping company?"

"Well, not all the Yankees were fools. They liked their little luxuries, too, and Elisha had European connections."

"I suppose," he said almost to himself, "that war always promotes profiteering."

"Profiteering? Why would you say a thing like that! The man took enormous risks. And where's it written that you have to go bankrupt to be a patriot?"

"I'm not saying it's reprehensible to make a profit. A man has to look out for his family. I was just trying to understand how Granddaddy established the shipping company." And now he seemed to be speaking in his mother's voice, infinitely reasonable, struggling to define the question, on the defensive.

"I swear, Lawrence, sometimes you're as featherbrained as your mother."

"One could hardly describe Mother as featherbrained."

Carlotta sighed. "I guess now you're a university man you're gonna land on me like a ton of bricks if I don't express myself in just the right words. You *know* what I mean. An' I don't want to talk about all that old stuff. I want to hear about you. Tell me, have you had to beat off those Yankee girls with a stick?"

"I haven't time to see girls."

Angelique squirmed in his lap. "I bet they have time to see you." He wasn't pleased with her precocious flirtatiousness and eased her off his lap.

"Angelique," Carlotta said, "run on out and get us some sherry."

"I'll just pull the bell rope an' get Maggie."

"No. Run on out yourself," Carlotta told her. When Angelique had gone, Carlotta said, "You can tell she's gonna break some hearts, can't you? Now we're alone, you can tell me. I know a tad about men, Lawrence. Whom have you been seeing?"

"I just told you, *Maman*. I haven't had time to see girls."

But he did see them. Saw them everywhere—in shops and theaters, on trolleys and ferries, walking in parks, riding in carriages, and when he wasn't actually looking at them, tantalizing memories of their hips, eyes, earlobes, and breasts flooded his mind and destroyed his concentration when he tried to study. His lust was so intense and constant that he wondered if it was normal. He sometimes believed that he could love any one of them. The knowledge that it would be years before he could even think of marriage made him desperate. His roommate, George, teased him about being a virgin, though Lawrence had never admitted as much, and one night after he'd been out drinking with George and a friend of his, George had directed the cabbie to take them to a house on the outskirts of Boston.

The house was at the end of a dark and muddy street. A single porch lamp illuminated a battered rocking chair and a nervous mongrel dog, but the sound of music temporarily elevated his hopes. A middle-aged woman opened the door, let them into a shabby parlor, and brought a pitcher of flat beer. There were only two girls; both were fully dressed. One played a dirgelike rendition of "The Man on the Flying Trapeze" on the harmonium, the other slumped on a chair. He'd gulped the beer, poured another, and tried to reconcile his fantasies to reality. He'd imagined dim lights, exposed shoulders and thighs, smoldering glances followed by . . .

The girl on the chair got up. George's friend cleared his throat and followed her out of the room. The harmonium player struggled through another chorus. George winked and said he could go first. The older woman touched the harmonium player on the shoulder, and as she turned, he noticed that the women resembled one another. The fact that they were probably mother and daughter further depressed him.

Without looking at him, the younger woman headed for the stairs. His heart pounded. The possibility of bodily contact excited him so much that he came erect as he followed the woman upstairs, but as they reached the landing, he heard a baby cry, and when she told him to put his five dollars on the dresser and drop his pants so that she could inspect him, the possibility of desire, let alone performance, deserted him.

An excruciating five minutes of wrestling on the lumpy mattress followed. The woman's indifference turned to impatience. He got up and put another dollar on the dresser and sank onto the only chair. She smiled for the first time, said, "We can wait a while before we go back down," then took a pair of little scissors from the dresser, slipped off her carpet slippers, and began to pare her toenails. He closed his eyes. How stupid he'd been to imagine prostitutes as a lustful subspecies of womankind. Here was an ordinary woman, at best uninterested in sex, either stupid or down on her luck. When he heard her put away the scissors, he got up and followed her out.

In the parlor downstairs she said, to no one in particular, that they'd have to rake hell to come up with the likes of him. So hypocrisy—or was it genuine compassion for his failure?—could also be bought.

On the way back to the college he'd pretended to fall asleep, sick with disgust and humiliation. How could he, who'd had the shining example of his parents' loving marriage, who had been taught to hold women in high esteem, have fallen so low? Even now the memory of it made his skin prickle with shame.

"Youth is fleeting," Carlotta was saying. "What's the point of being young if you haven't time for enjoyment? I know your mother thinks you're a scholar, but I know better. When I was your age, younger than your age . . ."

Angelique brought in sherry and little cakes. She climbed up onto the bed, nuzzling close to Carlotta, and began to lick the icing from a petit four. Lawrence told her to go play in the garden or go up to her room and read.

"But I want to be with you-all," Angelique said. It was a statement, not a request. What a self-willed little miss she was. He wondered how Julia, who'd always managed to order his days, had lost control of Angelique.

The sherry was cloyingly sweet, Carlotta nattered on about family friends, parties, and girls. His eyelids were heavy, but his knee bounced with uncontrollable restlessness. He had looked forward to coming home, but now he knew that he'd have to negotiate his way through the next five days, reassuring each of them of his affection. None of them seemed to notice how much he had changed. He was his own man now, much as he loved them. But he'd never taken the full measure of how much they'd all influenced him, how easily and involuntarily he slipped into their mannerisms and ways of talking.

The light began to fade, and the room was suddenly stultifying, smelling of dust, sweets, perfume, and, if he wasn't mistaken, a whiff of urine. He was about to suggest that Carlotta turn on the gaslight and open a window when the new girl, Maggie, announced that his father had come home. He got up quickly, almost knocking over the chair. Carlotta said it was time to dress for dinner. How useless she was, he thought as he bent to receive her kiss, always dressing and undressing, nibbling, sipping, gossiping. When he chose a wife, it would be a girl like his mother, someone with intellect and get-up-and-go, a "new woman."

He went to the main stairs, bounding up them two at a time, and knocked at his father's door. Charles welcomed him with the warm embrace he'd expected when he'd arrived, motioned him to a chair, and began to undress.

"It's been a helluva day," Charles said. "First old Vincent's funeral—sad to see a man die when he's never had the guts to really live—and then this damned meeting about the defense of the harbor. Not that the Spanish are likely to attack, but . . ."

"Stupid of me. I hadn't given a thought to the coastline defenses," Lawrence said.

"Nor has anyone in Washington, apparently. We don't want to be caught with our pants down." Since Charles was stripping off his own trousers, they both laughed. "I would have asked you to come with me," Charles continued, "but I knew your mother and grandmother would be hurt if I took you away."

"Yes. I should have liked to come."

"You'll come tomorrow. You know, assembling our first fleet is sure to exhaust the supply of vessels on the Atlantic and Gulf coasts, so I think . . ."

Lawrence was immediately caught up. Here were practical

problems that lent themselves to practical solutions, and he enjoyed the intimacy of his father padding about, shedding his clothes without a shred of prudery, talking to him man to man. Charles's midsection and jaw weren't as tight as they'd once been, but he still had a full head of hair and he moved and spoke with such an easy sense of command that it struck Lawrence that his father must be enormously attractive to women. Could his parents have had a falling-out because his mother was jealous of some other woman? Preposterous. His mother wasn't the suspicious type; his father would never give her reason to be.

". . . and it's crucial that commercial ventures be kept going during the war. I'm making arrangements to charter more ships, for our company as well as for the navy. Think what a massive operation this is going to be, Lawrence. Weapons, pack mules, wagons, medical supplies, foodstuffs, canteens, waterproof tents . . . Every time I turn around, I realize there's something else. They've given me authority to purchase more ships to transport the troops. I'll probably get them from the British. God knows, we haven't time to build them ourselves. I thought if we bought passenger liners and ripped out the staterooms and put in hammocks, we'd make the most effective use of space. What do you think?"

"Sounds like an excellent idea. We'd just as well get used to sleeping in a hammock on the way over."

"Rocked to sleep in the bosom of the deep." Charles laughed. He hit Lawrence on the knee and sat opposite him in his underwear. "By God, it's good to have you back, son. Didn't know how much I'd missed you till I saw you. I can't wait until this war's over and you come into partnership with me. I don't just want you because you're my son. I know what an asset you'll be. But let me tell you more about the meeting. Remember that old fart, Senator Togeland? He said . . ."

When Charles had gone over the high points of the meeting,

he suddenly got up. "Damn! Dinner. I'm supposed to be dressing for dinner."

He went into the bathroom, raising his voice louder than he had to for Lawrence to hear him. As a child Lawrence had sometimes been allowed into his parents' apartments when they were dressing to go out. The doors between their bedrooms had always been left open, and they'd moved from one room to the other, easily sharing common territory. Now, Lawrence was acutely aware of his mother's closed door. He knew she must be on the other side, listening, feeling excluded. What had gone wrong between his parents?

Charles came back into the bedroom wearing an expensive brocade dressing gown. "Is that a gift from *Maman?*" Lawrence asked.

"Strangely, no. You know how thrifty your mother usually is—well, now that you've met the cheeseparing Ridgeways, you know where she got it from—but I think after all these years she's finally loosening up. This dressing gown apparently caught her fancy, and she bought it for my last birthday. Said it made me look like an Eastern potentate. Now if she'd just become a bit more self-indulgent . . ."

"How is she?"

"She's fine."

"She doesn't look well."

"You know your mother." Charles made a show of searching for a tie. "She's been too active, as usual. Running off to spoon porridge down orphans' throats, raising money for suffrage clubs, setting up a home for working girls. . . . Then she stays up till all hours reading. You know." He picked up a hairbrush, then put it down. "Truth to tell, she's annoyed at me. She wants me to sell some property that common sense tells me I should hold on to. She means well, of course. She always means well, but she's become too involved in business affairs."

"That's not like her."

"Yes. Well. Truth is, your mother and I have had words, and she's being fairly stiff-necked about making it up with me. I've been away from the home fires too much. There's a great comfort in marriage, Lawrence, as I've always told you, but even a happy marriage requires negotiation from time to time."

He'd never thought that his parents negotiated. They talked, argued, discussed, compromised. Negotiations were for business. "But you look well, Father."

Charles took brushes in either hand and passed them vigorously through his hair, then stepped back, looking less than pleased with what he saw in the mirror. "Lucky I haven't lost much of my hair."

"What would a few hairs matter?"

"Symbol of virility." Charles laughed. "Remember Samson and Delilah?"

"Ah, myths." He was a university man. Self-abuse did not make you go blind; women did not sap your strength. "Why does it matter?"

"Don't you know that a man losing his hair is a disaster equal to a woman having her bosom drop?"

Lawrence looked down at his hands and wondered what any bosom—small, full, proud, or pendulous—would look like. Or feel like.

Charles turned, his eyes clouded. "We must both make a special effort to be kind to your mother. She's very upset about your going. Any mother would be, and as I said, I've been so busy I've been neglectful. But don't worry. I'll take special care to be comforting while you're gone. Now don't you want to go up and bathe? Get out of those traveling clothes. Dress for this homecoming dinner. By the by, do you need any cash?" Lawrence shook his head. "You're your mother's son, God bless you," Charles said with a smile.

The candles had burned low, the dishes had been removed, and Carlotta was still rabbiting on about Vincent and Yvette Liscomb. "It won't be long before Yvette will have to drive them away with a stick. A beautiful young widow like that. Rich to boot."

Lawrence had the impression that Carlotta's remarks were addressed mainly to his mother and meant to rankle her. "I almost forgot," he interrupted. "I brought you a new play of Mr. Ibsen's, Mother. Shall I go get it?"

With the delayed response she'd shown throughout the meal, Julia said that would be nice. Charles said, "Let's adjourn to the sitting room," but Carlotta wouldn't let go.

"Yes," she persisted, "Yvette almost fainted dead away when they laid him in the grave."

"Had the right man been there to catch her, I'm sure she would have," Julia said.

Lawrence laughed but was embarrassed. It was so out of character and so demeaning for his mother to make catty remarks. "All right, the Ibsen," he said. "Perhaps we could read some of it out loud."

"I hope you enjoyed the meal, Lawrence," Julia said.

"It was grand. You can't imagine how often I've thought of dinner at home."

"Good." Julia smiled. But she'd noticed that he'd hardly touched the oysters in cream sauce or the rice and beans that had been his childhood favorites. And who could blame him? She'd so much wanted his homecoming to be special, but she hadn't been able to rise to the occasion. Perhaps she would never be able to rise to any occasion again. She felt that her marriage, her entire life, was a sham. Her anger toward Charles had cooled and crusted into a mistrust that made every waking moment painful.

The morning after the party, Charles had come into her room

with a breakfast tray. She'd hardened herself against gratitude, knowing he was only trying to appease her. Sleeplessness had made her look haggard and weak-eyed, and somehow she'd held Charles responsible even for that. Without a word, he'd put the tray on the table by the window and sat down. She'd walked past him as though he weren't there, amazed at her control. He'd cracked the top off an egg, removed a fleck of shell from the yolk, brought the spoon to his mouth. She'd straightened things on her dresser. She'd brushed her hair and pinned it up. He'd finished the egg as though nothing were amiss, then said, "Julia, if you want . . ."

She'd gone to her wardrobe, taken out a dress, brushed it, and laid it on the bed. "All I want . . ." she'd begun, but questions and accusations had choked her. If she tried to talk to him, she would scream. If he lied, it would be horrible, but the truth might be worse. Besides, could she trust him to tell the truth? Could she trust herself to believe it? "All I want"—she became absorbed in getting a piece of lint from the hem of the dress—"is for you to get rid of the District properties." From the corner of her eye she watched him. The fact that he had no visible response confirmed the worst. He'd been to the District. "I've never asked you anything concerning your financial holdings before. But I'm asking you now." Her voice came out as ordering, not asking. Charles never responded to direct orders, and she knew it. But she didn't care.

"If we're going to talk, you might at least look at me," he said.

But she couldn't look at him. If she did, she might scratch his face or bury her head in his chest and ask him to love her.

Since she didn't want to dress in front of him, she went to her desk and sorted through the drift of letters. He drank coffee, bit into a *beignet,* wiped the powdered sugar from his mustache, and finished eating it without taking his eyes from her. The punishment of ignoring him was perversely satisfying. She actually became absorbed in searching for stamps and cleaning the nib of her pen.

"All right. If this is how it's going to be," he said as casually as if he were acknowledging that she'd said that dinner was to be at nine instead of eight.

He doesn't care, she thought. Nothing she could do would best him! But why did she think in terms of besting him, as though they were enemies? Because now they were enemies, just as surely as they'd been lovers. He didn't care if they were estranged. Estrangement would only give him more opportunity to live his own life. And what about her life? She felt dizzy. She dipped the pen into the ink and began to write. He ate another *beignet.* How could he eat! Then he left the room.

They had not spoken since, except in public.

"Very good," Charles said. "We'll read a play. We haven't done anything like that since you left, Lawrence."

Charles had no taste for gloomy Norwegian social drama (it was Julia and Lawrence who shared an enthusiasm for Mr. Ibsen), but at least reading the play would get them through to bedtime, when, no doubt about it, he would go to bed alone. He was at a loss to know how to scale Julia's wall of coldness, and he was almost to the point of not caring if he did.

When he'd woken up the other morning, memories of the previous night—the girl's, Katherine's, beauty, Abraham's horrible confessions, Julia's locked door—had flooded his mind. His first impulse had been to go to Julia and tell her everything. Well, not everything, but the core truth. But how could he get into that without admitting that he'd gone to the District? Not that he'd done anything wrong. He'd been tempted, but he'd resisted. Surely that deserved praise instead of blame. But Julia wouldn't see it that way. No wife would. So how to be truthful and simultaneously shield her from reality?

It had occurred to him only when he was leaving the brothel, desperate to get out before that jovial Irish madam accosted him, that it was actually part of his holdings. He got the monthly statements ("Rents from properties on Customhouse and Basin streets") from the agent, but he'd never thought about them. Julia would, he knew, be quick to point out that scooping up profits without knowing where they came from was doubly reprehensible. If he sold off the houses, he'd have to square it with Carlotta, who looked on the real estate income as hers exclusively. But peace with Julia tipped the scales against Carlotta's wrath. Morally, Julia was right. He didn't want and didn't need tainted money. The way out of the whole sordid mess was to sell off the properties. He would take Julia a breakfast tray. That was the ticket. He hadn't taken a tray into her room since she'd been confined to the couch, swollen up with Angelique or, more happily remembered, since their honeymoon. Life had been easy then. Even fastidious Julia hadn't minded toast crumbs in the bed in those days.

He'd dressed and gone downstairs to the kitchen, standing at the sink, drinking glass after glass of water while the cook had made up the breakfast tray. The servants' warm looks had reassured him. Not many men were amiable enough to come to the kitchen and chat with the staff or carry up breakfast trays to their wives.

Disarmed by the servants' approval, he had not been prepared for Julia's coldness. How dare she pretend that he wasn't even there? And then her frontal attack, just when he'd been about to offer to sell the properties. How could he consider himself a man if he took orders from his wife? He'd eaten his egg and almost gagged on it. But fine. If this was the way she wanted it, this was the way she would have it. He could withstand her indifference. Plenty of other pressing obligations required his attention. If Julia chose to ignore him, it gave him freedom to come and go as he pleased, he could indulge his own thoughts without the obligation of including her. And the girl Katherine was always on the periphery of these thoughts, he admitted to himself. There must be some way to see her again, to find out how she'd been sucked into the swamp of prostitution. He could give her money so that she could try a better life. He told himself that his concern was mainly paternal, but when he remembered the curve of her throat, it made his skin tight.

"Then shall we adjourn to the sitting room?" Julia asked. They were all about to rise from the table when Maggie came in and announced that Leonce Lambre was at the door.

"Isn't that just like Leonce?" Carlotta bubbled. "He's so sweet and thoughtful to drop by."

"Even if uninvited," Julia put in before telling Angelique that it was her bedtime. Angelique begged to see Leonce, and Julia, too tired to argue, said that she might.

They all went into the sitting room, where Leonce, dressed in an elegant black suit, was waiting. "Well, Lawrence," he drawled, taking off his hat and running his hand through his hair, "I guess it's taken a war to get you below the Mason-Dixon Line. How does it feel to be back with us decadent Southerners?"

Lawrence said, "It feels just fine." He smiled as he watched Leonce kiss Carlotta's hand, bow to Angelique, and greet his parents with the elaborate politeness of a dandy in a drawing-room comedy. He knew he and Leonce no longer had enough in common to sustain an adult friendship, but he felt sentimental about their boyhood acquaintance. Leonce was not admirable, but he was harmless and amusing, and just now he was a welcome intrusion.

"Will you have a brandy?" Julia asked, reaching for the decanter.

"That would be most welcome," Leonce said. "I have just come from paying my respects to the widow Liscomb."

"How is she?" Carlotta asked in hushed tones.

Leonce frowned as though considering the question, then said, so archly that Lawrence laughed out loud, "Bereavement will be very hard for her; black makes her skin look sallow."

Charles said, "You weren't at the funeral."

"No. I have my own rituals for honoring the departed. Besides, there's so much rushing about now that war is going to be declared."

Lawrence hit him on the back. "So, you've enlisted!"

"Oh, no. No, no, no. I am a poet, not a fighter. You see, I can *imagine* eating wormy rations, sweating in an ugly uniform, sleeping on the ground, and having spiders and gunfire disturb my rest so vividly that I have no need to actually *go* to war."

Julia poured the brandy, thinking how strange it was that she, who was so against the war, found Leonce's attitude disgusting and unmanly.

"You'll miss the greatest adventure of your life," Lawrence told him.

"Oh, I may go, but as a correspondent. I've got something in the works at the *Picayune*. If they come up with the money . . ."

"Oh, for you the money wouldn't be enough. They'd have to come up with a manservant, a chef, and a portable feather bed," Lawrence joked.

The glasses were handed round, and Charles proposed a toast. "To our brave young fighting men."

"An end to Spanish tyranny," Lawrence added.

"To feather beds," Carlotta toasted. "After all, what is civilization about?"

"To feather beds," Leonce repeated, winking at her. "And what do you toast, Mrs. Randsome?" he asked Julia.

"A speedy end to the war and the return of the men."

Leonce tossed off his brandy. "But tell me, Lawrence, why didn't you enlist down here?"

"My roommate, George, signed up with a special unit and persuaded me to do the same. The secretary of the navy, Mr. Roosevelt—I believe you know the family, Mother—is heading it up. We're to be called the Rough Riders, though George is such a city boy that he thought a stirrup bar was where you had drinks before you rode off." They all laughed.

"The war will unite the country," Charles said. "Northerners and Southerners fighting together."

"With the Southerners in front," Carlotta predicted, "so watch your back, Lawrence."

Charles began to talk of the logistical problems he'd described to Lawrence earlier, and Julia rose, telling Angelique to say good night. Angelique looked to her grandmother to protest.

"Now, now," Carlotta told her, "that naughty Coco Robicheaux wants to stay up, but you're a good girl who wants to go to bed."

Angelique hugged her brother and father, then offered her cheek to Leonce. "Remember," she told him, "you've promised to marry me when I grow up."

"Did I?" Leonce pretended to be shocked. "I'd entirely forgotten."

"Men are notorious for breaking promises," Lawrence said. "You should have sealed the bargain by getting a ring."

Leonce kissed Angelique's hand. "Very well, I shall bring the ring when next I visit."

"And when will that be?"

Julia put out her hand. "Angelique, please come now."

"I'll take her up," Charles volunteered, thinking he shouldn't miss any opportunity to be attentive. "I'll even read her a story."

"I'm too old for stories, Papa. But you can tell me about when you were young."

"That may tax my powers of remembrance, but I'll try. Shall I take her up, Julia?" From the corner of his eye Charles saw Leonce shift impatiently, bored with these petty domestic decisions.

Though Julia wanted to leave the room, she felt she shouldn't reject any kindly gesture from Charles. She sat back down, and Charles led Angelique out.

Carlotta asked Leonce to tell her if he'd enjoyed the party, and Leonce, settling languidly on the settee, recalled various guests' clothes and behavior in amusing detail.

He can talk to women so easily, Lawrence thought, better than I ever can. At least to women like Carlotta, and Carlotta's preferred topics were what most women wanted to talk about. His mother, being no better at small talk than he, had dropped out of the conversation entirely, her eyes taking on a soft, melancholy look, her mouth drawn tight, as though she were tasting alum.

"We were about to read a play by Henrik Ibsen," Lawrence said when Charles returned. "You have dramatic flair, Leonce. You'll be a welcome addition."

"It's kind of you to ask, but I'm afraid I have another engagement. In fact, I dropped by to see if you could come with me, Lawrence. I've taken new apartments on Esplanade Street, and some fellows are dropping by to see them. You know all of them, and they're anxious to see you. Won't you come?"

"It's my first night at home. I'm afraid I can't."

"Ah, I thought you arrived yesterday, otherwise I wouldn't have interrupted."

Julia looked up sharply. How smoothly Leonce lied. He'd mentioned the date of Lawrence's arrival the other night when he'd said, almost as a threat, that he planned to give him a bon voyage celebration. She was sure Lawrence could see what a slippery, unprincipled young man Leonce was and wouldn't waste time on him.

Charles said. "Go on if you'd like, son."

"Yes," Carlotta said. "Why would you want to read a silly play with the family when you can enjoy the pleasure of your young friends' company? It'll be ages before you see them again."

Lawrence turned to Julia. She knew the slightest word or gesture would keep him at her side, but he looked so eager. If she'd been able to create a more welcoming atmosphere, he might have wanted to stay home. "Yes, Lawrence. Go if you'd like," she said. "We'll have plenty of time together." Her heart began to beat faster as she imagined an hourglass with the sand trickling down quickly and irrevocably.

"You really don't mind, Mother?"

"I said I don't."

"And your mother *always* tells the truth," Leonce said with a sly smile. "So, dear fellow, get your hat and let's be off."

"I shan't be out too long," Lawrence promised.

"You're a grown man, off to the wars," Charles told him. "Stay out as long as you like."

As Leonce's carriage pulled away from the house, he laughed and slapped Lawrence on the knee. "Clever of me to effect your rescue, wasn't it? And don't tell me you aren't grateful, just reward me with a bottle of champagne." The moonlight glinted on his eyes and teeth, giving him a devilish look. "And now for our night on the town."

"Aren't we going to your apartments?"

"Oh, yes, we'll go there first and pick up Henri and Lavouisseur. You should count yourself fortunate in your friends, Lawrence. We've pooled our money to buy you a very special bon voyage present. Just wait'll you see her."

It must be admitted that such places are necessary in ministering to the passions of men who otherwise would be tempted to seduce young ladies of their acquaintance.

Editorial, *New Orleans Mascot*, June 1892

awrence felt a desperate need to leave and an equally powerful desire to stay.

It was so much as he'd imagined it would be that he had a sense of having been there before. The room was dimly lit, heavily carpeted, and draped like an opulent tent. It smelled of good cigars and perfume and women's bodies. The piano's seductively insistent rhythm reverberated through the wall. Lavouisseur swayed with a tall blonde whose hair was coming down. Leonce sprawled on the opposite divan, a girl on either side. The one with the frizzy hair—was it Rose?—had her skirts hoisted to show a garter and a handful of smooth white thigh; the other girl, Zoe, was almost prone, and as she leaned to whisper God knew what in Leonce's ear, her breast oozed from her bodice.

With tremendous effort Lawrence pulled his eyes away from her puckered nipple and looked toward the door. Anything was better than looking at "his girl," Katherine. She sat near the sideboard, hands in her lap, smiling faintly as though waiting for him to ask her to dance. What was a girl like that doing here? More to the point, what was *he* doing here?

He'd planned to slip away from the others when they'd left Leonce's apartments, but he didn't want to look like a hopeless prig, and curiosity being strong, he'd decided he would go along but leave as soon as the others went upstairs. Henri had obliged by choosing a girl as soon as they were ushered into the front room, but Leonce had reminded the madam that he'd reserved a room for a private party. Three girls had gotten up and followed them into the Turkish parlor. "A banquet of the senses requires the proper hors d'oeuvres," Leonce had told Lawrence as he'd closed the door.

"Right," Lavouisseur agreed, "let's get our money's worth. Let's have all the hors d'oeuvres before the main course of scagmo."

Everyone laughed, but the vulgarity of the remark so offended Lawrence that he downed a glass of champagne to cover his embarrassment. He had another glass to fortify himself for departure, but then the madam came in. "And here's your young lady. Here's Katherine," she announced. The other girls were young and pretty, but sluttishly so. He could have resisted them, but this one . . . would any man in his right mind pass up a girl like her? The memory of the lank-haired woman who'd played the harmonium in the Massachusetts house flashed through his mind. Katherine was no more like her than Venus was like a dwarf. Perhaps, he thought grimly, virtue was just a matter of aesthetics. Against all will and judgment, he accepted another glass of champagne and moved to sit alone on a divan.

He was just sober enough to realize that he was about to lose control. Perhaps he *was* a hopeless prig. Perhaps there was something wrong with him and he was impotent. But it was wrong to buy a woman's body, worse to have one bought for you. Was he such a coward that he couldn't risk the jeers of his friends? Was he so lacking in moral fiber that he couldn't walk away from temptation? How would he feel on his wedding night, knowing that he hadn't saved himself for his bride? He must leave.

He started to get up, but the divan was upholstered in slippery stuff and so low to the floor that he slid back. Trying to make his clumsiness look purposeful, he rested his head on the pillows and stared up at the painting of a pasha and a dancing girl, studying it as though he'd come upon it at an exhibition. It was quite ghastly. As though reading his thoughts, Leonce rolled up his eyes to the painting and said, "I grant you it isn't a Rossetti, but an element of the obvious is essential to eroticism, don't you think?"

"I think . . ." he began, but he thought nothing. The skin around his hairline and on his back was prickly, his palms were damp. He felt sick to his stomach.

Katherine crossed the room and sat down next to him. "Are you all right, Mr. Randsome?"

"I've been traveling for days. I've just come home"—let him not remember the disappointment of the homecoming—"and I didn't have a proper dinner."

"I could fetch you something. We have an excellent cook."

"You're very kind, but no. Perhaps if I went outside and took some air."

"There isn't any outside. I mean, there's only the street or the yard out back, and the yard faces onto the alley."

The slope of her shoulders was exquisite. He could kiss those shoulders. He could gently take the pins from her hair. These feelings of tender longing were at war with other, more violent ones. He could say, "You, upstairs. Now." He could do anything he liked with her. As possibilities flashed through his mind, the blood pounded in his groin. He couldn't get up now.

The door opened and the madam, Mollie, came in, carrying another bottle of champagne. "Everything all right, gentlemen?"

"Ah, more champagne." Lavouisseur let go of the blonde and reached for his glass.

Leonce said, "Let us sail on a sea of champagne into the harbor of pleasure."

"Eat, drink, and be merry," Lavouisseur cried, "for tomorrow we die."

"Die?" echoed the blonde. "I sure hope nobody's gonna die."

"Not I," Lavouisseur assured her, leaning over to rub noses with her. "It's Lawrence here who's going off to face the Grim Reaper."

Zoe tucked her nipple back into her bodice and gave Lawrence a come-hither smile. "Oh, I love soldiers. Are you really going off to war?"

Lawrence smiled. "Yes, but I don't intend to die." He looked into Katherine's great amber eyes. What if he died a virgin? The prospect seemed more terrible than death itself.

"Sure, he's off to a glorious victory," Mollie said.

Green as grass he was. About to bust his britches with lust and embarrassment, and just as finicky as his father. He'd never guess that the money that let him have such delicate sensibilities came from whorehouses. It always galled her to cater to these rich young men. They sucked in their sense of entitlement with their mother's, or more likely their mammy's, milk, and grew up to be mindless buffoons like Lavouisseur, ready to haggle over a dime, buying girls as they bought waistcoats or top hats or watches. Or they were like Leonce Lambre, all stylish, "poetic" degeneracy. But she had to admit that Lawrence Randsome was cut from a finer cloth. Even though he was squirming inside, he still had that patina of confidence that only those born to wealth had. He put his hand over his glass and said, "No more, thank you, ma'am," as though she were one of his mother's friends serving tea. And despite the fact that customers were piling up in the front parlors and Lawrence's inability to make a move was holding up the show, Mollie couldn't help but feel a certain tenderness toward him.

"Kate," she suggested, "why don't you take Mr. Randsome into the back room and have a little chat?"

"A chat!" Lavouisseur guffawed. "After what we paid, you'd better do more than chat, Lawrence."

Damned men, Mollie thought, it's always a contest with them. "I'm sure when Mr. Randsome gets to Cuba, he'll lead the charge," she said. "I can tell by lookin' at him that he has great courage."

"There are all kinds of courage," Leonce drawled. He slid his fingers under Rose's garter and squeezed her thigh, but his attention was totally fixed on Lawrence. " '*O Seigneur! Donnez-moi la force et le courage de contempler mon coeur et mon corps sans dégoût!*' "

Mollie didn't understand what he'd said, but it sounded like a challenge and it made Lawrence blush to the roots of his hair. She had always known Leonce was a snake in the grass, and as she bent to refill his glass, she saw the sick love/hate of envy on his face. It was the sort of look a cripple might give an athlete, and she knew in a flash that he was more interested in Lawrence than in any of the girls.

"And you, Mr. Lambre," she said, not bothering to keep the impatience out of her voice, "have you made up your mind yet? Is it to be Rose or Zoe?"

"Ah, Mistress Mollie . . ." Leonce circled the waists of both girls, but he was still fixed on Lawrence. "I'm so indecisive that I believe I'll have to have the pair of them."

"One on either side." Lavouisseur laughed. "Like bookends."

"Don't bite off more than you can chew." Zoe giggled and nibbled Leonce's ear.

Mollie knew this sort of saucy talk would be aphrodisiac for most men, but it was likely to make young Randsome bolt for the exit. She signaled Kate with her eyes. Kate got up and moved to the door.

"Yes, you two go and *chat*," Lavouisseur teased. "Lawrence can tell you about all those books he's read in college."

"Aw, leave him alone," said the blonde. "Still waters run deep."

Lawrence made it to his feet and went to the door. "Look at 'em," Lavouisseur persisted, "don't they look like the Gibson girl and her lovelorn suitor?"

"No," said Rose, who was sentimental, "they're like a prince and a princess getting married."

"Perhaps we celebratory peasants will knock on your chamber door to see you're getting the job done," Lavouisseur said, laughing. Mollie gave him an icy look.

" '*Donnez-moi la force et le courage de contempler . . .*' " Leonce began, but let his voice trail off. He and Lawrence locked glances, then Lawrence left amid another burst of boisterous laughter.

The light from the hall chandelier stung his eyes, the raucous voices from the front parlors assaulted his ears. What if someone recognized him? Holding on to the wall for support, he followed Kate down the hall to the rear of the house.

Moonlight streamed through the undraped window. "You said you needed some air," she said, going to it and trying to raise it. "I'm afraid it's stuck. It's just been painted."

He came up behind her, reaching around her, his mouth so close to her ear she felt his breath. He jerked the window up, and she turned, all but in his arms. "There's a bit of a breeze," she said, though she was most conscious of the shouts of men gambling in the alleyway.

He dropped his arms and stepped back, rigidly tense, his hands balled into fists. She could see he was in agony, but he wouldn't touch her. He's like his father, she thought, stung by the rejection. He's too high-and-mighty to do it with a whore. She felt angry and ashamed and respectful: this was the way any real gentleman would feel. She could see he was poised for flight. What would she do if he left? Would Mollie have to refund the money? She realized with a frisson of shock that it wasn't just the money or proving she could get him. She had never been with a man this young or handsome, so bursting with virility but so painfully contained. If she was the first woman he'd had, he would never forget her. It wasn't just the money; it was him. She wanted him.

Her breath was coming hard, and a pulse beat between her legs. She couldn't bear it if he left. Copying a gesture she'd seen Zoe use, she fanned her neck and caressed her bosom. She made her voice husky and said, "We'd be cooler if we went upstairs and took off our clothes," then closed her eyes and offered her face to be kissed.

His voice cracked. "I'm sorry." He took another step back. "I don't feel well."

How could she have been so stupid as to be bold with him? "Some water, perhaps?"

His hand shot up as though warding her off. "No. No, nothing. I think I'd better be going."

Her heart beat wildly. She had to make him stay. "What did Mr. Lambre say to you in there?"

"You don't understand French?" She shook her head. He passed his hand over his face. "It's a quote from Baudelaire. He said, 'O Lord! Give me the strength and the courage to contemplate my heart and my body without disgust.' "

She thought he was going to be sick. He turned abruptly and moved to the door. She took a step after him, putting out her hand. He spun around and grabbed her so swiftly that they staggered against the wall. He covered her face, her hair, her shoulders, with kisses, his hands were everywhere. She could feel him stiff to bursting through her skirts. He half lifted, half dragged her to the couch, laying her down, ripping at his clothes as though they were on fire. A button *ping*ed from his shirt and rolled across the floor. He struggled with her skirts and fell on top of her, burying his face in her neck.

"Does the door lock?" he rasped. She told him yes, and he staggered up.

"We could go," she began, but heard the lock click. His voice was low and desperate.

"No. Now."

She opened her legs. He unbuttoned his trousers and under-trousers, pulling them down together, clutching his penis as though trying to choke it. He found her place and thrust into her with bullish force. A few more thrusts, the last so powerful that it forced a cry from both their throats. And then it was over.

He lay stunned, gulping air. The sounds from the alley flowed in. He put a foot on the floor and grabbed the back of the couch to steady himself as he got up, then sank to the floor in a kneeling position. The breeze from the open window iced the perspiration that lathered him from belly to thigh, and he arched back so far that she thought he would topple over. His face was contorted, mouth open, eyes squeezed shut. He seemed to have forgotten her entirely. A tiny part of her brain wondered if he'd stained her dress. He shook his head as though trying to clear it, then moved to her, holding her wrist gently as though he were taking her pulse.

"Are you all right?"

She nodded. He was silent for perhaps a full minute.

"Then could we go upstairs?" he asked, as though he needed her permission. She nodded again.

Wordlessly, they rearranged their clothes. They went to the door. He didn't have to tell her what to do. "I'll go first," she said. "It's the second door to the right on the first landing."

XII

What is it men in women do require?
The lineaments of Gratified Desire.
What is it women do in men require?
The lineaments of Gratified Desire.

William Blake

She was curled into him, one hand on his chest, feeling its slight rise and fall, listening to his breathing—steady and deep, though he'd fallen asleep only a short time ago. The first light was coming through the window, and she knew he should go. She whispered his name, but he didn't stir. She repeated it, just to feel it in her mouth—"Lawrence"—and raised herself on both elbows to look at him.

She'd never thought a man could be described as beautiful, but there was no other word for him. His arms and legs were long and sinewy, his chest and pubic hair silky, his belly flat, joining into his hipbones as though his torso were a breastplate, like that statue of the young Roman that Shakespeare so admired. But he didn't feel like marble, he felt like finely sanded wood, smooth and hard. How strange that he, who'd used her body all night as it had never been used before, who'd touched and licked and probed every part of her to satisfy his own desires, should be the one who'd make her feel cherished, not used. He'd made her feel that thing they all talked about—cum, climax, the peak—but there wasn't any word for it, that surge to breaking, the spasms of release so complete that it seemed desire would be satisfied forever, but then desire came back like the tide, wondrous, unstoppable, as though there'd been no climax at all.

By the time he came into the room, she'd taken off her clothes and was lying on the bed. She thought he would undress and mount her again, but he just stood, looking at her. "Your hair," he said. She'd forgotten to take down her hair.

She started to take out a pin, but he pushed her hand away and began to take out the pins ever so gently, streaming her hair onto the pillow. He sniffed at it, kissed her lips as lightly as a butterfly, ran a finger down her neck to her breastbone. He rotated her nipples, his hands swam over her belly and her flanks all the way to her feet. He turned her over, passing his hands over her back, kneading her backside, licking the backs of her knees, massaging the soles of her feet. Her buttocks and her teeth clenched, her toes turned in. His touch was firmer, insistently demanding. Her whole body felt stiff as she rolled herself onto her back, her pelvis thrusting up of its own accord. She reached for the buttons on his fly, hot to get at him, wanting to see him naked and explore him, too. As though reading her mind, he stood up and slowly took off his clothes, dropping all shyness as he shed them until he was standing, legs apart, shoulders back, naked, erect, and proud.

He buried his face between her legs, and when he slid up to cover her, she tasted herself on his lips. She bucked like a filly, wave after wave of ecstasy so acute that it was almost painful.

They lay side by side without touching. His breathing slowed. He opened his mouth, inhaled a slow, lung-expanding breath, then, wordlessly, he was at her again.

When they finally rolled apart, bodies slick with sweat, hair flattened, he gave a little laugh. "When I was four, we went to Grand Isle for the summer. Mother did her best to teach me to swim, but I was afraid of the water. Then one day when she wasn't around, my cousin, Etienne—he was a nasty boy, about twelve then—threw me in. I sputtered and sank. I was in terror that I'd drown. But then—"

"The same thing happened to me!" She marveled at the coincidence. "My brothers threw me into the river. I went right down to the bottom. I knew I was going to die for sure, and when I came up, I had mud in my ears and my mouth. It was awful. I wanted to kill them."

He hadn't realized till then just how young she was. No more than four or five years older than his sister. "Poor little Katherine," he said tenderly.

"My name's just Kate."

"Poor little Kate. Mud in her ears, mud in her mouth." He licked at her ears, ran his tongue around the inside of her mouth, and pretended to spit out mud, then he tickled her until she quivered with laughter, begging him to stop. Pushing him away, she lost her balance and fell off the bed onto the floor. He scrambled after her, and they rolled about, cuffing and pawing each other like puppies until they were both breathless. She sat up, taking a bit of carpet thread from her mouth.

"I never did learn to swim," she told him, "but I still love the river. My grandfather was a riverboat captain, and we used to sit on the dock at sunset and watch the river turn blood-red, and he'd tell me stories about the old days." It was against Mollie's policy for girls to talk about their lives, but she couldn't stop herself. "When he died," she went on, "I thought he'd gone to heaven, but I don't believe in heaven anymore, do you?"

"I never did. Until tonight." He took her hand and kissed it. "Don't be sad, Kate, don't be sad."

"I loved my grandfather more'n anyone in the whole world. Who do you love best?"

He wanted to say "You," but honesty compelled him to say "My mother," and as soon as he'd said it, he felt sad, too. Families had no place here; the past and the future had no place here.

"I never did learn to swim," she said dully. "It seems like forever since I've been outdoors."

"I could teach you." He took her hands and raised her to her feet. "Tomorrow. We'll go out tomorrow. I'll take you for a carriage ride. My great-grandfather had rice plantations north of the city. We could go there. We could have a picnic with the ghosts."

They both knew he was saying silly things that would never happen, but she loved him for saying them just the same. He said he was hungry, and she said, "Let's have a picnic now."

She put on Mollie's dressing gown, went into the hall, and found the boy who changed the towels and asked him to bring them some bread and cheese. When she came back in, Lawrence was stretched on the bed, hands laced behind his head, a thoughtful, closed expression on his face. She knew why. While they were making love, they'd been oblivious, but once she left his side he'd looked around, he'd heard the noises and realized that they were surrounded by other couples in other rooms, in a brothel.

"It doesn't matter," he said, smiling up at her.

She smiled, too. It was remarkable that they understood each other's thoughts as easily as they understood each other's bodies.

He sat cross-legged on the bed while she curled at the end of it. He ate the bread and cheese while she asked him questions. He was going to design great buildings, he told her, like Stanford White. She didn't know who Stanford White was, nor had she ever heard of the famous buildings he mentioned, but he described them so vividly that she felt she could see them.

She said, "I know you'll do something grand." It was obvious that he was going to be a great man.

He said, "I've never told anyone else what I'm going to do." He'd discussed his ambitions with his roommate, George, but he would never have spoken to George with such passion. They looked at each other with grateful intimacy. Talking was fine, but making love was better.

Together they swept up the crumbs and smoothed the sheets, and when the bed was rearranged, they looked at it and laughed and threw themselves down as though they were flopping into a pile of hay. He gathered her into his arms. All sore tenderness now, he rocked into her with slow, sleepy rhythms that culminated in a climax that was no more than a shudder and a sigh. He kissed her forehead, arranged her body to accommodate his, whispered "Good night, sweet Kate. God bless you," and dropped off as quickly as if he'd been hit on the head. She lay awake, sticky and sore and blissfully happy. When she realized that she might never see him again, it was as if a shaft of iron had been driven into her heart.

She ran her hand over his chest and into his groin, capturing his damp, snaky penis, his balls. He groaned and shifted, his hand covering hers. She whispered his name again, and he came awake, sitting up with a lurch. She said, "It's almost morning."

He was on his feet, one hand raking his hair, looking around in disbelief. Dear God. He had to get home before any of them woke up. His mother . . . dear God, his mother . . .

Kate raised herself and nodded toward the chair. "Your clothes are over there." He began to pull on his undertrousers, but she said, "Wait," and got up from the bed. She went to the washstand, wet and wrung out the towel, started to give it to him, then knelt to wash him herself. He put his hands on her head, feeling her skull, combing her tangled hair with his fingers and holding it out to its full length. As he stiffened, his hands cupped her chin, slid to her shoulders, and raised her up. She dropped the towel. They backed up to the bed and fell across it.

"I *must* go," he told her. The sky had gone milky, the sun was about to rise. She said, "I know." He wiped himself with the towel and hurriedly began to put on his clothes. Pulling on his shirt, he saw the place where the button was missing and smiled down at her. "I have to go to a dinner party tonight, but can I come back this afternoon?"

"It's not regular."

"I'll ask . . ." What was her name? "Mollie."

"She'll still be asleep. I'll ask her as soon as she gets up."

He had no idea how he was going to get away that afternoon, he only knew that he would manage it somehow. And he'd have to have money. How much? That sobering thought was submerged as he put on his shoes. Fully dressed, he looked about, thinking he'd forgotten something.

"Judas will have your hat. He's the man with the big ears and the shaved head. He'll be sitting by the front door. He'll let you out."

He didn't dare kiss her again. Didn't dare even look at her. At the door he said, "I'll be back this afternoon."

She closed her eyes and pulled up the crumpled sheets. He was going to come back. She floated off to sleep with a rocking sensation, as though she were still a baby at her mother's breast.

He walked for blocks without finding a cab. He had to get home, certainly he had to bathe, because he reeked of it—that marvelous smell. His mind was teeming with plans, arrangements, excuses. He'd have to lie to get away this afternoon, but he felt no remorse at the prospect. Amazing to himself, he felt no shame about what he—they—had done. No shame at all, just powerful joy. How had he learned it so quickly? But you couldn't really say you learned it, you just gave way. *"O Seigneur! Donnez-moi la force et le courage . . ."* You had the courage and the strength to contemplate the desires of your mind and your body without disgust. You acted on them, and the knowledge flowed through you. The world wasn't divided into rich and poor, honorable and dishonorable, but only into those who knew this great secret and those who didn't. He had been initiated and transformed. Men who sniggered and showed dirty pictures and said hateful things about women had never been initiated, even if they'd done it. And women . . . They weren't supposed to feel it, but that was a terrible lie. Kate felt it. At first he'd been afraid she was faking, but that suspicion had been quickly swept away. To believe she didn't feel it was like denying that the sun came up. And the sun *was* coming up, turning the shadowy street gold, warming the air with smells of the river and flowers and coffee and horse manure. He was a man now, and the world had never been so beautiful. He saw a cab midway down the block and ran for it, his shout shattering the stillness.

He let himself in through the front door and moved up the stairs like an Indian padding through the woods. Passing his mother's door, he thought he heard a sound, but he kept on, mounting the stairs to his room with a gliding stealth. Everything in him cried out against secrecy. He was so boundlessly happy that his impulse was to tell someone. Tell someone? Lack of sleep must've unhinged his mind. But he didn't feel tired, he felt gloriously energetic. He got into the tub and began to wash, thinking of her with every touch. If respectable girls didn't like making love, how could he ever marry a respectable girl? Now that he'd had it, he could never do without it again. His member was rubbed raw, yet it rose again in memory of what they'd done. Things no other lovers had done, certainly. Things he'd never heard of or imagined. But, he reasoned, he was being naive. The variety must be infinite. Sore as he was, he wanted to slide into her, ever so slowly, centimeter by centimeter. Her juice would soothe it like magic ointment, and he would just stay in her, not moving, just looking into her eyes. Yes, that's what they'd do next time.

His parents were already at the table when he went downstairs. He glanced from one to the other, trying to determine if there'd been any thaw in their relations. Both were reading, but this was no indication that they weren't speaking. His mother often disobeyed her own rules of etiquette and carried a book to the breakfast table, and this morning his father, who usually concentrated on his food, was immersed in a stack of contracts.

"Ah, Lawrence," Charles said, and smiled. "We didn't think you'd be down this early. Didn't hear you come in."

Lawrence kissed Julia's cheek and took his place. He knew that his father wouldn't have been listening for him to come home, but his mother's worn expression suggested that she hadn't slept much. She smiled and asked if he'd had a pleasant time. He knew what that cheery greeting cost her, and it made him love her all the more.

"Who all was at Leonce's apartments?" his father asked.

"Lavouisseur, Henri LeCompe." He interrupted himself to tell Maggie that he'd have sausage, eggs, and biscuits and, hoping to head off further questions, volunteered that Lavouisseur had gone into his father's business.

Charles grunted. "Yes, I'd heard that. Old Lavouisseur had problems before, so I expect that fool son of his will push him into bankruptcy."

"He's all right in his own way," Lawrence said. This morning he could even be kind to Lavouisseur.

Charles asked what he had planned for the day, and Lawrence told him that he wanted to shop for some things to take to Florida. Julia reminded him that they were to lunch with Beatrice Ravenal and, sensing his disinclination, said, "You know she's very fond of you."

"And I of her," he answered. He wanted to see Beatrice, but how could he juggle his time? "Tell me, is she still so fat?"

"Let's put it this way," Charles said, "when she walks down the street, which she doesn't very often, the street looks narrower."

Though Julia prized physical fitness and had often said herself that Beatrice should control her appetite, she now rose to her friend's defense. "Food is her only comfort," she snapped. So, Lawrence thought, his parents hadn't made it up.

"It would be mine, too, if I had time to enjoy it," Charles said, putting the last of a biscuit into his mouth.

"You'll enjoy your dinner tonight. I know you like the Dewitts' cook."

"I like the Dewitts' cook a damn sight better than I like the Dewitts," Charles grunted. "Truth to tell, I'd clean forgot we were dining with the Dewitts."

"But I told you last—"

"I'm sure you did, dear, but I'd been hoping for an early night. We're all exhausted. What time did you say you got in, Lawrence?"

Just when he thought he'd cleared that hurdle! "Can't really say." Lawrence shrugged. "Around one, I think."

Julia looked up as though someone had just pinched her. He knew he'd been caught in a lie, and he made it worse by adding, "It may have been later." He'd do anything in the world not to deceive his mother, not to cause her anxiety. Anything except not see Kate again.

Charles wiped his mouth with his napkin, gathered his papers, and got up. "I'm sorry to be rushing off again," he apologized, resting his hand on Lawrence's shoulder. "Perhaps you can come by the office this afternoon. We'll continue that discussion we were having before supper yesterday." Lawrence nodded and said he'd see him later.

"Try not to be late," Julia called as Charles walked away. As soon as the words came from her lips, her hand shot up to cover them. She hated to nag. Charles came back and kissed her cheek. The kiss appeared to be more warm than dutiful, but she did not respond.

Lawrence looked into his coffee cup. If only his parents would make love, he thought (for making love now seemed the solution to most of the world's ills), they wouldn't be able to stay angry with each other. As a boy he'd been aware that there was a physical bond between them. There had been mornings when they'd come downstairs arm in arm, talking softly, exchanging glances, an aura of contentment about them. And evenings when they'd said they had to go to bed because they were tired, but he'd sensed a palpable expectation between them. He'd watched for these times, not just because it was good to see his parents so happy, but because he had known those were the best times to ask for special privileges. He wondered, with some discomfort, what their relations were now. Perhaps they were too old to really care about it anymore. He hoped he never lived to be that old. Of course, his father had the concerns of the world to occupy him, but his mother—he looked at her over the rim of his cup —had a brooding look. She wasn't exactly prudish, just shy and moralistic. He'd heard of feminists, albeit a fringe element, who were free lovers, but his mother would never approve of love outside the marriage bed.

"What are you reading?" he asked.

"A history of the Philippines. I know so little about them, except that now we'll be at war there, too."

"Yes. I'm glad I won't be going that far away from home." He didn't want to upset her with further discussion of the war, and he felt deeply sorry that she'd caught him in a lie. He had planned to shop or go back to his room for a catnap, but he said, "Would you like to go for a bicycle ride before it gets too hot?"

"That would be lovely."

"Good, then. Let's go." By riding with her, by being in her presence, he could show his affection, but they wouldn't have to talk about anything.

Beatrice Ravenal received them on her gallery. She did not get up from her chair. She was, Lawrence thought, more like a natural wonder than a woman, like some great volcano that had erupted decades before, the lava rolling down and hardening into cascades of fat. He liked her enormously. Since she had such a prodigious appetite, he assumed lunch would be served, but they talked on and on. Beatrice was a witty conversationalist, and he enjoyed watching the intimacy between her and his mother, but after a time his knee began to jiggle with impatience.

"Unless you're in a particular hurry, I thought we'd have a late lunch," Beatrice said.

"No," Julia assured her, "we're in no particular hurry."

"I didn't think so." Beatrice smiled. "I didn't think Lawrence came home to the South to be rushed." His heart sank. Beatrice scanned his face and chuckled. "I declare, Lawrence, you've not just grown, you're actually different. What have you been up to?"

By the slant of the sun and the heat in the room, Kate judged it was about two in the afternoon. The house was as quiet as a dead man. She went into the bathroom, locked the door, and poured a sinful amount of rose crystals into the tub. Floating, daydreaming, sudsing up the hair on her head, under her arms, between her legs, playing with her swollen labia, she stayed in the water until the skin on her fingertips was puckered. He had said he liked her smell, but she thought it was too ripe and musky. Yet she hated to wash it away, because it was his smell, too.

She got out and patted herself dry, humming as the water gurgled down the drain. Dusting herself with powder, she felt like a sugar doughnut. She was kneeling over the tub, rinsing her hair with vinegar water and testing a strand to hear if it squeaked, when the door handle rattled.

"Who's in there? How long y' gonna be?" Zoe demanded.

Kate said she'd be out in a minute, but she wasn't in a mood to be hurried. She dabbed rosewater on her wrists and behind her ears and wrapped a sheet around her.

Zoe pounded on the door. "You're not the only sow who needs to wallow in the waterhole."

Kate opened the door and curtsied.

"It's about time," Zoe grumbled as she shoved past her. "Cheerist, I need steam. I feel like that two-headed calf at the parish fair. I got a bad case of the horrors this mornin'." She turned on the faucets, stripped off her shift, and yawned. "Sure smells good in here. An' I sure need somethin' to make me feel good. Me an' Rosie was up till all hours. We like' to stand on our heads trying to please that Leonce Lambre. Finally ended up pleasuring each other. I swear the ones who can't do it tire you out more'n the ones who can. How was yours?" Kate shrugged. "He looked like a dream." Zoe yawned. "But I think Mollie shoulda put him with someone older. Someone who knew how to break him in. Y' know, Mollie always sez . . ."

Kate left her talking to herself.

She sat on the edge of the bed brushing her hair dry. What could she wear? The only day dress she had was the checkered cotton she'd come to town in, and she'd known the morning she'd gone to Madame Destault's and seen other girls on the street that it marked her as a hayseed. Besides, she wasn't a skinny kid with knobs on her chest anymore. The dress was tight across her breasts now, and it wasn't just because she was eating better.

She could see the change in her body, but she really couldn't think of it as a baby.

She drifted into a fantasy: By rights it should be Lawrence's baby, because he was the one who'd made her feel like a woman. Lawrence's baby, conceived in love. As she tore the flowers and the feather from her hat (nice girls dressed plain in the daytime, and she knew just how Lawrence would like her to look), the fantasy blossomed until it was full-blown, more comforting and, therefore, more real than the truth.

Mollie's bedroom door was ajar, and when Kate approached, she heard Lady Caroline's voice. She knocked on the jamb and stepped in, her cheeks dimpling at the sight of them. They were such an odd pair—Mollie in her nightdress, slack-breasted, hair streaming—and Lady Caroline, coiffed and hatted, tightly laced into ruffled mauve batiste, his big, mittened hands folded carefully on the handle of an upright parasol. Seeing Kate, he said, "My, don't we look rosy this morning!"

Mollie removed a speck of sleep from the corner of her eye. "I'm takin' it that everything came off fine?"

Lady Caroline said, "You can tell that by lookin'. She's got so many whisker burns around her mouth you'd think she'd been in the raspberry patch."

Mollie yawned wide enough to show where some of her back teeth were missing. "Lawrence Randsome is such a pup he doesn't have whiskers."

Lady Caroline said, "I wish I could say the same," and they both laughed.

"Yes," Kate said, "everything went fine." They were old and disgusting and vulgar, and it took all her patience to be polite. "Mr. Randsome will be coming by this afternoon. He was going to ask permission himself, but you were asleep, so I told him I would."

With a sudden flare of anger, Mollie hit the mattress. "I won't have it! You know the rules: No men before nine o'clock at night. Having a customer around in the afternoon is like havin' a rooster in the henhouse. It riles up the girls, and I won't have it."

"But we won't be here, at least not at first. He's taking me for a carriage ride."

Lady Caroline made a moue. "A carriage ride. Well, la-di-da."

"Are y' crack-brained?" Mollie demanded, roiling about in the sheets. "You know you can't go out of the District, Kate. It's too risky. You could be arrested."

"I told him I hadn't been outdoors in ever so long, so he said . . ." She'd never been mad at Mollie before, but now she felt the resentment of any girl coming up against her mother's authority.

Lady Caroline rolled his kohl-accented eyes in her direction. "Go on, Kate. You know better than to come at Mollie first thing in the morning. Go on and have your breakfast and come back later." His look promised that he would soften Mollie up.

"I should've known," Mollie said, putting on the crown of thorns of the aggrieved mother as soon as Kate had gone. "It's always the same. At first they're grateful, and butter wouldn't melt in their mouths. Then they start makin' your life a misery."

"She's fallen for the boy. That's as plain as the nose on your face."

"And haven't I heard that one before! Some Romeo gives the girl a bunch of flowers and a little sweet talk, and before you know it, he's gettin' it whenever he likes, without her makin' a dime. I won't have her taken advantage of."

"It's not like he wants to be her pimp. You said he's going off to the war, so what's the harm? The kid's gotta have some love in her life."

With the special vehemence that comes from accusing someone of a weakness to which you yourself are prone, Mollie said, "You're a sentimental fool."

Lady Caroline shrugged. "She's young. This is maybe the first time she got it good. You gonna tell me you didn't want to give it away when you were young and you were gettin' it good?"

"Ah, sure. And I'm here to tell you that every time I did, it landed me back in the bog. He goes off to war, then what? She's moonin' around the house, not wanting to take customers. She's pinin' for him. She's dreamin' about a life that can never, never be. I know Kate. She's only fifteen, and she doesn't know what's goin' on half the time as it is. She gets the idea she's in love . . ." Mollie harrumphed. "In love! You show me a whore in love, an' I'll show you a miserable woman."

Lady Caroline examined his mittens. "It'd be mean not to let her go with him."

"And what if she's arrested?"

"Have a brain. She won't be arrested with a boy like that."

Mollie put her hands to her temples and shook her head. "I have a great sense of foreboding," she said with Gallic drama. "A premonition. Don't give me that look. I do have premonitions. Something terrible is going to happen."

"If you'll forgive me, dearie, that feeling of foreboding is just a case of the katzenjammers. If you stayed off the sauce . . ."

"I admit I'm a sot, but this is real. Didn't I tell you I found a voodoo doll on the front doorstep when we opened up last night? Horrible, ugly thing with pins in its head! And didn't I tell you I found one there three nights ago? I know that Vivian Lefevre. She's out to get me. She wants to ruin my business. She wants to see me dead. You know we all swore that we wouldn't use any voodoo against each other, but swearing don't mean anything to the likes of Vivian Lefevre."

"Well, that's what I'm here to tell you. I'm sending Eulalie Echo 'round this afternoon. She'll scrub down your doorstep with brick dust, and that'll drive away the evil spirits."

Mollie looked at her altar. "I can't be gettin' into any voodoo. I'm a Catholic."

"Well, whatta y' think Eulalie is? But when you're in a war, you use the weapons at hand, and I swear by Eulalie. She learned from Marie Laveau, and she can put a hex on anyone. Mollie, are you listening to me?"

Mollie had reached down to massage her foot, a faraway, sorrowful expression on her face. "I'm listening," she muttered.

" 'Member that time I was about to be prosecuted?" Lady Caroline went on. "Well, Eulalie did me some fine gris-gris. She stuck pins in a lamb tongue, and when that judge got ready to sentence me, he couldn't get a word out of his mouth. He didn't put me in the lockup, I just got away with a fine." He patted the back of his hair and smiled. "Okay. Maybe they couldn't figure out whether to put me in the men's or the women's lockup, but I do swear by Eulalie, and I'm sending her 'round this afternoon, so there's nothing to worry about. Nothing to worry about with Kate, either. Let her have her fling with the pup. You couldn't hook the father, but you got the son. Okay, so it's not gonna lower yer rent, but what the hell? Oh, I know what I forgot to tell you. . . ."

Lady Caroline's eyes flashed, and he wiggled to the edge of the chair, eager to tell all. "The reason you couldn't hook Charles Randsome is because he loves his wife. Can you feature it! I heard it from Alma Heflin, who heard it from Phillipa Cotrane. Not exactly from Phillipa, but Alma and Phillipa have the same hairdresser, so that's how I know. And the wife—you'll love this—is a suffragist, from Boston no less. She's tall and flat-chested, and she rides around on a bicycle, and all the society dames laugh at her and think she's touched in the head because she's always worryin' about the poor an' the underdog an' all that, though Phillipa said she's really all right. She says Charles Randsome is devoted to her, but—this is the best part, you'll really love this—Julia Randsome tried to get up a petition to close down the District! Don't that beat all?"

When this bit of gossip didn't produce the expected response, Lady Caroline got up. "I can see you're in a funk, so there's no use me hangin' around. Besides, I got things to do. And you'd better get crackin', too. We aren't lucky enough to have a war every day, Mollie. If it keeps on long enough, it'll pay for our retirement. You can get your rose-covered cottage in the Emerald Isle like you're always jawin' about and serve tea to the nuns till you croak. But you're not a member of the Women's Christian Temperance Union yet, dearie, so give the kid a break and let her have some romance, will ya?"

Kate sat in the kitchen picking at the straw of her hat while Sophronia mashed sweet potatoes. She had an empty feeling in her stomach, as though she hadn't eaten in a long time. It was almost four, the girls would be down for their main meal any time now, and though Mollie had relented and said she could go out with him, it looked as if Lawrence wasn't going to come.

A drop of sweat fell from Sophronia's chin into the bowl. Wiping her face with the corner of her apron, she looked at Kate, then banged the masher on the tabletop. "What you have that hat for, Kate? You're drivin' me wild with sittin' there pickin' on that hat."

"I told you. I'm waiting for someone."

"And I'm about to serve a meal, so either you stop actin' like a boy gettin' ready to bury his dog and help me get it on the table, or you get outta my kitchen."

"I'm waiting for Mr. Randsome," Kate said to herself.

Sophronia did a double take. "Mr. who?"

"Mr. Randsome. Mr. Lawrence Randsome." The name already had the taste of disappointment.

"Mr. Lawrence Randsome?"

"That's what I said."

Sophronia's rhythm, steady as a metronome when she was preparing a meal, stopped abruptly. Her face was impassive, but a whistling sound came through her teeth. "Mr. Lawrence Randsome."

Kate looked up. "You know him? How could you know him?"

"Not from here I don't know him. My mama works in his grandmama's house. If his mother knew he'd been here . . ."

"Are you gonna tell her?"

"You see this scar on my neck? This come from someone who just *thought* I was gonna tell something he didn't want anyone to know. I'd be a dead woman long time ago if I told what I know. Lawrence is getting ready to go off to the war, isn't he?"

Kate nodded. "So you know all about him? Did you know him when he was a little boy and all?" If she couldn't be with him, talking about him was the next best thing.

"Kate, I just told you. I don't flap my gums with gossip. My mouth be glued so tight I don't give out my recipes. Now take over mashing these sweet potatoes while I see to the rice and beans." Kate took the masher and began pounding it into the bowl, her face blotched with disappointment. "Now, Kate, I'm sorry he's not coming, but you gotta learn you can't expect men to do in the daylight what they promised in the dark. It's not their nature." She shook her head, saying softly to herself, "Little Lawrence Randsome," then, "Shake a tad of cinnamon on those sweet potatoes."

Rose hurried in, holding the front of her kimono together. "I was just comin' down the stairs an' I heard a knock on the front door, so's I went to it and . . ." She winked at Kate. "Guess who's . . ."

Kate flew out of the room.

Lawrence stood on the threshold of the open front door, hat in hand, feeling vastly uncomfortable. This morning the prospect of lying hadn't bothered him, but when he'd actually lied, excusing himself from Beatrice's on the pretense of going to his father's office, then sending a boy to the offices with a note saying he'd been delayed, he'd felt unmanly. The sight of Mollie's house further increased his unease. In the bright sunlight it looked sordid and somehow threatening, an impression that was reinforced by the presence of the old Negro woman kneeling on the stoop. Her bony head was tied with a bright blue *tignon,* and a basket of what appeared to be feathers, bones, and dirt was at her side. As he mounted the steps, she looked up, her eyes seemingly sightless, their whites yellowish. She tapped her chest as though introducing herself, muttered what sounded like "You are an echo," then crossed herself three times and went back to rubbing the reddish dirt into the steps. Now, as he waited, staring into the foyer, he could still hear her behind him, muttering incantations. Part of him wanted to turn around and leave, but that, too, would be unmanly. Besides, Kate was coming toward him. She looked smaller than he remembered, and dowdy in her country-girl dress. I might pass her on the street without noticing her, he thought, but then she smiled and said, "You're here," and his heart tripped.

"I'm sorry to be late."

"It doesn't matter." She reached for his hand, realized she was still holding the masher, and said, "I've been in the kitchen."

"I'm afraid that it's too late to go for that ride."

"It doesn't matter." They couldn't sit in the parlors because the girls would be coming down for their meal. "I'll just take this back to the kitchen. You could go up to my room."

He glanced out the door as she closed it, his discomfort at the sight of the voodoo woman shifting to Kate. He wasn't frightened by such things, but what about her? "I'll go up," he told her, moving to the stairs, hoping he wouldn't have to see anybody.

She came into her room and locked the door. They looked at each other, smiling tentatively, and then she was in his arms. He flattened his cheek against hers, and she lowered her head to his chest. "I was afraid you wouldn't come."

"I had to . . . It doesn't matter what I had to do. We're together now."

He kissed her gently, wanting nothing more than to comfort and reassure her, but when their tongues touched, desire rippled through him. He took her hand, and they sat side by side on the bed. He hadn't imagined the stimulation of seeing her in full light. No artist could capture her coloring—the tawny, chestnut, auburn, and gold of her hair, the dark brown-and-gold flecks in her eyes, the blush on her cheeks, and the moist red of the inside of her lower lip. Why hadn't he thought to bring her flowers to brighten the room or—he swept back her hair—earrings or—he began to unbutton her dress—a necklace to hang between her breasts? He cupped them in both hands, marveling at the tender pink of the nipples, lowering his head to tongue them till they stood up, brighter pink, erect.

She caressed his head, then lay back on the bed, staring up at the ceiling. "I'm sore," she told him as he pushed up her skirts and eased down her bloomers.

He hesitated, but when he looked into her eyes, he saw not admonition but expectation. "I am, too."

His fingers combed her pubic hair, parted her swollen lips, dabbled in her silky, slippery juice, stroked her hard little button till she squirmed, squeezing her eyes shut.

"I'll be gentle."

"Yes."

"When I was in the bath, I thought about going into you so—"

"Slow. Yes."

He eased himself in, lifting her legs to his shoulders so that he might thrust in up to his hilt. They were joined in a throbbing stillness, cemented at the center of their being. She groaned, thrusting up involuntarily. He held her more tightly, restraining her, and when she had calmed, he pulled out almost to his tip, easing in again, then again, in long, slow strokes that brought him to the breaking point, till she restrained him, squeezing his head with her knees, pulling on his hair, digging her nails into his back until they held another, final moment of stillness. He could contain it no longer. He arched back, driving into her for the final plunge. They bucked and moaned, flooding each other. She stuffed her hand into her mouth and bit it to stop from crying out. I love you. I will always love you.

As Lawrence came out of Kate's room and hurried down the stairs, he found Mollie lying in wait. She motioned him into her bedroom, gestured to a chair, and offered him a glass of schnapps. Unnerved by the surroundings (who would have thought a madam would have an altar to the Virgin next to her bed?) and frantic because he was late, he refused the drink and nodded impatiently while she blathered on about what a lovely girl Kate was.

"Kate told me you were plannin' to take her fer a carriage ride. Now that's a lovely thought, Mr. Randsome, but if y'll consider it twice, I think y'll realize that it's not a good idea. You've got yer reputation to consider, and though it's not likely, 'cause I give the police a little somethin', Kate could be arrested. Seein' as how y're such lovebirds, I expect y'll be wantin' to be with her as much as y' can before y' leave. I can arrange fer that exclusivity, and I don't mind yer comin' by when I'm not officially open."

He said, with as much dignity as he could muster, that he did want to see Kate as much as possible and that he would be by again late that night.

She smiled and smiled, but there was a hint of condescension and even hostility in her voice when she said, "Sure, I know Kate'd never bother y' with the story of her life, but it must be clear to y' that she wouldn't be here had she not been entirely destitute. Thanks be to God, Mr. Randsome, you'll never know what it's like to be wantin' money, but Kate's a workin' girl, an' regardless of her tender feelings fer y', y're takin' advantage of her services."

A working girl? Her services? The euphemisms made him hot with humiliation. Seeing his reaction, she added with simpering gentility, "Sure, she's a beautiful girl. So fresh an' innocent she's the talk of the District, and if y'll inquire amongst yer friends, y'll get an idea of jest how much her services are worth at this particular time."

Dear God, he thought, she's talking about Kate as though she were a novelty exhibit at a parish fair. Was she going to present him with an annotated price list of every carnal act known to man?

He got up, desperate to leave, unsure of what to say or how to address her, and she supplied, "Mollie. Just call me Mollie," and got up, too. "Sure, I can see y're anxious to be off. I know a young gentleman like you always has pressing social obligations, and now we've had this little chat, I know I can rely on y' to do the right thing by her. She'll be waitin' fer y' tonight."

He assured her that he would do the right thing, and stiffened as she patted his shoulder. "Ah, it's an imperfect world, son," she told him as he edged toward the door. "There's some that rant about free love, but even love isn't free, now is it?"

He bowed and put on his hat. She trailed after him, calling "God bless you" as he went down the steps.

He strode along the street, propelled by anger and disgust.

What a sordid conversation with that appalling Irishwoman! She had actually called him "son." And to think Kate had told him that she was fond of her. How could he have been so stupidly naive as to forget about the money? He probably didn't have enough to pay for Kate's "exclusive services" before he left, and what would happen to her afterward? She was a virtual prisoner in that house. Any man who had the price could do anything he liked to her. She could be arrested if she tried to leave the District, and in any case, where would she go? If he didn't do everything in his power to get her out, then his love was no more than lust. He would have to set her up in a small apartment until he returned. But how much would that cost? And where in the world would he get it? Mollie had been right to condescend to him: he never really thought about money. There had always been more than enough. His father provided a generous allowance, his mother had instilled a sense of thrift that curbed extravagance, and he was confident that in a few short years he would make lots of money himself. The problem was, he needed it now, tomorrow at the latest.

As his mother's son, he'd been raised with an attitude of compassion and generosity toward the less fortunate, but until this moment he had never understood the desperation of not having enough money. The thought of Kate, alone, in a strange city, without a soul to turn to, made him break out in a sweat. The horror of her situation almost made it possible for him to forgive what she . . . Forgive? Who was he to forgive?

He passed a saloon. The beery smell and raucous male voices disgusted him. He had to get her out of that house. At the end of the block he saw a hack driver putting a bag of oats under his nag's muzzle and raced toward him.

CHAPTER

XIII

It has been said that the love of money is the root of all evil. The want of money is so quite as truly.

Samuel Butler

*T*t was after seven, the light was fading, and Julia, dressed in the claret gown that Charles said flattered her coloring, sat at her dressing table putting the finishing touches on her hair and trying to calm her anxiety because Charles and Lawrence had not come home. Hearing voices on the stairs, she stopped, hands in midair, and listened. Charles was going into his room. Now he must be sitting on his bed and taking off his boots. Now he was going into the bathroom and turning on the faucets.

How humiliating it was to sit, ears cocked, playing the spy in her own room. Though it had been going on less than a week, it already had the force of habit, so if a week, why not a month, or a lifetime? There were couples, Abraham and Alcesta, for example, who continued to live together in hopeless misery. Love and trust were forever gone, like a limb that had been chopped off. Surely it was better to forget about guilt and blame, surely it was better to forgive. But could she will herself to forgive? If she went to him now . . . Yet she knew it would only be minutes before she lost control. She'd demand to know where he'd been the other night, she'd insist that he sell the District properties, and then they'd be swept into another hurricane of anger and accusation. But this listening to him through the wall was insupportable. She got up abruptly, knocking a book onto the floor, and without bothering to pick it up, left the room. She would wait in the garden until the rest of the family was ready to go to the Dewitts' for dinner.

Passing through the dining room, she saw Marie carrying a pitcher of hot water into Carlotta's room. Since Carlotta had arranged the dinner at the Dewitts', she was obliged to go, but if she was just beginning her sponge bath (she believed that anything more than occasional immersion in a tub was bad for her skin), it would be another forty minutes before she was ready. Julia bit her lip and went to the French doors. Hearing the front door open and close, she moved back into the hallway and saw Lawrence bounding up the stairs. She had assumed that he'd come in with Charles. If he hadn't been with Charles, where had he been? That question went unasked in the flurry of their tardy departure.

As the servant put down the soup plates, Mrs. Dewitt toyed with one of her ruby earrings and smiled around the table, her glance settling on Julia. "I do hope the meal isn't entirely ruined."

"I'm sorry we . . ." Julia let the apology die. She had already apologized when they'd arrived, though their lateness was none of her doing.

She took a sip of soup but found she couldn't swallow. The scene was so gratingly predictable that she wished she'd had the sense to plead a headache and stay home. Orson Dewitt was talking about the war.

"Dammit, Charles," he sputtered, wiping his blubbery lips and pounding the table, "it's our destiny to pursue a policy based on principles of commerce. You know and I know that we should've taken over the entire Caribbean years ago. There's sugar in Cuba, coffee in Nicaragua, bananas . . . there's bananas all over the place. After the war we must build a canal so we can transport 'em."

Charles neither agreed nor disagreed but spooned into his soup with relish. Nothing interfered with Charles's appetite, Julia mused. She'd always thought that showed a healthy constitution, but now it seemed evidence of a fundamental insensitivity. Carlotta and Mrs. Dewitt were nattering about Vincent Liscomb's death and "poor little Yvette," but their attention was focused on the young people, ready to fan any flicker of attention Lawrence might show Adeline. But Lawrence seemed as distant as she, so preoccupied that he picked up a teaspoon and took several mouthfuls of soup before realizing his mistake. The part of her that would always think of him as a child almost signaled his faux pas.

Seeing his fine, high brow in the candlelight, she remembered his face when he was a boy—how, during their summers at Grand Isle, she'd rubbed butter onto his little nose and stroked back his sun-bleached hair. In those innocent days she'd always been able to read his face. She'd known at a glance how he felt, even what he was thinking. She'd answered his questions and kissed away his hurts. But he was a man now. Day after tomorrow he would go off to war, and so far they had not shared a single loving moment. Why hadn't she had the sense to restrain herself from criticizing him about the war? This afternoon at Beatrice's it had cut her to the quick to see how eager he was to get away from her. Again she tried to swallow, but her throat constricted.

Half listening to Adeline's twittering, Lawrence looked across the table at his mother. Her neck was taut and her mouth closed so tightly that she seemed about to gag. He felt a pang of guilt because earlier in the evening, when he'd come home late, he'd thought it was just as well that she and his father were on the outs, because that made it less likely they'd compare notes on his whereabouts.

He turned back to Adeline, whose eyes were filled with cowlike adoration. His own eyes were heavy from lack of sleep, but his mind was racing.

He would need seven hundred dollars, possibly a thousand, to set Kate up in an apartment, and every possible source of money seemed more ghastly than the last. Fool that he was, he'd refused his father's offer of money just yesterday. What possible explanation could he come up with for wanting it now? His father had never denied his requests; then again, he'd never requested so large a sum. His father was out. There was Carlotta. She'd be only too happy to hand it over, but she'd know it was for some illicit purpose, and she'd turn it into some sort of conspiracy against his mother. There was Leonce Lambre. He could imagine Leonce's sly remarks, the arch of his eyebrow and the curl of his lip when he said he'd make arrangements with his banker. Leonce would know it was for Kate. Taking from Leonce would be like taking from Carlotta: it would put him in his power. He could ask for a little from each of several friends, but then it would be all over town and sure to get back to the family. And it was really such a paltry amount. Those ruby earrings Mrs. Dewitt kept playing with were probably worth more.

". . . and I'm sure you agree, Lawrence," he heard Adeline say.

He'd lost even a nodding involvement with the conversation. He blinked, said he most certainly did agree, and took another spoonful of soup. Dear God, he was tired—so tired he couldn't imagine feeling any stirring of desire. But he still had to sleep with Kate, to wrap his arms around her, kiss the pale soft flesh of her shoulder, smell her hair, tell her everything would be all right, feel the roundness of her buttocks against his groin. A poem he'd always liked was going round and round in his head:

"Western wind, when will thou blow, / The small rain down can rain? / Christ, if my love were in my arms, / And I in my bed again!"

A servant was removing the soup plates, another putting down a silver platter of thin slices of duck in a red berry sauce, while another refilled the wineglasses. Realizing that Adeline had once again finished a sentence with the upward inflection that implied a question, he said, "I'm sorry, Adeline. I didn't hear what you . . ." Adeline's cowlike eyes changed to those of a bull about to charge.

"I'm afraid Lawrence is finally having to admit to the effects of his long journey home," Julia said.

"Nonsense," Carlotta remonstrated. "At his age I could dance all night and go to the races in the morning. A few glasses of brandy and a game of cards will brighten him up."

But Charles, much to Lawrence's relief, took Julia's cue and said that despite the fine company and the excellent cuisine, the Randsomes were taxed to the limit and would have to beg for an early night.

No longer consciously tired, but jittery as a racehorse at the starting gate, Lawrence stood at his bedroom window looking down on the moon-drenched garden and rotating his thumb over the face of his pocket watch. It was after one, they had been home from the Dewitts' for more than an hour, and given the general confessions of fatigue, he supposed they were all asleep. Still he hesitated, glancing at the bureau where the pistol Carlotta had given him lay.

He had decided to pawn the pistol, his watch, and the stickpin he'd been given for his eighteenth birthday. Since he usually gave things an intrinsic rather than monetary value, he had no idea how much they would bring, but at least it would be a start. He knew that selling gifts was tawdry, and he could hardly imagine

Carlotta's wrath if she ever found out about the pistol, but his misgivings were overshadowed by imagining Kate's relief when he set the money before her. In the morning he would definitely have to go to his father's offices. How to transport the pistol? What excuse would he manufacture when he left to find a pawnshop? And where would he find one? There must be pawnshops in or around the District. He would simply inquire from shop owners until he found one.

A cloud passed over the moon, and he took the gathering darkness as his cue. Pocketing the watch, he moved to the hallway, closed the door with an almost inaudible click, and felt his way down to the second-floor landing. Seeing a light from the entrance hall, he froze, feeling like a villain in a melodrama, before remembering that Robert, who was enamored of the novelty of electricity, sometimes left the entrance-hall light on overnight.

Reaching the downstairs hall stand, he was about to take his hat when he felt, rather than heard, someone behind him. Turning, he saw his mother, barefoot, in nightdress and peignoir, coming down the stairs. To his surprise, he wanted to laugh. First he'd felt like a stage villain, now he felt like the leading man in a French farce, always on the verge of a hasty departure and always foiled in his attempts.

As she came to his side, he said, "I couldn't sleep, so I decided to come down and get something to read." How easy it was to lie, even to his mother. The frisson of satisfaction that came from knowing he could get away with it turned into an inward shudder of fear. Being caught out was frightening, but there were other, more subtle dangers. Lying corroded your trust and made you cynical: if you could lie so easily, others must, too. But under the circumstances he had no other choice.

"I hope I didn't waken you," he said, his voice low and serious, asking for absolution.

"No, you didn't wake me. I knew you weren't able to sleep. When you were a child—at Christmas or Mardi Gras—or whenever you got too excited, you wouldn't be able to sleep. If you'd like, we could talk."

There was no way of refusing, so he followed her into the library, where she turned on the light, closed the door, and sat on the divan, tucking her feet under her and tossing back her long braid with a gesture that made her seem young.

"You're not cold?" he asked.

"Good heavens, no. It's already hotter than I like. You know, I think people in tropical climates are intellectually sluggish because the blood doesn't circulate to their brains. When you return to Boston, I shall visit you. We'll walk through the snow and have stimulating conversations. But I don't suppose you'll be back in Boston this winter."

"I plan to be. I expect the war will be over long before that."

She didn't say that expectations of quick victory were usual at the onset of a war but asked if there was anything she could do to help him pack. He thanked her but said no, and covered a yawn, hoping she'd take the hint.

"I finished reading the Ibsen by myself," she told him. "It's a pity that I shall have no chance of seeing a production. I find it quite remarkable that Ibsen is still so virulently attacked. I can almost tell if it's worth talking to someone by asking them how they feel about Ibsen."

Under normal circumstances, and knowing how starved she was for this sort of conversation, he would have enjoyed listening to her. She was thoughtful and often original, and she sometimes used a discussion of plays or books to reveal more intimate things about her life. At the moment he couldn't even fake an interest but sat stiffly, clasping and unclasping his hands, willing her to stop. Her need to prolong their time together was so strong that she kept talking, hoping to involve him, until, unable to ignore his inattention, she interrupted herself and said, "I know you must have a great deal on your mind."

"Yes."

"Tonight at the Dewitts' I couldn't help but see how distant you were, but then you have as little tolerance for small talk as I, and Orson Dewitt's bombast is enough to make anyone want to flee the room."

"I should have been more gracious, especially to Adeline."

She smiled. "As the daughter of one of the richest men in town, she feels entitled to any young man's undivided attention."

"I'm sorry."

"Oh, I don't mind. Had she had anything substantive to say, I'm sure you would have listened. And I certainly don't expect you to court Adeline. That's Carlotta's idea. I don't think Adeline is nearly intelligent enough for you."

"I don't suppose intellect is the only quality that recommends a girl."

"No, but in your case I'm sure it would be one of the principal attractions."

"Was it his intellect that attracted you to Father?" He'd tripped her up on that one, and he watched as she drew in her breath and considered how to phrase an honest but sufficiently delicate answer. But he wasn't really interested. In his mind's eye he saw the hands of a clock, stubbornly stalled, then spinning wildly out of control. It must be one-thirty by now. He would have to run from the house to the nearest thoroughfare and hope to find a hack. Even if he was lucky enough to get one right away, it would be after two before he got to the District. Then he would have to negotiate the raucous crowds. Just getting from Mollie's front door to Kate's room would be like running the gauntlet. He heard, "What are you thinking about?" and, caught off-guard, he answered:

"Money."

"Money," she repeated, as though it were a foreign word whose meaning she wasn't completely sure of. "Do you mean to say that you need money? I should have thought that your father—"

"He did, but I didn't . . . that is to say . . ." He was hopelessly entangled. "The money's not for me. It's just . . . I'm sorry. I do need some rest. My brain is addled. I didn't mean to—"

"It's not for you?"

"I'd rather not discuss it."

"Do you mean . . . ?"

"It's for a friend. A friend who is in desperate circumstances."

"What friend?" she asked gently.

"You don't know"—he had enough presence of mind to change the pronoun—"him," and, trying to extricate himself, added, "He isn't from here."

"Is it your friend George?"

"Really, Mother . . ." He got up and began to pace. "I don't know why I mentioned it. I surely didn't intend to. It's a delicate matter, and I'm not at liberty to discuss it. It's just that it's on my mind."

"Yes, I can see that it is. And if it's a matter between you and your friend, I can understand the difficulty of your position. One must never violate the trust of a friend, and one should do everything in one's power to come to a friend's aid." She paused. "How much do you need?"

"Five hundred," came out. He was appalled by what was happening, but part of him was calculating: five hundred added to whatever he got from pawning the goods was sure to be enough.

"Five hundred. Well. It is a substantial sum. But if your friend needs it, I suppose I can manage it."

He had never even considered asking her, but she was the obvious choice. Who but his mother, who was so frugal that she darned her own stockings, would be trusting enough to take his request as its own justification, to hand over cash without any prying questions? He was already in so deep that he saw no reason not to plunge on.

"I'll need it by tomorrow afternoon. I'll pay it back as soon as possible, though I don't suppose my army pay—"

"Your army pay! Dear boy, I shouldn't think your army pay would buy you a handful of beans. I'm sure your friend George will make good on it, and when he does, you can return it to me." She was so relieved that he'd confided in her, however obliquely, so happy that she could be of use to him. "I wish you'd told me sooner. You should have known that I'd do anything in my power to help you. I won't be able to go to the bank until the afternoon, but I assume you'll take it with you to Florida, so wouldn't tomorrow evening be ample time?" He nodded. "Then I'll give it to you tomorrow evening. I'm certainly glad we'll be here at home." She put her hand to her forehead and closed her eyes. "I still can't believe that you'll be leaving day after tomorrow. Or rather, tomorrow. I am muddled. What time is it now?"

"Getting on to two. We must go up to bed." Flooded with relief and gratitude, he went to her, taking her hands and bringing her to her feet. "Dearest, dearest Mother, what would I do without you?"

Her hands gripped his back, and she was racked by a single sob. He brought her head onto his shoulder and felt her body, so fragile yet so indestructible, and thought, I came from this body. The realization filled him with awe. He stepped back, placing his hands on her shoulders.

"You mustn't worry about me, Mother. We will walk in the snow in that bracing Boston cold, and we'll talk and talk." She wiped her eyes and nodded, showing him a stoic smile. "I'll go up, then," she said. "I'm sure I can sleep now."

He smoothed her brow and kissed it and told her goodnight, and when she left, he leaned against the door, counting the minutes until he could leave.

CHAPTER

XIV

*One of the striking differences between a cat and a lie is that a cat
has only nine lives.*

Mark Twain

*T*he following day, April 24, 1898, war was formally declared,
and as Lawrence went in search of a pawnshop, the mood on the
streets pulsed with such collective excitement that, despite another night of much lovemaking and little sleep, he picked up
his step, already imagining heroic deeds.

The first words out of the pawnshop keeper's mouth were,
"By Jove, we'll get 'em now!" And when Lawrence told him that
he was leaving for training camp the next morning, the deal was
concluded quickly and so favorably that Lawrence bought a necklace with a small gold heart for Kate. He was still six hundred
and twenty dollars richer when he went to his father's offices,
where he found Charles in high good spirits.

"No turning back now," Charles told him. "You're on the eve
of a great adventure. And I've had a piece of interesting news
myself. Have you ever heard of a New York law firm called
Sullivan and Cromwell?" Lawrence said yes, and Charles offered
him a cigar and took one for himself.

"I received a letter from William Nelson Cromwell today," he went on after relishing the first puff. "He's lobbying for a group that wants to buy the unfinished French canal works on the isthmus in Panama. I've had dealings with many of the men in Paris, so he's asked me to come to New York to discuss the enterprise with him. The time's ripe now, my boy. All forward-looking men see the need for a canal under American control. Just think of it! It'd be larger than the Pyramids!"

Lawrence said, "You look larger just talking about it," and Charles, who enjoyed being kidded when he was in an expansive mood, laughed.

"Granted, it's not as exciting as going off to war," he said, "but we old men of commerce must find our romance where we can. I tell you, Lawrence, this idea tickles my fancy as nothing has in years. It's not enough to make money; a man wants to feel that he's contributing something, that he's part of a great enterprise. Of course, if I become involved, I'll be traveling to Paris, and I'll want to visit the site in Panama as well."

"I hope Mother won't be left alone for too long."

"She could come with me. I've often told her so, but she's always so involved with her committees and such here at home."

Lawrence didn't point out that Julia's involvements were due, at least in part, to the fact that his father was away so much of the time, and he couldn't quite feature Julia tromping through Panamanian jungles. "It's just that I know she's anxious about my going, and since the two of you have seemed less close than usual . . ."

"No need to worry about that. Marriage is a lifetime proposition. Bound to be ups and downs. And she's not the type of woman who'll let you patch things up with an apology and a gift. You know, Lawrence, even when a man loves a woman, he doesn't always know how to approach her. I've been so damned busy I just haven't had the time. And speaking of time . . ." He looked at his watch and snuffed out his cigar. "Let's go home right now and surprise her by being early for a change. By the by, I think we should keep any discussion of the war to a minimum. And don't get your mother started on any discussion about exploited factory workers or women's rights."

Lawrence smiled. "All right. I'll confine myself to talk of cabbages and kings." He had grown up thinking that his parents were united in their beliefs, but during the past few years he'd come to realize that his father echoed rather than shared his mother's progressive opinions. Charles was no hypocrite—Lawrence was sure that he would never do anything unethical or even shady—he was just more concerned with society's good opinion than with its welfare. He believed that a wife should set the moral tone, and the husband should try to live up to it but shouldn't have too much trouble forgiving himself when he didn't. It wasn't an attitude that Lawrence was prone to criticize, at least not today.

As they left the offices and walked to their carriage, they were greeted by a host of passersby, and he felt very satisfied to be the son of a man who was not only respected, but so well liked. When they reached the front doors of the house, Charles stopped, took out a hundred-dollar bill, and pressed it into Lawrence's hand.

"I hear the señoritas are very beautiful," he said with a wink. "When you get to Havana, have a drink for me."

After he'd bathed and dressed, Lawrence sat on his bed playing with the necklace he'd bought for Kate. Upon closer examination he saw that it was a rather common-looking thing, but, he thought as he heard a knock at the door and pocketed it, at least it was a memento.

"Supper's almost ready," Julia told him. She stepped in, took an envelope from the folds of her skirt, and handed it to him. "And here's the money you need."

He said "Thank you!" not once but twice and, realizing that

his guilt was making him sound too effusive, quickly moved on to another topic. "Did Father tell you that some New York lawyer wants to enlist him to lobby for a canal in Panama?"

"He's still dressing for supper. We haven't had a chance to talk."

"I know he's eager to discuss it with you. He said that if he takes it on, he'd like you to travel with him. You know you should, Mother. Angelique is surely old enough to be left in the care of the staff."

"Oh, I doubt that Angelique would miss me. Well, I'm glad you had time with your father." She couldn't help but wish that more of that time had been spent with her but comforted herself with the knowledge that she was the one Lawrence had come to for help.

"He does love you, Mother. You know that, don't you?"

"Yes, I know." She gave him a smile that took years off her age.

"He said that when I marry, he hopes I can find a girl who's half as fine as you." He saw nothing wrong in embroidering his father's remarks; in fact, playing Cupid to his parents made him feel wise and kind and very mature.

When the family had assembled at the table, he saw that his efforts had had some effect. As his father helped his mother onto her chair, he let his hand rest on her shoulder, and she smiled up at him, arching her back ever so slightly to acknowledge his caress.

A succulent bouillabaisse was served. Angelique, who had a little package near her plate that he guessed was a going-away present, was on her best behavior. Even Carlotta displayed an uncharacteristic sweetness, asking how Julia was feeling and complimenting her on the menu. Lawrence smiled around the table. He could keep an easy rein on his impatience tonight. He had accomplished everything he'd set out to do: he had more money than he'd hoped for, and he'd even had the presence of mind to arrange for a hack to be waiting around the corner at midnight. It was only a matter of hours before he would be with Kate.

As the next course was put before them and he let go of Angelique's hand to drain the juice from an oyster, Carlotta said, "I'm happy to see you've found your appetite. It will be a long time before you'll have another feast like this."

Eager to avoid any reference to Lawrence's departure, Charles said, "I'll never forget the Christmas when Lawrence insisted on carrying the coconut cake to the table and dropped it. It was such a big cake and you were such a little boy. You looked as though you'd fallen into a snowbank."

"Oh, yes," Julia joined in. "And when Belle—you remember old Belle, don't you, Lawrence?—when Belle took you upstairs to wash you, you said, 'Do I have to wash it off? Couldn't I just lick it off like the cat does?'"

Everyone laughed. The remembrance prompted stories of other holiday meals. Every family must have these silly anecdotes, Lawrence thought, and they trot them out like the olios in a vaudeville show to keep the conversation away from important or unpleasant topics. But he was in such a tolerant mood that he dredged up some stories himself, while relishing the rack of lamb, curried rice, and pureed yams.

By the time the fruit and cheeses arrived, Carlotta, who usually took a dim view of sentimental stories, was telling Angelique about the time Lawrence plucked a feather from Robespierre's tail.

"I would never do that," Angelique said, "because I love Robespierre." She eyed the package near her plate that had occupied her attention through most of the meal and asked if she might not give it to Lawrence. "It's a locket with a curl of my hair," she told him as he lifted it from the wrapping. "*Maman* cut it off this afternoon because a girl gives her sweetheart a lock of her hair when he's going away so he won't forget her."

Lawrence pulled her to him. "There's no chance I could forget you, my pet. But now you must go off to bed so that you can be up first thing in the morning to see me off."

"*Oui, ma petite,*" Carlotta said, cutting off any objection. "Off you go to Blanket Street."

Angelique gave kisses all around, took Marie's hand, and went off. Carlotta rose and, with such uncharacteristic sensitivity that it almost made Lawrence suspicious, said, "I believe I shall toddle off, too. I'm sure you want some time alone with your parents."

The three of them retired to the parlor. Charles sat beside Julia and held her hand, talking about the Panama venture. When that topic had been exhausted, Lawrence talked about his favorite professors and his roommate, George. Finally Charles yawned, gave Julia a tender look, and suggested they all retire.

Lawrence said goodnight to them at his mother's door, and when he reached the upper landing glanced back and was pleased to see his father follow her into her room. Whistling "Plaisirs d'Amour," he went into his room to wait. An hour later he left the house as casually as if he were going out for an afternoon ride.

The District was in the throes of wild revelry. The boisterous crowd had spilled over the banquettes into the center of the street, flags and half-naked women hung from windows, trumpet players stood at the doors of rival saloons, blasting at each other in frenzied competition, and an organ grinder and his monkey and a Negress hawking love potions were doing a brisk trade on Mollie's stoop.

Lawrence pushed his way up the stairs and through the doors. The place was packed, a pounding rendition of "Camptown

Races" barely audible above the noise. Lawrence craned his neck. A small, silver-haired man stood next to him, surveying the scene with a jaundiced eye and muttering, " 'But make you ready your stiff bats and clubs, Rome and her rats are at the point of battle.' " Catching Lawrence's look, he said, "If you prefer a more patriotic quote, how's 'There is a tide in the affairs of men, which, taken at the flood, leads on to fortune'? Are you looking for anyone in particular?"

Lawrence said, "I'm looking for Mollie."

The man pointed in the direction of the Turkish parlor. "Thither she stands, surrounded by rhetoric and cigar smoke."

Lawrence thanked him and shouldered his way to her. Mollie, looking the worse for wear, excused herself and motioned him to follow her into her room. As soon as she'd closed the door, someone pounded on it, and she yelled, "Hold yer horses fer chrissake, I'm comin'," then lowered her voice and began a palaver about how brave he was to be going off to war and how much Kate would miss him.

He peeled off some bills, said, "Will three hundred settle my account?" and without waiting for either approval or objection, opened the door and asked, "Where's Kate?"

"She's in her room. And Mr. Randsome, if y'd like to—" but he was already pushing his way through the crowd and up the stairs.

Kate would be waiting, her beautiful hair loose, wearing nothing but a negligee that would slip to the floor at his first touch, and they would make love with exquisite tenderness.

He tapped at the door, already feeling the precious moments slipping away. He heard a man's voice bellowing for more whiskey and, glancing down the dimly lit hall, saw a heap of soiled linen piled next to a door and a naked girl, her rump jiggling as she darted into the bathroom.

He knocked again and tried the handle. It rattled and seemed about to give way. To think that nothing but a rickety lock stood between Kate and this pack of ravenous beasts. He brought his mouth close to the door and said, "Kate, it's me."

The door opened and he slid in. The room was stuffy, illuminated only by a bedside lamp. He saw with disappointment that she was fully dressed, and when he tried to take her in his arms, she turned her head away. "Kate, darling, what's the matter?" She moved to sit on the bed.

"I know," he said, taking off his hat. "It's a madhouse out there. It's like some painting by Hieronymus Bosch."

"Who?"

He stripped off his jacket and waistcoat, circling the bed to go to the window, deciding that the whisper of air was worth the annoyance of hoots and shouts from the street. Why weren't they in a clean, spacious room overlooking a garden?

"Who?" she asked again as he knelt behind her on the bed, cupping her breasts and kissing her neck.

"Doesn't matter," he whispered, fumbling with the pins in her hair.

She pulled away, stroking up a strand of loosened hair and pinning it into place. "If you say something I don't understand, the least you can do is explain it to me."

He sat beside her and took her chin in his hand. "Katherine, Katie, my Kate, what's the matter?" Her face had a closed and suspicious expression. "What is it?" he asked again. "Please tell me."

"Nothing," she said dully, looking straight ahead, her eyelashes casting shadows on her cheeks.

"Kate." He took her by the shoulders and turned her to him. Why tonight of all nights, with time draining away, was she behaving like this? Surely she must know that he felt the sordidness of their surroundings and the pain of their impending separation as much as she did. "Kate, I've been waiting all day to see you."

"I've been waiting, too. I've been—"

He stopped her mouth with a hard kiss. At first she was woodenly resistant, but then he felt her give way, her lips parting, her hands clutching his back, tiny springs of excitement uncoiling in both their bodies.

His hands moved over her, foundering in an ocean of skirts, frustrated by the cage of whalebone stays. He pressed his cheek to hers. "Get undressed, won't you, darling?" When she didn't move, he eased her dress from her shoulders, buried his face in her breasts, and moaned, "Don't you love me? Don't you trust me?"

To his amazement she pulled away and stood up. "What's the matter?" he demanded, impatience rising in his voice. She was breathing hard, but she looked as though she were about to cry.

"I want you to undress me. Undress me properly and carry me to the bed."

He stood unsteadily and took her in his arms, kissing her and simultaneously trying to undo the row of tiny buttons at the back of her dress. His fingers felt as clumsy as if he were wearing woolen gloves, and the din from the open window and a sudden shriek from another room grated on his nerves. Exasperated by her passivity and his own lack of finesse, he muttered, "I'm all thumbs tonight."

She stepped back, said, "Oh, all right," and reached around to unbutton herself.

He sat on the chair to take off his shoes, then stood, hurriedly yanking off his cravat—this was not the way it was supposed to be—pulling off his shirt—why was she angry? Why wouldn't she explain?—unbuttoning his trousers—it was their last night, his heart was bursting with love, but she . . .

He lowered his trousers, then pulled them up. No matter how much he loved her, he wouldn't let her treat him as though he were some goatish customer. He had some pride, and he would leave unsatisfied before he would sacrifice it. He turned to tell her so, but when he saw her, dress gone, camisole partly undone, bending to step out of her petticoats, he stopped.

He had thought she could never be more beautiful than she had been in the daylight, but the lamplight glowed on the heap of white at her feet, outlined her breasts and shoulders, burnished her hair to copper gold. The thought that other men would see her like this made him sick, and as she struggled with a knot in her stays, a frown of concentration creasing her forehead, she seemed so oblivious of his presence that his jealousy changed into a violent need to possess her.

He lunged, lifting her off her feet, ignoring her gasp of surprise as he threw her on the bed. By God, he would have her. He moved with demonic purpose, tearing at clothes, grabbing her arms and legs and moving them into position. As he was about to enter her, he groaned, "Kate, Kate I love you. Look at me."

She opened her eyes and stared up at him, and what he saw froze his heart. Her look said, "You can do anything you like to me, but part of myself I keep only to myself."

He pulled away and sat on the edge of the bed. Neither of them moved or spoke. There was a shout from the street, and a band struck up "There'll Be a Hot Time in the Old Town To-night." His breathing came back to normal, he wiped his hand over his face and went to his pile of discarded clothes.

"I have some money for you," he said. "I've already paid Mollie. This is just for you. I thought you wanted to get out of here. That is . . ." He couldn't bear to look at her. "*I* thought you should get out. I realize now that I don't really know what you want, but"—he dropped the roll of bills onto the bed—"this money is for you. And there's this." He placed the necklace next to the bills. "It isn't worth much, but I wanted you to have something from me."

He pulled on his trousers and sat on the chair to put on his shoes. He wanted to leave but was overcome with such a feeling of desolation that he couldn't move. He heard the bedsprings creak as she reached for the money. And then he heard her crying, not as a woman would cry, but with the uncontrolled, squeaky sobs of an abandoned child.

"Don't go," she cried. "Don't leave me. Please don't leave me."

She was a terrible sight, her camisole half off, her bloomers down around her knees, one stocking on, her face twisted. He went to her, and she clung to him, shaking her head from side to side, sobbing, "Don't go, please don't leave me." He wiped her cheeks and kissed them, tasting the salt of her tears and thinking for a single wild moment that he should take her and run away, but he took her by the shoulders, shaking her gently.

"Kate, you know I have to go."

"You'll never come back."

"I will come back. You must believe me."

"I know you won't. I'm just a whore and you're—"

"Don't say that!" He shook her. "You must never say that. You must believe in your own strength and dignity, you must . . ."

The words might have come from his mother. Something more than an exhortation to dignity was needed. His word of honor. A promise. But he couldn't bring himself to say that he would marry her. "I love you. I'll take care of you. I'll send you money. When the war is over, I'll . . . You must believe that I love you."

"I've spoilt everything. I wanted tonight to be perfect, and I've spoilt it all. Because I thought you didn't love me, because you're leaving."

"No, no. It's all right. I understand."

Given the circumstances, it was inevitable that they would fight, that she would act coldly in order to protect herself from the pain of their parting; after all, who else was there to protect her? "If only I'd had another day, I could've found a place for you to live. You will leave here, Kate, won't you? You must leave. Promise me you'll leave."

"I promise." She started to cross her heart, but her hand was clenched around the necklace. She opened her palm, offering it to him, then bent her head and held up her hair so that he could put it on. "I'll wear it for my whole life," she said as he centered the heart on her breastbone. "I don't have anything to give you."

"Please don't cry. You've given me everything. You've given me yourself. And while I'm away, I shall remember this"—he slipped the camisole from her shoulder, caressed her collarbone, her neck, her breasts—"and this"—he swept her hair back from her forehead—"and this. . . ." He laid her back, stroked her arms, pulled them around his neck, moved to lie next to her, and stared deep into her eyes. The look there was so full of trust and love that it swept away all other sights and sounds. They were nothing but two souls on the planet.

"And this . . ." he went on, skimming his hand over her belly. He kissed her navel and smiled up at her. Her belly was so tight and smooth, yet, slim as she was, it had a slight convex curve that reminded him of an infant's.

She grabbed his hand. "Oh, Lawrence, there shouldn't be any secrets between us, should there?"

"No, darling, never, never any secrets."

"I have to tell you . . ."

"Tell me that you love me. Only tell me that."

She began to cry again, seizing his head and pulling him up to kiss him, sobbing, "Just make love to me."

The light was on in the foyer, as he'd expected it would be, and as he noiselessly closed the front door, he felt something close to peace. There was no more plotting and planning; he had done all he could do. He imagined Kate, already asleep. He would get a few hours of sleep himself, and then he would be off. He'd purposely neglected his packing, knowing that last-minute activity would cut short any lingering or sentimental good-byes, and he'd forbidden any of the family to come with him to the train station. Robert would take him, and Robert would have the sense to say little or nothing. Looking at the staircase, he felt like a long-distance swimmer who's finally sighted the shore. He took a breath and moved toward it.

As he put his foot on the first tread, he heard an insinuating hiss of "Lawrensss" and froze as though the tip of a knife had been thrust into his back. Turning, he saw Carlotta, fully dressed, in the door of the front parlor.

"I thought you'd never come home," she called to him. He moved to her, gesturing for her to lower her voice, having trouble finding his own.

"Why are you up?" he asked in a strangulated whisper.

"Because I shan't get up in the morning, and I wanted to say good-bye to you alone," she said as loudly and innocently as if she were defending herself across a crowded room.

He took her by the arm and steered her into the parlor. "Please, *Maman,* it's almost dawn."

"It surely is, and I admire your stamina." She gave him a leering smile. "But surely you have enough energy left to share a bon voyage toast with your poor grandmama." She shrugged off his hand, and he watched, too shocked to move, as she turned on the light, crossed to the sideboard, and picked up the brandy decanter.

"No, please, *Maman.*" He shot after her, shaking his head and moving his arms in ineffectual protest. "I don't want anything to drink. I want to go to bed."

"I expect you've already been to bed, but you didn't get any sleep, did you?"

She must be drunk. "Be quiet," he whispered angrily. "You'll wake them." He looked around, saw the open door, and made a move toward it, but she outdistanced him and swung it shut with a resounding bang. Her movements were so swift and purposeful that he realized she couldn't be drunk.

"What," he asked, incredulous, "are you trying to do?"

"Why, you can see what I'm doing. I'm fixing us a brandy." She went back to the sideboard and began to pour. "Come, come, my pet, don't play shy with me. You might deceive the others, but you didn't think you could deceive Carlotta, did you? I've known since that first night when you went off with Leonce."

"How . . ." was all he could get out.

"After a certain age one does not have the pleasant exertions of the chase to make one tired. One sleeps very lightly. Oh, yes, I've known from that first night."

It was like some terrible childhood dream; he was transfixed as the monster moved toward him; he struggled to wake up; the monster still advanced.

"Why do you look so glum?" she asked, holding out the glass. "You can't imagine that I have any objection to your nocturnal adventures. No, no. I find it rather amusing. All these years she's tried to turn you into a bluenose, and here you are, lascivious as a monkey and sly as a fox. I know she's trained you to thrift, too, but I didn't suppose your breeding would incline you to anything but the most expensive goods. So where is he getting the money, I asked myself, since he's at it night and day? And then, this afternoon, she canceled one of her famous committee meetings and went off to the bank and I thought, Ah-ha!"

"Stop it." His whisper was half command, half plea. "Stop it."

"I toast your resourcefulness, my boy." She raised the glass and took a sip, eyes glittering. "I don't suppose you feel too guilty, knowing that your pleasures have used up her contribution to orphaned darkies or dissatisfied women." She took another sip. "Yes, the situation is most amusing and, for reasons you cannot fully understand, so full of—what is that word she is so fond of?—irony. Yes," she said, chuckling, "irony."

"I am going to my room. Good night." He moved to the door, his heart thudding.

"Surely you won't leave me when you've been so neglectful of me," she pouted. "You know your secrets are safe with me. So tell me, did you taste the nectar of one particular *putain,* or were you a busy little bee sampling many blossoms? In my day . . ."

As he opened the door, his heart seemed to stop. His mother stood on the threshold, her mouth open. "I heard the door slam," she said, "and I wondered—"

"Lawrence was just saying his final good-byes," Carlotta said, and as Julia's eyes went up to Lawrence's hat, she added, "Well, we can't expect a man of his age to confine his good-byes to the family, now can we? It's only human nature that some of his *affections*"—she pronounced the word with lewd innuendo— "would be engaged elsewhere."

She had such a look of triumph that he understood immediately: waking Julia was what she'd been aiming for all along.

"You," he said, and the words came out with spaces between them, "are an evil woman."

"What a thing to say to your poor old grandmama! You didn't get that self-righteousness from my side of the family. And how, dear Lawrence"—her eyes focused on him—"am I evil? *I* haven't lied to anyone, have I?"

She looked from one to the other, and when she was sure that Julia had taken in the situation, she yawned and put down her glass. "Well, as you have pointed out, it is almost dawn. I believe it is time for all of us to go to bed. I mean, to go to sleep."

She offered her cheek, first to Julia and then to Lawrence. When neither of them moved, she shrugged and sighed. "No? No, I suppose not, though when I was a girl, members of the family always kissed each other good night. As I said, I shan't get up in the morning, so"—she raised her hand and made the sign of the cross near Lawrence's face—"bless you in all your endeavors, my dear. You will write to us and tell us how things go in the war."

He could only stare after her, and not being able to look at his mother, he bowed his head. "It is very late. I'm sorry to have disturbed you. I'll bid you good night."

"Last night," Julia said after an agonizing pause, "when you were up, it wasn't because you couldn't sleep. It was because you were going out."

Her tone was so flat that he couldn't tell if it was a question or an accusation. Not that it mattered. "It's very late," was all he could muster.

She walked a few steps, her hand to her mouth. "And the money you asked me for, it wasn't really for your friend George."

He didn't even consider lying. "No."

"It was for . . ."

"It was for a girl. Mother, if you met her . . ." It was hopeless. He couldn't explain. Not now. Not ever.

"I didn't believe you were capable of deceiving me. And I never believed that you would . . ." Her voice became inaudible, again her hand came up to her mouth, she shook her head, gently, as though she were puzzling out a problem, and he heard her say something about "the District."

"Mother," he said after a dreadful silence, "I'm leaving in the morning."

"Yes. I know. Good-bye."

"But Mother—"

"I said good-bye, Lawrence."

She moved past him as though sleepwalking. When she had almost reached the stairs, she said almost as an afterthought, "I don't believe I shall get up tomorrow morning either."

Julia closed her bedroom door and leaned against it. Hearing her, Charles stretched like a great cat, opened his eyes, and said, "You're up. Why are you up? It's scarcely daylight."

His features, blurred with sleep, took on a look of dreamy contentment as he remembered their reconciliation and its consummation. "Here," he whispered, holding back the sheet. "Come back to bed."

She moved past the bed to the window as though she hadn't heard him. "Darling, what's the matter?"

"Lawrence has just come home."

"Oh." For a split second that seemed to be a perfectly natural state of affairs.

"He spent the night in the District." Her voice sounded so strained and otherworldly that it reminded him of a spiritualist Carlotta occasionally brought to the house to conduct seances. "He has been spending the night in the District ever since he came back."

He sat up, disoriented, struggling to understand. "What makes you think . . . ?"

"I heard them and I went downstairs."

"Heard whom?" What in God's name was she talking about?

"Lawrence. And Carlotta."

"I can't follow what you're saying."

"I think you can."

"And I tell you I can't," he said impatiently. "I was asleep, you burst in and start telling me God knows what, and . . ."

He got out of bed and started to go to her, but, suddenly feeling uncomfortable in his nakedness, he went instead to the chair where he'd flung his clothes. She stood staring out the window as he pulled on his trousers.

"Now, Julia," he began, "tell me what—"

"I was awake. . . ." I was awake, she thought, listening to you breathe, my arms wrapped around you, so grateful that we'd been able to make up and make love, so grateful that we had been able to comfort one another because our son was going off to war. "I heard noises. Carlotta had apparently waited up for him. I heard them and I went down." She paused, considering. "She's known all along. Have you known, too?"

"Carlotta?" He tried to fit the pieces together. He was not altogether surprised to hear that Lawrence had gone to the District, but that Julia had found out, and Carlotta had somehow been instrumental in her discovery . . . "I still don't understand," he stalled.

"I told you. She's known all along. She finds it vastly amusing, but then, it's a way to humiliate me, and I suppose"—she turned to face him—"that she's pleased that some of the money her grandson spends on vice will find its way back into the Randsome pockets."

"Carlotta is a mischief maker," he said angrily.

"Oh, she's much more than that, Charles, though I don't suppose you will ever face it," she went on in a dull voice. "She's like a spider, spitting out a web that covers everything. She's down there now, gloating over what she's done, knowing what we're saying as surely as if she were in the room."

"Julia, darling . . ." He started to reach for her but knew he dared not touch her. "If this is true . . ."

"It is."

For the life of him he couldn't think what to say. To admit that he didn't think it was a terrible thing for Lawrence to go to the District was out of the question. "*If* it's true," he began, though through his confusion he was already sure that it was, "try not to judge him too harshly. He's young. And he's going off to war."

"Oh, boys will be boys? They're entitled to lie, to go to brothels?"

"I only meant that under the circumstances . . . If you could find it in your heart to understand. If not to understand, then to forgive."

"Am I always the one who must understand and forgive!" Her eyes blazed as though a match had been struck. "I didn't expect you to understand. I even think you approve."

"It's not a question of approving, but—"

"Of course you approve. How could you not? If it weren't for people like you who make a profit from the District, it wouldn't be there. Young men wouldn't be tempted."

"How can you be so naive?" he flared up. "How can you possibly connect . . ." The argument was reeling out of control. "I told you I would dispose of the District properties as soon as I could. I've hardly had time to—"

"But you had them in the first place. And you never told me. You lied to me for years. Oh, it makes me sick. Sick to my soul. You will go on being blind, you will go on ignoring your complicity . . ."

"You are being totally unreasonable. I understand that you are upset, but—"

"Upset?"

"Not just upset . . ." Wounded, angry, betrayed. Oh, what a look on her face! "But you can hardly hold me responsible for something you believe Lawrence has done."

"Tell me something." Now it was she who made an abortive movement, as though she would grab him by the shoulders. But her hands dropped to her sides, and only her eyes held him. "Tell me, and may your soul be damned if you don't tell me the truth. . . ."

Recklessly trying to inject some levity, he said, "But Julia, darling, you don't believe in an immortal soul."

"Tell me! The night of the party, when you went with Abraham, where did you go?"

He felt as though the bars of a cage had clanged down around him. "I don't see what—"

"Tell me!"

"If you'll remember, Abraham was very drunk." He began to pace. "So drunk that he confessed that Alcesta had told you terrible things about their private life." Dammit, he would not be trapped! "And why didn't you tell me about that?" he demanded. "Because that's what started all this, isn't it? That miserable woman!"

"If she is miserable, it is because her husband made her so, with his whoring and his lies."

He snorted. "She would be miserable if she'd married the archangel Gabriel. Why didn't you tell me what she'd told you?"

"She spoke to me in confidence. I felt I couldn't repeat it, even to you, without betraying . . ." She shut her eyes. He was purposely trying to deflect her question, to outmaneuver her. *"Did you go to the District?"*

Frustration made him as breathless as if he'd climbed a hill. "Yes. I took him there. But I didn't—"

"I knew it! I knew it that night. But I didn't want to believe . . ."

"I didn't do anything to be ashamed of," he bellowed, "and I won't have you treating me as though I did. *I won't have it!*" No sooner had he grabbed her wrist than he let go. Suddenly he saw them, a bullying man and his accusing wife, their faces twisted in the early morning light. "I am going to bathe and dress. Then I am going downstairs to breakfast and to say good-bye to my son. I suggest," he added with a dignity he did not feel, "that you do likewise."

"I never want to see him again. I never want to see either of you again."

"That," he said, "can be arranged."

CHAPTER

XV

It was a splendid little war.

John M. Hay
Secretary of State, 1898

*J*ust a week later, Admiral Dewey defeated the Spanish fleet
at Manila Bay, the United States claimed the Philippines, and
Mollie literally had to bar the door. She felt like a besieged
general herself—the customers came earlier, stayed later, and
were so rowdy that she had to hire Judas's brother to give him
a hand. The laundress couldn't keep up with the extra work, so
she had to buy new linens. The girls were exhausted and cranky
and using too many stimulants. Sophronia was so busy preparing
fancy suppers for the guests that she had to feed the girls with
buckets of spaghetti from the Italian restaurant next to Sean
Hanratty's saloon.

"I don't want no dago food for breakfast," Zoe complained,
looking around the kitchen table to see if any of the others would
join her in a mutiny.

"You'll eat it or go without," Mollie told her. "Just think of
the money you're makin', and keep pullin' your weight like the
rest of us."

"What about her?" Zoe pointed a fork at Kate. "She ain't pullin' her weight."

"It's my time of the month," Kate said quietly. Every time she tried to get up her courage to tell Mollie that she was leaving, she was overcome with fear. She had no idea where she should look for a place to live, and the wild crowds on the street frightened her.

Ida, a girl with a flat face and a huge bosom, most of which was exposed by her loosely wrapped dressing gown, said, "Gee whiz, Kate. If you've had the curse for over a week, something must be wrong with your parts."

"Yeah," Hortense advised. "Better get you an herb woman or talk to Sophronia when she comes in."

"She ain't got the curse," Zoe scoffed, spearing a meatball from the bucket and eyeing Kate as she chewed. "She's gone mushy for that rich boy who was drillin' her before he went off. She don't wanna work." Kate pushed aside her plate and got up. Zoe said, "See?"

"It's her loss." Mollie was sour. "A body who's willin' to work now can make enough to retire on." Her glance followed Kate as she left the kitchen, then she turned on Zoe. "For God's sake, keep your mouth shut when you eat."

"Yeah," Ida agreed. "Talkin' and eatin' at the same time is unladylike."

"Well," Zoe shot back, "danglin' your tits in your grub don't exactly make you look like Mrs. Astor."

Vera banged down her coffee cup. "Just shut your mouth, Zoe. You look like a cow chewin' her cud."

"Listen, sister, if you don't want a plate of spaghetti in your face . . ."

"That's enough," Mollie shouted. "All of ya shut up and eat, and when you're through, get upstairs and pick up your rooms."

Rose whined, "That's the maid's job."

"She's doin' her best, but she can't keep up, and I won't have my place lookin' like a pigsty." She glared 'round the table. "Anyone don't like the rules can leave. Holy Mother, I feel like I'm runnin' a kindergarten. I'll be back in an hour. I want the rooms cleaned. I want all of you cleaned. And no arguments."

She bounced out the door and caught up with Kate at the foot of the stairs. "I'm goin' to Our Lady of Victory to say a wee prayer for the boys." Kate said she would get her hat.

They knelt in the front pew, Mollie with her head bowed, muttering over her beads. I'll bet she's not praying for the boys, Kate thought. She's here because she's guilty about all the money she's made this week.

Kate supposed it must be comforting to pray, but she couldn't do it. If there was a God, Spanish women must be praying for their sons and lovers, too, and she didn't see why God would choose sides.

She sat back on her haunches, thinking about Lawrence, feeling sick and miserable. She followed Mollie's gaze to the altar. Its marble base was carved in an elaborate bas-relief of bodies writhing in flames, their arms outstretched in supplication. "That's what it's like to be in the life," Mollie whispered with great gloom.

"Like hell?"

"No. That's purgatory. Purgatory feels the same as hell, but when you've served your time, you can get out." She tried to imagine the cottage she'd have beside Dingle Bay. It would be cool and green and quiet. She'd hear nothing but the waves, and her only customers would be birds. "Oh, my feet are killin' me." She struggled up. "Come on, we have to go back."

When they went through the front door, the maid said that Monsieur Leonce Lambre was waiting in the front parlor. Mollie rolled her eyes in exasperation. "Damn, it's not even dark yet.

It's bad luck to see men before it's dark." She gestured for Kate to go upstairs.

Kate was about to step out of her petticoats when Mollie knocked and came in without waiting to be asked. Her jaw looked as if it were set in concrete. "Mr. Lambre came by special. He booked you for tonight."

Kate wrapped her arms around her breasts and looked as though she'd smelled something noxious. "And he's supposed to be Lawrence's friend."

"It may not have come to your attention"—Mollie's voice oozed sarcasm—"but I'm not running a dancing school here. He doubled your price. Two hundred dollars for an overnight. You've got to take him."

"I can't."

"Don't play with me, my girl. You've pushed my patience to the limit. You work tonight or you leave."

"I'll leave, then," Kate shot back. "I was planning to leave anyway."

"Oh, so you were planning to leave. And where were you planning to go, little Lady Muck?" Mollie's glare became a stare, then her face went apoplectic. Good God, how could she have been so blind? She, who could spot every condition known to woman.

As the realization broke across her face, Kate spat it out. "Yes. I'm going to have a baby."

Mollie threw back her head and howled like a dog. "You stupid little cow!" Her hand flew up and landed flat and hard on Kate's face; she reeled back, wheezing, instantly contrite.

"Go ahead. Slap me. I don't care. I've been hit before." But she hadn't believed Mollie would ever do it. "I don't care what you say or do to me."

"How far along are you? Tell me the truth or I'll flay the skin off your deceitful backside."

"Three months." Kate hesitated. "Maybe a little more."

"Goddamn you to hell! Why didn't you say something when there was still time to do something about it?"

"Because I was . . . I tried to, but . . . It doesn't matter. I'll go away. Lawrence gave me money to go away."

"Gave you money? How much?"

"Almost seven hundred dollars. Enough till he gets back."

"Bet you didn't tell him you had a bun in the oven, did you? Of course you didn't. You idiot! Where do you think you're gonna go? You think that paltry amount will see you through having a baby? Not unless you're gonna drop it in the gutter, it won't. And you still owing me for your fancy-assed clothes. Who'd y' think's goin' to be with you when you drop this kid? Oh, I could kill you!"

But the anger had gone. Mollie sank on the bed and shook her head. "You don't know. You don't know what it's gonna be like."

The memory was buried deep, and she wanted it to stay that way. She'd been not much older than Kate. She'd never known who the father was, though she'd always thought it was that boy from Ohio who'd spent a whole month of his army pay before he'd gone off to Vicksburg. She'd worked right up through her seventh month, around the camps where you didn't take off your clothes, so hardly any of them had noticed. She'd left the baby with the Sisters of Charity. She hadn't seen it long enough to remember anything about it except that it was born with a full head of hair.

"Don't be mad at me, Mollie. Please, don't be mad at me."

Mollie knew what she was about to do was totally unprofessional, but if she turned the girl out, the weight on her conscience would be even worse. Besides, she couldn't help it—she loved the girl. "There's that attic room I keep for storage. I'm always saying I'll clean it out, but I never do. You can move your things up there. You'll pay me room and board outta what he left you. You can leave if you like, but if you think about it, I think you'll decide it's best to stay."

There was a sharp rap on the door. "Mollie," Sophronia called, "you in there? Iceman come with just three blocks of ice. I know I order five. Customers gonna be mad as hornets they's no ice in the drinks. Better come talk to this iceman."

"I'm comin'," Mollie yelled. "I swan," she added wearily, "it's all as hopeless as peein' against the wind."

A few days after Lawrence had gone, Charles slipped a note under Julia's door saying that he hoped she was feeling better and that he was leaving to go to New York, then to London, on private and government business.

It's come to this, she thought, now we communicate with notes slipped under doors. For the first time in their married life, she did not supervise his packing but continued to stay in her room. To avoid gossip among the servants, she said that she was coming down with influenza, and just hours after she heard Charles leave, that white lie became a prophecy. The fevers, aches, and chills were nothing compared to her mental anguish. She relived her parting scenes with Charles and Lawrence; when she slept, she had nightmares of bloody battles and floods. Though she normally enjoyed excellent health, it took her weeks to recover, and even when the physical symptoms had disappeared, she was so listless that she felt she was under a spell. With a tremendous act of will, she resumed her regular activities, arranging her days to avoid any contact with Carlotta. She was so successful that she sometimes felt she was living in a hotel.

She got up at dawn, and as soon as she'd breakfasted with Angelique and attended to household tasks, she left. At committee meetings she was so dazed that she had to refer to notes to remember the agenda. She volunteered at the orphanage, but the presence of a society lady who rolled up her sleeves instead of writing checks made the staff so uncomfortable that she gave it up. She went to the library and to art exhibits. She sat in parks and fed the birds—anything to keep out of the house. She rode her bicycle everywhere. Since it was considered unladylike for a woman, let alone a woman of her age and position, to cycle alone, people in the streets looked at her as though she were mad, but she didn't care.

She returned to the house at nightfall and took supper in her room. She declined all social invitations, but sometimes, after she'd tucked Angelique into bed, she had Robert drive her to Beatrice Ravenal's. They sat on Beatrice's gallery, sipping sherry, lemonade, or iced tea. Sometimes they talked till after midnight. They talked about the war, politics, the nature of love. They gossiped, recited poetry, told each other their dreams. When conversation went slack, they just sat, breathing in the smells of the garden, listening to the insects, and looking at the moon. One night, when she was so miserable she couldn't restrain herself, she told Beatrice about the District properties and her terrible fights with Charles. It was so unlike her to discuss such intimate matters that, even as she spoke, she felt shamed. She was afraid that Beatrice would commiserate in a way that would make her feel diminished or, worse yet, blame her, as she often blamed herself, but Beatrice just studied the tip of her little cigar and said, "Dearest Julia, you know my heart goes out to you. I feel sure Charles will do the right thing. I only hope he does it soon." Julia felt so grateful that she was tempted to tell what had happened with Lawrence, but, even with Beatrice, she couldn't bring herself to expose that wound.

She felt sure that Lawrence would write to her. Initially, when she was still hurt and angry, she imagined that she would return his letter unopened, but after a month, when no letter arrived, guilt overcame her: she had let her son go off to war without saying good-bye. She must write to him and beg his forgiveness. She wrote page after page, pouring out her pain, so shaken that she sometimes lost control of the pen. What started as an apology invariably ended as an indictment, so she tore up the letters.

She wrote again, determined not to accuse, not to be emotional, agonizing over the choice of words that would express her thoughts about integrity, trust, the relations between men and women. But the letters sounded as dry as a dissertation on morals, so she tore them up, too. She tried chatty letters, assiduously avoiding any but the most trivial topics—the weather was now so hot that she'd had to give up cycling; Angelique had mastered a simple Chopin nocturne; Boodles had had a litter of kittens—she couldn't even finish those. They were so superficial as to constitute a lie—they were like the letters Charles wrote to her. She had opened the first letter with trembling anticipation but immediately saw that Charles was determined to pretend nothing had happened. He began with his usual "My dearest wife," closed with his usual "Your devoted husband," and mentioned nothing more important than the weather, the quality of his accommodations, the results of business meetings. He continued to write from London, and she wrote back, her letters so vacuous that she felt like a hypocrite. She felt she had to write, partly because it was her duty to keep him informed about Angelique, but mainly because he was in touch with Lawrence, and sandwiched in between Charles's banalities, there was news of her son. The training in Florida was over, the troops were eager to get under way, but no firm date had been set for the invasion. She knew that much from the newspapers. The important thing was that Lawrence was safe.

In late June, two months after Lawrence had left, when the heat of the city became unbearable, she decided to take Angelique and her governess, Miss Branioner, to Grand Isle. The day they left New Orleans, she heard that the American force had landed in Cuba, and she could think of little else. The holiday was not a success. The sight of families on the beach made her miserable, the cottage was too small to afford her any privacy, Angelique whined about being away from Carlotta, Miss Branioner was bitten by sand fleas and the bites became infected. After a week she decided they should go back.

The morning the donkey cart came to take them to the ferry was hot, bright, and breezy, with cottonball tufts of clouds in an azure sky. As they approached the dock, she saw a large crowd, dancing and shouting, throwing their hats into the air. A young man with a pockmarked face ran by the cart, so excited that he ignored the presence of women and children and yelled, "We licked the bastards! We licked 'em!" A newsboy hawked papers, crying, "Victory in San Juan! Rough Riders lead the charge!" She bought a paper and, clutching Angelique's hand, moved through the crowd. Voices hit her like waves—"Thank God, oh, thank God!" "Whipped the whole damn Spanish empire!" "Hip hip hurrah!" "Three cheers for Teddy and the Rough Riders!"

She found a place at the prow of the ferry, and as Miss Branioner read the newspaper account of the battle, she gripped the rail and took deep breaths. Angelique said, "Is the war over, Mama?"

"Almost over. The men will have to sign treaties first."

"Does that mean Lawrence will be coming home?"

"Yes. Lawrence will be coming home."

"Soon?"

"I think so. Yes, soon," she assured her. But her own fears could not be so easily put to rest. Still, she was so relieved about the victory that she couldn't even hold a grudge against Carlotta, and when they arrived home that afternoon, she followed Angelique into Carlotta's room.

"You must've heard—"

" 'Course I've heard," Carlotta interrupted. "The whole world's heard. I hope this will bring you out of your funk. Everyone's been talking about your behavior."

With that, Carlotta opened her arms to Angelique. Julia left the room, wondering how she could have been so foolish: with Carlotta there could never be an armistice.

As she headed to the stairs, Marie came to her, pressed her hand, and said how happy she was that the war seemed to be over. She also said that Carrie Bonisett had sent a note inviting Julia to an impromptu victory celebration. Julia asked her to send word that she appreciated the invitation but declined.

She went to her room and undressed. She planned to take a bath, but when she sat on the bed, she eased back and fell into the calmest sleep she'd had in months.

In the middle of the night she woke, as she had when the children were babies—when she'd get out of bed and go to the crib before she was consciously aware of the sniffle or whimper that had roused her. She found herself standing in the corner where the crib had once been. There was an armoire there now, and she stood before it, holding on to it, disoriented.

Lawrence was in danger. She knew it as surely as she had ever known anything in her life. She turned on the lights and walked about the room, trying to explain away her fear. She was a rational woman. There was no such thing as a sixth sense. She had no psychic powers. No one did. Her anxiety about Lawrence had dredged up a powerful memory of when he was an infant and had almost died of scarlatina. It was no more than that.

Yet the feeling persisted, ever-present and as undeniable as the fear of being pregnant. It persisted the next day and the day after that, so that late that evening, when she knew Carlotta was in bed, and she went down to the library, she had the sense that she was keeping an appointment.

A little after ten she heard a carriage. Maggie told her that

Senator Togeland was at the door. She hardly heard his apology for having called on her so late, but she noted that he didn't come into the room with his usual cocky stride but advanced cautiously, as though he weren't sure of his footing. He took her by the wrists, and she stared at the freckles on the backs of his hands.

"Julia, it's about Lawrence." She nodded. "He's . . ."

She nodded again, and when he couldn't speak, she said, "He's dead, isn't he?"

"I'm afraid . . . Yes. He's dead."

"When?"

"A few days ago. At the big battle. I took the liberty of sending a telegram to Charles. He'll take the first ship back from England."

She heard herself say, "Thank you for being so kind as to notify him." She felt an implosion, not in her heart but lower, in her belly, an inward bursting, that turned the world dark, made her buckle under its force. "Will you be kind enough to—"

He caught her as she sank to the floor.

George Armister, Lawrence's friend and college roommate, stood at the doors of the house on Poydras Street, his nervousness about the meeting momentarily eclipsed by the size and grandeur of the house. He had come out of a sense of duty sharpened by guilt (after all, he had encouraged Lawrence to enlist), but he dreaded what he knew would take place. There would be tears, perhaps even hysteria. Lawrence always said that his mother was an exceptional woman, but George knew that any woman who'd lost her only son was bound to give way to uncontrolled feminine emotion. He squared his shoulders in the jacket that, since he'd suffered from dysentery, was now too large, and raised the knocker.

Julia Randsome opened the door, introduced herself, and

thanked him for coming with such controlled dignity that his initial impression was that she was very cold. She apologized for the absence of her husband and her mother-in-law, saying that Mr. Randsome was in transit from London and her mother-in-law was indisposed with grief, then ushered him into a sitting room. She offered him food and drink, suggested that the chair directly under the ceiling fan was the coolest place to sit, and did everything she could to put him at his ease. When he put the stained rucksack that contained Lawrence's belongings on the table, she glanced at it only once, then fixed her clear gray eyes on him, taking in his sunken cheeks and jaundiced complexion. "I can see that you are not well, Mr. Armister."

"Touch of fever, ma'am. I'm on the mend now."

"It's very kind of you to have taken the trouble to come to New Orleans. I know you must be eager to rejoin your family. You're from Philadelphia, isn't that what Lawrence told me?"

"Yes, ma'am." It was so humid an atheist would have prayed for a breeze. "I wanted to come. Lawrence asked me to come."

"You mean he asked you because he knew he was dying?"

"No, ma'am. We made a pact when we were in training: if anything happened to either of us, the other would pay his respects to the family."

"I see. Are you sure I can't offer you a lemonade?"

He shook his head. He could see now that she wasn't unfeeling but struggling, successfully, to protect him from any display of emotion that would require his response.

"I would be most appreciative of any information you could give me, Mr. Armister," she said after a pause. "When one knows nothing of the circumstances, one's mind conjures so many things." She had woken from nightmares where she saw Lawrence, screaming with pain, lying deserted on the battlefield. Even in her waking hours the visions persisted—in some he was felled by a single shot, in others he was slashed with a saber or riddled with bullets. "Please speak frankly, Mr. Armister. And please don't try to spare me. I want the truth. Anything you can tell me, no matter how painful, will be a greater help than you can know."

He cleared his throat. "He was wounded in the first action we saw, ma'am. We charged up the hill against their fortifications. We were on foot, and as we crested the hill, the firing began and he was shot in the leg. I was beside him when he went down."

"In the leg?"

"The thigh, really." So close to the groin that they'd made jokes about it, saying that if it had been a few inches higher, it wouldn't have been worth surviving.

"Then how did he . . . ?"

"He died from loss of blood. They removed the bullet that afternoon. He was conscious for quite a while. He died that night around midnight. He spoke of you, ma'am, and his father. But mostly of you."

"So you were with him when he died?"

"Yes, ma'am."

"And he knew that he was dying?"

"I believe so. He was very weak, but he was lucid. I don't believe he was in pain. He was just very weak, and he went to sleep. Peacefully. He . . . went . . . to . . . sleep." That was the bare bones of the story and all he was willing to tell. He had changed a few details, but that was what anyone with a heart would do. In fact, Lawrence had not died from loss of blood, and he had not died that night. He had died several days later of yellow fever and the beginnings of gangrene. Most of the men had died not from their wounds, but from fever or tainted army food; but what place did stomach cramps, teeth-rattling chills, cries for water when there wasn't any water pure enough to drink, and the smell of men lying in their own ordure have in a hero's story? And he hadn't been with Lawrence when he died. He'd been in a cantina swilling rum and looking for an example of the much touted Spanish pulchritude. It was later, when he'd staggered back to the church that was being used as a field hospital and couldn't find Lawrence's pallet, that he'd been told that Lawrence had given up the ghost. He'd found his body on the ground in back of the church, in a long row of the dead who'd been laid out and were waiting to be buried. He'd sobered up enough to claim Lawrence's rucksack and volunteer to dig graves.

"He always spoke so highly and lovingly of you, ma'am," George told her. "Right up to the last." His nose tingled and his eyes watered, and he tilted back his head, swallowing tears.

She handed him her handkerchief as calmly as if she'd been handing him a cup of tea. "Is there anything else you can tell me, Mr. Armister?"

"Only that he was one of the finest men I've ever known. I don't say that because he was your son or my friend. He was . . ." He wiped his eyes and blew his nose, snorting at the irony: he'd been afraid that *she* would lose control! Ashamed that anyone should see him behave in such an unmanly fashion, he got up. "I must be going, Mrs. Randsome."

"You are most welcome to stay with us, Mr. Armister."

"Thank you kindly, but no. I'll be leaving for Philadelphia first thing in the morning."

She couldn't bear to let him go. There were so many things she wanted to ask him. Even if he had no more to add, it would ease her heart to go over the story again. Doing her best to keep any pleading out of her voice, she said, "Perhaps you would like to come up to Lawrence's room with me and see if there's anything of his you would like to keep as a memento." She had gone into Lawrence's room with the intention of packing things up, but the objects themselves, his clothes and books, all seemed to be evidence that he was coming back home.

"No, ma'am. Thank you, ma'am." Lawrence had been given the bullet they'd removed from his leg. He'd said he was going to keep it as a souvenir, and after he'd died, George had searched the floor near the pallet, but apparently it had been swept up and thrown away. "There are a few of his personal effects in here, Mrs. Randsome." He touched Lawrence's rucksack. "He told me he was writing to you, right after they removed the bullet. The letter's in here. It's all sealed up, but I guess he didn't have time to address it." The handkerchief she had given him was drenched. After a moment of indecision he pocketed it.

"Mr. Armister, I am most grateful. Most grateful." Seeing that he was anxious to leave, she got up and offered her hand.

"He acquitted himself with the utmost bravery, ma'am."

"I won't detain you, Mr. Armister. I must tell you again how very kind of you it was to come. You have my deepest gratitude, and I wish you all good fortune in your future life."

Marie was coming through the hall when Julia turned from seeing him out the door. Without being asked, Marie said that Carlotta was asleep. More likely in a brandy-induced stupor, Julia thought, but she almost envied her that. She said that she was not to be disturbed and carried the rucksack up to her room. She had had a rocking chair brought from downstairs and placed near the window and sometimes sat in it for hours at a time. She sank onto it, holding the rucksack in her lap. The clasp was rusted, and she broke a fingernail opening it. There was a belt and holster, a tin cup, a photo of her and Charles, the locket containing a curl of Angelique's hair, a book of architectural principles, and the sealed envelope wrapped in a bit of oilcloth. She opened it slowly. Some of the ink was blurred. The heading read "July 2, 1898, after the Battle of El Caney." The tin cup fell from her lap as she read the salutation:

My dearest Kate,

I am lying on a pallet on the floor of a church. It is very cavelike and gloomy, but I judge by the light coming through the open doors that it is late afternoon. The altar has been moved to the entrance and turned into an operating table. I took my turn on it some hours ago, for I was wounded in the battle this morning.

Do not be alarmed, my dearest one. The bullet has been removed and I've been told that I will soon be moved to the hospital ship *Olivette*. I feel weak, but I have every confidence that I will recover very soon. Truth to tell, I didn't know that I had been hit. I will never have the artistry to describe the battle—one simply cannot describe the confusion and the noise of it—but due to the chaos and the horrendous din, I didn't feel the bullet enter my leg, but continued to charge forward until I buckled and reached down to find my hand wet with blood. What occurred between that and the present moment I can report with only faltering accuracy. It seems that my good friend George was at my side when I went down. I remember cursing when I was put onto the stretcher. Apparently I cried out for my mother. I regained consciousness what must have been hours later as I was lifted onto the altar, then they put a sponge soaked with ether over my nose, and whether from the ether or from shock, I lost consciousness again. The bullet they removed is beside me. We'll keep it as a souvenir. It hardly seems credible that something so small could do so much damage. It almost shattered the femur. I think of you kissing the scar and making it better. At least I know I won't be a peg-leg. If my luck holds, I will return to you hale and hearty.

They have given me some morphine. I'm not in pain, just thirsty and feverish. The lemonish light from the open doors reminds me of an Impressionist painting. I imagine taking you to Paris and showing you all the museums and galleries. My thoughts are full of all the things we will do together.

But let me tell you about the battle. We marched most

of the night in the direction of Santiago de Cuba. We knew that the Spaniards were waiting in the trenches and that the battle would be a decisive one. We sang and talked as we trudged through the jungle and finally made camp, George and I sharing a single strip of rain-soaked canvas. I haven't woken up with such astonishment since first I lay with you. The foliage dripped moisture, and the land had a sour smell.

I went down to the stream, and while I was filling our canteens, I saw General Lawton moving through the underbrush. He had come to the stream as I had, to relieve himself and wash. Though he bears no real resemblance to my father, I thought of my father as I watched him, because it struck me that, despite his experience and his age, he was only a man and must share some of the same thoughts and apprehensions as the rest of us.

It was too damp to light fires, so we had no real breakfast. We formed into lines of march and began to move, George complaining that he wanted coffee. There were plants and tropical flowers, crimson and yellow, and land crabs with leprous blotches. As we approached the Spanish fortifications, we were bound together with a thrilling anticipation. Some older veterans, who've been Indian fighters on the frontier, laughed and spat as we chanted, "Rough, tough, we're the stuff. We want to fight, and we can't get enough. Whoopee!" And Teddy Roosevelt was up front, his spectacles glittering in the sun, looking as happy as a boy on a picnic.

As I said, it is beyond my powers to describe the battle itself, though by the time you receive this, you will already know that it was a great victory. A journalist talked to me (actually woke me up because I'd dozed off) just minutes ago, and told me he has already sent a dispatch describing the battle, though he changed the name of the hill we actually charged, Kettle Hill, to San Juan Hill because he said it sounded more Spanish and romantic! The name isn't important. The important thing is that we have ended four

centuries of Spanish tyranny and brought democracy to the
people of Cuba at last.

As always, my thoughts are with you. You have been at
my side through the training and the voyage and the landing.
Whenever I saw something beautiful, like the scarlet flowers,
I thought of you. I see your face, I gather your hair in my
hands, I kiss your eyelids. I have long pondered what our
future might be. I confess that, after I left, I was ravaged by
a terrible jealousy when I thought of your being with other
men. The feeling was so strong that it almost overpowered
my understanding of the circumstances that brought you to
that terrible life, and I even thought to abandon you. I confess this with great shame, but we agreed that we would
always tell each other the truth no matter how shameful,
and because I know that I will never have such thoughts
again. I will never abandon you. Being close to death has
changed me. I believed I had become a man when we made
love, but now I know that I am truly a man because I understand what is important in life. I saw a little boy, not ten
years old, dead in the field. I hear some two hundred died
in the battle. I don't know how many were wounded. I would
like to block my ears and not hear the groans of the men
lying around me.

I mean to make you my wife, Kate. I am not so sanguine
as to suppose that we could make a life in America. Our
youth, our circumstances, my family, and all society would
be against our love. But a plan begins to form in my mind
that after the war we should come back here. Despite the
land crabs, the torrential rains, heat, and terrible poverty,
the people and the country have great beauty. There is so
much to be done here, and I know that with you by my side
I can and will do great things.

I am very feverish, and thirsty and feel I have been writing
for hours. It is almost too dark to see. Just now, against the
orange light coming from the open doors, I saw the figure
of a woman. She seemed to be offering me something. At

first I thought it was my mother, then I thought it was you. Then I realized that she was too short and thick-bodied to be either you or my mother. I think she is a peasant woman trying to sell something. I feel very weak and the pen keeps slipping from my hand, so I must finish this. My darling girl, I know all will be well. The future belongs to those of us who will seize it with love.

> Devotedly, your future husband,
> Lawrence

A wail of pain tore through the still, humid air. Julia ran from chair to bed, scattering the objects in her lap, and threw herself down, trying to stifle her cries in the pillows. She sobbed and moaned, calling his name.

The door opened, but she was beyond hope or need of control. Marie was standing by the bed. Beatrice Ravenal was with her, breathing hard from climbing the stairs. "Dear Julia," she wheezed, "I don't mean to intrude . . . forgive me. . . . Are you . . . would you like me to go?"

"No. No. Don't leave me." Julia wrenched herself up, clutching at her friend's skirts. Beatrice sat on the bed and pulled Julia's head to her bosom. "It's all right, my dear, it's all right."

"I . . . he . . ." she sputtered, and hiccuped. "It's . . . a letter from Lawrence. His friend . . ."

"Yes. Yes, I know. Marie told me he'd been here."

"A letter . . ."

"Oh, my dear, I'm so glad. At least now you have a final word from him."

She shook her head. Her nose and eyes were streaming. Beatrice produced a handkerchief, wiped her cheeks, and told her to blow. "He died in a church. He bled to death. The letter . . ." Her voice was strangled. "It's not to me. It's to a girl. A girl he was in love with."

"Blow," Beatrice said firmly, putting the handkerchief to her nose.

She did so, then pushed Beatrice's hand aside and wiped her still-streaming nose with her hand. "He . . . he was in love with . . . a girl from the District. . . . You see . . ."

"Yes, yes, my dear, I see."

"I don't . . . I don't even know where to find the girl. I have to find her. He would have wanted me to find . . . He loved her, and I don't . . ."

Beatrice held her, rocking and shushing her, her eyes catching Marie's. "Marie, perhaps you could bring some brandy."

Marie had her hand over her mouth. She brought it down slowly and said, "Mrs. Ravenal, I know where to find that girl. My daughter Sophronia's a cook in the house where she stays."

Though denizens of the District rarely greeted anything with surprise, those few who were on Customhouse Street late the following afternoon—a saloonkeeper supervising the unloading of beer kegs, a laundress carrying a pile of fresh sheets on her head, a boy from the apothecary's delivering an emergency order of headache powders—all stopped and stared when the carriage pulled up to Mollie Q.'s and two society ladies, dressed in black and heavily veiled, alighted. Even Banjo Annie, who was sitting in the gutter cleaning her nails with a silver toothpick she'd filched from a soldier who'd passed out in Anderson's saloon, squinted against the sun and watched as they went up the stairs. One of them was tall and wraithlike and stared straight ahead, the other was a behemoth who had to grip the railing and pause for breath on every other step. The door was opened, and they went inside.

"Ladies," Mollie said in her softest voice.

"I'm Mrs. Ravenal," Beatrice provided, "and this is Mrs. Randsome."

"And I'm—" She almost said Mollie Q. "Mrs. Quinn." The

old black dress she'd taken out of mothballs was so tight she could barely breathe. "I want to express my condolences for the death of your son, Mrs. Randsome. Sure, he was a fine young man. The finest."

"Thank you, Mrs. Quinn." As Julia raised her veil, her eyes rested, ever so briefly, on a statue of a naked nymph—someone had stuck an American flag in the hands that demurely covered its mons—then focused on a potted plant.

Mollie could've kicked herself. She'd been so busy getting herself and Kate ready that she hadn't thought of the host of objects that the ladies would find offensive. "Say, would you like some tea or coffee?"

Julia said, "No, thank you," too firmly and too quickly, and Beatrice, seeing that Mollie's feelings were hurt, said:

"I'd be happy to take coffee with you, Mrs. Quinn, but I believe that Mrs. Randsome . . ." She turned, offering Julia the floor.

Julia patted sweat from her upper lip. The heat and stale smells were so overwhelming that she thought she might swoon. She had never consciously imagined what the inside of a brothel would be like, yet nothing surprised her, except that she was actually standing in one. "I would like to see the young lady."

"Katherine. Sure, she'll be down in a minute. She's not feelin' the best, as you can imagine."

Mollie hailed a Negro girl who was running a feather duster along the banister and told her to get Katherine, then ushered them into the front parlor, where a table had been set with her best china. They all sat down.

"Are y' sure you wouldn't like . . . ? No, I suppose not." She hadn't counted on the presence of the fat one, but she should've realized that respectable women, like nuns, rarely went anywhere alone. "My, it's swelterin' today, isn't' it?" The fat one nodded, but neither spoke, so she plunged in.

"I can't tell you how grateful I am that you sent 'round that note and that you've come, Mrs. Randsome. Y'see, Lawrence had been writin' Katherine regular, and she's been miserable since the letters stopped. We'd heard a rumor that he'd been hurt, but she didn't want to believe it; on the other hand, she didn't believe he'd stop writin' if he was all right. So she's been almost dead with worry." She realized that wasn't a happy choice of words but blundered on. "They were in love, y'see. You know yer son. He wouldn't fall for just anyone. Kate's an exceptional girl. She's not like . . . I mean, she's very sweet and young, and she's only been in town a couple of months. She's an orphan, poor thing, though from what I know of the treatment that was handed out by her father, we can't take that as much of a loss. She was here but a few days when she met Lawrence, and, well, it was his first time here, too, and the minute they set eyes on each other it was love. I swear on m' mother's eyes they were in love." She'd rehearsed what she was going to say, but Julia's impassive gaze so intimidated her that she was getting it all arse backward.

Beatrice raised her eyebrows a fraction. This Mrs. Quinn was laying on the blarney very thick; to hear her talk, you'd think the girl had been found under a rosebush. "I think Mrs. Randsome would just like to speak to . . . is it Kate or Katherine?"

Julia said, "It's Kate."

"Sure, sure. She'll be right down. She's been in such a state she won't come out of her room, and I daren't let her alone with a kitchen knife." Still no reaction. "I know y're a gentlewoman, Mrs. Randsome, an' I hope you'll be gentle with Kate. She's in the family way, y'see." Now she saw a reaction. Julia Randsome looked as though someone had doused her with cold water. Mollie paused, then added, not too obviously but enough to make the point, "She's about two months gone."

It was too much to suppose that she could convince her that Kate was pregnant with Lawrence's child—the woman wasn't so innocent that she couldn't figure out the odds—but since Julia

Randsome was reported to be such a tender-hearted philanthropist, there was at least the chance that she could engage her sympathies enough to pry some cash out of her. She looked from one woman to the other. She guessed they must be very close friends for Julia Randsome to bring this Mrs. Ravenal along, but she knew the fat one wouldn't have the final word. You could tell by looking at Julia Randsome that she was the type who made up her own mind, elseways she wouldn't have been bold enough to come in the first place.

"Are y' sure I can't tempt you to some of these pastries?" she asked, touching the plate.

"No, but perhaps a sherry," Beatrice said, "or better yet, a brandy."

"Ah, sure! I didn't think to ask." Mindful of the strain in the armholes of her dress, Mollie wiggled to the edge of her chair and reached for the little bell she'd torn the house apart to find. She only hoped the maid would remember she was supposed to come when she heard it. "I have some fine Napoleon brandy."

"From Beluche Distributors?"

"As a matter of fact, yes." Mollie smiled, believing she'd found a conversational wedge.

Beatrice grunted. "Paul Beluche is my brother-in-law."

Mollie's smile wilted. She could hardly say that Paul Beluche gave her a discount because he was a sometime customer.

The minutes ticked on. The fat one looked around with open curiosity, but Julia Randsome just stared straight ahead. Mollie had thought that if Julia got high-hat with her, she'd tell her that the Randsomes owned the building and watch her shrivel, but looking at her now, all she felt was sympathy. Sometimes you could tell when a woman had been hit so hard that she would never be young again. She forgot her speech about the fate of the poor little unborn baby. She wanted to say something to comfort her, to tell her that her husband was faithful, and her son had really been a fine young man, that she understood that if husband and son were so fine, it must be because Julia was an exceptional wife and mother.

"You have my deepest sympathy in this, your time of bereavement," she said, but that sounded all wrong, as if she were reading it off a card. "What I mean to say is, my heart goes out to you. Really and truly it does. It's so hard when a young person dies. He had his whole future before him, and a brilliant future it would have been, and . . ." Oh, clumsy as a cow stepping on her own udder. "A young lady of my acquaintance, Agnes by name, died just a few days ago of consumption, so I know how you feel. I pray for her soul, just like I'm going to pray for your son's soul, Mrs. Randsome." Where was that maid? "Mamie! Ah, here she is." Hearing a sound at the door, she turned.

It was Kate.

Beatrice was shocked. She'd expected something pert and saucy, but this girl, her eyes swollen from crying, her hair hanging to her waist, a makeshift mourning band attached to her checkered dress, which showed a bulge around the middle, looked as new as a peeled egg.

Julia stared at the girl with no change of expression and took the letter out of her purse. The girl dropped her head, then raised it, staring back.

Beatrice lumbered to her feet and moved to the door. "Mrs. Quinn, I believe we should leave the ladies alone."

Mollie wanted to oversee the interview and guide Kate's responses, but when Beatrice beckoned, she felt she had no choice but to leave. Where in the hell was she going to put Mrs. Ravenal?

"It's all right," Beatrice said as Mollie came to her side. "I've always wanted to see an establishment such as yours. Won't you show me around, Mrs. Quinn?"

Shaken and surprised, Mollie touched Kate's cheek and gave her a little shove forward as they left. Beatrice closed the door after them.

"Good afternoon, Kate. I'm Julia Randsome."

"Yes, ma'am."

"Please sit down." Kate did so. "As Mrs. Quinn may have told you, I have a letter that rightfully belongs to you." Kate's eyes begged a further explanation. "A friend of Lawrence's came to the house and brought me some of his things. This letter was among them. I realized as soon as I opened it that it was not for me. I must apologize for having read it."

She handed her the envelope. Kate tore the letter from it, began to read, then looked up apologetically. "It's all right," Julia told her. For reasons she didn't completely understand, she had hoped the girl would read the letter in front of her. "Go ahead."

Kate began to read, looking up once to say, "I'm sorry I don't read fast," and later, this time to herself, "He asked me to marry him."

When she finished, she folded the letter, smoothed it, and tried to hand it back, but Julia shook her head. "It's yours."

"Yes, but—"

"No, it's yours." She started to give Kate the details she herself had been so anxious to discover. "Mr. George Armister, Lawrence's friend, said that Lawrence died later that night from loss of blood. He said that . . ." But she saw the girl was totally uninterested in the details.

Kate shook her head and sank to her knees next to Julia's chair. "Thank you, Mrs. Randsome. Oh, thank you. I can't believe you came to see me. I can't believe—"

"Please get up. Don't be offended, but please get up. It's just that I can't bear to see a woman in a submissive position."

Kate didn't understand, but she felt her way back to her chair.

"I can't believe you came. Lawrence told me about you. He said you weren't like other women. He said—"

"You have the advantage of me. I know nothing about you." Her voice sounded supercilious, which wasn't at all what she felt. "How old are you, Kate?"

"Fifteen. Lawrence said you were different, but I didn't think . . . He told me . . ."

"Told you what?"

It had only been on that final night that he'd started to talk about his family. He'd told her he'd wanted to keep families out of it, but now that he knew he loved her, he didn't see how he could. She couldn't tell him that she'd already met his father, so she'd asked lots of questions about his mother. She couldn't remember all the fine phrases he'd used to describe his mother's character, so she said, "That you're from Boston and you like to ride a bicycle, and you tried to teach him to swim at Grand Isle, but you can't really swim yourself."

"I can see that you were very intimate with my son. I mean," she amended, embarrassed, "that you shared an intimacy beyond the physical. I should like to know something about you, Kate. Please tell me about yourself."

Some half an hour later, when Mollie knocked on the door, Julia rose. "Thank you, Mrs. Quinn. Thank you, Kate. I'm happy to have made your acquaintance," Julia said formally, lowering her veil. "Are you ready, Beatrice?"

Beatrice nodded, offered her thanks to Mrs. Quinn, took a long departing look at Kate, and followed Julia to the door. Mollie followed, trying to stop them with condolences and thanks, but they left without another word.

"Did she say anything about money?" Mollie asked as soon as the door was closed.

Kate shot her a look of contemptuous amazement. "She didn't mention it, and I didn't ask."

"Didn't I tell you what to say! Didn't I!"

"She wouldn't go for anything like that. She's a great lady."

"She may very well be, but you're not. How the hell do y' think y're goin' to manage? Have y' no sense a'tall!" It was only with great effort that she stopped herself from mentioning that Kate was taking up valuable space, that the cash Lawrence had left her couldn't hope to cover expenses, so the only thing Kate could do was to have the child and hand it over to the Sisters of Charity. "You had a chance," she hissed, "and you just let it walk out that door!"

"Lawrence asked me to marry him."

Mollie threw back her head and flung out her arms. "And what difference on God's green earth can that possibly make now!"

"You don't understand anything!" Kate cried. "Nothing, nothing." And with that, she spun around and ran up the stairs.

The women rode in silence until they were well out of the District. When Beatrice could contain herself no longer, she asked, "What did you think of the girl?"

Julia took a long time to answer. "I'm going to ask her to come and live with me."

"Oh, Julia, no," Beatrice blurted. The consequences of such an action were so obviously disastrous as to render her temporarily speechless. "Give her some money if you wish. I'll even contribute something to help her, but you can't possibly think of bringing her to live with you."

"Money is what that deplorable Irishwoman was angling for. Giving money is often a way of salving one's conscience and shirking responsibility. How could money alone insure the girl's well-being, let alone that of her child? You saw the conditions she's living in."

"But you can't assume responsibility for—"

"I told you that the Randsomes own property in the District. The girl's wretched state is partly the result of their greed."

"But there are thousands of girls who—"

"Lawrence loved this particular one."

"You have no way of knowing that the child is Lawrence's."

"I am aware of that. But they spent several nights together, so there is more than a possibility that it is. In any case, he loved her, she is pregnant, and she is in need. I believe this is what Lawrence would want me to do."

"Julia, you can't bring her to live with you. Carlotta simply wouldn't permit—"

"Carlotta does not deserve, nor will she ever again receive, any consideration from me. Perhaps it would be best if I took the girl to my parents' home. I've been thinking of going back to Boston for some time now."

"When did you say Charles will be back?" She could only hope that Charles would be able to dissuade Julia.

"In three days. But he plans to leave again almost immediately. The affairs of state are even more demanding than the affairs of business," she added with some bitterness.

"I'm sure he's coming home as fast as he can."

"Yes. But I shan't wait for Charles's decision. I shall write to the girl tonight."

Beatrice mopped her forehead, struggled to remove her glove, and took Julia's hand. "Dear Julia, I must be frank. You are in a state of grief. You know I understand your feelings as only a woman who has lost her son can, but I beg you to reconsider. When one is grieving, it is impossible to think clearly. You know so little about the girl. Taking her is . . ." The words *insane, pigheaded,* and *stupid* rushed through her mind, but she came up with one that had always had particular weight with Julia. "Unreasonable."

"Reasonable people always accept the world as it is," Julia said quietly. "Therefore, all progress depends on unreasonable people. I will do my best to save that girl. To save Kate, and her child."

Waves of August heat shimmered from the pavement, creating the quality of a mirage, and as Charles Randsome was driven toward the house on Poydras Street, he felt as though he were still traveling through unfamiliar territory. Until the death of his son, he'd had no direct experience of suffering. Now it seemed that his former life had been not only charmed, but enclosed in a bubble. A shimmering bubble that had burst. How did one reconstruct a bubble?

As the carriage drew up, Angelique ran down the steps. Dressed in black, she looked like a miniature woman, but she said, "Papa, Papa, I didn't think you were ever coming home," with a childish lisp he hadn't heard for years, and she held up her arms as though wanting him to carry her. He kissed her, took her hand, and walked into the foyer.

Julia was standing, still as a statue, at the foot of the stairs, but when he opened his arms, she came into them. Their embrace was fierce but strangely disembodied, as though they were shipwrecked strangers clinging to the same spar. "You've lost some weight," she said, stepping back and composing herself.

"I don't think so. Perhaps."

"Perhaps not." He wasn't thinner, but there was a gravity in his expression that drew down his features and hollowed his eyes. He opened his mouth to speak but could find no words. Alone in his bereavement, he had believed that no one could feel the loss as he did, but, seeing her, he knew that her pain was perhaps even greater. Given their estrangement, how would it be possible to comfort her?

Angelique asked, "Papa, did you bring me a present?"

"Don't I always?"

"Always?" Angelique repeated dubiously. Since her brother had died and her mother and grandmother had stopped speaking to each other, "always" had lost its meaning. She tugged at his arm. "*Maman*'s waiting in her room, Papa. She's been terribly sick, and she's longing to see you."

Julia turned toward the stairs. He felt he should follow her, but Angelique repeated, "Papa, *Maman*'s waiting."

"Go in and see her," Julia said with what appeared to be genuine unconcern. Then she asked, as politely as if she were a servant, "Shall I unpack your things?"

"If you would. I'll be up directly." As she mounted the stairs, he called after her, "Julia, there's a present for you in the leather pouch where I keep my shaving things."

Steeling himself for what he knew would be a scene, he followed Angelique into Carlotta's darkened room. As soon as she saw him, Carlotta began to whimper, then she pulled him down and he was suffocated by kisses and the cloying smells of perfume and sherry. When he pulled back, her whimperings rose to a wail.

"Thank God you're home. Oh, Charles, I thought I'd never see you again. My dear little boy is dead. Buried in alien ground. You know how I loved him. You know I shall never, never recover from this loss."

She thrashed about, beating the pillow, crying over and over again that she would never get over it. Though he knew she felt genuine grief, he was also aware that, like a child convulsed in a temper tantrum, she derived a perverse satisfaction in acting out the drama. Everything she said about Lawrence related to her: she had lost her only grandson, she was bereft, she was so ill she didn't think she could survive the requiem mass the bishop would say now that Charles had come home. How, he wondered, had he managed to tolerate her selfishness? Indeed, had he actually encouraged it?

When she began to sob that Lawrence's death meant the end
of the Randsome line and that if Charles had married a younger
woman there might be another son, he slid his eyes over to
Angelique and indicated that Carlotta should restrain herself.
"You don't know what that woman has done," she cried. "She
has taken leave of her senses. Just yesterday she brought—"

"That's enough," he said, getting up.

"A man who is not master of his own house, who cannot control
his wife—"

"That's enough," he said more sharply. "I am going up to see
Julia now."

"When you find out . . ." she threatened. As he walked out,
he heard her whimpering for spirits of ammonia.

He found Julia brushing off one of his jackets and hanging it
in the wardrobe. She had sorted his things into piles, one of items
to be laundered, another of things needing repair, just as she
had done a hundred times before. This illusion of normalcy filled
him with gratitude, and wanting to preserve the illusion, he began
to talk as he would have when coming home from any trip. He
mentioned meeting a mutual friend in London, asked about the
servants, said he'd had an uncharacteristic bout of seasickness
during the crossing, all the while thinking that Julia would in-
terrupt him and they would begin to talk about Lawrence's death.
Julia was always the one who introduced discussions of the important things, and he wished with all his heart that she would
do so now, but she kept on, methodically unpacking his things.

"I shall have to go to the office and send some telegrams this
afternoon," he said, picking up his valise. His business concerns
immediately flooded his brain. He had always been rather lack-
adaisical about business, but since Lawrence's death, work had
assumed a great importance. It wasn't just because he was now
involved with truly momentous affairs that would affect the fate
of the nation, but because work was the only thing that kept

depression and a sense of powerlessness at bay. Placing the valise on his desk, he saw a pile of letters bordered in black.

"Notes of condolence," Julia explained. "I've already responded to them, but I thought you might like to see them."

He touched them but couldn't bear to pick them up. His heart thudded, and he felt the constriction in his throat that came when he fought back tears. He cleared his throat. "Carlotta told me that the bishop will say a requiem mass tomorrow."

"Yes. I've arranged for refreshments to be served afterward, but I shall not attend."

He was tempted to say that she might, for the sake of appearances, make the effort, but he did not. "I suppose you've been deluged with callers."

"I've seen very few people."

"I'm sure they understand."

"I don't care if they do or not." The calm with which she said it was more chilling than defiance. "Beatrice has been a great comfort. And Carrie Bonisett, and," she added, almost to herself, "Abraham Davenport has been most kind." At least Abraham had understood that there was nothing to be said. He had sat silently in the parlor with her. She had let him hold her hand. "In some ways he is a man of great sensitivity."

The mention of Abraham Davenport brought to mind their awful parting fight. He didn't want to talk about Abraham Davenport. "Here," he said quickly, opening the pouch in which he kept his shaving gear. "I brought you these ivory combs. I thought you would appreciate the workmanship." He ran his finger over the intricate carving. "I know you like water lilies."

She came to his side. "They're very lovely."

In times gone by he would have put them in her hair, she would have thanked him with a kiss; now he handed them to her and went back to the suitcase. "And there's a music box for Angelique somewhere in here. Did you find it already?"

"I was wondering . . ."

"Yes?" He turned expectantly.

"If you kept the letters Lawrence wrote to you."

"Of course." He found the bundle of letters tied with his favorite cravat and gave them to her. His voice was hoarse. "Julia, I wish with all my heart that I'd been here with you when you received the news. If only I'd been here . . ."

Her shrug was not dismissive, it only implied that his presence would not have made a difference, that nothing would have made a difference. She turned Lawrence's letters over in her hands and sat down. "I've been thinking," she said in a low voice, "that I might go back to Boston for a visit."

"No. You mustn't do that." He had to stop himself from saying that he would forbid it. "How long would you plan to be gone?"

"I don't know. I haven't thought it through yet."

"I don't want you to go."

"I must tell you that I can no longer tolerate being in the same room with Carlotta. And you won't be here. You wrote that you'll be going to Paris almost immediately, didn't you?"

He knew it was unreasonable to ask her to remain during his absence, but the idea of her leaving made him feel that events were once again spinning out of his control. He repeated, "I wish you would reconsider. I don't want you to go."

She bowed her head and looked down at Lawrence's letters. "Lawrence's friend, George Armister, came to the house last week. He brought a letter from Lawrence. It was the last thing he wrote." Charles made a move toward her, but she shook her head. "It wasn't for me. Or for you. It was for the girl he was . . . For the girl. He was in love with her. As a matter of fact, she's upstairs." He stared at her openmouthed. "I went into the District and found her," she went on. "Please sit down and let me explain."

———

When Kate had entered the house, she'd felt like the peasant girl in a fairy story who has finally been brought to the prince's castle. She had never imagined that such riches could be gathered in one place. As Julia had led her out to the garden, where an old Negro woman sat brushing a little girl's hair, she'd taken in the tapestries, paintings, carpets, statues, mirrors, the fireplace that was big enough for a man to stand in.

"Kate, this is Sophronia's mother, Marie," Julia had said. "And this is my daughter, Angelique."

Marie kept brushing Angelique's hair, but her look gave Kate to understand that she knew the whole story. Lawrence's little sister asked, quite boldly, "Is she coming to work here?"

Julia said, "No. She's a friend of mine. She will be staying with us."

Angelique took Kate's measure, decided that even if she weren't a servant, she looked like one, and went back to selecting ribbons for her hair.

Julia ushered Kate through a dining room that was large enough to seat a hundred people. A portrait of a beautiful woman in a ball gown, with a parrot on her wrist, hung above the fireplace. Pausing to look at it, Kate felt a presence, and when she turned, she almost jumped out of her skin. An old woman in a nightdress, her hair elaborately puffed and curled, stood in the door. She bore no resemblance to the woman in the painting, but her ruby necklace and the parrot perched on her wrist were the same. She stared at Kate with such malevolence that Kate was transfixed.

"Kate, this is my mother-in-law, Carlotta de Lesseps Randsome. Carlotta, this is—"

The old woman turned and went back into the room. Julia told Kate to follow her upstairs. Kate wanted to ask if she might see Lawrence's room but didn't dare to ask.

Her fright at the sight of the old woman was forgotten when Julia showed her the bathroom, all pink-veined marble with gleaming brass fixtures and a bed-size tub, and the room in which she was to sleep. Julia brought her books and, at suppertime, carried up a tray and sat with her while she ate.

"For the time being," Julia said, "I think it best for you to remain in your room. I hope you won't feel too confined."

How, Kate wondered, could she feel confined in a room that was larger than the house in which she'd been born? Julia said she would inform her of "our plans" as soon as Mr. Randsome came home. At the mention of Charles, Kate felt sick. What, she'd asked Mollie, would she do when she saw Charles Randsome? What if he recognized her? She would, Mollie had instructed, do absolutely nothing, and, Mollie was sure, Charles Randsome would do the same. Kate had protested that it wasn't that simple.

"I'll tell you what's simple," Mollie had said, capping the argument, "if you don't want your little bastard born in a brothel, you'll go with Julia Randsome."

And, after all, it turned out as Mollie had predicted. Toward evening Julia tapped on Kate's door. Opening it, Kate saw Charles Randsome standing directly behind her. There was no more than a slight widening of his eyes when he recognized her, and when Julia introduced them, his discomfort was no greater than that of any respectable man who had returned home and found a pregnant whore in one of his upstairs bedrooms. He spoke to her very briefly, inquiring if she was comfortable, then told Julia that he would wait in the dining room.

Carlotta took supper in her bedroom. Angelique, Charles, and Julia sat at the dining-room table. Charles ate little and remained silent for most of the meal. When the dessert had been served, he turned to Julia and said, "I've reconsidered the trip you were discussing this afternoon. I think that, under the circumstances, it would be best for you to go."

XVI

. . . full of crooked little streets; but I tell you Boston has opened, and kept open, more turnpikes that lead straight to free thought and free speech than any other city.

Oliver Wendell Holmes

*K*ate lay in the narrow bed in what had once been Julia's brother's room and thought, Please God, don't let it be six o'clock yet. The room was still so gloomy that she could barely make out its spartan furnishings, but she could hear the cook's heavy tread as she came down from her attic room, so she knew it was six o'clock. She must get up. One did not lie abed at the Ridgeways'. One slept and ate because these were functions needed to recharge and refuel the body, not because sleeping and eating were pleasurable in and of themselves. She must get up and wash and dress and tend to the baby, because in half an hour, before the fire had had time to take the chill from the dining room, the Ridgeways would be sitting down to breakfast, and not even Emily Ridgeway, whose hands were crippled with arthritis, would complain about the cold. Emily might complain about imperialism or backward politicians or conditions in the city's slums, but she would not complain about a minor personal misery like being cold.

Kate pulled the quilt up to her chin and closed her eyes. The day stretched before her in tedious detail. She knew that after they had bowed their heads and thanked Providence for the porridge, toast, and tea, the Ridgeways would begin to talk, briskly and reasonably, as though sleep had been only an interruption of the previous night's conversation. Joshua Ridgeway, an eighty-year-old with a shock of white hair and the vitality of a man twenty years his junior, would read the paper, calling their attention to items of interest. His particular interest was the continuing war in the Philippines. He was outraged that the United States had now turned its force against the native insurgents it had ostensibly set out to liberate. Emily Ridgeway, who managed to look straight-backed despite a dowager's hump and who covered her hair with a cap even when she was in the house, would discuss the day's plans with Julia. Joshua would leave for his office, and, weather permitting, Kate and Julia would visit the library or walk in the park. When they returned to the house, Julia would help Emily with her correspondence, or they would visit the settlement house they were helping Dr. Lockman to establish, and Kate would come back up to the room to care for the baby.

I must get up, she told herself, but she burrowed deeper into the bed.

She knew no one would chastise her if she were late to breakfast, but the looks of concern would be worse than a reprimand. She didn't want to disappoint Julia. Julia had done everything in her power to save her. And she couldn't disappoint the Ridgeways. They had taken her in as few respectable people would have done, and she wanted to conform to their rules and routines. She didn't know if Julia had told them that she had been a whore or that she and Lawrence had been lovers, but she almost believed that the old couple would have helped her if she'd simply knocked on their door and said she was in trouble. The Ridgeways "acted on principle," and, she supposed, people who acted on principle were by nature somewhat distant in personal relations. They never pried into her past. The only things they questioned her about were her opinions and beliefs, and even in that she felt she disappointed them because she didn't have any opinions or beliefs, at least not any she could express. But there was no question that she owed them a debt she could never repay, and her feeling of gratitude was especially strong toward old Emily Ridgeway.

She had always thought that Julia would be the one who would be with her when her time came to deliver the baby, but on her second day of labor, in this very room, when she'd writhed and screamed obscenities, Julia had become so upset that Emily had ordered her out of the room. It had been Emily who had gripped her hand and told her to push while Dr. Lockman, a stocky woman who was a frequent visitor in the house, had pulled a head that felt the size of a football from her. And it had been Emily who had helped her to a chair, sponged her body, packed the towel between her legs, helped her into a clean nightdress, and changed the sheets. And when she'd sobbed and said she didn't want to see or hold the baby, that she just wanted to die, it had been Emily who'd said "I know" as if she'd meant it.

With tremendous effort she threw back the covers, tucked her hands into her armpits to keep them warm, and went to the crib. The baby, a girl, had been born two months ago, just before Christmas, and a sprig of holly tied with a bit of red ribbon still decorated its crib. She'd hoped it would be a boy, because a boy would have reminded her of Lawrence and a boy would have an easier life. She sensed that Julia would also have preferred a boy, though, as usual, she couldn't read Julia's feelings. But the old couple's acceptance of the child was complete. Emily rocked and cuddled it and knitted it dresses and caps, and when Joshua held it, his voice, which usually sounded as though he were reading an editorial, softened to gurgles and coos. Kate had wanted to call the baby Mollie but knew that wouldn't sit right with Julia. Emily had suggested Christabel, which was the name of a young Englishwoman whose family championed women's rights, so Christabel it was. A Unitarian minister, also a frequent guest, had performed a ceremony in the sitting room to welcome the child into the world, and a letter had come from London, from Miss Christabel Pankhurst, saying she was pleased to have another "little crusader" as her namesake.

Shivering, Kate bent over the crib. Mother love was supposed to be the strongest human emotion, and sometimes, mostly when Christabel was sleeping, she did feel a powerful love. She could hardly believe that anything so perfect had come out of her. But the baby's crying drove her mad, its throw-up and dirty napkins made her gag, and when it gummed her nipple, she felt a confusion of arousal and disgust. Emily told her that new mothers were often melancholy, but in her heart of hearts she knew that the natural maternal impulse hadn't shown itself in her because she was a whore. She picked up the baby, struggled to pull the quilt around her shoulders without dropping her, unbuttoned her nightdress, and gave Christabel her breast.

A drizzly rain was falling. It would turn the snowbanks into slush, so that meant they wouldn't be going out for the usual morning walk. She'd be a prisoner in the house for the whole day, and Julia or Emily would find some task, like addressing envelopes or helping the cook, to keep her busy. Perhaps she could sneak up to her room and read. The Ridgeways thought reading was a worthy occupation. Most of the books they gave her were difficult and boring, but she'd discovered that with some effort she could read and enjoy Shakespeare. He wrote about things a regular person could understand, like love and betrayal, murder and plotting, and there were even risqué jokes.

Sometimes, to her delight, she recognized things she'd heard Billy Shakespeare quote. *Romeo and Juliet* was her favorite. "Spread thy closed curtain, love performing night! That rude day's eyes may wink and Romeo leap to these arms, untalked of and unseen." That was how she'd felt when she was waiting for Lawrence. If only the baby had been Lawrence's, maybe she would have loved it more. If only she could have been like Juliet and had the courage to kill herself when Lawrence had died. She decided that she would plead a headache this afternoon and come up to the room and read the play again, but then she remembered that she couldn't escape to her room because a meeting was scheduled and some famous old suffragists were coming to speak.

People, mostly women but occasionally like-minded men, were always dropping by the house, and every Tuesday there was a regular meeting of the National American Woman Suffrage Association. Last week one of the women had brought a cartoon from the newspaper. It showed a group of fierce, cigar-smoking feminists dressed like men; they had a puny-looking man on a leash, and the man was carrying a baby. It had made the women very angry, but she just thought it was silly because it was so wide of the mark. None of the women who came to the meetings were anything like that. As far as she could see, the only characteristics they shared were that they were educated, generally dressed more plainly than their finances would allow, and were far too ladylike to smoke. Most were married. A few, like Dr. Lockman, were spinsters, and a smaller contingent was in pairs. She could tell they were "married," but the other women were either too innocent to see or too polite to acknowledge that the couples were anything more than best friends. All the women talked tirelessly and endlessly about politics and books. They exchanged pamphlets and letters from women in other states and foreign countries. They discussed tactics and strategies about changing laws and improving education and getting the vote. They listened to each other more seriously than she'd ever heard women listen to each other, but, for all their plotting and planning, she didn't think they understood much. How could they expect men to give up their privileges and treat them as equals? Men didn't care what women thought. Lawrence had been the only man who'd ever listened to her, and that was only because he was in love with her. And she couldn't see why it was so important to get the vote anyway. Politicians would always do what they liked once they were elected, and no one would ever elect a woman, no matter how smart she was.

The discussions about the vote and settlement houses and divorce and property laws were bad enough, but once she'd had to sit through a discussion about prostitution. All agreed that prostitutes were victims of men's depravity, though some were so naive that they thought girls were actually drugged and shanghaied by white-slave traffickers. Some said that if prostitution were legalized, the girls would at least be checked for disease and given some protection, but others said that legalization would only help it to spread. It was generally agreed that if there were a more just and equitable economic order and women could find decent work, they would never stoop to such an evil. One of the more outspoken women had talked about "free love" and predicted that the day would come when women would have the same right to express bodily love as men. That had caused a real furor. Some said that sexual desire was against woman's nature, others argued that free love would only lead to greater exploitation of women, and that radicals like that shocking Emma Goldman, who preached it, harmed the cause of women's rights. Besides, who would take responsibility for babies? Neither Kate nor Julia had said anything. Kate thought that all of it and none of it was true. These women couldn't imagine a girl like Agnes, who actually preferred it to any other work she could have hoped to get, or girls who were poor, simpleminded, addicted, or just greedy. They didn't understand that there would be a demand for it as long as there were armies or any groups of men without women, or that most men, and even some women, liked quick, illicit coupling without any social obligations. She believed that it would always exist, that hell would freeze over before a man would be prosecuted for it, that it would always be seen as the woman's sin.

She yawned, moved her feet to keep the circulation going, and changed Christabel to her other breast. The sun was struggling, unsuccessfully, to break through the clouds. How she hated Boston. Everything in Boston was brown and gray, gloomy and cold.

She thought about Mollie's. They'd all be going to sleep about now, and when they got up in the afternoon there'd be Sophronia's wonderful breakfast—café au lait, cinnamon buns, spicy sausage, ham and eggs and grits—and the girls would wobble down from their rooms, cranky and defenseless, still recovering from the previous night, but at least they wouldn't have to pretend that they were brisk and proper and eager to face another day. She wondered what had happened to her magnolia satin dress. Mollie had said, rightly, that there wouldn't be any use for it here, so probably some other girl had it by now.

As Christabel stopped suckling and she moved her into position to burp her, Kate realized she was singing ever so softly, "Oh, dem golden slippers! Oh, dem golden slippers! Golden slippers I'ze gwine to wear, because dey look so neat!" She missed the music even more than she missed the long baths or the food or the pretty clothes. At Christmas, carolers had come to the door, and once, when the Ridgeways had people for dinner, one of the guests had played the piano and they'd all sat, hands folded, ankles crossed, politely appreciative. Well, you couldn't imagine them clapping their hands or swinging their hips, or wailing about being so sad they could die or having the itch for someone. Not in Boston. She felt so miserable she even missed Monkey. She decided to crawl back into bed, just for another five minutes. She settled Christabel in the crook of her arm and stroked her head, crooning, "Golden slippers I'ze gwine to wear to walk de golden street."

Ever since she'd been a child, Julia had slept soundly and woken up smartly, mind instantly alert, body eager to move. Now she slept only fitfully, and when she woke, she had to make a conscious effort to get up. But get up she did, on this morning as on every other morning. Here in her parents' home there was a routine, and she was grateful for it. Routine sometimes gave the illusion of purpose.

She shook herself like a wet dog and went to the window, glancing at the letter from Beatrice that lay on her desk but resisting the temptation to reread it. She opened the window, hoping that the shock of air would stimulate her; but the air wasn't bracing, it was just bone-chilling damp. What a long winter it had been. Every drop in temperature seemed like a personal insult, every snowstorm a conspiracy. And this morning it was drizzling rain. That meant she wouldn't be able to take Kate out for a walk. But, she reminded herself, there was a meeting this afternoon, so she wouldn't have to worry about inventing activities to keep Kate occupied. Since both Miss Anthony and Mrs. Cady Stanton were to be guests of honor, there was bound to be a large turnout.

She shut the window, touched her toes a hundred times, and made her bed. She dressed and brushed her hair . . . ninety-eight, ninety-nine, one hundred times. Counting seemed to calm her, as did writing in her diary, balancing the household accounts, or doing algebraic equations.

She twisted her hair into a rope, pinned it to the top of her head, and fixed a cameo to the throat of her dress. Hearing her parents on the stairs, she thought she would go and help Kate with Christabel. She had never been sentimentally fond of babies, indeed she had trouble feeling much affection for children until they began to talk, but she felt a deep fondness for Christabel, perhaps because the little mite had been born into such unhappy circumstances. But she decided against going to Kate's room. Kate might think she was nagging her to get up. And seeing how unhappy Kate was always made her feel powerless.

With the wisdom of hindsight she saw how rash she'd been in taking on responsibility for Kate and the baby. She also saw that her motives had not been altogether pure. She had wanted to show Carlotta and Charles that she would do the right thing, and she'd wanted a reason to get away from New Orleans herself. On the other hand, she couldn't have left the girl in a brothel or let her farm out the baby to an orphanage, not when there was even the possibility that it might be Lawrence's child. But now she had to help Kate start a new life, to find some work that would give her a sense of purpose and provide her with some money of her own. There was no question that the girl was bright, but she'd gone no further than the fifth grade, and now that she was a mother, there was no possibility of her returning to school. Employment as a servant or in a factory or a shop was the only possibility open to her. Such jobs would pay no more than a pittance. Dr. Lockman had suggested that Kate and Christabel come live at the settlement house, where she would train Kate as a nurse, but Julia had her doubts about that. Dr. Lockman would be a stern taskmaster, and the atmosphere of the settlement house might be oppressive to a girl who didn't have a real calling for the work.

It was such a heavy problem that whenever she thought of it she actually felt weighed down. She began to pace. She must

resist the terrible depression that had sucked her down after
Lawrence's death. She must think clearly and decide on a course
of action, not just for Kate, but for herself. She picked up Beatrice's letter and carried it to the window.

February 14, 1899

Dearest Friend:

How happy I was to receive your latest correspondence
and to hear that the child is thriving and your beloved parents
are well. Your description of the park after the snow was
lovely. I am not, however, writing about the weather. I have
been sitting here, pen in hand, wondering how to approach
an unpleasant topic, and I see there is nothing for it but to
plunge in.

Impossible as it may seem, some extraordinary gossip
about you has been circulating. I heard it from Carrie Bonisett, though its source is our own town crier, Phillipa Cotrane. Not content with fobbing off dubious members of
European aristocracy on gullible New Orleanians, Phillipa
took her latest lapdog, Sir Harry, on a tour of our major
cities. Apparently, she was in Boston and saw you in a park,
wheeling a baby carriage. She claims that she hid behind a
tree to make sure that it was you, and having determined
that it was, she was too taken aback to approach you. She
has now returned and has been spreading the most viperous
rumors. To wit, that during one of Charles's many absences
you took a lover, conceived a child, and ran away to Boston
to hide your shame. That you are the least likely of all the
women we know to indulge in an illicit affair means little.
You have always been, dear Aardvark, an outsider, and you
must understand that a woman who holds unpopular beliefs
is suspect, particularly in her private life. The fact that you
spoke in favor of the single standard has now been twisted
into claims that you are in favor of free love. The men who
have been put forth as your possible paramours would make

you laugh. Because you publicly showed that you like him, poor, bumbling Abraham Davenport has been mentioned; because you publicly showed that you *didn't* like him, Leonce Lambre is also a candidate. Of course, it is all preposterous, but foolish people will believe things simply *because* they are preposterous. Naturally, Carrie doesn't believe any of it, though your sudden and unexplained departure and the fact that you have remained away for almost six months baffles her. She is so deeply concerned that I was almost tempted to tell her the truth, though you know that I would never betray your secrets.

I make it a point not to give advice unless it is solicited, and even then I take no pleasure in meddling, but I must tell you that I believe you should come home, not just to put a stop to the rumors, but because it will be best for you. I saw Charles at one of the Dewitts' tiresome dinners. He told me he is about to go to Panama. He did not look well. Yvette Liscomb was fawning over him in the most tasteless fashion. When he was asked about you, he maintained that you were staying in Boston due to your mother's ill health. I think that a brief absence can make the heart grow fonder, but a woman who leaves her husband alone for too long is tempting fate.

Think, dear Julia, what your future will be like if you continue this separation. I can understand your reluctance, nay, revulsion, at the prospect of having to live with Carlotta again, but even Carlotta is not immortal. I wouldn't have the slightest scruple in hastening her demise if only I could find a reliable voodoo woman. Perhaps you could convince Charles to let you have a house of your own. That would set tongues wagging but would at least be an improvement on the current gossip of desertion, bastardy, and impending divorce. Please consider it.

Mardi Gras is almost upon us, and there's the usual mad flurry of preparation. I hear that Carlotta, who has claimed to be too ill to rise from her bed, is planning a ball. Also, you'll be amazed to hear that Lucretia Asbury has taken up the banner for women's suffrage. This can hardly be explained as a change of mind or even a change of heart, since Lucretia lacks both; rather, it is Judge Asbury's idea. As you know, the legislature has passed the "grandfather clause," which restricts the right to vote to men whose grandfathers were voters in 1867, and thereby effectively disenfranchises Negro men. Apparently, the good judge thinks that if white, conservative women got the vote, their numbers would offset any future threats by the Negroes. Sad to say, he's probably right.

Again, forgive my meddling, but surely now that Kate has delivered the child and your parents have so lovingly accepted it, she could stay with them in Boston and you could come home. I know you don't think of New Orleans as home, but since it is your husband's home, it must be yours. I confess that I also write from selfish motives: I haven't had a stimulating conversation since you left.

I remain always,
Your devoted Hippo

No, Julia thought, refolding the letter carefully, I don't think of New Orleans as home, but I don't think of Boston as home, either. Perhaps she was doomed to be "the only animal of its kind in the zoo," always longing for the place where she wasn't. It had been naive to suppose that she, a middle-aged, married woman, could slip back into the life she'd known here as a girl. She loved and admired her parents more than ever, but she couldn't help but think that they were a bit too rigid and austere. Why should they content themselves with such unappetizing food? Why had they looked disapprovingly (though they'd never said a word) at her purchase of the matching fur hat and muff? Why did they think that going to the theater was frivolous? Granted, it was comforting to be surrounded by people of good-

will and like mind, but she had no friend here who was as close
to her as Beatrice, and she missed a host of things, many of
which—the smell of honeysuckle, the sound of Negro voices,
spicy food, and good wine—she hadn't even been consciously
fond of. She felt guilty at having left Angelique alone for so long,
though she knew Angelique was well cared for and was even
grateful for her absence. Mostly she missed Charles. She'd believed that her love had been snuffed out forever, but it wasn't
true. She thought of him constantly. She rarely woke, and never
went to bed, without thinking of him, and throughout the day
memories of how he said this or how he would see that flooded
her; she longed for his company and his touch.

She opened the desk drawer and took out the pile of his letters.
They had come from New Orleans, New York, Washington, and
Paris. She had read and reread them, finding nuances and hidden
meanings, even though she knew that Charles was nothing if not
straightforward. The tone of the letters had changed from apologies to expressions of love. In his last letter he had sounded
impatient, all but ordering her to return. He had also said that
he was thinking of running for Congress. The thought that he
wanted her back because the scandal of their living apart might
interfere with his ambitions had crossed her mind. She knew
such suspicion was unworthy of her—Charles was not the sort
of man who lived his life for mere social advantage—but she also
knew that, now, she would always question and suspect his motives. That worm was in the apple for good.

And yet, as Beatrice had pointed out, what would her life be
if she didn't go back? Her own mother had counseled her to
return. She'd told Emily that her marriage was foundering, and
she'd told her about Kate and Lawrence, but she hadn't told her
about the District properties or how badly Carlotta had treated
her. She believed she'd withheld that information because it
would upset Emily, but she now saw that she hadn't told her

because at the back of her mind she'd always thought she would go back to New Orleans. Charles was her husband. She might never trust him again, but she still loved him.

She made up her mind that she would speak with Dr. Lockman that afternoon and arrange something for Kate. And then she would write and tell Charles that she was coming.

Despite the rainy weather, it was the largest gathering Kate had ever seen in the house. The sliding doors between the sitting and dining rooms had been pushed back to make one big room, the furniture had been moved, and extra chairs had been brought from every corner of the house, but it was still so crowded that many women were left standing. There was a pervasive smell of wet wool, occasionally relieved by a whiff of lavender or rosewater, and the mood was one of controlled excitement. Kate stood behind the refreshment table pouring tea and moving her head to see the guests of honor. Miss Susan B. Anthony and Mrs. Elizabeth Cady Stanton were famous, Julia had told her, throughout the world. They had been friends and comrades for over fifty years, but they were "like two old generals who've fought many battles together but no longer agree on how to fight the war." Miss Anthony was still singularly committed to getting the vote, but Mrs. Stanton no longer believed that the vote would appreciably change women's lives. Mrs. Stanton now thought that real change could be achieved only when the influence of organized religion had been destroyed.

Judging by her appearance, Kate found it hard to believe that Mrs. Stanton thought, let alone wrote, such things. She was a pillow-shaped woman with a decidedly maternal air, natural enough since she was the mother of seven. She wore a fashionable garnet-and-gray-striped silk dress, and her hair was bunched in clusters of white curls on either side of her benign and fleshy face. When Kate handed her her tea, she smiled and said, "Oh, aren't you pretty. Two lumps, please."

Miss Anthony was a spinster and looked it. She was tall, angular, and wore a plain brown dress, and her sparse hair was drawn tightly into a bun. Her eyes had the look of a schoolmarm's whose patience was about to reach its limit. She came up to the refreshment table with Dr. Lockman, saying, "No, the fight will continue to be more difficult here in the East. The frontier, by its nature, lessens the differences between the sexes. Women and men have to work together in order to survive, so men are more likely to accept women as equals." Kate poured Dr. Lockman's tea but didn't look at her. Dr. Lockman's presence always intimidated her, partly because the doctor had such a brusque way of talking, partly because Kate remembered shrieking all those obscenities while she was in labor.

Emily touched Miss Anthony's arm and suggested that they call the meeting to order. Miss Anthony said, "Let Elizabeth speak first," but Mrs. Stanton, who was comfortably settled in an armchair, said, "No, Susan, you're the president of the association now. Please, let's hear from you."

All conversation hushed as Miss Anthony took her place at the front of the room. "Friends and fellow citizens," she began. She pulled down her cuffs and pushed her spectacles more firmly onto the bridge of her nose. "The Declaration of Independence, the United States Constitution, the constitutions of the several states, all alike propose to protect the people in the exercise of their God-given rights. But how can the consent of the governed be given if the right to vote be denied?"

Kate felt her way to a chair. She had never thought of it that way before; in fact, she hadn't thought of it at all, but what the old woman was saying did make sense.

"It was 'we, the people'—not 'we, the white male citizens,' but we, the whole people—who formed the Union. It is a downright mockery to talk to women of their enjoyment of the blessings of liberty while they are denied the only means of securing them provided by this democratic-republican government—the ballot. Discrimination against any class on account of color, race, nativity, sex, property, or culture can only embitter and disaffect that class, and thereby endanger the safety of the whole people. Clearly, then, the government . . ."

How brave she was, Kate thought. How sure of herself in every way. She exhorted, she reasoned, pausing to make sure her point had been taken, at one juncture staring directly at Kate and giving her a quick nod of recognition when she saw that Kate understood. It was as though Kate had seen an orange and couldn't think of what to call it, and Miss Anthony had said "That's an orange" and she didn't feel stupid anymore. And the pleasure was heightened because she knew that all the women in the room were sharing the same thoughts and feelings. Miss Anthony talked about dignity and freedom and working together for the common good. Kate had never worked for a common good, but she thought it must be a fine feeling. She caught the eye of another woman, and the woman smiled and she felt that, after all, she did have something in common with her, with all of them. She began to feel that she wanted the vote; she wanted dignity and fair treatment. She felt expansive and energized, as though she were taking deep breaths for the first time, and when Miss Anthony concluded, her voice reverberating with quiet but forceful conviction—"Nothing can stand in our way. We shall prevail"—Kate was one of the first on her feet, clapping until her hands tingled.

"I see Miss Anthony has impressed you," Emily said when the applause had died down and the women had begun to talk and circulate.

"Oh, yes," Kate answered, "she was"—she almost said

"damned good" but changed it—"enlightening." She wanted to tell Julia how much she'd enjoyed the speech, but Julia was standing in the alcove, engaged in what appeared to be a private conversation with Dr. Lockman, so Kate went into the kitchen to fetch more tea.

"Did you hear the speech?" she asked the kitchen maid.

"Part of it," the girl said. "My priest says it's not good for a girl to listen to that sort of thing."

"I think it's best," Kate countered, feeling very mature, "to listen to everything and to keep an open mind."

"But y' notice," the girl went on, putting another kettle on the stove, "that there's never any men at these meetings."

"There is sometimes. Besides, women can say things when men aren't around that they wouldn't say in front of them. Look, I'll finish up inside, then I'll collect the dishes and help you wash them." Determined to make her point, she added, "Women should help one another."

"Sure, it's women's work, i'n't it?" the girl snapped. "An' any girl who don't know that is never likely to find herself a husband." She gave Kate a look that said she knew Kate would never find one in any case, that she knew all about her and her bastard baby.

Kate turned away and busied herself with the cups. The girl was ignorant, but she was right. Even if she met a man, how would she explain Christabel? She was "damaged goods"; no respectable man would ever want her.

She went back into the dining room and moved among the women, asking if they'd like more tea. The rain had started again, and since most were reluctant to leave, it provided an excuse to linger. She wanted to tell Miss Anthony what an honor it had been to meet her, but she felt too shy. She ran upstairs to check on Christabel, and when she came down, some fifteen minutes later, the rain had stopped, Miss Anthony had already gone, and most of the women were in the hall, gathering up their umbrellas and cloaks, kissing each other good-bye. Only a handful remained, Mrs. Stanton among them. She sat on an armchair, engaged in conversation with a few intimates, and, catching Kate's eye, indicated that she should join them. Gathering her skirts around her, Kate pulled up a footstool. A woman in a maroon dress was saying that she took great comfort in the Bible and didn't understand Mrs. Stanton's objection to it.

"As a work of literature, it may have some merit," Mrs. Stanton replied, "but how can one take comfort in a book that teaches that woman brought sin into the world and is responsible for the fall of the human race?" Kate nodded and Mrs. Stanton smiled, encouraging her to speak.

"I once heard a minister say," Kate faltered, remembering the time she'd gone to church with Gertie and Herbie, "that all women are daughters of Eve. That we're all tainted with sin."

"And did you remain in his congregation?" Mrs. Stanton asked.

"No. I haven't been to church since," Kate replied, wondering what the women would say if they knew where she had been since.

Mrs. Stanton laughed. "I see we have a rebel in our midst." She turned back to the woman in maroon. "The Bible also says that man shall rule over his wife. It promotes servitude, not love. And, you'll remember, Southerners often used the Bible to justify slavery."

"But," the woman countered, "our cause is already so unpopular. If we attack religion—"

"Not attack," Mrs. Stanton corrected. "Question."

A woman with a heart-shaped face said, "But Eve was cursed, at least in part, because of her curiosity."

The discussion went on until they were the only ones left in the room. "Perhaps," Mrs. Stanton concluded, her eyes twinkling, "we should confine our reading of the Bible to the Song of Solomon. I'm very fond of that because my husband used to quote it when he was courting me. 'I have compared you, my love, to my filly among Pharaoh's chariots.'" She chuckled. "Well, that was many years ago. I'm no filly now." As she got up, she smiled at Kate again and said, "It's always good to see a fresh face. And such a pretty one."

When everyone had gone, Kate moved around the room, stacking dishes. She felt buoyed up with hope. What did it matter what the kitchen maid had said? The kitchen maid was ignorant, but educated women treated her with respect. Mrs. Stanton was such a large-spirited woman; she might accept her even if she knew about her past. As she walked to the kitchen, Julia came in from the hall, where she'd been saying good-bye to the last of the guests. "When we've finished straightening up, Kate, I'd like you to come to my room," she said. "There's something I want to talk to you about."

They sat in Julia's room, Julia at her desk, Kate on the only other chair. Julia said, "You look very well today, Kate."

"Because I feel well," Kate answered. She never tried to pretend, because Julia could see through any pretense, so it felt good to be honestly cheerful, as she knew Julia wanted her to be. "I was very gloomy when I woke up this morning," she confessed, "but meeting the ladies, particularly Mrs. Stanton, picked me right up. And it was a great honor to hear Miss Anthony speak."

"I'm glad you enjoyed it. The first time I met Miss Anthony I was about your age and, I confess, I found her rather formidable. But now I understand what she's been through . . ."

"What has she been through?" Kate wanted to know.

"Well, she and Mrs. Stanton have been struggling for the vote for over forty years."

"Forty years." Kate opened her eyes wide. "My mother didn't even live that long."

"Miss Anthony has been scoffed at, arrested, spat upon, vilified in every conceivable way. She's a woman of great courage."

"Besides which," Kate asserted, "she's right."

Julia smiled more warmly than she'd smiled in months. "Yes, Kate. She is right."

"Oh, Mrs. Randsome," Kate said in a gush, "I'm so very grateful to you. If it hadn't been for you—"

"I've told you to call me Julia."

"Julia," Kate said as warmly as a child would say "circus" or "taffy apple." Julia smiled again, and Kate felt approval shining on her like springtime sun.

"Let's talk about you, Kate," Julia said. "I've been thinking about your future, wondering what you might do to put your talents to use. Dr. Lockman has come up with a possible solution. She thinks it might be a good idea for you to come and work with her at the settlement house. She knows what a bright girl you are, and she could train you as a nurse. Would you like that?"

"I don't know," Kate faltered. But she did know. She wouldn't like it a bit; in fact, she would hate it.

"Just turn it over in your mind, Kate. Let me know what you think. I believe it would be a fine opportunity for you. You would learn something useful that would ultimately provide you with a means of support. And you'd be helping others. That's always a source of satisfaction."

Kate got up. "I'd better go and see to Christabel."

"Would you like me to watch her for a while? You did so much work and were so helpful this afternoon. Perhaps you'd like a little rest before supper."

"No, I'm all right."

"You're a fine girl, Kate. Life doesn't always treat us fairly, but if we are resolute and persevere, we can overcome." She put her arms around her and held her close, resting Kate's head on her shoulder, then, embarrassed by the surge of emotion, she held her at arm's length and smiled. "I'm going downstairs to talk to Cook about supper. I don't think it would be excessive if we had both Indian pudding and mince pie for dessert, do you?"

Kate ran to her room and threw herself on the bed. She was cursed. Whenever she thought things were going right, it was a sure sign that they were about to go wrong. She could never be a nurse. She hated sickness and death. When her mother and grandfather were dying, all she wanted to do was run away, and when Agnes had started to spit up blood, it had only frightened and disgusted her, even though Agnes had been her friend. And she hated being around poor people. She had visited the settlement house only once, but she knew she would rather die than work there. Everything about it repulsed her —the bare walls, the dormitory with the rows of iron beds, the women, all widowed or deserted—lank-haired, swollen-bellied, missing teeth, their eyes either pleading or conniving—and their nose-leaking, lice-infested children, and the dispensary reeking of disinfectant, and the big institutional cooking pots belching smells of cabbage and soup bones. Julia said that helping the poor was a source of contentment, but anyone who'd been poor knew that it was like an infectious disease. And she hated Dr. Lockman's square hands and the way she began sentences with "Now tell me . . ." when she already knew the answer. And she knew that even though Dr. Lockman treated her well when Julia was around, she secretly looked down on her, thought she was scum.

But how could she disappoint Julia? Julia was Lawrence's mother, and she'd done so much for her. If she told Julia that she didn't want to study with Dr. Lockman, Julia would think she was weak, lazy, ungrateful. She knew Julia wouldn't force her to go, but what other choices did she have? Either she worked at the settlement house and took care of charity cases or she stayed on at the Ridgeways', a charity case herself. And no matter how kind the Ridgeways were, she couldn't stay indefinitely. She wasn't a member of the family, but she wasn't a servant, either. She was useless, a freeloader. She would never fit in, never be able to earn her keep, let alone that of her child. A life of loneliness and dependency stretched before her like an endless tunnel. She would never wear pretty dresses again, or dance, or meet men.

"Oh, Mollie," she sobbed into the pillow. "What shall I do?" But she already knew what she would do.

She pulled herself up and went to the drawer where she kept her underwear. There, tucked in the pair of silk bloomers she'd brought from Mollie's, was the money she'd kept hidden all these months. A hundred and two dollars—all that was left from what Lawrence had given her after she'd paid room and board at Mollie's and bought a suitcase, two respectable dresses, and a pair of boots. One hundred and two dollars. Surely that would be enough to get her back to New Orleans, but what if it wasn't? It crossed her mind that she might steal something. But she couldn't do that to the Ridgeways. She might be a whore, but she wasn't a thief.

Christabel started to whimper. She picked her up, whispering, "Don't cry, Mama's here." As the words hit her, she began to cry herself. She had done some terrible things in her life, but nothing as terrible as this. Abandoning her child was the worst thing a woman could do, the one unforgivable thing.

The baby squalled louder. "Please don't cry," she begged, holding it tighter, pacing the room as its wails reached a deafening crescendo. "Shut up! *Please!*"

With horror she realized she was rocking her daughter so violently that she'd frightened her. She opened her arms, dropping her onto the bed. The shock silenced the infant momentarily. Kate stood, sick with self-loathing, thinking, I'm not fit to be a mother. Even if I had the money, I'm not fit. As the baby began to sputter and wail, she lay down next to it, murmuring,

"I'm sorry. I'm sorry," pulling it to her, unbuttoning her dress, giving Christabel her breast, trying to soothe her. "They'll take care of you better'n I could. I wouldn't go if I didn't know that," she told her, her hand trembling as she stroked her small head. Calm, suckling, the baby stared into her eyes. When she said "I do love you; what I'm doing is for the best," the infant almost seemed to understand.

That night Kate hardly slept, and the next morning her nerves were so raw that she jumped when she heard the cook's tread on the stairs. It might be days before the opportunity for escape presented itself, but she would have to stay alert and be ready to go when it did.

The chance came that very morning. Emily did not come down to breakfast. Joshua said she was feeling poorly, and Julia said she would stay and care for her if Kate wouldn't mind going for a walk alone.

"But I know how much you like your exercise," Kate said. "Why don't I stay and you go?"

But Julia demurred, and Kate ate her porridge, feeling as though she were swallowing gobs of cement. She excused herself while Joshua was reading the editorials and went to her room. She put on an extra pair of bloomers and tucked the money into her bodice, then went to the Ridgeways' bedroom, ostensibly to find out how Emily was feeling, but really to say good-bye.

Joshua sat on the edge of the bed, holding Emily's hand. "Just a touch of pleurisy," Emily told her, but she could see that the old woman was pale and struggling for breath. She looked for some opening in the conversation where she could say thank you but said nothing because she was afraid she would start crying.

Julia was waiting at the front door with the baby in her arms. "It's such a nice day I thought you might take Christabel, too."

She put the baby in her carriage, tucked the blankets tightly around her, and told Kate to be sure the canopy was positioned so Christabel wouldn't get sun in her eyes. "Oh, Kate, look at this lovely day!" Julia exclaimed as she opened the door. "Everything's been washed clean. It's fairly sparkling. I wish I were coming with you."

Because she couldn't bear to look her in the face, Kate pretended to squint at the sun. The morning was dazzling, the air brisk and fresh. She walked once around the park, then came back to the house and left the carriage on the sidewalk while she went down the steps to the tradesmen's entrance to peek in the window and make sure no one was in the kitchen. Easing the carriage down the steps and moving it to the alcove near the door, she bent down for one quick, furtive kiss. She looked around, then hurried down the street. At the end of the block she began to run, and when she saw a hansom, she hailed it, breathlessly telling the driver to take her to the train station.

With the instinctive feeling for effect that would never again desert her, she told both the ticket seller and the conductor that she was going to the funeral of an aunt who'd died unexpectedly. She'd barely had time to situate herself on a corner seat before the stationmaster yelled, " 'Board!" She was sweating, but she pulled her cape tighter around her chest, because she hadn't given Christabel her morning feeding and her breasts were leaking. She hoped they wouldn't stain the front of her dress before she could go to the ladies' room and tear up her handkerchief to make pads for her nipples. She wondered if they'd found Christabel's carriage yet and how Julia would feel once she understood that she'd gone. She should have left a note, but there hadn't been time. Besides, what could she have said? The train lurched forward, and all guilt was momentarily swept away by the excitement of having escaped.

As they trundled through the outer suburbs, a suave-looking man at the end of the carriage lowered his newspaper and glanced at her, then raised it with such conscious absorption that she knew he had taken her in. It didn't matter that she was dressed like the daughter of a proper bourgeois: he could tell. She wondered how long it would be before he approached her.

By the time they'd reached the outskirts of Worcester, they'd exchanged enough looks to have an understanding. He moved up the aisle and swept off his hat. "May I sit down?"

XVII

Rags were royal raiment
When worn for virtue's sake,
But diamonds were moving briskly, too.

Heywood Hale Broun

It was early afternoon when she finally arrived at Mollie's. The street was as quiet as she'd expected it to be and dirtier than she'd remembered. She had to knock a long time before Judas flung back the door, scratching at the armpit of his long johns. His face went from surly to pleased but registered little surprise. "You're back," he said after a yawn. "Guess you wanna see Mollie. Wait in the front parlor an' I'll wake her."

Judas's knock on Mollie's door was followed by a predictable aria of curses, then Mollie came into the parlor, pushing back her rat's-nest hair, sputtering, "Oh, my God . . . oh, my God, Katie. What a surprise! What in the name of heaven . . ." She pulled Kate to her. "Oh, my God, I never thought to see you again." And fond as she was of Kate, part of her had hoped she never would. "What are you doin' here? Tell me what—"

"Ever been to Boston?" Kate said as though she were telling a joke.

"Sure, I told you that's where I landed when I first come over. Haven't seen it since I was knee-high to a duck."

"Well, don't bother to go back. It's one dead town."

"But tell me—"

Kate cut her off. "I wanted to see you."

"Now isn't that grand." But nobody came back to the District for old times' sake. A host of questions bubbled up, but Kate's expression was as bold and resistant as that of a criminal who'd been caught red-handed, so Mollie knew this wasn't the time to ask. "It's grand to see you, too. Just grand. This calls for a celebration. Pop us a champagne cork, will y', Judas? Turn, turn, around, girl. Let me get a look at you." She took in Kate's peacock-blue redingote, beaver toque, high-button shoes, and kid gloves. "You look like the cat who got the cream! And you've grown up so much. You look like a real lady. Where'd you get the dress?"

"New York."

"So you been to New York, too?"

"I met a man on the train, and I went to New York with him for a coupla weeks. He was a gambler. He wanted me to stay with him." And she'd thought she might, until he'd started introducing her to his friends and hinting that her favors might be offered in lieu of his debts. She'd stolen fifty dollars from him, gotten herself a hotel room, and hunted for legitimate work until she'd seen that it was hopeless. She'd gone to see some of the great buildings Lawrence had told her about, then the money had run out and there was nowhere else to come but here. "I left him a note," she went on casually. "I told him, 'You're a gambler; I'm not.'"

"You were smart to leave," Mollie agreed, knowing there was more to the story. "Gamblers ain't a reliable source of income. So take off yer hat and stay a while. Sure, you're a sight for sore eyes."

"Oh, Mollie, I've missed you so much." It would have been stretching the truth to say that Mollie looked well. New clusters of broken capillaries brightened her doughy cheeks, and there was more gray in her hair and a glob of egg yolk on her nightdress. "I've been thinking about you for so long, wondering how you are, how everybody is."

Mollie flopped down on the sofa and patted the place next to her. "Oh, me. I'm the same as ever, only worse. Business has been steady. Not so good as during the war, but steady. And let's see . . ." She took the champagne from Judas and told him to go back to bed. "Let's see. Silt—the old professor—he's gone. He got sweet on some gal who does a sister act in a darkie vaudeville show—think he's sweet on the sister, too. Anyhow, he left town with them, so that left me without a professor, and you know a high-class house has got to have music, so against my better judgment I let that damned Monkey come in. Oh, you wouldn't recognize him. A regular King Midas he is. He's bought himself a suit and spats and a gold watch. Bein' as how he's so young and ugly, the customers think he's a novelty and give him big tips. He's makin' more'n some of the girls, but they all still treat him like a pet. A pet python, I say." She took a long swallow. "That silly bitch Bertha's crazy in love with him. Vivian Lefevre found out about it and she beat Bertha up an' kicked her out. Bertha wanted me to take her in, but I wouldn't take the risk. Not with Vivian still leavin' dead cats on my doorstep and puttin' the gris-gris on me so's I can't get a decent night's sleep. So Bertha got herself a room up near Congo Square. She says Monkey's keepin' her, but I know it's the other way round. He's pimpin' for her, sure as God made little apples. And what else . . . well, the ceiling in the little back room is fallin' down again. And one of Lena Friedman's girls went berserk and bit part of another girl's finger off. And Rose is gone. Went to visit her cousin in Chicago and never come back. She had someone

write me a letter sayin' she's workin' at the Everleigh Club."
Mollie snorted. "Hell, I know those Everleigh sisters from when
they spelt their name E-v-e-r-l-y. They're up to all kinds of tricks,
trying to get a reputation as the fanciest sportin' house in the
country. Rose says they let loose a box of live butterflies in the
parlor. Imagine tryin' to impress the customers by wastin' money
on bugs! Well, it's like Billy says, good taste is where the cost
don't show."

Kate brightened. "Oh, Billy. How's Billy Shakespeare? I
thought about him all the time."

"Sad to say, he's gone, too. Company of actors came through
town, and when they offered him a part, he took off like a scalded
cat. Prob'ly woulda gone if they'd offered to let him sweep the
stage. You know actors are worse than whores, they never get
out of the life. Sez he'll some back when the tour's finished, but
y' never know."

"That's too bad." Kate stared into her glass as though it were
a crystal ball. "I wanted to see him."

"Well, think how I feel. Apart from missing the pleasure of
his company, the books are in a terrible mess."

"And Sophronia?"

"Sure, she's still here. Regular as a hundred-dollar timepiece,
God bless her. And I got a coupla new girls. One—Conchita—
can't talk English too good. She's from some bordertown in Mex-
ico, but we say she's from Cuba 'cause of the war. Makes the old
coots who stayed at home feel like they were in on the fightin'."
She knew she'd put her foot in it by mentioning the war. "Say,
are you hungry? Sophronia'll be in any time now. What I mean
to say is"—and now it was Mollie who stared into her glass—
"are you wantin' to stay and go back to work?"

"If you'll have me."

"If I'll have you? Kate, I always told you you were sittin' on
a gold mine. 'Course I'll have you, it's just . . . what I mean to

say is . . . I'm sorry it didn't work out. I was hoping that when you went off with Mrs. Randsome . . ."

"It wasn't her fault. She's the finest woman I've ever known. I—I just didn't fit in. Guess I'm not cut out for the respectable life."

"Was it a boy or a girl?" Mollie asked gently.

"A girl. Christabel."

"Now isn't that a pretty name."

"I'd just as soon you didn't mention it again."

"Sure, sure. I understand. It's best to put the things we can't change behind us. Think of the future, that's what I always say. When I get low, I think about my cottage in Dingle Bay, about smelling the ocean and the new-mown hay and . . ."

It was as familiar as a bedtime story, and suddenly Kate felt very tired. She listened up to the description of the imaginary garden, then said that if Mollie didn't mind, she'd like to take a nap.

"Sure, sure. Go on into my bed. I'll see about fixing up a room for you. Can't get your old one back. Zoe took that territory soon's you left. I'll find something. My sheets is clean. My sheets is always clean. Haven't seen Sean Hanratty for—well, God knows how long. Can't tell if that makes me glad or sad, but in my case"—she laughed—"it's a change of life for sure. And Katie . . ." She kissed Kate's cheek. "Welcome back."

Kate felt a hand on her shoulder and woke to see Sophronia standing near the bed. "Sophronia. I'm so glad to see you."

"Bet you be just as glad to see the biscuits an' sausage I'm cookin'. Here, have some coffee."

She handed Kate a cup. The coffee was hot and rich and sweet, and after a long, delicious swallow, Kate asked, "How's your mother?"

"She be fine. You don't have to be so polite askin' 'bout Mama.

I knows you want to know what's goin' on over there, but I want to know what's goin' on in Boston. I hear Miz Julia's mama's serious ill. You know that 'fore you runned away?" Kate shook her head. "Miz Julia want Angelique to come be with her, but Mr. Charles won't let the child go. Think he's holdin' her 'cause he's thinkin' it'll bring Miz Julia back. She wantin' to come back?"

"I don't know."

"An' you prob'ly wouldn't tell if you did, 'cause you lie like a snake."

"I'm sorry I lied to you about taking your herbs and that pill, Sophronia. I just couldn't do it."

"I 'spect you'll outgrow it. Only a few born liars, rest jus' doin' it 'cause they cain't figure out what to say. You tell Miz Julia you was leavin'?" She could tell by Kate's face, which had an expression not so much of guilt as of failure, that she hadn't. "I sure hope she come back soon," Sophronia went on. "Mama thinks it's such a shame, me workin' in sportin' houses, but it way better'n that place on Poydras Street. That crazy ol' woman an' her parrot runnin' things now. House always be in a uproar. No man like his house in a uproar. Miz Julia don't come home soon, Mr. Charles'll find some woman to straighten it out fo' him." Feeling someone behind her, she turned. Monkey and Bertha were at the door.

Monkey said, "Well, I'll be jiggered if it ain't Kate."

"What you doin' here so early?" Sophronia demanded.

"Piano tuner's comin' 'round."

"Don't expect no free breakfast," Sophronia warned as she pushed past them.

"We come 'cause we knew you was here," Bertha said, smiling as widely as her puffy, bruised lip would allow.

"How'd you know?"

"News travels fast in the District." She was still wearing the hat, now bedraggled, that Kate had delivered to Vivian Lefevre's.

"Judas told the maid, the maid run into Eulalie Echo at the French market, and I met Eulalie—"

"She don't need chapter and verse," Monkey cut her off.

"Guess you didn't make out up north, huh?" Bertha said with satisfaction.

Her arm was looped through Monkey's, and he shrugged it off, grumbling, "Why you always hangin' on a body?"

"I wasn't hangin'!"

"Like a damn leech." He smoothed the lapels of his jacket.

"I was just—"

"Well, don't. Go in the kitchen an' get me somethin' to eat."

"I wanna talk to Kate."

"Y' can talk to Kate anytime. She ain't goin' nowhere."

Kate could tell this was a typical refrain—Bertha begging, Monkey bullying. She guessed that Monkey had given Bertha the fat lip. "Both of you go. I'm taking a nap."

"Scat!" Monkey ordered, and Bertha did as she was told. He looked at Kate with the same longing and resentment Bertha had when she looked at him. "Seems like you been gone a long time." He tilted his straw boater over one eye and strutted around like a bantam rooster, showing off his striped trousers and gold watch. "Reckon you heard I been doin' pretty good. Pretty damned good."

"You look like you belong to an organ grinder."

"Yeah? Well, I guess you wouldn't've dragged your tail back here if J. Pierpont Morgan had proposed. One of these nights I just might come up with your price."

"You'll never be that rich, Monkey. Go away and shut the door."

"You heard her," Sophronia said as she came in with a tray. "Get yo' sorry self outta here."

"I don' take orders from no woman, 'specially no woman black as shoe polish." He swiped a biscuit and left.

Sophronia set the tray on Kate's lap. "Special treatment fo' today only. Tomorra you comes to the kitchen like usual. Don't be layin' in the bed the whole day. Prob'ly Miz Julia try to teach you discipline an' that why you runned away. I'm not raggin' on you. I know what it's like to be livin' in somebody else's house, but you gotta take yo'self in hand, Kate. Otherwise you end up like that pitiful Bertha, always lookin' fo' someone to treat her bad jus' so she know she alive. How you like that sausage?"

"You're the best cook in the whole world, Sophronia."

"You get rich, you stake me to a restaurant." Sophronia watched, satisfied, as Kate mopped up the gravy with a biscuit, then, hearing the girls coming downstairs, she left.

Kate put the tray onto the floor and rolled onto her side. Whenever she lay in that position, she imagined Christabel next to her, but she knew she would never see Christabel again. Thinking about Christabel would only make her miserable, just as listening to Sophronia talk about the Randsomes made her miserable. She had to put all that behind her, or she could never go on. She'd forbid Sophronia to ever mention the Randsomes again.

Pulling a pillow to her breast, she heard Bertha's shrill voice calling good-bye. Poor Bertha had deteriorated faster than her hat.

Kate saw herself, hatbox in hand, following Monkey into the District for the first time. It seemed as far away as her very first memory, of hanging on her mother's skirts while her mother bent over the washtub. She remembered Monkey buying her a waffle and how happy she'd felt being out of doors. Monkey had said that the District was like flypaper, that once you got stuck, you pulled and pulled but you never got free. She hadn't understood what that meant then, but she did now.

She'd once told herself that she'd be a whore for only a little while, but now she was trapped, just like the rest of them. It was fine for Julia and those Boston women to talk about dignity, but how could you have dignity if you didn't have money? But that wasn't the whole truth, either.

She sat up in bed, trying to puzzle it out. Money alone couldn't give you dignity. There were rich people who were no better than whores, and people like Shakespeare who had dignity, even though they were poor. She remembered Emily reading to her from Mr. Emerson's essay on self-reliance: every man must take himself for better, for worse, and till in that plot of ground which is given to him to till. Emily said that "man" meant woman, too, though Kate didn't see how that could be, and she was sure Mr. Emerson hadn't had whores in mind. Still, she understood, as Julia would say, "the principle of the thing." If the District was to be her plot, she would have to learn how to till it. She mustn't get stuck like some damned little fly and end up drinking, or crazy, or a slave to cocaine, always dreaming about a future that wouldn't come true. Shakespeare said that the difference between a whore and a courtesan was discipline. She'd have to get discipline. She'd promised Lawrence that she would get out, but until now she'd never promised herself. By God, she would get out. She just didn't know how or when.

Spring turned to summer and summer to fall. Kate marked the passage of time not by the seasons, but by counting the money she'd earned. She kept it in a small metal box under her bed, and counting it became her greatest pleasure. She worked hard, and the cash mounted up. She knew how real ladies looked and acted, and her successful mimicry of their behavior earned her the nickname "Ice Princess." "You couldn't find a finer specimen at a debutante ball of New York's Four Hundred," Mollie bragged. Downstairs she was the perfect picture of the debutante; upstairs she coolly perfected her technique, so that the time between the closing and reopening of the bedroom door was cut to a minimum. Customers often felt outfoxed, but that only increased her desirability. She was unique, not just because of her looks, but because, unlike the other girls, she never bothered to fake desire. Men began to make bets to see who could thaw her, but that was one of the few games where a woman had the advantage. On those very rare occasions when a man aroused her, she didn't let it show.

The core of dignity, she began to understand, was to make your own rules. You never explained them, but you never disobeyed them. One of her rules was that she wouldn't take an overnighter. At first Mollie said she'd kick her out if she didn't conform, but Kate stuck to her guns—no customer could pay her enough to sleep with him. When she went to sleep, she thought of Lawrence. Another rule was that she wouldn't take Leonce Lambre. He came sniffing around as soon as he heard she was back and doubled and tripled her price, but she still refused. On New Year's Eve she wouldn't take anyone at all. She joined in the celebration, but when midnight came, she went up to her room and toasted in the new century all by herself.

The other girls thought she was uppity, and she kept their resentment at bay by loaning them things and listening to their problems, but she didn't bother to correct them when they said she thought she was better than they were, because secretly she believed she was. For one thing, now she had a life of the mind, whereas they thought a whore who read books was as odd as a dog who could sing. Julia had taught her that books were not just an escape, they were salvation. Tales of adventure and travel books were her favorites, transporting her to Paris, darkest Africa, Samarkand. She also knew she was smarter than the other girls when it came to money, which was even more important. She helped Mollie order supplies and balance the books, partly because she was interested in business, partly because Mollie was drinking so much that she was forgetful, and Kate wanted to make sure she was getting the full percentage of her earnings. She didn't drink or snort her money, didn't buy the tacky trinkets that were peddled from house to house, and when customers gave her gifts of jewelry, she always pawned them.

Still, she never saved as much as she'd planned to. Apart from the investment she had to make to keep up her appearance for the customers, she developed a weakness for fine things that were exclusively for her own consumption. She had a conservative dress and hat made, so that when she walked out on her day off, she looked like a proper lady. At first she was too nervous to venture beyond the French Quarter, then she began to move among the shops on the periphery of the District. Once she looked in the window at Madame Destault's, and the Spider, not recognizing her, gave her a fawning smile. That gave her the courage to go even farther afield. After all, there were no border guards, and if you knew how to dress and act, you could "pass" without too much risk. She went to bookshops, apothecaries, and dressmakers. She could no more resist buying books than Mollie could resist buying soap or decorations for the house. She also bought bath salts, perfume, imported chocolates, a bottle of Napoleon brandy, and a wildly expensive kimono embroidered with yellow, white, and orange chrysanthemums, which she wore only when she was alone. She would slip into it after the last customer had gone, pour herself a tot of brandy, and read her books, isolating herself in blissful solitude.

Almost a year had gone by when Shakespeare came back, penniless. He said he'd left the theater for good. He was too old to put up with flea-infested hotels, drafty dressing rooms, inedible food, fellow thespians who had reached the outer limits of sanity, and a manager who had the gall to censor the Bard. He got back his old job at the Versailles, and occasionally, on his day off, he accompanied Kate on her forays. Sometimes he played her grandfather, at other times her uncle. He said her performances were better than Sarah Bernhardt's, that she might have been an actress, though her features were not bold enough to have an impact beyond the footlights and her diction was too poor, a failing that he tried constantly to correct.

Occasionally a man wanted to take her as his mistress, and as summer dragged into fall, she had an offer to which she gave serious consideration. A Mr. Gershon, who claimed to own half of Detroit, wanted to take her away. Mollie checked out his bona fides and found that he *did* own half of Detroit, and Kate was tempted. He was an unprepossessing man, physically unremarkable except for an unusual growth of hair—no more than a mouselike fuzz on his head, but dark tufts sprouting from his ears and nose. His appearance wasn't the obstacle—she was long past any consideration of how men looked and could put her mind elsewhere during the act—but he was jealous and crushingly possessive. He didn't even want her to sit downstairs with the other girls, he quizzed Mollie about everything she did, and he made jokes about putting her under lock and key. "You can't be a bird in a gilded cage," Shakespeare advised. "You're like one of those New Women, much too independent." Her independence, she wanted to point out, was no more than an act, but her fear of being in a strange city, literally under lock and key, was too much of a risk, so she turned Mr. Gershon down.

The only other event that stood out from the petty pace of her nights was the appearance of Frank Staughton. One night, as she started to go into the front parlor, she heard a laugh that stopped her in her tracks. Staughton had backed Ida into a corner and was regaling her with a story of how he'd just made a big sale. Kate went straight to Judas.

"That man in the corner—the one with the reddish hair—kick him out." Judas's "Why?" was stopped by her steely look. "Twenty dollars for you, and I'll square it with Mollie, just kick—him—out."

Judas obliged. She waited at the top of the stairs, straining to hear Staughton's protest, disappointed when Judas's threats of violence didn't materialize and Frank, with whining objections and demands to see the madam, slunk away.

Later she dug her fingernails into a customer's back. He took it for passion till he saw her eyes, then he finished up fast, buttoned up his trousers even faster, and told her she was sick in the head. After he'd gone, she spread her savings on the bed and counted it twice.

"I earn more'n you ever will, Frank Staughton," she muttered. She swigged straight from her bottle of brandy. When she'd finished almost half of it, she wondered how much it would cost to have him killed. Then she passed out.

XVIII

Best friend, my well spring in the wilderness!
George Eliot

"$\mathcal{I}$f Muhammad won't come to the mountain, then the mountain must come to Muhammad. Arrive Boston, Tuesday the 25th, 11:45 A.M. train. Love, your Hippo."

Beatrice blotted what she had written, turned to her companion, Grace, who had just come into the room, and said, "If you've finished the packing, will you be kind enough to take this to the telegraph office?" Seeing the dubious look on Grace's face, she added, "Believe me, this is the best way to proceed. If I wrote and asked if we should come, Julia would only say that the journey would be too much for me."

Grace said, "I'm afraid it might be."

"And so am I. Nevertheless, we're going."

Beatrice pulled herself up from her desk and retied the sash of her dressing gown. "The worst of it will be having to lace myself into those abominable corsets. Oh, my flesh feels like lava that has flowed over a doomed city." During the last years it had become a chore to leave the house, but when Julia had written that Charles was suing for divorce, Beatrice had known that she must go to her. "Go and fetch your hat, Grace. And come back in before you leave."

She lit a little cigar and strolled out onto the gallery. It seemed only yesterday that she and Julia had sat here together, though it had been nearly two and a half years. At the time, she would never have believed that Julia and Charles's marriage would break apart. Sometimes there was an inexplicable downward spiraling of events that the wisest soul could neither predict nor change. Her mind went back to the War Between the States—her vain hope that it could be averted, her even vainer hope that the South would see a speedy victory, the years of struggle, the final humiliating defeat. Julia had suffered a similar downward spiral —her discovery of the District properties and subsequent estrangement from Charles; the terrible shock of Lawrence's death; the girl, Kate, in whom she'd placed so much affection and trust, running off. Even when that had happened, Beatrice had still hoped that Julia would leave Kate's child with her parents, return to New Orleans, and patch things up with Charles. But fate had conspired against her yet again: her mother, Emily, had fallen ill. Julia had nursed her until she'd died, then, as was often the case with devoted, long-married couples, her father, Joshua, had succumbed, and Julia had been left with the sole responsibility for Christabel. And now Charles was asking for a divorce.

It was useless to speculate how, at any of these turning points, Julia might have acted differently. She felt Julia had been foolish in taking Kate on, but since she'd done it with the best intentions, Beatrice couldn't bring herself to find fault with her.

But she could, and did, find fault with Charles. She had known him all his life and had always been extremely fond of him. In many respects she still thought him a fine man, but it seemed that when the chips were down, he was an emotional coward. At every turning point he had failed to act. Why, she wondered, hadn't he sold the District properties as soon as Julia found out about them? He might have lost money, but money didn't mean that much to Charles. He wasn't a greedy man. Of course, he would have had hell to pay with Carlotta, and standing up to Carlotta had never been easy for him. But she didn't really think that was it. No, Julia's discovery had destroyed the comfortable blanket of half-truths and compromises they'd woven over the years. It had roused the struggle for dominance that slumbered in even the happiest of marriages. Julia had shamed him, and people were rarely shamed into doing the right thing. Charles might support Julia's independence in theory, but he didn't propose to have her tell him what to do.

But if Charles had wanted to assert himself, why hadn't he tried to stop Julia from taking the girl and leaving New Orleans? The fact that he had so quickly given his consent was still a mystery to her. And, at the very least, she thought he should have gone to Julia when her parents had died. Julia had seemed to accept his excuse of "pressing affairs of state," but that only showed that she was still in love with him.

"Poppycock!" Beatrice muttered, puffing on her cigar. "Pressing affairs of state" had been invented to keep men from the messes of birth and death. It wasn't as though Charles were commander in chief of the nation, though over the last years he had shown an ambitious drive that hadn't formerly been evident. If only he and Julia had shared the loving trust they'd once enjoyed, they might have comforted one another when Lawrence had died. Instead, they'd moved farther apart, Julia turning inward while Charles tried to escape his pain by focusing on the larger world. The last time she had seen him, she'd been amazed at the change in him.

Some six months ago, hearing that he was in town, she'd accepted an invitation to one of Mrs. Asbury's garden parties, thinking he might be there. She'd sat, sweltering under one of the green-and-white-striped tents on the Asburys' lawn, sipping lemonade until she'd felt her bladder would burst, feigning laryngitis so she wouldn't have to participate in any of the tiresome conversations. At last, just when she'd whispered to Grace that she would like to leave, Charles had made his entrance.

In the old days she would never have thought of Charles as making an entrance—his presence in a crowd had been felt gradually, like the sun breaking through clouds. Now his arrival burst with a sudden brilliance. He had always been an important man in the city, but now he was an "Important Man," capital letters, connected to the most powerful lobbyists and the biggest financiers in New York and Paris. As he strode across the lawn, handsome in his white suit—energetic, obviously harried—people surged toward him. He moved through them, smiling, greeting, shaking hands with his old easy charm, then stopped near the tent where she was sitting, waved away a lemonade, accepted a bourbon, and stood, legs apart, joking with the men who clustered around him. After tossing off his drink, he wiped his mouth, turned to Senator Togeland, and got down to business with Yankee alacrity. She overheard him say, "No, Senator, Cornelius Vanderbilt's old Nicaragua crossing won't work for us."

Senator Togeland protested, "But the Nicaragua site would only require a sixteen-mile channel cut across dry land, so the cost—"

"No," Charles insisted, "Panama is, without question, the most desirable site."

Even his voice sounded different, filled with an aggressive emphasis that brooked no disagreement. He went on, making his point while the men nodded, his eyes scanning the crowd and coming to rest on her. "I'm sure that by the time the vote comes up, Senator, you'll see the wisdom of my argument. And now, if you'll excuse me, there's an old friend I must speak to."

He came to her side, kissed her hand, and asked if he might sit down. His manner was intense but hesitant, reminding her of the way young gallants had acted toward her when she was a girl; but she knew it was because she was Julia's friend. "I've been having a little difficulty convincing Senator Togeland about the merits of my argument," he said, taking a seat.

"Senator Togeland isn't worth the powder it would take to blow him up, though I expect his vote will cost you a bit more than that."

He laughed. "Beatrice, it's always a pleasure to see you."

They danced around the preliminaries—his travels, her health, the weather—until she turned him to more personal concerns by asking, "And how is Angelique?"

"Thriving. At least, I think she is. I only arrived yesterday morning, so I haven't spent much time with her yet."

"Julia misses her so. I know she was hoping you'd send her up to Boston."

"I was planning to, but, under the circumstances . . . Julia's parents . . ." he foundered. "I thought Julia had her hands full."

"She certainly did. But Joshua's been dead for several months now."

His face, already florid from heat and drink, became even redder. "I'd planned to go up to Boston myself, but something always intervenes. You can't imagine how busy I've been."

"I think I can," she agreed, but her look said she'd known him since he was a boy and his excuses wouldn't wash with her.

"I know I've been remiss, but you must know that I've written countless times asking her to come back."

"Yes, I know that." She also knew that he wrote less frequently and that he'd suggested that Julia leave Christabel in Boston, which Julia was not prepared to do. "Correspondence is all very fine, but for a man and woman it has its limitations. I feel sure that if you saw one another face to face—"

"Charles Randsome! Wherever have you been?" Yvette Liscomb descended on them in a billow of pink flounces. "I swear, you're like the Flying Dutchman! Carlotta told me you were coming home, but I said I didn't think you knew where New Orleans was anymore." She smiled prettily, twirling her sunshade, but Beatrice detected a note of genuine upset beneath her affected peevishness. Perhaps she really is in love with him, Beatrice thought. Certainly his newfound celebrity, which would only have embarrassed Julia, made him even more desirable in Yvette's eyes. "When did you arrive?" Yvette asked.

"Just last night," Charles lied.

"I should hope so. Otherwise, I should have expected you to call. Then again, I'm afraid you've forgotten your old friends. You've surely forgotten your manners. You haven't even greeted Lucretia, and she is your hostess." Yvette held out her hand. "Do come and say hello to her, Charles."

Beatrice couldn't tell if he was irritated or relieved by the interruption. He got up and bowed to her again. "Beatrice, if you'll excuse me. Perhaps we could continue this discussion at another time. May I call on you?"

"Of course you may. I shall look forward to it." She watched as they moved through the crowd, Yvette's face turned up to his. Surely Charles couldn't be so changed as to be seduced by the likes of Yvette Liscomb. But Charles was a lusty man, and deprivation often obscured good judgment. If a woman was separated from a man she loved, her desire might lapse into quiescence—this, she was sure, was true for Julia—but the same was rarely true of a man. She wondered, with a sick feeling, if it wasn't already too late. Perhaps things had already spun out of control; perhaps Charles had already formed another alliance. Some lines from Ecclesiastes (the only book of the Bible she could tolerate) floated into her mind, and she muttered, " 'To every thing there is a season, and a time to every purpose under the heaven.' " What if the time for Julia and Charles had passed?

"Did you say something?" asked Grace, who had drifted to her side.

"Yes," Beatrice answered, "I said I'd like to be taken to the commode."

As Grace pulled the chain, handed Beatrice her cane, and rearranged her skirts (ah, the indignities of old age!), Beatrice decided that it was imperative that she speak to Charles again that day. But when she returned to the garden, she saw that he'd been captured by another group of admirers.

A week passed, then two. She gave up hope that he would call even before she heard that he had left the city. Why, she chastised herself, had she told Charles that things could be mended if only he looked into Julia's face? No man, let alone one who was daily showered with adoration, wanted to look in the face of a woman who had made him feel shame.

In the six months that followed their meeting in the Asburys' garden, she had seen him only once, briefly and quite by accident. Just two weeks ago he had literally bumped into her on the banquette outside the Ringrose Emporium. He'd reached to steady her, apologizing before he realized that it was she, then said, "Good God, Beatrice!" and became even more flustered, spewing out a string of explanations—he'd just gotten off the train, hadn't been home yet, had forgotten to buy Angelique a present so had come by the Emporium—he'd held out a package as evidence—had to get home, late already, they were waiting for him. He would definitely call on her. She could tell he couldn't wait to get away from her. She'd said she'd look forward to seeing him, but even as she'd watched his retreating back, she'd known he wouldn't call. There was something about his demeanor—he wasn't just embarrassed and harried, he was downright guilty. She hadn't fully understood why until, a few days later, she'd received Julia's letter telling her that he had asked for a divorce.

Much as she dreaded the prospect, she decided that she would go to the house on Poydras Street. She had no clear idea what she could accomplish, she only felt that she must go there before she wrote to Julia. She sent round a note and received one in reply: Carlotta would be *à la maison* on Thursday afternoon and would be happy to receive her.

Grace helped her to the door, then returned to wait in the carriage. A servant she didn't recognize took her through the dining room, which was in a state of chaos, into Carlotta's bedroom. The sun shone through the closed windows, exposing the bloom of dust on the mirrors and tabletops and making the room insufferably stuffy. Carlotta was propped up amid the pillows. She was perfectly groomed but somehow looked disheveled, her shoulders hunched in her lace peignoir. Angelique, still in her nightclothes, sat at the vanity examining a powder puff.

"Dear Beatrice," Carlotta cried, "how very kind of you to come. Don't be alarmed to find me in bed. I'm not really sick. . . ."

"I know," Beatrice said.

"We're just recovering from a little dinner party we had last evening, aren't we, Angelique? You remember Mrs. Ravenal, don't you, darlin'?"

"Yes, ma'am," Angelique said, sliding a sideways glance in Beatrice's direction. "She was Mother's friend."

Beatrice said, "I still am your mother's friend." She thanked God that Julia wasn't here to see Angelique, still in her nightclothes in the middle of the afternoon.

"As I said," Carlotta went on, "we're recovering from our little party. I would have invited you, Beatrice, but I know how reclusive you've become."

"Quite so. I've brought you these." She gave Carlotta a bunch of flowers and was submitted to another of her rituals of dismissal. Carlotta sniffed them, gushed over their beauty, then tossed them onto a table littered with coffee cups and plates smeared with cream cake.

"Will you take some tea or coffee?" Carlotta asked, but made no move to ring for a servant.

"No, thank you. But I should like to sit down." All the chairs were piled with clothes.

"Angelique, be a darlin' and take those things from the chair." Angelique swooped up an armful of clothes and dropped them onto the floor. "No, no, darlin'," Carlotta cooed. "Go and get Marie to come and hang them up."

As Angelique passed her, Beatrice said, "I'll be writing to your mother soon. Is there anything you'd like me to tell her?"

Angelique considered, then said, "Tell her that I'm going to a Mardi Gras party as Coco Robicheaux."

"Isn't she the little miss?" Carlotta laughed. "You can tell she's going to break some hearts, can't you? Go on now, darlin'. Go on and leave the ladies alone." Angelique, precociously swinging her hips, went out the door.

Carlotta patted her hair. "I expect you were hoping to see Charles, too, but unfortunately you just missed him. He left early this morning. That's why we had the little party last evening. He's off to Panama again. 'Course, he hates being away."

"Yes," Beatrice said archly, surveying the room, "I can see where he'd miss the comforts of home." But why was she allowing herself to sink to Carlotta's level? What was the point of trading snide remarks, when she could see by the triumphal look on Carlotta's face that she already knew about the divorce? She gripped the arm of the chair, set her cane on the floor, and started to get up.

"Oh, Beatrice, before you go, there's something I want to show you."

Carlotta felt under the pillows, found a small paper-covered book, and put it on the edge of the bed. The cover title read

Blue Book—Tenderloin 400. Bending forward, breasts and pearls dangling, Carlotta leafed through it, and Beatrice, despite herself, leaned closer. There were lists of addresses, photos of girls, advertisements for saloons and Mardi Gras balls.

Finding the page she was looking for, Carlotta speared it with a yellowish fingernail and said, "Look here."

Beatrice didn't recognize the girl in the photograph until she read the caption: "Gentlemen! When you come for an evening of sport at Queen Mollie's, don't fail to enjoy the beautiful and accomplished Katherine. She has a form equal to Venus and the manners of a society girl. She's guaranteed to please the most discriminating . . ."

Beatrice stood up. She thought age had inoculated her against the devastating emotions, but a wave of disgust, more powerful than hate, twisted her guts and dried her mouth.

"As I once told Julia," Carlotta said, "you can't change human nature. I knew the girl was trash as soon as I saw her. Leonce Lambre brought me the book. He's such an amusing young—" She stopped, then with mock alarm asked, "Beatrice, is anything the matter? I didn't mean to offend. I just assumed you'd reached the age when you'd be amused rather than shocked."

"I am not shocked," Beatrice said softly. "Shock would affect the heart, whereas you, Carlotta, are only capable of affecting the stomach. You merely sicken me."

She didn't think she could walk without help, but she did. She got all the way to the front door and began hitting it with her cane before a servant came to assist her.

She didn't think anything could destroy her appetite, but for the next two days her bowels ran and she could take nothing but clear broth and boiled rice.

"Will there be anything else?" Grace, dressed to go out, came onto the gallery, rousing Beatrice from her reverie.

"You've packed the teddy bear for the child?" she asked. Grace nodded. "Then perhaps on your way home from the telegraph office, you might stop by the confectioner and get another box or two of the bittersweet creams. Then you might go to the tobacconist's for an extra box of my little cigars. And perhaps some brandy, and some coffee with chicory from the French market. After all, we're going to Boston."

Beatrice stepped down from the train, the conductor bracing one of her elbows, Grace supporting the other. The platform was streaming with people, and Grace, in a rare outburst, muttered, "Never thought I'd see this many Yankees any place outside of hell."

They spotted Julia almost immediately. She came to them with the same brisk, arm-swinging stride that from a distance made her seem like a young woman, but as she came closer, Beatrice saw the pinched look on her face and the new streaks of gray at her temples.

"My dear Beatrice, you've come!" Julia blinked back tears. "Oh, I'm so glad to see you. I was afraid the journey would be too much for you."

"I'm fit as a country boy's fiddle," Beatrice assured her. "And we thoroughly enjoyed the journey, didn't we, Grace? The country's so vast and beautiful, I wonder that I've never bothered to see it before."

In the carriage, Julia pointed out Boston landmarks while Beatrice told her the latest New Orleans gossip: young George Lavouisseur had finally been snared in Mrs. Dewitt's marriage net and was set to wed Adeline Dewitt in September; Carrie Bonisett had delivered her first child, a boy; Phillipa Cotrane had gone off to England to care for Lord Harry.

"Apparently," Beatrice explained, rolling her eyes, "the old boy is riddled with gout. He has one foot in the grave and the other on a banana peel, and since we know Phillipa would rather play cards than play nurse, I expect she hopes to give him the push and be mentioned in his will."

Julia laughed until her shoulders shook. Dabbing her eyes, she said, "Beatrice, you're such a gift. You can't imagine how long it's been since I've laughed."

Beatrice patted her hand and said, "I think I can."

When they arrived at the house, Grace went upstairs to unpack and Julia ushered Beatrice into a sitting room and helped her onto the largest chair. A decanter of sherry, a box of cigars, and a dish of chocolates had been placed next to it, and Beatrice felt her eyes mist at Julia's thoughtfulness.

"Now put up your feet," Julia said, taking Beatrice's cane and arranging her feet on a stool. "And you must be chilly. Let me close the windows. I always open them at the first hint of spring, but it's been unseasonably cold this year."

"Julia, do stop fussing and sit down. Let me look at you." Julia took a chair, laced her fingers in her lap, and offered her brightest smile, but Beatrice noticed a twitch in her left eye. "How is your health?"

"My health? All right, I suppose. The occasional headache." She couldn't bring herself to admit the depressions that often made it impossible for her to get out of bed in the morning. "I suppose I think of my body the same way I think of the house. I hardly notice it unless something goes wrong. It just feels empty. It isn't that I listen for my mother's voice or walk into a room expecting to find my father. I got over that. I nursed them for so long, and I knew they were going to die, so we had time to say good-bye. It's Kate I still expect to see." She shook her head. "I still can't believe she ran off without leaving so much as a note."

"You forget the impetuosity of youth."

"Perhaps I can't remember it because I rarely felt it. The only impetuous thing I ever did was to marry Charles."

"My guess is that Kate decided to leave quite suddenly and felt too guilty to say good-bye, even in a note."

"She's in my thoughts almost daily. I suppose I shall always worry about her and wonder what became of her."

Beatrice grunted. She had already made up her mind not to tell Julia about her visit to Carlotta. Julia was sick with doubts and uncertainties, but in this case truth was not the cure. If Julia knew that Kate was back, whoring in the District, and Carlotta was crowing about it—her mind would never be free. "I shouldn't worry too much about the girl. She seemed to have enough grit to survive. She was not without resources."

"No, she wasn't. That's the worst part of it. She had so much to offer. Everyone who met her was impressed by her. She had an innate feeling for the finer things, a natural intelligence. And of course," she added, catching Beatrice's look, "she was very beautiful. I understand why Lawrence fell in love with her. I never thought I would come to see it this way, but I'm even glad he had . . ." She stopped, embarrassed, and looked down at her hands. "I mean, I'm glad they were together, like that, before he died. But I shall never, never understand how she could go off and leave Christabel."

"Raising the child must be a terrible burden for you."

Julia's head snapped up. "Christabel, a burden? Oh, no. You won't be able to say that when you see her. Would you like to see her?" Beatrice nodded. "Then I'll tell Clara to bring her down."

Julia stepped into the hallway, summoned a maid, then reentered the room, closing the door behind her. "I told you Charles suggested I find some responsible couple and pay them to care for her, didn't I? That was the last straw. He simply didn't understand that I couldn't leave her. Of course I realized that I could never take her to New Orleans. The scandalmongers would never let us live that down, and, more important, I would never expose another child to Carlotta."

"Have you had any further word from Charles?"

"No. He now communicates only through his lawyers. Isn't it ironic that he should be suing me for divorce on grounds of desertion when I no longer know his address? I asked the lawyers to forward my letter to him. One of them told me that since Charles was offering such a handsome settlement, he didn't understand why I was contesting. He didn't understand that money is beside the point."

"Money is never beside the point. Take it, Julia."

"It isn't about money," Julia said irritably. "I would have thought that you, of all people, would understand that. I want custody of Angelique. If he won't go along with that willingly, I shall contest the divorce."

"Please think this through before you act," Beatrice cautioned. "You, or any woman, are bound to get the short end of it in any battle with the courts."

"I didn't expect you to counsel resignation," Julia said with a flash of her old spirit.

"I'm only reminding you of what you must already know," Beatrice said slowly. "The mere fact that you left your husband's home renders you guilty and unfit in the court's eyes."

"But you know—"

"Of course I *know*." Beatrice tried to control her exasperation. "Intelligent though you are, Julia, you have never understood that appearances are usually more important than reality." She couldn't bring herself to say that Angelique was a pawn already taken in Carlotta's game. "I'm only saying that you should consider things carefully before you proceed, that you should—"

There was a knock at the door. Julia put thumb and forefinger against her twitching eye, shook her head as if to clear it, then called, "Please come in."

A maid, carrying the child, stepped in. Christabel said, "Mama," looked from Julia to Beatrice, then buried her head in the maid's shoulder.

Julia said, "Thank you, Clara. Just put her down." The maid set Christabel on her feet and closed the door.

"Come on, Christabel." Julia smiled and held out her arms. "This is our friend Beatrice. Show her what a big girl you are."

Christabel wobbled across the floor, plunging headfirst into Julia's skirts. Julia picked her up and sat her on her lap, smoothing her pinafore and kissing the top of her head. "Sometimes," she said, "she makes me feel very young, but at others she really makes me feel my age. Since she's started to walk and open cabinets, I can't keep up with her. I usually let Clara take her for her walks and bathe and feed her. But I always tuck her into bed. That's when we read together, isn't it, Christabel?" Christabel put her thumb into her mouth and looked across at Beatrice with long-lashed, unblinking, amber-colored eyes, the whites of which were so clear as to appear faintly bluish.

"She's a beautiful child," Beatrice said.

"She is, isn't she? Perhaps it's my imagination, but I do think she looks like Lawrence."

Beatrice nodded, though as far as she could see, the child's barely formed features resembled only Kate's, and her reddish hair suggested an entirely unknown genetic contribution.

"That's our friend Beatrice," Julia whispered. "Why don't you go and say hello to her?" She eased the child off her lap and gave her a encouraging pat on the bottom, propelling her forward.

Christabel toddled over, looking up at Beatrice as though she were a monument. After studying her for a moment, she decided Beatrice was all right and raised her arms. Beatrice creaked forward.

Julia came to her side, urging, "Can you say 'Beatrice'?" and lifted her onto Beatrice's lap.

Christabel studied Beatrice some more, tentatively touched her cheek, then, emboldened, she began to puddle her fingers in Beatrice's double chins. "Bee-trith," she lisped, patting the massive bosom and putting her thumb into her mouth.

"Big girls don't suck their thumbs," Julia said, taking the child's hand from her mouth. Christabel smiled, eyes showing she already knew what she could get away with, and calmly reinserted her thumb. Julia sighed. "As you can see, she has a mind of her own. I've tried to break her of the habit, but so far I haven't succeeded. I think she does it because she was weaned too young. I remember I nursed Lawrence for almost a year. It was harder with Angelique. My milk didn't come in, and Carlotta wanted me to get a wet nurse. I resisted, but I had a terrible time of it. Forgive me," she said, wiping her eyes impatiently and straightening. "I seem to get weepy at the most unaccountable moments."

"There's nothing to forgive."

"You must be hungry. I'll go and tell them that we'll have lunch." On her way to the door, Julia turned. "Did I tell you that I'm learning to drive an automobile?"

"You didn't buy one, did you?" Beatrice asked with alarm. Though she'd greeted the electric light as a miracle and was equally delighted by the invention of the telephone, she had never ridden in an automobile and didn't want to. What was the point of putting on goggles and duster, climbing into a dangerous machine, cranking it up, and bouncing along in a mess of noise and dust, when one might just as well sit behind a companionable horse who could listen to directions?

"No, I didn't buy one. They're far too expensive. A friend of mine, Dr. Lockman, has loaned me hers. It's a self-starter. A new Baker Electric. You don't even have to crank it. After lunch, if

the weather holds and you're feeling up to it, I thought we might
go for a spin."

"I've never seen a woman drive a motorcar," Beatrice said,
stalling.

"For shame, Beatrice. How can you be so old-fashioned? Why
shouldn't a woman drive a motorcar?"

Stuck for an answer, Beatrice muttered, "Why, indeed?"

It took both the maid and Grace to heft her onto the red plush
passenger seat. She tucked the woolen blankets around her legs,
adjusted her goggles, tied the ribbons of her bonnet more se-
curely, and wondered if it would be better to hold on to the seat,
the dashboard, or the wooden door. Julia swung onto the driver's
seat, pulling a motorman's cap firmly onto her forehead. "I wear
the cap for good luck," she said, reaching for a knob. The motor
jumped into life. Julia clasped the wheel and squared her shoulders. "Ready?" Since her tongue had swollen to twice its normal
size, Beatrice could only nod.

"Then," Julia cried, pulling away from the curb and waving
good-bye to a stricken-looking Grace as the car lurched forward,
"we're off."

When they had purred along for a few miles, Julia yelled "Do
you like it?" over the roar of the motor, and Beatrice nodded
again. Having calmed herself with philosophical thoughts about
the benefits of sudden death, Beatrice found it was really quite
pleasant—like a carousel ride when she was a child—the buildings and trees and people whisking by. She felt slightly sick, but
excited, and by the time they'd reached the outskirts of the city,
she was actually enjoying it. But then Julia turned down a dirt
road, honked at a plodding horse cart, swerved around it, and
pushed the accelerator to the floor.

"I'm a road hog," Julia yelled, "and I have a lead foot. Do you
mind?"

Beatrice shook her head until her wattles shook. "Is that a rhetorical question?" she bellowed, knowing that even if she could be heard, she had no chance of being listened to.

Julia gripped the wheel more tightly, the countryside rushed by in a blur of blue skies, brown-and-green earth, the wind bit into their faces. As they ascended a hill and hurtled down into a valley, Beatrice shut her eyes and held on for dear life.

"Look there." Julia pointed. "Lilacs." She pulled to the side of the road under a giant chestnut, switched off the motor, set the brake, and yanked off her goggles. "Don't get out," she said, jumping down. "I wouldn't know how to get you back in without help." In the sudden quiet, Beatrice thought she could actually hear her heart beating. She pulled off her goggles, wiped her eyes, and took long, deep breaths.

"Are you all right?" Julia asked, climbing back into the automobile and putting a spray of lilacs on her lap.

"Frankly," Beatrice wheezed, "I can't tell yet."

Julia touched the lilacs. "They're only just coming into bloom. Don't they have a delightful scent? When we were first married and I moved to New Orleans, I missed the spring flowers so. Charles once had some packed in ice and shipped down. They didn't last the journey, but it was such a loving gesture. I told myself that no matter what happened, I would never, never leave him."

She looked out at the countryside as though she were in an alien land. Her eyes brimmed, and she fumbled in the pocket of her duster for a handkerchief. "I loved him so. Sometimes I think I still love him. Night after night I turn it over in my head. What should I have done? How could I have prevented . . ." She wiped her eyes and threw her head back. "I'm sorry. You know it's not like me to be like this. I didn't even cry at my father's funeral. It's just . . . seeing you . . . there's no one else who cares so much about what I think and feel, no one else who'll really understand. . . ." She rubbed her hands over her face as though she wanted to take off the flesh. "I simply must stop this! I'm losing all self-respect." She shivered, straightened, and said, "I'm sorry. I didn't mean to burden you. We should go back. You must be cold."

Beatrice said, "I'm all right." But the truth was that her nose was beginning to run, and her hands and feet were numb.

"Well, I'm cold. It seems as though I've been cold for years. Winter used to be my favorite season. I liked the idea of things being stripped down. I felt it was a time when one's real character showed, when one's will and endurance could be tested. But since I've been back, I've barely ventured out. I don't want to test my endurance because I know I'll fail the test. Even my heart seems to be frozen."

" 'A woman's heart must be of such a size and no larger, else it must be pressed small, like Chinese feet,' " Beatrice said. "I think you must leave everything and go away, my dear. Simply go away. Find a warm, easy place. Go to Italy or the south of France."

"You mean I should follow Charles's example—keep myself in a state of perpetual motion so I can avoid responsibility?"

"You know I don't mean that," Beatrice said. "I only suggest that you allow yourself time to thaw out."

Julia placed her arms on the steering wheel and put her chin on her hands, staring straight ahead. "I have had invitations from friends who live abroad, but how can I leave my obligations here? There's the settlement house and the Women's Suffrage Association." She sighed. "To tell the truth, neither of them is going well. I always believed that I was dedicated, that I had courage and staying power, but now I know I don't. I marvel at women like Susan B. and Elizabeth. They've held on through decades of setbacks and disappointments. But I'm not made of that mettle. I'm weak. I have to see tangible results. 'The summer soldier and the sunshine patriot will, in this crisis, shrink from the service of their country.' I know it now. I am only a summer soldier. I can't remember who said that, can you?"

"No doubt some stiff-necked Yankee such as yourself."

"I know who said it," Julia cried, hitting the dashboard. "It was Thomas Paine."

"Well, he's dead," Beatrice muttered, "and I'm alive, and I'm telling you that you must get out from under all of it, at least for a time. When you travel, you'll find yourself in new situations. It will call forth energy you no longer believed you had. You've made me living proof of that. But just now I'd like to take a nap. And no hell-for-leather ride back, if you please. I don't want to be buried in your Yankee soil, lovely though it is."

"Beatrice, I do apologize."

"If you apologize one more time, I shall leave tomorrow morning. Now let's go back and have a nice toddy and a nap, like civilized human beings."

Much as she cared for Julia, much as she believed she knew her, she couldn't guess if Julia would emerge from this swamp of troubles. People, some of the best, went down in despair. She hoped and prayed that Julia would not. She took her hand. "I know declarations of affection embarrass you, but since none of us will live forever, I take this opportunity to tell you I'm exceedingly fond of you, Julia. And since none of us will live forever, I really don't care how you drive. Just take the wheel."

CHAPTER

XIX

Flee as a bird to your mountain,
Thou who art weary of sin;
Go to the clear flowing fountain,
Where you may wash and be clean.

Hymn, Mary Stanley Bruce Dana
1842 (?)

*T*t was never clear in Kate's mind whether it was the smell
or the noise that woke her.

The night had ended like hundreds of other nights. She'd said
good-bye to her last customer and gotten ready for a bath. When
she came out into the hall, she heard the piano and went to the
top of the stairs to listen. Monkey was playing a gentle, bouncy
rag, and she had to admit he was pretty damn good. After her
bath she went back to her room, locked the door, tossed back a
measure of brandy, lit a cigarette, and started to read.

Sometime later she heard doors slam and shrieks, not of passion but of alarm, and the smell of smoke pricked her nostrils.
She pulled on her kimono and flung back the door.

Men and girls in various stages of undress were streaming to
the stairs. Hortense, wild-eyed, yelled "The house is on fire!" as
she darted past. A man, trying to run and pull on his trousers at

the same time, fell, righted himself, and was knocked back down by another.

Kate dashed back into her room, grabbed her money box from under the bed, scrambled to find her shoes, realized there wasn't time, and ran. Billows of smoke enveloped the downstairs foyer. As she stumbled down the stairs, Zoe, who was just in front of her, wailed "My jewelry!" and turned back.

Judas bounded up, yanked Zoe by the arm, and pulled her after him. "Get out, you dumb whore. You wanna burn to death?" Flames were shooting out of Mollie's bedroom.

"Mollie!" Kate screamed. "Where's Mollie?"

"She's out. Get out!" Judas thrust her into the mass of bodies that were pushing, shoving, wailing, and coughing, trying to get out the front door. A man elbowed her in the breast and shot out ahead of her. She stumbled down the stoop, gasping and wheezing, and fell to her knees.

A crowd clotted the street, pointing and shouting as though it were a fireworks display. A naked man yanked a sheet away from Conchita, leaving her naked and screaming. Kate got up and shoved her way through the melee, calling for Mollie. She spotted her on the banquette across the street. A drunk stood beside her, sloshing a mug and yelling, "Let's put it out with beer."

There was a roar as the draperies at the front windows caught and a great wall of flame went up, then a loud popping noise as the windows shattered.

Mollie's face was streaming sweat, orange in the flames. She clawed the air, crying, "Sweet Mother of God!" And then she was a limp body collapsing, her head hitting the banquette.

"Help her," Kate cried, trying to lift her. "Somebody help her!"

There was a clanging of bells and a great disturbance at the end of the street as fire wagons tried to get through. A horse reared, knocking someone down. Some men lifted Mollie by her armpits. "Take her to Hanratty's," Kate yelled. As they pushed through the chaos, there was a clap of thunder. The skies opened just as the fire wagons pulled up to the house.

They met Sean Hanratty halfway to his saloon, and he went ahead of them, shoving people out of the way. He pushed back the swinging doors and led them through the bar into his office, sweeping everything off his desk and telling the men to put Mollie there.

"She's out cold," he said, slapping her cheeks and pulling back her eyelid. "For chrissake, someone get a doctor."

Kate went back into the bar. The customers were lining up, and the bartender was pouring so fast his hands were a blur. Zoe was on a chair, crying uncontrollably. The bully who'd ripped the sheet from Conchita was pleading for someone to give him some clothes.

"Sean says to get a doctor," Kate yelled to the bartender. A ruddy-faced bald man put down his glass. "I'm a doctor," he told her, and followed her into the office.

She leaned against the wall and watched as he pinched and poked at Mollie's body. Sean asked him over and over again if Mollie would be all right. "She'll have a lump the size of a turkey egg on her head tomorrow, but I think she'll be fine." Sean rewarded the diagnosis with a glass of his best whiskey.

The doctor sidled up to Kate, putting his arm around her. "And how about you, sweetheart? You feeling all right?"

She pushed him away and turned to Sean. "Can you get some men to carry her to Lady Caroline's?"

She led the small procession down the street. In the misty rain the firemen stood about, exchanging jokes with the onlookers. The house was still standing, a faint flop and crackle coming from deep inside its guts. As she passed it, she realized that she'd lost her money box.

"Give me a drink, will ya?" Mollie lay in Lady Caroline's four-poster with the lavender satin canopy, one flabby white arm flung up to cover her eyes, her great breasts sagging into her armpits.

Kate moved to open the draperies, but Lady Caroline said, "Don't get her a drink. And for God's sake don't open the drapes. I wouldn't let the devil himself see me like this."

Lady Caroline did look a sight. It was the first time Kate had seen him without wig or paint. His short-cropped hair was gray and his unshaven chin bluish. He held a chip of ice wrapped in a lace hanky to his eye. When, hearing the fire engines, his customers had started to rush out to the street, he'd caught one trying to lift some silver, and the customer had landed him a well-aimed punch.

"Will y' get me a drink?" Mollie groaned again.

"Shut up, Mollie. Just shut up," Lady Caroline snapped.

"Then get me a priest."

"No drink and no priest."

"All gone," Mollie muttered. "Everything gone."

"Don't be so dramatic." Lady Caroline's voice was shrill. "We already told you, it's not *all* gone."

Kate gingerly wiped Mollie's forehead with a damp cloth. Mollie's eyes were red-rimmed. A bruise the color of an eggplant stained the left side of her face, and blood matted the hair on the knot on her head.

"Remember, I told you," Kate said gently. "It's not all gone." She had gone back to the house first thing in the morning. Judas was sitting in the front hall with a shotgun across his lap to scare off looters. Kate had picked her way through the rubble and gone upstairs, where some of the girls were scavenging what they could from their own and others' rooms. "The upstairs is hardly hurt at all. Just your bedroom, the parlors, most of the dining room, and . . ." Her voice trailed off. It was the worst mess she'd ever seen.

"The Turkish parlor. My God, the money I spent on that. And the piano? The piano, too?" Mollie rolled one marooned eye up to Kate and shut it as Kate nodded. "Holy Mother of God, I'm ruined. I knew that Vivian Lefevre would get me. I knew she would. She started the fire. She ruined me."

"It wasn't Vivian Lefevre," Kate began, but couldn't bear to go on.

"The fire captain said it started in your room," Lady Caroline said. "You must've gone to sleep with the candles burning on your altar. You prob'ly knocked one of 'em over and it caught on the carpet. Just be glad you weren't so sloshed you didn't wake up, otherwise you'd be roast pork."

Mollie's eyes narrowed as though trying to see in the dark, widened for a second as the truth dawned, then squeezed shut again. "No. *She* did it," she cried vehemently. "I know she did. She's in league with the devil."

"Listen, Mollie—"

"Don't even try to explain. She's delirious."

"I want to get up," Mollie said suddenly. "I want to go to confession."

"You can't go to church in a ripped-up old nightdress, now can you?" Lady Caroline got up wearily and shoved Mollie back down. "You're supposed to rest. Get it? Just lie still, shut up, and rest."

"Oh, Jesus, I've got such a headache. My brains are oozin' out of the pan. I can feel it. I need extreme unction."

"Get her a drink. Anything to shut her up. Here." Lady Caroline fished in the pocket of his dressing gown and came up with a key. "You know where the cabinet is, if the bastards didn't raid that, too. Get us all a drink."

When Kate came back with the bottle, Mollie was asleep. "I wish Shakespeare would get here with the doctor."

"She'll be all right. She's just got a worse than usual case of the horrors. Well, who wouldn't?"

"No. Something's wrong. See how she keeps nodding off so fast? She's passing out."

"Let her pass out. Maybe we'll get a minute's peace. Just sit here with her while I take a bath and get dressed, will you? Shakespeare oughta be back by then."

Kate pulled up a chair and took Mollie's hand, stroking it and speaking in low, soothing tones. "It's all right, Mollie. Everything's going to be all right."

She was talking for her own benefit, but it didn't do any good. How could anything be all right? They were ruined. She'd lost her savings, and Mollie was out of her head. She took a gulp of whiskey and shuddered as it went down. It was all hopeless, as Mollie would say, as peein' against the wind. Her mind kept going round and round like a hamster pawing at a wheel, wondering where she'd dropped her money box. Probably she'd left it on the banquette when Mollie had gone down. Damn you, Mollie! she thought. Damn you, you stupid old drunk!

Mollie came to. One of her eyes twitched, the other roamed around the room. "Where's all my girls?" she asked.

"Zoe and Hortense are over at Sean's. Mabel Kranz has taken Conchita and Ida in. I think Emily's at Lena Friedman's. I don't know about the rest."

"Round 'em up for me, Katie, there's a dear. That Lena Friedman's always had her eye on Emily. She'll try to get her away from me, sure. You say the upstairs is all right? Get 'em upstairs. Get a bucket of spaghetti from the Eyeties. Get 'em back to work."

"Yeah, sure, I'll do that." She couldn't keep the sarcasm out of her voice.

"Oh, my head does ache so, Katie."

"I'll get you some ice. You want some ice for your forehead?"

As she started out the door, she ran into Shakespeare. After exchanging looks, Kate shaking her head, he took off his hat and moved to the bed. " 'How now, most wretched queen,' " he said, looking down at Mollie.

"Can you stay with her a while, Billy? I want to go back to the house and get the rest of my clothes. Then I'll go over to Mabel Kranz's and see if she's got anything that'll fit Mollie."

"Go along with you, then. The good doctor will be here presently, and in the meantime I shall entertain our patient."

"Just pray with me, Billy," Mollie said, clutching at his hand.

"Dear lady, I cannot pray. I'm here to entertain. Now what shall it be? Tragedy, comedy, history, pastoral-comical, historical-pastoral . . ."

When Kate returned some hours later, the house was eerily quiet. Reggie, Lady Caroline's fancy man, waved her into Lady Caroline's bedroom without a word. Lady Caroline was slumped on a chair, staring into space. Shakespeare knelt by the bed, clasping Mollie's misshapen feet. Mollie was stretched out, hands folded across her chest. As Kate saw the crusted blood that ran from Mollie's ear, Lady Caroline said, "Yeah, she's dead. Gave it up about an hour ago, just before the doctor got here."

Kate shook her head. It couldn't be true. Mollie couldn't die. Not Mollie. Mollie was battered, dinged up, beyond repair—but she was indestructible. She'd seen her stretched out like this morning after morning, just sleeping it off. If it weren't for that trickle of blood near her ear . . . She took the handkerchief from her pocket, wet it with saliva, and reached to wipe away the blood, but her hand shook so violently that she sank down onto the chair.

Lady Caroline said, "She once told me she didn't want no men looking at her when she was dead. You think you can dress her?"

Kate stared at the fly swimming in the dregs of Mollie's whiskey. "Kate! You listening to me?"

A shaft of iron had been driven into her heart. If she opened her mouth, she would scream.

"I said, can you dress her? Think that dress you got from Mabel will fit?"

She looked at the dun-colored dress in her lap. Her voice came out soft and tremulous: "I'd like to put her in something better than this."

Lady Caroline was all business. "No time to go shopping. Reggie's already told the undertakers and the priest. We'll bury her tomorrow morning. Unless we're gonna send her out buck naked, same way as she come in, it's Mabel's dress. Gotta move fast on account of the heat."

But no one moved.

Kate watched as the fly lost the struggle, then she fished the fly out of the glass and wiped it on the edge of the bedside table. Shakespeare's shoulders were shaking. Lady Caroline moved to the bed, gently pried his hands from Mollie's feet, and helped him up. He swayed slightly and smoothed back his hair. "I'm used to inattentive audiences, but I've never had anyone die on me before." He laughed till he cried, and Lady Caroline led him from the room.

Kate watched from the window as a hearse drawn by two white horses with black plumes on their heads pulled up, and the undertaker and his assistant yanked the coffin from its bed and struggled up the stoop with it. She had combed Mollie's hair as best she could and dabbed some rouge onto her cheeks. Shakespeare had come up with a rosary, which she'd twined in Mollie's hands, and a shamrock-shaped brooch that she'd pinned to the neck of Mabel Kranz's brown dress. Except for the amethyst earrings, Lady Caroline's parting gift, Mollie looked like a peasant. It broke Kate's heart to bury her without shoes, but Shakespeare said Mollie had always been miserable in shoes, so she wouldn't mind. Kate looked at her for the last time and bent to kiss her forehead. The undertaker and his assistant eased the coffin to the floor. "Gawd, she weighs as much as a ton of bricks," she heard one of them say as she left the room. Kate put on a hat she'd borrowed from Lady Caroline and listened to the thud of the hammer as they nailed the coffin shut. Lady Caroline, heavily veiled, came and offered his arm.

The sun was high and hot. Two nuns waited on the stoop. One had a waxy, expressionless face, which she shielded with an umbrella. The other was a mere girl, who greeted them with a beatific smile. Mabel Kranz and several of her girls huddled close to the wall, seeking shade. Lena Friedman, flanked by Zoe and Conchita, hurried to join them, the jet beads on her hat shivering as she walked. No one spoke. The men loaded the coffin into the hearse. The driver told the horses to gee-up, and Kate and Lady Caroline fell in behind it. As they advanced up the street, doors opened and women and girls, all in black, some carrying flowers, joined the procession. Kate stared at the coffin, but she was aware of the gathering throng. It grew larger with each block. A hundred, two hundred, three. No sound but the horses' hooves and the shuffling of feet. Kate felt she was in a dream.

"The whole damn District is turning out," Lady Caroline whispered. "Wouldn't Mollie be proud?"

Kate thought, I didn't know there were this many whores in the world. They were a great dark sea, growing ever larger.

The priest was waiting at the grave in Metairie Cemetery. As he intoned his blessing, sweat ran down Kate's face and her legs felt as though they'd melt from under her. She had never fainted since that first day at Vivian Lefevre's, but now she thought she might.

The men lowered the coffin into the grave. Alma Heflin gasped and shrieked. Lena Friedman gave Alma a frosty look, stooped to gather a handful of dirt, and threw it onto the coffin.

"That's a Jewish tradition," she muttered to Kate, and it seemed so right to Kate that she followed suit. One of Violet Johnson's girls began to sing:

> *Flee as a bird to your mountain,*
> *Thou who art weary of sin;*
> *Go to the clear flowing fountain,*
> *Where you may wash and be clean.*

Her voice was high and pure. Some of the other girls joined in.

> *Fly for th' avenger is near thee,*
> *Call and the Savior will hear thee,*
> *He on his bosom will bear thee,*
> *Thou who art weary of sin,*
> *O thou who art weary of sin.*

Women moved by the grave, tossing in flowers. There were sniffles, sighs, comments: "Mollie was the best"—"You could always count on Mollie"—"Gawd, I need a drink"—"Remember the time she . . ."

Conchita sat on a gravestone, wiping her eyes with her sleeve and crying, "*Madre*. She was *madre* for me. Better than my own."

Lena took off her hat and held up a twenty-dollar bill. "C'mon, girls, let's chip in and buy her a gravestone. C'mon, don't be stingy. Here's my twenty to start it off."

At the edge of the crowd some girls were harmonizing, "In the sweet by and by, / We shall meet on that beautiful shore." The band waiting near the cemetery gates took up the refrain, slow, mournful, slightly off-key. A trumpet player with skin as dark as eggplant held the final note, bending so far back it seemed he would topple over. There was a moment of silence. The trumpet player spat, stomped his foot, said "A one, a two . . ." and all hell broke loose—a wild cacophony of bouncy, joyful sound. Monkey wailed on his harmonica and did a do-si-do with a cornet player, the drum emblazoned "Abyssinian Social Club" pounded, a barefoot boy in a bright blue suit and hat twirled in circles, shaking a tambourine.

They moved out, raising dust, brass and sweaty faces shining in the sun. A small army of laundresses, maids, pimps, barkeeps, and restaurant owners fell in behind them. Shakespeare had Banjo Annie on one arm and Sophronia, wearing a dress that had cost two months' wages and a hat as big as an ostrich's behind, on the other. The girls streamed out of the cemetery gates, prancing, cakewalking, jigging, swirling their umbrellas.

"Over to Hanratty's," Mabel Kranz yelled. "Drinks on the house. Drinks for Mollie Q."

When Mollie's wake threatened to turn into a bacchanal—Conchita dancing the hootchy-kootchy on a tabletop, strangers who'd never even met Mollie toasting her so they could soak up the free whiskey—Kate and Shakespeare left Sean Hanratty's and walked, without speaking, to the waterfront. They found some crates on a deserted loading dock and sat down. The sun was setting, turning the river silver and the sky to opalescent pinks like the inside of a shell.

"It's beautiful," Shakespeare said. Kate nodded, but he could tell that she was in a fog of depression, looking but not seeing. "What will you do now?" he asked.

She undid the top buttons of her dress and rested her hand on her collarbone. "Did I tell you that my grandfather was a steamboat captain? Before the War Between the States, he did the St. Louis–to–New Orleans run. He could read the river like you'd read a book—a ripple on the surface showed a changing channel, a floating log meant a rising tide. When I was young, we'd go down to the dock 'most every evening and watch the sun go down, and he'd tell me all about New Orleans. He always said he'd bring me here. Just before he died, he'd get confused and call me his first mate and tell me to take the wheel." She could see him quite clearly, tall and impressive as an Old Testament prophet, with a long, uncombed beard and gravy spots on his vest. "He died right after my mother. Then my brother Newland lit off, and my other brothers and sisters were farmed out. I was afraid to stay in the house with my father, so when Frank Staughton came along . . ." She sighed. "No. I don't know what I'll do."

"You'd be welcome in any white house in town."

"I know. I've already had some offers. I just can't imagine living with anyone but Mollie. Not just 'cause I loved her. She let me do what I wanted. I was pretty much running the house. I won't be able to do that anywhere else. But I have to get back to work, what with my money gone and all."

"Would that I were in a position to give you something more substantial than moral support." The young woman who sat beside him now was a world away from the frightened kid he'd met at the Versailles. She'd bedded hundreds of men, but she was still enough of a country girl to have kept her savings in a box under her bed.

As if reading his thoughts, she said, "I always meant to put it in the bank, but I was afraid they'd ask me where it came from."

"Bankers are not noted for curiosity about their customers' source of income."

"It wasn't just that. It made me feel good to count it. I counted it all the time. Like a miser. Maybe that's why it was taken from me. As a punishment."

"It sounds as though Mollie infected you with her superstitions about divine vengeance. If there is a Supreme Being, I should think He'd be aiming his lightning bolts at the Carnegies and the Rockefellers instead of arranging for the theft of your measly stash."

"It wasn't measly. It was over two thousand dollars—the most I've ever had."

"And what were you planning to do with it?"

"I dunno. I just figured when I had enough, I'd leave. I didn't have a real dream like Mollie had. Poor Mollie. She had that house all planned out, right down to the color of the curtains and the kinds of flowers she'd grow in the yard."

"Mustn't be sentimental about that," he warned. "When a dream lives long enough to have that many particulars, it can never come true. I think Mollie would've been bored to tears in her little Irish cottage. The natives would've spotted what she was. They would've ostracized her or run her off. It's better this way. She didn't go out in a blaze of glory, but at least she went out in a blaze." He got up. "Come on. I'll escort you back to Lady Caroline's before I go off to the Versailles to help the human flotsam and jetsam find their harbor for the night. At least you'll be safe at Lady Caroline's. Lovely though you are, you won't appeal to the particular tastes of Lady Caroline's clientele." She didn't move, so he took her hands and gently raised her to her feet. "All is not lost, my dear. You have youth and beauty, two things for which I would make a pact with the devil." But, he thought as they headed back to the District, Kate's beauty meant nothing to her at the moment, and as for youth, that, he remembered dimly, was often a time of desperate confusion.

Lady Caroline was in his kitchen, drinking coffee and trying to sober up after Mollie's wake. "Good you left when you did," he said. "Alma Heflin got coke-jagged and turned hysterical, and some booking agent started talking to Monkey 'bout going to Chicago to play the piano, so Bertha ended up saying she was gonna kill herself. Oh, this is for you." He pushed a letter addressed to Kate across the table. "Delivery boy brought this round. If you hadn't come in the next ten minutes, I woulda opened it. Looks like it came from the court of Louis the Fourteenth."

The stationery was creamy, heavy, and sealed with a blob of red wax. Kate read it and handed it back to Lady Caroline. "I am, as always, at your service. Will you come to my apartments this evening at ten?" It was signed "Leonce Lambre."

"He doesn't mean he's at my service. He means he wants me to be at his. And I won't."

"C'mon, Kate, be practical."

"He's like a vulture."

"So he's like a vulture, so what? You got no money. You've got no place to live. Maybe he'll wanna keep you. Maybe you could stay with him while you're sorting things out. You gotta be practical, Kate."

This time the call to practicality sounded stronger than a suggestion, and a feeling of panic, familiar as the sweats of a recurrent fever, swept over her: she was homeless again, her survival totally dependent on the good graces of others. For the last two nights she'd been sleeping in Reggie's room, and Reggie had been bunking with Lady Caroline, who'd let it be known that he was just as devoted to sleeping alone as Kate was. Another few nights and she might outstay her welcome.

Shakespeare had been wrong about Mollie's dream. It wasn't just a fantasy about respectability and lace curtains; it was the need to have that most basic thing—a place you could hide in, a place where no one could tell you to get out.

"Gawd, Kate, if you don't change that expression, Leonce Lambre will have to give it to you in the dark. Now go on in and give yourself a bath. Use as much of my jasmine salts as you like. That'll make you feel better. And, Kate," Lady Caroline called after her as she left the room, "get the money up front. Mollie always said Leonce Lambre was slippery as a greased eel."

Kate arrived at Leonce Lambre's apartments at a little after ten. He opened the door himself, wearing a black silk dressing gown and Persian slippers that turned up at the toes. Instead of kissing her hand, he turned it over and licked her palm. She followed him, wiping her hand on her skirt, into a dimly lit room that looked as though it had been hit by a hurricane. Paintings and books were stacked against the walls, clothes and bottles strewn about. A candelabrum dripped wax onto a table littered with papers, ink bottles, pens, a half-eaten chicken, and a bowl of figs. He pressed her down onto a chair, then traced the line of her chin, neck, and breast with a finger.

"I knew one day you would come to me, Kate. It was only a matter of time." He yawned and giggled, moving across the room to lie on a chaise longue. There was a hookah on the floor, and he reached for it, sucking in a mouthful. "Would you like some opium first?" She shook her head. "Then disrobe, my goddess. I want to study you. I want to admire you."

"I don't undress until we've settled on the price."

"Ah, I see I didn't get you in time. A few short years ago you were a maiden, now the romance has gone from your soul. You are hard-bitten now, but then all women are hard-bitten at bottom, aren't they? You pretend innocence, but you seduce, you tempt. You cannot help it. It is your nature. 'And the Lord Yahweh said to the woman, "What is this that you have done?" And the woman said, "The serpent beguiled me and I ate." ' Would you like to eat, Kate? No? Ah, you are as silent as my muse has been of late. But *you* shall be my muse. You will call my spirit forth." He smoked some more, staring up at the ceiling, then closing his eyes, silent for so long that he seemed to have forgotten her presence. "You must be feeling sad, Kate. You've lost Mollie, sorry old baggage that she was. Are you feeling sad, Kate? Has Thanatos overcome Eros?"

"About the money . . ."

"Why are you so pitifully mercenary? I do not want your person just for the night. I want you as my mistress. All my worldly goods will be yours, my Sheba. I will dress you in jewels and furs. You will inspire me, and I will enlighten you. Would you care to hear one of my poems? No, again?"

"If you like," she said, understanding that part of the reason she was here was to be his audience.

He staggered up, riffled through the drift of papers on the table, then swept them onto the floor, sinking down beside them and reaching for the hookah again, gathering the dressing gown around his exposed crotch in a parody of shyness. "But what do you know of poetry? Eros and Thanatos are intertwined. But, I don't expect you to understand. You are woman, the primeval ooze against which man's will must always struggle. You are Lilith and Circe, you are . . ."

He raved on. She had no idea what he was talking about, but she remembered something Agnes had told her: the would-be poets and writers were always the worst. They bashed your ears before they bashed your body, and you had to pretend that you were enthralled. But pretense was beyond her. As he crawled toward her, arms outstretched, mewling, "I adore you. I worship at your shrine," she stared at the candelabrum, her mind reverting to useless speculation about where she'd dropped the money box that held her savings.

She barely felt him pawing at her skirts, clutching her buttocks, but there was an insidious tone in his voice that she couldn't shut out. "I know you are secretly full of lust," he whispered, "because I saw you that night. I saw you panting for him. You were a little bitch in heat then. Re-live that night, Kate. Tell me everything

he did to you and I will do it. Close your eyes and call me by
his name. Let me be . . . Lawrence."

For a moment, she was completely still. Then she wrenched
up, toppling him, furiously slapping and punching. His arms flew
up to protect his head. "You filthy whore! I'll have you prosecuted!" She backed away, bumping into a doorjamb, turning and
running, flinging back the front door as he screamed, "Come
back! Name the price. Just come back!"

She ran through the streets, jostling the crowds, hearing men
curse and call after her as she bumped into them. Catching sight
of a policeman, she forced herself to slow down, but she walked
with such purpose that men stepped aside, hooting and protest-
ing. At last she was in front of Mollie's. The house seemed to
be dark, but as she climbed up the steps, she saw a pale light
shining through the gaping hole where a window had been. She
pounded on the door. Judas opened it. "What the hell . . ." he
said as she pushed past him.

"I have to stay here tonight, Judas."

"You can't. It stinks. It ain't safe." He raised a kerosene lantern,
and slow-witted though he was, once he saw her face, he said,
"If you have to, you have to. Wait and I'll fix you another lantern.
You wanna go up to your old room?" She nodded and stood in
the dark, holding on to the banister while he padded to the rear
of the house and came back with another lantern. "Go on up,
then. Want me to come with you?"

She shook her head. "No. Just let me lie down. Let me lie
down alone."

She put the lantern on the bedside stand. Seeing her hands black-
ened with soot, she started to go to the bathroom, then remembered there wasn't any water. The curtains had been ripped from
the window. Her quilt and mirror were gone. She supposed one

of the girls had scavenged them. She didn't care. She took off
her shoes and lay back on the bed. The sheets smelled of smoke,
but she didn't care about that, either. Her mind drifted far, far
away. She was back on the dock with her grandfather, looking
down at the water, listening to him explain how you judged the
depth and telling about a shipmate who'd drowned himself. Why
would anybody want to do that? she'd asked. That was terrible.
Not always, her grandfather had said. "He was rocked to sleep
in the bosom of the deep." She thought about one of Alma
Heflin's girls, Eve, a seemingly jolly girl with a strawberry birth-
mark on her neck, who'd killed herself just two weeks ago. Lots
of whores killed themselves. Suicide was a plan even the most
helpless could carry out. Two bottles of sleeping syrup and a
bottle of whiskey. Rocked to sleep in the bosom of the deep. It
was a comforting thought, better than a pile of money because
no one could take it away from you.

At first, the knock on the door seemed to be part of her
dream—a dream in which she'd lost the use of her legs and
couldn't get up, and a line of customers, hundreds of customers,
snaked from her door down the stairs and out into the street.

"You awake?"

Judas put down his lantern, struck a match, and lit the lantern
on the bedside table. He jerked his head in the direction of the
hall, where a man stood in the shadows. "Gentleman came to
see his house. I told him you were here."

He picked up his lantern and shambled out, and Charles Randsome stepped into the room. He took off his hat and passed his
hand through his hair, shocked at the dingy chaos of the room
and Kate lying motionless on the bed. "I had no idea you were
here. In New Orleans, I mean."

She made a motion with her hand, and when she spoke, it
sounded like her mother's voice apologizing to a neighbor who'd

come by unexpectedly. "Please sit down. I'm sorry I've nothing
to offer you." Nothing to offer. Except herself. She didn't suppose
he'd come for that, but you never knew.

"You're not hurt, are you?" She shook her head. He found
the chair, pulled it up to the bed, and sat down slowly, averting
his eyes. When he finally spoke, it was as though he were explaining something to himself. "My property agent told me about
the fire. I couldn't sleep, so I came by to inspect the damage. I
didn't expect to find anyone here." After a pause he looked at
her. "Are you sure you're not hurt? The fire chief told the agent
no one was hurt."

"Only Mollie. We buried her today." Had it been that day?
"What time is it?"

"A little after midnight."

"Then it was yesterday." She muttered something about Mollie's being barefoot. He wondered if she was still in shock.

He said, "I was told that everyone had gotten out safely."

"She did. But she fell and hit her head."

"I'm sorry." He remembered that the driver of the hansom
had told him something about a funeral—"regular jamboree of
whores, y' never saw so many whores in yer life." He straightened
his back and cleared his throat. "I was told the fire started in
Mrs. Quinn's room. That she herself had probably started it." At
first he'd been afraid the fire had started because the building
was in disrepair, but, thank God, he'd been absolved of that.
And he couldn't by any stretch of the imagination be held responsible for the woman's death. Yet he felt the need to explain,
to distance himself from the entire sordid catastrophe. "I've been
meaning to sell the house for years, but circumstances . . . I
inherited it, you see, along with several other properties. One
doesn't think about the things one inherits." His excuses meant
nothing to her; they didn't mean anything to him, either.

Shouts and hullabaloo from the street flowed through the open window. He wanted to leave but couldn't seem to get up from the chair. Seemingly oblivious of his presence, Kate lifted the hair from her neck and covered her eyes with her hand. He studied the curve of her arm, the slight rise and fall of her breast. It crossed his mind that she and Lawrence might have made love in this very bed, and he surprised himself by saying, "I'm sorry I didn't acknowledge you when Julia brought you to the house."

"You'd only seen me the one time. I wasn't sure you'd remember."

"I remembered. I thought about you afterward." Thought about, fantasized, lusted after. "But when I saw you in my house, I couldn't, under the circumstances . . ."

"I know. Mollie told me that even if you remembered me, you wouldn't say."

"It was a great shock to come home and find you there."

"It must've been." Her tone was flat, uninterested, without any hint of sarcasm or reproach.

"I was afraid . . ." he began. But he had never for a moment been afraid that she would expose him, had never for a moment considered how she felt. He'd only wanted her out of his house and out of his life.

When Julia had written that Kate had run off, he'd felt nothing but relief and a less than honorable sense of vindication; Julia had gone beyond the bounds of reason in taking her on; somehow Julia had gotten what she'd deserved. At the back of his mind he'd always known that Kate would drift back into prostitution, but he'd imagined her at a safe distance, in New York's Tenderloin or San Francisco's Barbary Coast. Over the past few years he'd stopped thinking about her, yet just a few weeks ago, at a party in Panama, where most of the women were dark-complexioned, he'd seen a girl with the same fair skin and beautiful chestnut hair, and he'd wondered what had become of Kate.

He said, "I just got back from Panama," and, as was usual when he mentioned Panama, everything else was pushed from his mind. He saw the dense jungle, the rotting hulks of machinery the French had abandoned two decades before. He thought about the herculean task of clearing the jungle, hauling the machinery away, beginning again. It would be the greatest engineering feat in human history. The excavated soil would build sixty-three pyramids the size of Cheops! "Have you heard about the plans for the canal?"

She had no idea what he was talking about, but it didn't matter because he seemed to be talking to himself.

"Sometimes," he went on, "when I'm at the site, I imagine Lawrence standing next to me. I remember a letter he wrote the first time he saw the Brooklyn Bridge. 'A great engineer is also a poet. He uses steel and concrete to uplift mankind.' Lawrence wanted to be an engineer."

"Yes. I remember him saying that." That first night they'd made love, when they'd sat cross-legged on the bed, eating bread and cheese.

"He told you?" Somehow he had never imagined them having a conversation.

"Yes. Julia told me, too." She had kept her promise not to ask Sophronia about the Randsomes, but now she couldn't stop herself. "How is Julia?"

"I believe she's in France. I don't know. Julia and I are divorced." She turned and looked at him for the first time, her face so stricken that he added, "You had nothing whatever to do with it. Julia didn't go back to Boston just because of you. She never liked New Orleans. The divorce was inevitable."

"Inevitable?" she repeated as though it were a word she had never heard before.

"Yes. Inevitable." It has taken him several years to come to that conclusion, but now he was convinced: he and Julia had been mismatched from the start. There was nothing he could have done to prevent the dissolution of their marriage. He had never been able to measure up to Julia's standards. Even if he'd taken her part against Carlotta, it wouldn't have made any difference. A man couldn't live with a woman whose very presence was a reproach. "At one time a reconciliation seemed possible, but . . ." His voice trailed off. He stared at the lantern flame. It had been around the time of Julia's father's death that he'd given up on it. By then he'd virtually forgotten that he'd encouraged her to leave. He'd known only that his wife had deserted him and disrupted his life, that when he came home, sorely in need of comfort, he found only chaos and an empty bed. And comfort had been readily at hand in the person of Yvette Liscomb. At the back of his mind he'd known that Yvette would try to exact the highest price, marriage, for what was ostensibly offered for free, but loneliness and the prospect of finally having her had almost overwhelmed that consideration. Strangely, it had been the thought of Julia that had stopped him from dropping the second shoe.

He'd escorted Yvette to the opera. They'd been planning to go to a supper party afterward, but Yvette had said she wasn't feeling well. At her door she'd swooned against him, asking if he would help her to her room. Since her servants were conveniently absent, he'd known that she had made up her mind to go to bed with him. Tight with anticipation, he'd guided her up the stairs, helped her onto a chaise, and kept up the pretense by searching her dressing table for spirits of ammonia.

When he'd turned, she had been stretched out, her chest heaving, the top buttons of her gown undone. He'd dropped the spirits of ammonia and topped her, smothering his face in her bosom, feeling himself get hard. Deftly undoing the rest of her buttons while simultaneously easing off his shoes, he'd heard her whimper, "You've conquered me. I'm helpless against you."

He couldn't tell if she was still play-acting for his benefit or if she'd actually convinced herself that what was about to take place was beyond her control, but as he'd heard his shoe drop, he'd remembered a night long ago, when he and Julia had been in a particularly playful mood; he'd stalked her around the room like a villain in a melodrama, twirling his mustache and growling, "Ah-ha, me pretty, I have you in my power now!"

Julia had backed away, falling on the bed, lisping, "Oh, sir, you've conquered me!"

They'd rolled about, laughing, but as he'd started to enter her, she'd turned serious, putting the flat of her hands against his chest, staring into his eyes, whispering, "I don't want to be conquered. I want to give of my own free will."

Remembering that night, desire had left him. He'd eased his foot back into his shoe, handed an amazed Yvette her spirits of ammonia, and bade her good night.

The incident had made him realize how vulnerable his desire made him. Upon returning to Panama, he'd met a pretty mulatto girl, the niece of an overseer, and had taken her as his mistress. He did not love her, or rather, he loved her only when he was making love to her, which was a marvelous simplification. The fact that he had slipped back into the habits of his forefathers did not cause him great remorse—it was the way of the world, after all—but he had broken his marriage vows. He knew he could never face Julia again. He'd convinced himself that it was all for the best. And now that the divorce was final, he was free to make a more lasting and socially acceptable arrangement. He had already been introduced to a girl from a fine Colombian family. Mercedes Contreras D'Abeyal was doe-eyed and convent-trained, a bright girl with no thoughts beyond fulfilling her obligations as a wife.

"When we're young," he said, coming back to himself and realizing that Kate was there, "we think we can change things, but when we grow older . . ."

A flash of lightning turned the window silver blue, a gust of wind blew into the room. As rain began to fall, he got up to close the window, glancing over his shoulder. In the dim light Kate's face was strained and begging. The child! He'd forgotten to mention the child. He searched his mind for its name—Christine? Isobel? "You needn't worry about the child. Julia has accepted it as her own and taken it with her. She's a very good mother."

And, like any good mother, she'd fought for custody of Angelique. But she'd never had a chance. The courts had only one opinion of wives who deserted their husbands, and Angelique had relieved whatever guilt he'd had by insisting that she wanted to live with Carlotta. "So you needn't worry about"—finally it came to him—"Christabel."

He expected that would comfort her, but she rolled onto her side, wrapped her arms around her breasts, drew up her feet as though a sudden pain had seized her guts, and sobbed, "My baby," then, "Oh, Julia, poor Julia!" Her cry hit him like a hurricane wind, knocking down his flimsy shelter of excuses and rationalizations. He braced his hands on the windowsill and felt the rain drench them. *I am not responsible,* a voice inside him insisted, *not responsible for Julia or this miserable girl.* But another voice said, *You, great man of action, haven't acted at all. Your sins are the coward's sins of hypocrisy, procrastination, and denial.*

He slammed the window shut, shaking water from his hands, demanding, "What happened to the curtains?"

"They're gone. Everything's gone," she sobbed. "Mollie, my baby, Julia, Lawrence."

He moved back to the chair, sat down heavily, and wiped his hands on his pants. "You loved my son."

She uncurled, rolled onto her back, and stared at the ceiling. "He was the finest thing that ever happened in my life."

"What I said about Julia . . ." he began slowly. "It wasn't true. The divorce wasn't inevitable. Only death is inevitable." He put his elbows on his knees and bent forward, hiding his face in his hands. "The truth is, I left Julia long before she left me. I left her alone in her grief, just as I'd always left her alone in her struggles. The strange thing"—his head moved slowly from side to side—"is that when I think of her, I still get angry. It's easy to feel anger at someone when you know you've done them wrong." The rain came down in sheets, lashing the window, drowning out his voice.

"I have a mistress now," he went on after a time. "I bring her trinkets and she pretends not to notice my gray hair. And there's another woman, a girl really. If I marry her, I might have another son. At least I know that she will accept me as I am. I know I will never feel what I felt with Julia. That hope, that yearning toward another soul, that's only for the young." He could see Julia quite clearly, eyes bright, jaw determined, but a crease of uncertainty in her forehead as she raised her arms, wanting him to teach her how to dance. "No doubt about it, we were an unlikely pair." He started to laugh. "I married a Yankee reformer who didn't know how to dance." The laughter stuck in his throat, turning into a great ache. "No one will ever know what we had, what we were really like. Sometimes, when we were alone . . ."

He stopped, embarrassed. He had been baring his soul as he'd never done in a confessional. But Kate didn't seem to have taken it in. She lay still, fingering a little necklace. Feeling his eyes on her, she said, "Lawrence gave me this."

He wanted to take her in his arms but dared not. If he touched her, his impulse to comfort would be tainted with desire. That was his nature. Accepting one's nature wasn't always cowardice. He stood up. "I'm sorry, I must leave." He put on his hat and looked about the room. "Where will you go now?"

"Nowhere. I don't know. This was my home." She bit her lower lip and squeezed her eyes shut. "Oh, Mollie, I buried you without your shoes."

"You can't stay on here. Even if the house was repaired, there's no one to run it."

"I could run it. Mollie taught me how."

"But you're so . . ." He was going to say "young," but that was ridiculous. There was no correlation between this girl's age and her experience. "Is that what you want to do?"

"Yes, but . . ."

It came to him as suddenly as the lightning that had illuminated the window: he could help her and finally rid himself of the property. Make a clean sweep of the whole sorry mess. "I'll sign the house over to you. I'll send the agent around tomorrow. The insurance settlement for the fire will help you to refurbish it. Or you can sell it if you like. Go off somewhere and start a new life. Anything you like, just . . ." Now that he'd made the decision, his desire to be out of the room, the house, the District, never to see or think about any of it again, was so strong that he started to the door.

"You'd give me the house?" she asked, rising up in disbelief.

"That's what I said." He turned back, looked down at her for the last time, put his hand on her head. "I hope life will treat you kindly, Kate. Good-bye."

She lay, stunned, listening to his footsteps, then the rain. She shivered but didn't move. When the storm subsided, she got up, put on her shoes, picked up the lantern, and walked out of the room and down the stairs. Judas sat near the front door, the shotgun across his legs.

"Judas, you know the boardinghouse where Shakespeare lives?" Judas nodded. "Then go there. Wake him up. Tell him to come."

"I can't do that. It's the middle of the night. It's wet out there. And I gotta protect the house."

"Just go," she told him, taking the shotgun. "I'll guard the house. It's going to be my house now." She let out a cry. "My house."

CHAPTER

XX

Legislature voted the District down . . .
Legislature voted the District down . . .
Damned good way to spread the hookers over town.
Tell me how long will I have to wait?
Can I have it now—
Or must I hesitate?

"Hesitation Blues," 1917?

"So what shall it be? Hathaway? Nesbitt? Cavanaugh?" Shakespeare pushed aside the ledgers in which he'd just totaled the week's accounts, folded up his spectacles, and looked over at Kate, who sat at her dressing table taking down her hair. "I fancy Ca-va-naugh. It has a refined, respectable ring to it." He spoke the name slowly, as though he were announcing the arrival of a grand dame at a state ball. "Mrs. Katherine Cavanaugh."

Kate said, "I'm not Mrs. anything."

"If you're going into society, you must be either a man's daughter or a man's wife. You're a bit old to play an unmarried daughter . . ." He studied her reflection in the mirror. With her hair loose, dressed in her peach satin negligee, she was a lovely sight, but her features had a closed-off look that threatened to settle into a permanent hardness.

"I'm only twenty-eight," she said irritably.

"So you'll have to be a wife," he went on, "or, rather, a widow. There's nothing more delectable than a young widow. Now let me see . . . Your late husband, Mr. Cavanaugh—Augustus, we'll call him—has been dead for two years. Being a good woman, you still mourn him. But you are restless. Your heart yearns for a pure and noble love, a man's gentle touch upon your hand, and, given the right inducements, you might be persuaded, might foolishly succumb, to a less gentle touch in more intimate parts of your anatomy. Yes, Mrs. Katherine Cavanaugh. I think it suits."

"I'm too tired to play games," she said, whipping the brush through her hair. "I'm just plain Kate."

Billy sucked in his cheeks and rolled his eyes. "For a girl who was once advertised in the *Blue Book* as a society debutante, I think it very mulish of you to call yourself plain Kate. Besides, a new life requires a new identity."

"A new life," she snorted. "Next you'll be trying to sell me snake oil and telling me I can shed my skin."

"You must shed your skin, Kate. And this is the perfect time to do it. You said that woman from Chicago has offered you a good price on the house. Since the chill wind of reform has already swept through that fair city and she's on the run from the police and desperate to set up shop here, I should think you could drive a hard bargain. With the sale of this house . . ."

"That wouldn't be enough to—"

"Plus your savings and stocks—"

She slammed down the brush. "Billy, go home. The sun's coming up and I'm too tired to play games."

"I only remind you," he said gently, "that you're not getting any younger."

"I've been the youngest madam in the District for ten years. I'm still the youngest madam in the District."

"I do not mean to imply that you are decrepit. Quite the opposite. You are at the height of your beauty. That's why this is the most opportune time to leave."

She got up. "For chrissake, just let me look at the books." She picked up the ledger, running her finger down the columns, turning the pages, muttering, "I'm not paying that laundry woman. She sent back a heap of stained towels. And this new girl, Edna . . . look at this: she only took three customers last night. I thought she was all right, but she's an air walker—so doped up on morphine she falls asleep in the front parlor. I gotta get rid of her. Gotta get rid of Frankie, too. I told her no pets when she moved in, but she's been keeping a little hairless dog up in her room. I didn't mind when it messed on the carpet, but it bit one of the johns the other night. She's gotta go."

"Don't be mean, Kate. She needs the dog. We all need something on which to lavish our affection."

"Bullshit. I just need people who are reliable. This new professor, for instance. He didn't turn up Tuesday night. Dammit, I've gone through three professors since Monkey left. None of 'em can hold a candle to Monkey. When Monkey was here, customers came in just to hear him play."

"If memory serves, it was you who asked him to leave."

"He kept grabbing my ass," she reminded him. "I'm the boss. I couldn't have some damn piano player who was my employee grabbing my ass."

"He couldn't help himself. It wasn't just lust, it was love."

"Love?" she said in a cynical voice.

"Well, admiration coupled with frustrated desire. That's what generally passes for love. You were the only woman he ever wanted that he couldn't have. Why else did he stay on all those years when he could've earned more money elsewhere?"

She slammed the ledger shut. "An' Judas is slowin' down, and Sophronia's talkin' about setting up a restaurant. Christ, if it isn't one thing, it's another!"

"You sound like Mollie."

"Why shouldn't I sound like Mollie?" she asked, pouring a glass of champagne. "I try to give people a square deal and they—"

"I mean you sound like Mollie when you say you don't have enough money to get out. When you first took over, you said you'd be out of the life in five years, then you upped it to seven, now—"

"Shut up, Billy. Just shut up! I told you I've had enough for one night." She took a gulp, realized the champagne was flat, and hurled the glass into the fireplace.

He raised his eyebrows and pulled on his gloves. "And now you're beginning to act like Mollie."

"And what if I did leave? Where would I go? What would I do?" she demanded, staring at the shattered glass. "Besides which, you'd be out of a job."

"It won't be too long before I shuffle off this mortal coil. My needs are simple and I've squirreled away enough to care for them. But you should get out now, Kate. Times have changed. If you read the papers—"

"I read the papers."

"Then you should know," he said coolly, studying his gloves. "A great tidal wave of reform has swept the country. The trusts and monopolies have been broken up, machine politics as we know them will never be the same—that's all to the good—but it won't stop there. Our fellow citizens are going through one of their periodic spasms of self-righteous puritanism. They'll try to reform private morals as well."

"Not in New Orleans," she said. "Never in New Orleans."

"It will take longer, but it will come." He put on his hat and took up his cane. "You've asked me to go and I shall. At least at this hour I shan't encounter any of those damnable street preachers who've been lurking on the outskirts of the District. What a perverse and abominable lot they are! Screaming hellfire and damnation, confessing their sins in public, and licking their crocodile tears with more pleasure than they'd feel when licking a lover's neck." He shook his head and squeezed her shoulder. "Remember what I've said, Kate. Screw your courage to the sticking place. Sell the house and get out."

When he had gone, she sat down at the desk, sorting the night's take, banding the bills, and stuffing them into the canvas bag to take to the bank. "Damn you, Billy," she muttered, but she knew he was right. Business was down. You couldn't open a paper without seeing some lurid, titillating story about white slavery. Congress had just passed the Mann Act, prohibiting transportation of women for immoral purposes. There was even talk of arresting the johns, though she knew that would never happen. She was tired, bone tired, of it all. With money from the sale of the house, combined with her savings and stocks, she could live comfortably into the foreseeable future. But where would she go? What would she do? Except for a journey to Philadelphia with a prizefighter she'd taken briefly as a lover, and a few trips to New York to buy clothes, she hadn't been out of the District in a decade. She felt like a prisoner who'd stared at her cell door for years, but now that it had started magically to swing open, the prospect of leaving seemed more like exile than escape.

"I've gotta make a decision," she said aloud. But she only got up and crawled into bed.

It wasn't until two days later, when she got a call to come and identify the body, that she made up her mind.

"I went down to the St. James Infirmary, to see my baby there, she was laid out on a table. She was so sweet, so cold, so fair. . . ."

There was Bertha, laid out on the table, not sweet or fair as the song lamented, but definitely cold, because they'd fished her body out of the river. "That's her," Kate said, though she couldn't quite believe it. Bertha had threatened to kill herself so many times—whenever Monkey ran off or found himself another woman—that she'd become "Do-Me-In Bertha," a standing joke in the District. But Monkey had always come back, at least long enough to mooch Bertha's meager earnings or brag about his exploits. This time he wasn't coming back. He'd driven off in his fancy new Mercer Raceabout, and word had come through the grapevine that he was making top money playing at the Goldfield Hotel in Baltimore and had married an eighteen-year-old girl.

Kate told them she would pay for the funeral and left. Walking back to the house, she felt more relieved than sad. Bertha couldn't have been more than thirty, but she'd looked fifty. By doing herself in, she'd escaped the worst of it. In a few years drugs, booze, disease, or violence would surely have claimed her, as they'd claimed so many others. Alma Heflin had given up the ghost to cocaine; Gertie Hauser had gone out raving, her mind destroyed by a three-cross case of syphilis; Conchita had died of a botched abortion; Zoe had been beaten to death by a mean-spirited pimp. Even the seemingly invulnerable Vivian Lefevre, who never left her house without a bodyguard, had been gunned down by an unknown assailant in front of Madame Destault's hat shop. (There'd been plenty of suspects, no convictions, and no tears.) Percentagewise, you died young and died bad if you stayed in the District.

When she got back to the house, she made herself a pot of coffee and sat at the kitchen table, watching it get cold.

"I'm late 'cause I went over the French market to see 'bout that li'l café I tolt you 'bout," Sophronia said when she came in. "Don't mean to be runnin' out on you, Kate, but the rent's right an' you know I always wanted to start m' own place."

"You won't be runnin' out on me," Kate said slowly. "I'm leaving, too."

She sold the house to the madam who'd been run out of her place in Chicago, then booked two first-class tickets on the *Lusitania*. Traveling was the answer, not just because she'd always wanted to, but because you could pass yourself off as anything when you traveled. At first Shakespeare said he wouldn't come with her—he was too old, and he didn't want her paying his way—but finally she convinced him that Katherine Cavanaugh was too ladylike to travel alone; she needed her dear old grandfather, William, to protect her.

They set off for New York, where she shed her corset and bought a wardrobe of the latest fashions—hobbled skirts a daring eight inches from the floor. They boarded the ship and were instantly accepted as part of the posh ("port out, starboard home") crowd. They were a charming duo—the still-young but world-weary widow who showed such a touching regard for her aged granddaddy, and the granddaddy who was rigidly protective when a man Kate didn't like was around but conveniently disappeared to his cabin when one she fancied caught her eye. By the time the ship docked in London, they'd collected invitations to country homes and villas.

They toured England, France, and Italy, and Kate confirmed something she'd always suspected: if you seemed rich, you rarely had to pick up the tab. She also discovered that, given the aphrodisiac of free choice and the dance of courtship, she enjoyed taking lovers. But she never kept them for long. Some men accused her of taking pleasure in breaking hearts; she didn't deny it. Her favors were never rewarded with gross cash, but gentlemen staked her at the gambling tables, hotel bills were magically paid, and "tokens of esteem"—rings, watches, earrings—were tucked discreetly into bouquets of flowers.

After two years of wandering around fashionable watering

holes and the less grand but more interesting artists' haunts, she decided that they should go back to America.

Though Billy would never tell his age, she knew he was well into his eighties and he'd had a case of pleurisy the previous winter from which he'd never fully recovered. His mind was still sharp—he could still size up people after three minutes' observation—and when the mood took him, he could still recite his soliloquies, though he now preferred Lear to Hamlet. But his lungs were weak, his eyes rheumy, his legs wobbly. She told him they would go from New York to Florida and that, after a month in the sun, he would be his old self, but she didn't really believe it. She saw the warning sign of his irreversible decline: he, who had always been so fastidious in his grooming, began to neglect his appearance. His hair and beard went uncombed, and he wore the same clothes day after day: tweed plus fours, a Norfolk jacket, and a little hunting cap, the flaps of which he usually kept down, saying that he'd had his life's quota of foolish conversation.

When they walked up the gangplank for the return voyage, he gripped her arm for support. He insisted on climbing to the top deck, and once they'd reached it, he stood, wheezing and shaking, looking out to sea. "I had always hoped to follow Molière's example and die after a performance of *The Imaginary Invalid,* but I believe that being tossed into the briny deep will have a comparable flair." She told him not to be silly.

"Then don't you be silly and spoil my final voyage by being sentimental," he snapped back. "For a queer duck who was born on a Kansas farm, I've had a full and remarkable life. We all have to meet our Maker sometime."

Kate arched her brows. "Meet our Maker? If you're turning religious on me, then I am worried about you."

"Figure of speech, and I grant you, not an eloquent one. I mean . . ." He drew in his breath, flung out his arm, and in a voice that sounded like the wonderful instrument it had once been, boomed, " 'Vex not his ghost. O let him pass! He hates him / That would upon the rack of this rough world / Stretch him out longer.' "

Two young girls, standing some twenty feet away, ducked their heads and stifled their giggles. As Kate gave them a disapproving look, it struck her that Christabel must be about their age. "You can't think of leaving me," she said lightly. "You're all I have in the world."

She watched, pained and helpless, as he was seized by a coughing fit that left him watery-eyed and trembling. He shrugged off her touch, straightened, and pulled down the flaps of his hunting cap. "I believe," he said, "that I shall go to my cabin now. And you had best go about your business and let that gentleman who's been eyeing you ever since we came on board make your acquaintance. Over there, near the signal deck. The one in the sable coat."

He turned casually, as though taking in the deck, then let his eyes rest on the man, who met his gaze and tipped his hat. Turning back to Kate, he said sotto voce, "A gentleman of the Jewish persuasion, if I'm not mistaken. Very prosperous, lonely, and, judging by the eyes, not a bad soul."

The ship's horn signaled departure, and more passengers streamed to the railing. "Now, my dear, take my arm and help me to my cabin," Billy told her. "I'm sure the gentleman will be touched by your demonstration of concern." She was aware of the man's eyes on her as she led Billy to the stairwell.

At the door of his cabin Billy kissed her cheek and said, "Now, off you go and let me rest. I shan't accompany you to dinner. The captain's sure to introduce you, though the gentleman may make his move first. I'd suggest you wear the burgundy crepe. And perhaps the garnets that buffoon in Rome gave you last summer."

She was long past the point of needing Billy's advice, but she'd never let on to it. They were closer than the relatives they pretended to be. They were a matched pair.

As she was opening the door to her suite, the man came up, removed his hat, and said, "Please allow me to introduce myself. I'm Mr. Julius Laveene." He was in his early fifties, jowly, but still robust. His eyes were shrewd but, as Billy had noted, kindly. "I couldn't help but notice that the gentleman . . . ?"

The upward inflection of his voice implied the question, and she saw the relief on his face when she supplied, "My grandfather."

"Your grandfather. Yes. I couldn't help but notice that he's ill. If there's anything I might do to be of assistance . . . ?"

"Mrs. Cavanaugh," she provided. "Mrs. Katherine Cavanaugh." She could tell he wanted to ask about Mr. Cavanaugh but couldn't think of a polite way to do so. "Thank you for your concern, Mr. Laveene. And now, if you'll excuse me . . ."

She found herself seated next to him at dinner and supposed that he'd arranged it with the captain. The other couples at the table, a banker and his wife from Detroit and a newly married English couple on their maiden voyage to the United States, relieved him of the task of asking her questions. When she said that she was a widow, she could see his thoughts as clearly as if they were fish swimming in a bowl. He said that he was a New York furrier, returning from a trip to Russia, where he had gone to buy pelts. When the banker's wife, noting his interest in Kate, asked rather pointedly if there was a Mrs. Laveene, he admitted there was and shot Kate an apologetic look. Because she was so used to operating on a combination of instinct and calculation, she was able to carry on a low-key flirtation while her attention was several tables away—on the young girls who'd been at the railing and now sat with their parents. Their faces were scrubbed, their ribbons in place, their eyes bright with the excitement of being allowed to dine with adults.

"I have no family," she heard herself say. "No one but Billy." Much to Julius's disappointment, she refused an invitation to play cards after the meal and went to Billy's cabin.

He was under the covers, still fully dressed and wearing his hunting cap. His hair was matted to his forehead with sweat, but his hands were icy. He refused to see the ship's doctor or to take any food, but he said he would have some tea if she put it into his special blue teacup. She called the steward, served the tea, then sat beside him, trying to cheer him up by imitating the banker's wife's midwestern twang and Julius Laveene's lovesick looks. "You could do worse than Mr. Laveene," he told her.

"No, Billy. He lives in New York. We need a sunnier climate. We'll go down to Florida and sit in the sun and bake this nasty pleurisy out of you. And when you're better, we might go back to New Orleans and visit the District. Would you like that?"

"I'd like," he said, his eyes tender as a child's, "you to read to me. My mother always read to me when I was going to sleep."

"Anything particular?"

"I've been reading the sonnets. This one, I think." He thumbed through his book, pointed out the page, then eased back onto the pillows. Closing his eyes, he mouthed the words as she read.

> *"Being your slave, what should I do but tend*
> *Upon the hours and times of your desire?*
> *I have no precious time at all to spend,*
> *Nor services to do, till you require. . . ."*

By the time she had reached "So true a fool is love that in your will, / Though you do anything, he thinks no ill," he was snoring. She tucked the covers around him and stood looking down at him. No one else had given her such complete and accepting love. She had no hope that anyone would ever do so again.

The next morning she knocked on his door and, when there was no answer, opened it. He was stretched out on the bed, wearing his best suit, his hair washed and combed, his mustache waxed. She knew he had been dead for only a short time because his eyes did not have a dead man's stare and, when she closed them, his face was still warm to her touch. She put his teacup and his volume of Shakespeare on his chest and called the captain. As they tipped his body over the railing of the ship, Julius Laveene was at her side, steadying her. Three nights later she let him make love to her.

Julius did his best to comfort her by setting her up in an apartment on lower Fifth Avenue. She moved into it on a gusty day in May, when a huge parade of suffragists was scheduled. She and Julius stood at the bay window watching as the phalanx of women on horseback who were leading the parade moved past. She leaned from the window and waved.

"You're not interested in that sort of thing, are you?" he asked.

"I once had a friend . . ." she began. But men did not keep mistresses because they wanted to hear their innermost thoughts. "I'm interested in you, Julius," she amended.

"And I," he said, kissing her neck and turning her from the window, "am in love with you." And, it appeared, he was.

Much to her surprise, the affair lasted for over five years. Julius claimed she was the love of his life and periodically told her that as soon as his children were grown, he would get a divorce. For her part, it was a comfortable and essentially undemanding arrangement: he paid her bills, visited her three times a week, and, whenever possible, took her with him when he traveled. But, finally, his wife got wind of the affair and threatened divorce. His son was furious ("more likely jealous," Julius stormed), his daughter wept about the scandal it would cause, but, Kate suspected, it was his wife's threats to bankrupt him that tipped the scales. Though Kate had grown fond of him, she was not altogether unhappy when it came to an end. Being a kept woman made her restless. She was thirty-five years old and wanted to put down roots, to have a place of her own. As a parting gift, Julius bought her some prize property in Florida. She decided to go down there and see about building a house, but first she would take a side trip to New Orleans. She was packing to go when she got a letter from Lady Caroline.

November 2, 1917

Dear Kate:

I was really looking forward to seeing you again after all these years, but I guess it's not to be. Impossible as it seems, they're closing down the District! The Secretary of the Navy wants to protect the virtue of his sailor boys, if you can feature that! He told Mayor Behrman "to close down the red-light district or the armed forces will." The no-nut city council knuckled under. Gertrude Dix is trying to get an injunction against the shutdown, but I expect the no-nut courts will turn that down, too. The cops came around last week and told all the madams that we have to be out by midnight, November 12. You know how much I've always hated coppers. I got so riled up I hit one of 'em and knocked out his gold tooth. Didn't know I still had the strength in me, but I was pretty tanked up at the time. They threatened to cart me off to the cooler till I reminded them that it was the madams' protection money that had put the gold in their pockets *and* their teeth. But there's no question about it— we have to get out. The insurance companies got wind of a rumor that some of the madams planned to burn down the houses, so they've canceled all the policies.

I tell you, it's like a zoo at feeding time around here. Girls running crazy, not knowing where to go, madams trying to set up shop in other parts of town, some just hightailing it out. There's moving vans clogging the streets and auctions in every house. Countess Willie Piazza had to sell her white piano for a picayune dollar and a quarter! Mabel Kranz is throwing in the towel and going to live with her widowed sister in Joplin. 'Course the District was going downhill even before you left. You were smart to get out. Lena Friedman saw it coming, too. She left for California about six months ago (or did I write you that already?). She has a cousin in the picture business who says Los Angeles is a good place to set up a house. Lena says I should come visit, and maybe I will. My arthritis is getting so bad I can't take this wet weather. Finally got me a white wig, so you can tell I'm growing old gracefully. Ha ha. I tell you, Katie, it's a helluva mess. So don't be coming back now, 'cause we'll all be gone.

Very truly yours,
Lady Caroline

P.S. Remember the good old days when Lulu White had thirty girls and the music played all night long?
P.S.S. If you could spare $500 for old times' sake, it would be much appreciated.

She wrote a check for a thousand and got on a train to Palm Beach. At the Breakers Hotel, she danced, played cards and golf, and let a young man who was heir to a soft-drink fortune think he had seduced her. But since Shakespeare wasn't around to share the plotting, the society game bored her.

She drifted down to the Keys, where the artsy, eccentric style was more to her taste. Still, she was restless. Leisure took more energy than work, and she was a working woman. She bought a ramshackle bar and transformed it into a chic nightclub. She called it The Limehouse. It was fun to play queen bee and be around musicians again. Business was good, but a couple of years later, when Prohibition came in, she put a peephole in the door and made a few payments to the powers that were, and business really boomed. Living just this side of the law gave life an added zest, a feeling that was apparently shared by the public at large. At the invitation of the bootlegger who ran her club's booze across the Gulf, she went down to Havana. *"Cuba libre"* had been the rallying cry that had sent Lawrence off to war; now "Cuba libre" was a cocktail. The mob controlled every brothel, bar, casino, luxury hotel, and politician on the island. After being squired around Varadero Beach, going deep-sea fishing for marlin and barracuda, and visiting the United Fruit Company's polo club, she went off by herself to search for Lawrence's grave. The night she gave up on finding it, she drank herself into unconsciousness. The next morning, after retching into the sink, she looked in the mirror and saw her first gray hair. As she pulled it out, it occurred to her that, unbeknownst to her, she might be a grandmother by now.

When she got back to the States, she hired a detective, and after a few weeks he reported that the Ridgeway house in Boston was currently occupied by a Mr. Jonathan Ridgeway, nephew to Julia Ridgeway Randsome, who still held title. Julia Ridgeway and her daughter Christabel were traveling in Europe. He asked if she wanted him to pursue the investigation, but she decided she'd undertaken it in a weak moment and told him no.

By the time Prohibition was repealed, she'd made a small fortune and her gray hairs were too numerous to pull out. She turned over management of The Limehouse to her maître d', sold the Miami property Julius Laveene had given her to one of Al Capone's lieutenants who wanted to retire to a warm climate, and took herself on a world tour. She saw the sun rise over the Ganges, rode in a rickshaw in Hong Kong, admired the cathedral windows at Chartres. In London she met a banker who wanted to marry her. He was her age (which seemed unaccountably old), widowed, attractive, and wealthy. Marriage, he told her by way of proposal, was a venerable institution; she told him she had no desire to be institutionalized. Respectability meant nothing to her, she was too old to have children, she had her own money. What was the point of marriage? By way of a change, she gave him a parting gift—a portrait, which made her look twenty years younger, painted by the most fashionable artist of the day—and sailed back to America.

She bought another property in Key West and turned all her energies to building a house. She designed plans, hired architects, climbed scaffolding, selected tiles for the pool, bought furniture and statuary, instructed gardeners about the placement of flower beds and shrubbery. When the house was finally finished—a rambling, Spanish-style mansion, named (incongruously but in memory of Mollie) "Dingle Bay"—she began to throw lavish house parties. Guests came from as far away as New York and Havana. At first she took satisfaction in knowing that she had the power to bring all the movers and shakers—society people, hot musicians, businessmen, politicians, ex-gangsters—together, but after a time she found she enjoyed the preparation more than she enjoyed the parties themselves. Often, after the guests were dancing, gambling, or swimming in the pool, she retreated to her room. Sometimes she stayed there for days—reading, sleeping, eating from trays—while the party went on around her. At one particularly large and raucous gathering, she came into her bedroom and found a seminude couple thrashing about on her bed. It suddenly hit her that she wasn't entertaining, she was being invaded. She slipped into her bathroom, showered, and waited until the couple were finished, then handed them their clothes and locked her door. Her days as a famous hostess were over.

She had a high wall built around the property and dismissed her live-in staff. On rare occasions, she had dinner parties for small groups of friends, but mostly she kept to herself.

One late September she woke with the night sweats. Wind whipped the trees and made the windows shudder. She got up and moved, naked, through the halls, switching on the lights. In the library she turned on the radio and heard through crackling static that there was a hurricane watch. She stood stock-still, trying to remember something. She didn't think of herself as a superstitious woman, but something, some presence, was calling her into the garden. The wind swung back the door with a bang as she stepped out onto the patio, rain bit into her flesh like needles, lightning cracked the sky, and for a split second she hoped that it would strike her. Something—not a thought, but knowledge, recognition—passed through her: Julia is dying.

She stumbled back into the house and fastened the doors. Going upstairs to find her robe, she muttered, "You've been alone too long, old girl. You're losing your mind."

She came back downstairs, fixed herself a toddy, put on a stack of jazz records, and listened to Monkey's rendition of "Basin Street" over and over again, till the storm knocked out the electricity. Then she sat in the dark, the storm raging around her, waiting for a plan to take shape.

In the eerie stillness of dawn, as the sky turned mauve-gray, it came to her: she should buy the house on Poydras Street, reclaim it for Julia, make it into Julia's place of honor. Perhaps in some way that was not yet clear to her, she would at last meet Christabel.

She contacted a Mr. Jack Gavier, a New Orleans attorney recommended by one of her Mafia connections, and asked him to make discreet inquiries about the house. He called her back to say that it was owned and occupied by Angelique Randsome and her husband, Leonce Lambre. She said, "Angelique Randsome married Leonce Lambre?" and laughed so long and hard that she could feel him on the other end of the line, wondering what was the matter with her. Resuming her businesslike voice, she asked for details.

"I'm not sure you'd want the property if you saw it," he warned. "It's in a sorry state of disrepair. The family lost their inherited money in the Crash, and Mr. Lambre has no means of employment, but I'm still not sure they would sell. These old Creole families place a high value on tradition."

"Everyone has a price, Mr. Gavier. You make them an offer and get back to me."

Six months later, warning that she was paying too much, he negotiated the purchase without revealing her identity. She remained similarly anonymous when she donated the house to the Women's Society, albeit with instructions that it was to be turned into a museum honoring New Orleanians, particularly Julia Randsome, who had been active in the struggle for women's rights. Mr. Gavier then informed the society that one of his clients was willing to finance most of the restoration, providing Julia Randsome's daughter Christabel gave her blessing and attended the opening of the museum.

After some weeks, word came that Christabel Ridgeway, who was now Mrs. David Witsworth and resided in Washington, D.C., had given the project her enthusiastic support. Kate then wrote to the society's chairman, Mrs. Carrie Bonisett, introducing herself and expressing her interest. Since she enclosed a large check with the letter (and people were seldom rude enough to question you when you were giving them money), no one ever asked how she had heard about the museum or why she wanted to be involved. Mrs. Bonisett wrote to thank her and tell her that, given the dilapidated condition of the house and the fact that building materials were in short supply because of the war, it was impossible to predict when the museum might open.

Later the society hired a Miss Abigail Ashburton to coordinate and supervise the restoration. Miss Ashburton sent her a monthly newsletter and, owing to her special interest (meaning sizable contribution), was often in touch with her personally.

Almost two years to the day after she'd bought the house, Kate was on the train to New Orleans.

And now she sat in her room at the St. Charles Hotel, waiting for the ghosts who had visited her throughout the night to disappear, knowing that in a few short hours she would see her daughter.

CHAPTER

XXI

Our deeds still travel with us from afar,
And what we have been makes us what we are.

George Eliot

*K*ate heard the soft thrump of newspapers being
dropped at the guests' doors and the muffled sounds of a radio.
She supposed her room must be above the kitchen, because the
smell of coffee and bacon mixed with the river smell coming
through the open window. She showered for a long time, turning
the faucets from hot to cold to revive herself, then smoothed
lotion on her body, put pads soaked in witch hazel on her eyes,
brushed her hair, called room service and the concierge. She
took her broad-brimmed hat from its box and unpacked her
clothes. When the concierge came, she gave her her suit to be
pressed. She drank her coffee slowly, pleased that the hotel had
gotten around war rationing and come up with the real stuff, but
found she had no appetite for the *beignets,* eggs, and bacon. She
read the newspaper: there had been a victory in the Battle of the
Coral Sea, the draft age was being lowered from twenty-one to
eighteen, daylight saving time was being instituted. She turned
to the back pages and read the never-ending story of corrupt

Louisiana politics. Had anyone observed her, they would have thought she was languidly calm, but the prospect of meeting Christabel made her heart beat irregularly, and when the telephone rang, pain squeezed her chest.

"Mrs. Cavanaugh? This is Abigail Ashburton. I hope I'm not calling too early."

"Not at all."

"And I hope you're feeling better."

"Much better, thank you. I apologize for abandoning you last night."

"Oh, I took your advice. I stayed and danced and had a fine time. I'm over at the Randsome house, and Christabel's just arrived. We thought perhaps you'd like to come over before the luncheon, and we could show you around."

"Thank you. I'll do my best to be there early."

"I'll look forward to seeing you. Good-bye, Mrs. Cavanaugh."

When the concierge brought up her suit, she started to dress. By the time she'd put on her slip, she had such a case of the jitters that she called down for a hair-of-the-dog prairie oyster. Her hand shook as she downed it. She sat and smoked two cigarettes, then started to put on her makeup. Though she usually painted her face with the same objectivity with which she'd arrange a vase of flowers, she kept stopping and staring into the mirror, searching for answers to questions she couldn't form.

At last she was ready, but she, who knew every mole and hair, who'd made it her life's work to emphasize this and artfully disguise that, didn't know how she looked. She walked away from the mirror, then turned back quickly, hoping to see herself with the same shocked objectivity you had when you caught a reflection in a store window and suddenly realized it was you. She walked slowly toward the mirror. In her pale lemon, broad-brimmed Schiaparelli hat, her white Balenciaga suit, cream-colored gloves, and high heels, she was the picture of an elegant matron *d'un certain âge*. The sort of woman any girl would be proud to call "Mother."

Abigail Ashburton opened the door. "Oh, Mrs. Cavanaugh, I'm so glad it's you." Abigail's red-and-white polka-dot dress was crisp, but her face was already shiny. "I was afraid it might be Mrs. Lambre," she went on. "She's been here every day, dragging in treasures from God knows where, rearranging things the minute I turn my back. And she's already called twice this morning. Forgive me, but I'm a nervous wreck. The caterers have shorted me on the desserts. I'm on the phone with them now, so"—she moved as she spoke, indicating that Kate should follow—"if you could just wait here in the dining room for a sec, I'll finish talking to them and then I'll take you upstairs to meet Christabel."

Four uniformed Negro women were setting the table. "Please," Abigail said to one of them, "put the programs at the head of the plates. And leave that centerpiece on the sideboard. It's too tall to see over. If I have time and I can find some smaller vases, I'll break it up." Her voice was irritable, and she bumped into a chair as she left the room. Kate suspected that Abigail's nervousness about the luncheon might be exacerbated by a hangover.

She introduced herself to the women and walked slowly around the room, glancing up at the portrait of Carlotta Randsome and her parrot. When she reached an open door, she stepped in. The smell of fresh paint dominated, but there was a hint of mustiness, coming, she supposed, from the once yellow, now ocher, velvet draperies. The floors were bare and polished, the furnishings slight—an armoire, a dressing table and chair, a large bed roped off with a silk cord and covered with an embroidered quilt. Several photographs arranged in orderly if unimaginative fashion were on the walls. One in particular caught her eye, and she stepped closer to examine it. It showed a fat old woman with a face so placid that she looked like a Buddha with ringlets. The plaque beneath it read "Beatrice Ravenal. 1824–1902. Clubs and organizations: Daughters of the Confederacy; Beautification Society; Equal Rights Association, founded 1884; Board of Advisers, Newcomb College (first women's institution for higher learning in the South, founded 1886); St. Anna's Asylum for Women and Children. Footnote: In 1878 a woman left $1,000 to St. Anna's Asylum. Because only women, but no men, had witnessed the signing of her will, the bequest was annulled and the money went to the state." Kate had the distinct feeling that she had actually met Beatrice Ravenal, but she knew that couldn't be.

Hearing the click of high heels, she turned and saw a middle-aged woman in a girlish lavender dress, the belt of which was cinched so tight that just looking at it made Kate feel she couldn't draw breath.

"Oh, I am *so* sorry," the woman gasped, clasping hands covered with black net mittens to her breast. "I had no idea anyone was in here." A bunch of silk violets was pinned to the lapel of her dress; another bunch sprouted from her hair, which was various shades of neglected brass; rouge called attention to the little hammocks of flesh that hung beneath her eyes . . . but in spite of it all, it was obvious that she had once been very pretty. "I'm Angelique Randsome Lambre."

"How do you do. I'm Katherine Cavanaugh."

"Oh, Mrs. Cavanaugh, what a delight to meet you!" she gushed. "For a second I thought I recognized you, but we've never met, have we? But the ladies on the committee have told me so much about you. Why, we couldn't have created the museum without your generous support! Do forgive me for walkin' in on you like this." She gave a little laugh and batted her eyes. "I came by early because I felt it was my last chance to be in the house. 'Course I know I can come by whenever I want, but after today the

public"—she made the word sound like an infectious disease—
"will invade, so it won't be the same. I was born here, you see.
Born right upstairs. I lived here all my life till a few years ago.
I even lived here after my marriage because my husband loved
the house as much as I did. My husband, Leonce, is a poet, so
he has that special eye for beauty. He's always said this house
was the crème de la crème. There are bigger houses, of course,
but none of them captures the essence of how we all used to live
better than this one does."

Kate drew in her breath and nodded. Angelique rushed on.
"This was *Maman*'s room. My grandmother. Carlotta de Lesseps
Randsome. You knew her, of course. But gracious, you look so
young, you couldn't possibly have known her! I mean, you know
of her. Everybody does. She was the last of the great ladies.
Have you seen the portrait of her in the dining room? Why,
'course you have. How *silly* of me!" "Silly" had the ring of self-
congratulation. "You had to walk through the dining room to
get here, didn't you?"

"Actually, I knew your mother. Julia."

"Oh. Yes. Mother." She dismissed the reference and plunged
in again, punctuating her sentences with little gasps, as though
drowning in her own stream of words. "Yes, the happiest moments of my life were spent in this room. 'Course, it doesn't bear
any resemblance to the way it was. Miss Ashburton even wanted
to take down those velvet draperies. Well, I s'pose the ability to
see what you should keep and what you should discard has to
be bred in the bone. Look at that quilt she's put on the bed!
Why, *Maman* would as soon lie down in a ditch as sleep under
a cotton quilt! *Maman* always had satin bedspreads, and carpets
all over the floor, and paintings. . . . Right on that wall above
the bed was the loveliest painting. The *Marriage of Venus and
Mars*. We had to sell it after the Crash. Had to sell so many
pretty things. I'm glad *Maman* wasn't alive to see it. 'Course, we

still have some property in the Quarter. New Orleans wouldn't be New Orleans if the Randsomes didn't own property. But when I think of the property Daddy just gave away because he was so civic-minded! I s'pose you've heard I have a little jazz club in the Quarter? It's called Coco Robicheaux—that was *Maman*'s pet name for me. I guess some people think it's not fitting for me to be runnin' a jazz club, but my husband, Leonce, has never enjoyed the best of health, an' bein' as he's so artistic, he's got no head for business, so someone's got to"—she interrupted herself with a fluty, embarrassed laugh—"put croissants on the table."

"I've always admired enterprising women."

"But no woman *wants* to be enterprising, does she? It goes against our nature. Now what was I tellin' you?"

Kate had seldom heard such a nervous spewing forth of personal confidences and jumbled recollection, but, given that she was married to Leonce Lambre, how could the poor woman not be a wreck? "You were telling me about the house," she said softly, hoping Angelique would take the hint to lower her voice and ease her pace.

"Oh, yes. We had some wonderful parties here, 'specially after Daddy went off to live in Panama. He wanted me to come down and live with him, but *Maman* said, 'Robespierre'—that was her parrot's name—'Robespierre might enjoy flitting around the jungle, but it's no place for a young lady,' so I just had to stay with her. Poor Daddy, he dedicated his life to that silly old canal, an' he didn't even live to see it open. Had a heart attack right there at the site. Only thing *Maman* could do to keep her spirits up was to have parties. The year I was crowned Mardi Gras queen, we had five hundred people here! And when I got married! Well, people are still talkin' 'bout my wedding reception. I was just eighteen at the time, but Daddy had died the year before, and *Maman* said, 'We just got to have a man in the house,' and, of course, I'd known Leonce since I was a bitty thing. The Lambres were one of the oldest planter families in the state, and Leonce was a particular friend of my brother, Lawrence, so it was the most natural thing in the world for us to—"

Abigail's voice trumpeted loud and clear as she came into the room. "Ah, there you are, Mrs. Cavanaugh. And Mrs. Lambre, I didn't know you were coming by early. I presume you've already introduced yourselves?"

"Indeed we have. Mrs. Cavanaugh was just asking me about the house. And I want to ask you something, Miss Ashburton: Where's that antique telephone I sent over?" She turned to Kate. "*Maman* abhorred, I mean ab-horred, most modern inventions, but she did love the telephone. I thought we should put it right there on her dressing table, along with the silver brush and comb set. Don't you think that would be an item of interest?"

Abigail looked at her watch and said, "The ladies will be arriving very shortly, so we'd best go upstairs right now, Mrs. Cavanaugh. And, Mrs. Lambre, would you be an angel and check to see that the name cards are in the right places at the table?"

"But I was just telling—"

"I'd appreciate your help so much." She gave Angelique her sweetest smile. Well, Kate thought, Abigail's been in the South long enough to have mastered the manners of diversion and deflection.

As Abigail and Kate left the room, Angelique called, "Don't forget about that telephone, Miss Ashburton."

"That telephone is so bashed up that it belongs on the trash heap," Miss Ashburton muttered under her breath. "And those damned musty curtains are coming down tomorrow morning. This way, Mrs. Cavanaugh."

As they ascended the stairs, Abigail put on her tour-guide voice. "We've turned most of the top floor into a library—books, some diaries, and personal correspondence of prominent women.

Because of the climate we've had to put them in glass cabinets, but scholars who want to use the collection will be able to have access without any red tape. As I wrote you, the third-floor bathroom is so marvelous I didn't want to do anything with it. After the luncheon you must let me show it to you. It's all pink marble and brass fittings, with a tub that would have done a Roman emperor proud. You wouldn't believe it."

Kate remembered sitting in that tub, looking at her swollen belly and crying into the bathwater. "I'm especially proud," Abigail went on, "of the restoration that was done on that window at the top of the stairs. There aren't too many artisans left who do that particular sort of leaded-glass work, but we managed to find one."

Kate was several steps behind her, holding on to the banister so tightly that her knuckles showed through her glove. "And this," Abigail said as they reached the landing, "used to be Julia's room." She knocked, heard a brisk "Please come," and opened the door.

Christabel got up from the desk and came toward them. She was tall, perhaps five feet ten inches, athletically trim but full in the hips. Her hair, thick and reddish (in a flash Kate remembered Frank Staughton's ruddy coloring), was ear-length and parted in the middle, so that its wings swept down to emphasize her wide-set amber eyes. My eyes, Kate thought. Her jaw was a trifle too large (Kate saw her grandfather), her complexion clear but freckle-spattered. She wore no makeup except a fire-engine-red lipstick. Her disregard of fashion—the haircut, flat-heeled shoes, and simple blue shirtwaist—was so complete as to constitute a style in itself. She moved confidently, but when she smiled and thrust out her hand, she had a certain girls'-school manner, direct yet gawky, that made her seem younger than her years. "Mrs. Cavanaugh, it's a great pleasure to meet you."

"I'm very happy to meet you, too, Christabel."

"Please call me Chris."

"Christabel is such a lovely name."

"But so old-fashioned. The only one who calls me Christabel is my husband, and when he does, he's either in a romantic mood or annoyed with me." She continued to hold Kate's hand but turned to Abigail. "Abigail, I could shoot you. You should have told me beforehand that you wanted me to read something from Mother's diaries." She smiled at Kate again, showing a slight gap between her front teeth. "Here I am in Mother's New Orleans house for the first time, all I want to do is snoop around, and Abigail has saddled me with this. And I'm as self-conscious about public speaking as Mother was. I've been poring through her diaries all morning trying to find something that's interesting but not too personal. You know what a deep sense of privacy Mother had." She supposed Mrs. Cavanaugh did know. Abigail had confirmed that Katherine Cavanaugh and Julia had been friends, though she didn't know any details of the relationship.

"I'm sure Mother must've spoken of you, but I honestly don't remember," she continued. "Since you've taken such an active part in creating the museum, I assume you must've been very close. Did you know each other here in New Orleans?"

"Yes. And briefly in Boston."

"You must've been very young when you knew her."

"Yes. Our acquaintance was brief, but she had a very important influence on my life." Kate realized that she was not only holding but gripping Christabel's hand. "Unfortunately," she said, releasing it and stepping back, "we lost touch."

"That was easy enough to do. We traveled so much. We'd lived in Paris, London, and Rome by the time I was eleven, and didn't come back to the States until I was twelve. After that we went back to Europe again."

"I would never have thought that Julia would become an expatriate," Kate said.

"I think it surprised her, too, but once she started traveling, she never stopped. The only place she wouldn't come to was New Orleans. When I found out she'd lived here, I used to beg her to bring me, but she only had negative associations with New Orleans." Christabel winked at Abigail. "Don't worry. I won't say that in front of the ladies."

"Oh, the ladies." Abigail checked her watch. "They'll be arriving any minute. I'll just leave you two alone. Do come down soon."

"I think she's done a marvelous job, don't you?" Christabel asked when Abigail had left. Mrs. Cavanaugh appeared not to have heard her but stared at her with such a curiously fond expression, as though they were dear friends who hadn't seen one another in years, that Christabel felt an unaccountable sense of recognition. How beautiful she must once have been, Christabel thought. What marvelous eyes. But there was something about those eyes, something she couldn't quite put her finger on, that made her feel uneasy. "Were you in the Equal Rights Association with Mother, Mrs. Cavanaugh?"

"If I'm to call you Chris, you must call me Kate."

"All right, then. Kate. You came in from Key West, didn't you?"

"Yes. And you came down from Washington? Is that your home?"

"Well, we're there for the present, but I don't call it home. I'm afraid my adult life has been a continuation of my childhood. My husband, David, is in the foreign service, so we've been posted all over the globe. We were married in Greece— that's where our first two children were born—and then we moved to—"

"You have children?"

"Three. Even the baby's almost grown now."

"Do you have photos of them?"

"Not with me."

"That's too bad."

She was surprised that Mrs. Cavanaugh sounded genuinely disappointed, because she didn't seem the type who'd want to see snapshots of children. "David was lecturing at Oxford when the Nazis invaded Poland, and our eldest son, Lawrence, was just starting university. After Pearl Harbor, we came back to the U.S. Lawrence is in the air force now, and David and the other children and I are living in Georgetown. David's in intelligence, and I'm doing my patriotic bit by teaching foreign languages to OSS trainees. And trying to squeeze in some research at the Smithsonian. One of these days, when the war's over and the children are grown, I hope to write a book about the suffragist movement in the South."

Since Mrs. Cavanaugh didn't seem disposed to give any comparable information about her life, Christabel stepped away and looked around the room. "Let me show you around, at least insofar as I'm able. I suppose you know this was Mother's room. It seems it was never really used after she left. After the divorce Father apparently insisted that it be left undisturbed. I don't suppose the loss of one room meant much in a house this size, though it does give one rather an eerie feeling, doesn't it? To be frank, the whole place gives me an eerie feeling. The city, the house, the Randsomes—they're all a bit too gothic for my tastes. I simply can't imagine Mother living here."

Kate Cavanaugh was still staring at her with that Mona Lisa smile. Christabel walked over to the desk and motioned for her to follow. "Abigail left it up to me to hang these pictures. Mother would've been the last person to have wanted anything like a shrine, but I do think they look nice, don't you? We haven't put up the descriptive plaques yet, but this one . . ." She tapped a photo that showed a group of women and children, all wearing aprons, ranged around a kitchen table. "This was taken at the women's hostel on the rue de Varenne, in Paris during the First World War. That's me—the skinny kid on the end. The woman standing next to me is Edith Wharton. Miss Wharton and Mother were close friends, and when Miss Wharton set up the hostel for women who'd been displaced by the war, Mother helped her. They worked terribly hard, but to me it was just an adventure. I loved rolling bandages and stirring soup and taking care of the younger kids. Since I was brought up as an only child, I've always loved babies. And this one"—she tapped another photo—"was taken in Massachusetts, when Mother was only eleven."

The picture was sepia-toned and age-spotted. It showed a girl bundled in coat, muffler, earmuffs, and knitted hat, standing in a snowbank, clutching the rope of a sled. "I like this one especially, because, even though Mother was young, you can already see her character so clearly. She looks so serious and determined, as though she could see all her life's struggles right there in front of her." Christabel swept back her hair and laughed. "Or maybe I'm reading in too much. Maybe she just looked like that because she was cold."

Kate stepped closer to examine another picture. "And this one?" she asked.

"Oh, yes . . . that's my all-time favorite." It showed a mature Julia, wearing a man's greatcoat and a felt hat, at the wheel of a large, sleek automobile, looking as though she were about to drive a chariot into battle. "Did you know Mother was crazy about automobiles? She said they came along at just the right time in her life, because she was getting too creaky to play sports anymore. That's an early Mercedes. Mother was rather tight about money, but when it came to cars, she had to have the best. She drove that one to the front during the First World War, and she once drove it in a race from Paris to Lyons. Came in second. Oh, she was a real terror behind the wheel. After I'd married, when she was living in this old mouse-ridden villa in Tuscany, we'd visit her and she'd insist on taking us for rides. She'd careen down those dirt roads, scattering dust and chickens, and when the peasants shook their fists at her, she'd just wave. The children loved it, of course, but it used to scare the life out of me."

"Did she always live alone?"

"After I went off to college, yes. When the Fascists took over and she had to leave Italy, David and I wanted her to go back to the States, but she insisted on coming to London because she wanted to be near us. But she wouldn't live with us. She didn't approve of mothers-in-law living with married children, I suppose because she'd had such a terrible time with her own mother-in-law." Christabel shook her head. "She told me that the only person she could never find it in her heart to forgive was her mother-in-law. God only knows what Carlotta did. Mother wouldn't talk about that. I once asked her if she got bored living alone, and she said, 'To say one is bored to be alone is to admit that one has no inner resources.' "

"Yes. That sounds like her." Kate smiled. "Tell me, when did she die?"

"About two and a half years ago. She was well into her eighties, you know, and I saw she wasn't well when she arrived in London. I tried to get her to slow down, but she was in the thick of it just days after she landed, helping some women's organization to evacuate children from the city. She must've had the cancer for some time—I found bottles of painkillers when I went through her things. For a while I was angry that she hadn't told me, though I don't suppose my knowing would have changed anything."

"No," Kate said, "I shouldn't think it could have."

"The last time I saw her . . . we'd had the most awful blitz during the night, and toward dawn, when they sounded the all clear, I went over to her flat to make sure she was all right. It was drizzling rain, but she was sitting in the garden, wearing an old mac over her nightdress. I'd never seen her look so frail. When I asked her what she was doing, she said, 'I've been communing with the souls of people I love,' which was totally unlike her. I told her to go to bed, but she asked me to check her calendar because she thought she had a meeting scheduled for that morning—at that point she couldn't remember things unless she wrote them down. When I came into the kitchen, she was making tea. The last thing I remember her saying was 'I wish we had some *beignets* to eat with this. I grew so fond of them when I lived in New Orleans.' Then she said she had to dress for the meeting and kissed me good-bye. About four o'clock that afternoon the housekeeper called and said she'd been rushed to hospital. She died a few days later."

"And this was . . . ?"

"It'll be three years next October. October sixteenth."

"Communing with the souls she loved," Kate said softly. "Yes, I remember." Seeing Christabel's questioning look, she added, "I think there was a terrible hurricane in Key West that night."

Christabel waited for her to elaborate, then, when she didn't, broke the silence by asking, "Do you have a cigarette?"

Kate nodded, opened her purse, offered the case, took one for herself, and lit them. Christabel looked around. "No ashtray. Well, it is a museum, isn't it?"

"More a museum than a house. That's what Julia always said."

"I suppose it's all right to use this little dish, whatever it is."

"It was used to hold hairpins," Kate told her.

"Shall we sit over there?" They went to the chairs near the windows. After taking a long drag on her cigarette, Christabel said, "I'm not usually this talkative."

"I'm glad you are. I've wanted to know what happened to Julia for a long, long time."

"Tell me, did you know my father at all?"

"I didn't know him well, but I know he was a fine man in many ways."

"I suppose he must've been, for her to marry him. I don't believe she ever recovered from the divorce. She said she was partly responsible, but I can't imagine that she initiated it. Abigail thinks there's a hint in the diaries that she might have had an affair, but I find that hard to believe."

"I shouldn't think she would have."

"Nor do I. You could tell the way she talked about him that Charles Randsome was the one and only love of her life. And she was always a bit rigid about sex."

Her initial unease had completely dissipated. She felt sure that Kate Cavanaugh was the sort of woman to whom she could say anything, and talking gave her a ships-passing-in-the-night intimacy. "Mother was very progressive about explaining the biological aspects of sex, but she was terribly shy about the emotional side. When I was in my early twenties, I went through a wild phase. God knows where I got it from, but I was absolutely man-crazy. It upset her terribly. I remember coming home from college in my flapper outfit. Oh, I thought I was the bee's knees— short hair, short skirts, hip flask, Cupid's-bow lips, lots of mascara. I understand now why she had such a violent reaction. I mean, when she was growing up, only prostitutes wore makeup. More to the point, she was afraid I'd get pregnant and ruin my life. And I was neglecting my studies, and she was adamant that I get a degree and have a career. She said she'd cut me off if I didn't straighten up, and I knew she meant it. I remember her banging her fist on my dressing table and saying, 'We didn't fight for the emancipation of women so the next generation could grow up to be jazz babies!' "

Kate threw back her head and laughed.

"Oh, yes," Christabel went on, her own laughter subsiding, "she was a crusader right up till the last. But she wasn't nearly so righteous about it. She came to a certain acceptance of people's weakness, though she could never forgive her own."

Kate said, "You seem to be a very accepting person yourself."

"Well, life's been a lot easier for me. Many of the things she had to fight for, I simply grew up accepting. And I've been very lucky. I have a good marriage and I also have work. That's what it's all about, isn't it? Love and work. Do you have any children, Kate?"

"It's hard to believe," Kate said quickly, "that you and Angelique come from the same family."

"In point of fact . . ." Christabel moved to the edge of her chair. She wanted to swear Kate to secrecy, but that wasn't necessary; even on this brief association, she felt Kate was someone she could trust. "In point of fact, we don't. I'm adopted. When I was an adolescent, I started to ask questions about my father, and I suppose keeping up the pretense was just too much for Mother's honesty. She told me that I was adopted, but she didn't know anything about my parents. At first I entertained all the usual fantasies—that I'd come from some illicit and perhaps royal liaison. But I doubt I was any duke's or prince's daughter. More than likely I was a foundling. Probably left in one of the settlement houses Mother supported. But you know how wise Mother could be. She turned the mystery into something positive: she told me that because I didn't know anything about my biological parents, I was free to invent myself. Oh, look—" She directed Kate's attention to the window. "The guests are starting to arrive." Several cars had drawn up in the drive, women were getting out, smoothing their skirts, adjusting their hats. Christabel stubbed out her cigarette. "Will you excuse me? I must read over this excerpt from the diary one more time, otherwise I'll stutter."

"I'll go downstairs."

"No, just wait a sec, and we'll go down together. You must know most of the women."

"I don't know any of them."

Christabel thought, fleetingly, that that was strange, but her mind was occupied with more immediate concerns. "Well, wait for me anyway, if you would. I'll just be a sec."

She went over to the desk and picked up a diary. Kate walked about, looking into a glass case that contained letters from Susan B. Anthony, a pair of ivory combs carved with water lilies "Believed to be a gift of Charles Randsome," and notes on an address to the Equal Rights Association concerning women's property rights. She glanced over at Christabel, who sat, elbow on desk, chewing on the end of a pencil, her other hand holding back her hair. When Christabel had first talked about Julia, calling her "Mother" in a way that made her love for her palpable, Kate had felt a twist of jealousy. Now she felt nothing but unalloyed gratitude. Julia had brought up her daughter to be just the sort of woman she would have wanted her to be.

"There," Christabel said, shutting the diary. "I think I have this under control. Shall we go downstairs?"

Kate nodded and moved to the door. As Christabel opened it, she reached up, took Christabel's chin in her hand, and kissed her on the forehead. "It's given me great pleasure to meet you at last."

"I'm not leaving until tomorrow morning. Perhaps we could have a drink together this evening."

"Yes, I'd enjoy that very much."

The foyer was so full of plumage, twitters, and caws of greeting that it seemed like a giant aviary. Abigail moved through the crowd and came to the foot of the stairs, bringing two women in her wake.

"This is Mrs. Carrie Bonisett and Lady Phillipa Dawes, wife of Sir Harry Dawes, though your mother knew her as Phillipa Cotrane. Carrie, Phillipa, this is Julia's daughter, Christabel, and our chief benefactress, Mrs. Katherine Cavanaugh."

Carrie Bonisett was in her sixties and had the look of a woman who'd led a placid, well-cared-for life. Her smile was sweet, her silver hair carefully waved, her navy suit, with fluted white cuffs and collar and matching hat, was expensive and tasteful, and as she greeted Kate and Christabel, her manners were as impeccable as her grooming. Phillipa was older, rail thin and frail, with lavender-rinsed hair poking out from her bottle-green, feathered Eugénie hat and lips so wrinkled that they seemed cobbled together over her tombstone teeth. "I was great friends with your dear, dead mother," she said in a quavering voice, taking Christabel's hand. "What an inspiration she was to all of us. So forward-looking in her attitudes. I always had the greatest admiration for her, and in my own small way, I like to think that I helped to further the cause."

Kate thought, There won't be any women here today who won't claim to have been close friends or to have furthered the cause, no matter what the reality might have been. She lingered long enough to appear polite, but as soon as she saw an opportunity, she moved away.

In the dining room she nodded, smiled, and kept moving, eavesdropping on conversations. They were principally about diets, doctors, and hats. She glanced up at the portrait of Carlotta, who seemed to smile down, confident that the ancien régime was still firmly in place. Which, of course, it was.

Abigail moved around the periphery like a frisky sheepdog, herding, nudging, nipping at the stragglers, until at last they were all seated in front of their cups of fruit cocktail. Christabel and Angelique were at the head of the table, Kate was to their right, with Carrie Bonisett next to her. As Abigail stepped to the lectern, Christabel flashed Kate a commiserating smile, indicating that she, too, would rather be somewhere else.

No sooner had spoons been raised to mouths than Abigail rang a little bell, thanked them all for coming, and explained that since they would all want to tour the house after the meal, the program would begin at once. Angelique muttered, "I don't think it's polite to be talkin' at people while they're eating," but Abigail went on in her crisp Yankee accent, going down the roll call of organizations and individuals "without whose invaluable contributions . . ." When she started to introduce Kate, Kate gave her a warning look, and Abigail kept her praise to a minimum. The fruit cups were removed, the coq au vin served.

"And it's my great pleasure to introduce Julia Randsome's daughters, Angelique Randsome Lambre and Christabel Randsome Witsworth. Mrs. Lambre will speak to us first."

Abigail took her seat and slid her eyes over to Kate with a "Dear God, let her not go on too long" look. But Kate barely listened as Angelique directed the company's attention to Carlotta's portrait and stumbled through her reminiscences.

It was hard for her not to look at Christabel. My daughter . . . my flesh and blood, kept going through her head. And there was another thought, insidious and persistent: Since Christabel already knows she's adopted, why not tell her the whole truth? There was every indication that she would accept it. Christabel was sophisticated and open-minded; she genuinely seemed to like her. There was no reason why they couldn't become friends. She had never understood the universal need to see a continuation of self in the next generation, but suddenly she wanted to meet Christabel's children, her grandchildren. Surely, if she told her the whole story, Christabel could accept. . . .

"Aren't you feeling well?" she heard Carrie Bonisett whisper.

She shook her head and began, mechanically, to cut up her chicken. Glancing around, she saw that the plates were already being removed. "And I know," Angelique gushed, "that Mother, and especially Grandmother, would be de-lighted to see the house restored to some of its former beauty and to see such a gathering of beautiful ladies sitting in this room, which has witnessed so many happy . . ."

When Angelique finally concluded, there was a warm round of applause. Abigail, relieved that Angelique had not stumbled off into a reminiscence of the Mardi Gras ball of 1923 or complaints about antique phones or substitute quilts, joined in the applause, then raised her hand for order. "Now, I'd like to introduce Julia Randsome's younger daughter, Mrs. Christabel Witsworth, who's come all the way from Washington, where she's contributing to the war effort by teaching foreign languages to young men who will soon be joining our allies in Europe." More applause. "Mrs. Witsworth is going to honor us by reading an excerpt from Julia Randsome's journals. Mrs. Witsworth."

Christabel rose to her feet to a smattering of applause. "I'm very appreciative of this opportunity to visit your lovely city for the first time and to be with you today," she began, speaking so softly that a whispered "No, no. I can't possibly have dessert," was heard from the far end of the table.

"I know," she began again, straightening her spine and squaring her shoulders, so that Kate could almost hear Julia commanding her to stand tall, "that some of the older women present today were in the Equal Rights Association with Mother, and I know that this was not always the most hospitable environment for women to be active in such an association."

She picked up a large book with a marbleized cover that looked like an old accounting ledger. "I'd like to read from one of Mother's journals. This was written in the spring of 1912, on the day of what was perhaps the first successful march for women's rights in the city of New York. We were staying with Mother's friend, Jane Carroll. I can remember the day very clearly myself, but I think Mother says it best." She smoothed the spine of the journal. " 'May 4, 1912: I know I shall not forget this day as long as I live. I woke early and was sorry to see that the weather looked dismal. I had had a restless night. There had been a late planning session for the march, and I had eaten only a fish-paste sandwich (which hadn't agreed with me) and some tea the night before. And of course I was anxious about the march.

" 'Since we are guests and I didn't want to disturb the household, I merely splashed my face with cold water, dressed, and went quietly downstairs, telling the maid that I was going for my morning constitutional. I hoped a healthy walk, if such a thing is possible in New York City, would help me to sort out my thoughts. I was still undecided as to whether I should ask Christabel to participate in the march. Like all mothers I want my child to share my convictions and reflect my beliefs, and I want her to play her part, however small, in history; on the other hand, I know that I have created much confusion in my life by wanting others to conform to my way of seeing things, and the furthermost wish from my mind is to raise a replica of myself. After turning it over, I decided that I wouldn't ask her to come. I felt gloomy, because I realized that I myself was participating in the march from a sense of obligation, but with little enthusiasm. I bought a bunch of daffodils on my way back to Jane's house, and that cheered me some.

" 'While we were lunching, Christabel asked how long women had been struggling for the vote. Jane said since before she was born, and Christabel said, "That long? If it's been over fifty years, we'd better speed things up," which caused us all to laugh. Then she said, "Mother, may I ride, too?" It was Mrs. Knoblauch's idea that a cavalry detachment of women should lead the parade. Her husband had been a Rough Rider, and she insisted that it was a good way for us to make our mark. I had not ridden in years, and the prospect of doing so in a public parade made me rather nervous. Jane said they had a horse for Christabel, so I told her she might come. I was touched by her decision, and when we went up to dress, I began to feel more hopeful. I have reached the point where I no longer believe in progress, but I still believe that human perversity can be diminished.

" 'We arrived at the George Washington arch around half-past three. Some of the sillier women insist on calling it the Martha Washington arch, but no matter. I was astonished and uplifted by the turnout. There were great crowds of women, as far as the eye could see, all ages and classes, all dressed in white with purple-and-green sashes. No matter how strong one's character, when one has been scoffed at for one's beliefs, it is a great comfort to be in a throng of like-minded people.

" 'Because the turnout was so much larger than we'd dared hope, there was much confusion and milling about. It was windy, and the women were having trouble with the banners. I was most anxious that we start on time, for I know that those who are against us take anything, even the inability to start punctually, as evidence of our inferiority. At a few minutes after four there were two blasts from the bugle and we mounted our horses. I had to suppress a smile, because Mrs. Knoblauch, who has the characteristics of a musical-comedy general, being short, stout, and perhaps too enamored of command, almost fell off; but I was proud to see my Christabel firm in the saddle. As we started clattering up Fifth Avenue, the sun broke through as if by magic. A little boy dashed into the street yelling "They're coming! They're coming!" The crowds were three and four deep, curious and not unfriendly, which relieved me greatly, since I'd been told that the women had been booed and pelted with eggs the year before. The band, which was marching just behind the cavalry, struck up "Everybody's Doin' It," a popular but, to my mind, rather vulgar song. (I had hoped they would play something more solemn or patriotic.) The crowd started singing the tune, there was a great burst of cheering; some men even waved their hats and called "Go get 'em, girlies" and the like. And women began to chant "The vote! The vote! Give us the vote!" I was bouncing along, the sun in my face, holding on to my hat. I haven't felt so alive, so young, in years. Suddenly, all over again, everything seemed possible.' "

A silence held the room, then Phillipa Cotrane Dawes, tears in her eyes, called, "Bravo, Julia!" and rose to her feet. Other women joined her. Christabel took a swallow of water and sat down, covering her mouth with her hand.

"Thank you so much, Christabel," Abigail said, raising her voice.

The clapping continued, and now it was Christabel who raised her voice and called, "Could we please give a special round of applause to show our appreciation to Miss Abigail Ashburton, whose tireless efforts have made the dream of a women's museum a reality."

The applause continued, but with diminished enthusiasm. Christabel shook Abigail's hand, and a newspaper photographer who'd been lurking in the corner started to snap pictures. Purses were gathered, gloves drawn on, hats adjusted, and the exodus to other rooms began.

"If the ladies on the steering committee could gather at the head of the table," Abigail called. "Mrs. Bonisett, Mrs. Dauveill, Miss Champlian, and, of course, Mrs. Cavanaugh." She looked around. "Where is Mrs. Cavanaugh?"

"She was here a minute ago," Carrie Bonisett said. "Perhaps she just went to the ladies' to freshen up for the photos."

But Kate was already walking down the driveway, past the parked cars and the lounging chauffeurs, her high heels crunching on the gravel. There were thunderheads in the sky, and the air was so still and heavy she felt she couldn't breathe. If there was one thing she'd learned, it was when to leave well enough alone.

What could she offer Christabel except half-truths or a whore's confession? And what girl, no matter how broad-minded, wanted to hear that her mother had run off and deserted her when she was a baby? She had met her daughter. Her daughter was everything she'd wanted her to be. That was enough. Leave well enough alone. What she needed was a taxi, and then a drink.

The band was warming up with a dreamy rendition of "All or Nothing at All." Kate sat at the bar and sipped her cognac. There were few things as comforting as being in a classy hotel bar on a rainy afternoon, sipping cognac and listening to a band warm up. You didn't care what city it was, what time it was, what year it was. But since she'd just changed her plans and made arrangements to be on the seven o'clock train, she asked the bartender.

"Little before five, ma'am," he told her. "Would you like some peanuts?"

She glanced at the three or four habitués nursing their drinks, then at the bandstand. A saxophone player wandered to his place, straightening his bow tie, nodding to his fellows, then eased into the melody as though he were settling into a warm bath. Waiters were putting candles on the tables. A lone couple, clinging to each other with honeymooners' exhaustion, moved on the dance floor.

"Hey, it's rainin' cats and dogs out there." A girl came up next to her and greeted the bartender with a too-bright smile.

"Hey, Doris," the bartender croaked, but he didn't look overly pleased to see her. "The usual?"

The girl shook her head. "Uh-uh. I need somethin' stronger tonight. Wild Turkey straight up." She turned to Kate and added apologetically, " 'Cause I got an awful toothache," then stripped off her rain-soaked jacket. Her breasts were tight against the pink satin blouse, with a rhinestone American flag pinned where the top button should have been. She climbed onto the stool, took a compact from her purse, grimaced as she inspected her face, pulled the scarf from her peroxided hair, and ran a comb through it. Kate recognized her as the blonde who'd put on the show jitterbugging with the sailor the previous night.

"I come here 'most every night," she explained, though Kate had given no indication that she wanted explanation or even conversation. "Because I love to dance. You like to dance? Only time I feel alive is when I'm dancin'."

The bartender put down her drink, and she opened her purse and counted out her money carefully. "I'm Doris," she told Kate, clicking her glass to Kate's and flashing an ingratiating smile. "Here's to dancin'. And victory." She knocked back the Wild Turkey, winced, and touched her jaw. "Ooh, this here tooth like to make me howl out loud. Marty, you got any aspirin?"

The bartender put two tablets on the counter and gave her a look that said, Watch your step. You know you don't belong here. You're bothering a lady who's a hotel guest.

"Ooh." She winced again, and Kate saw that she was in pain.

"Would you like another drink?" she asked.

The girl looked at her with surprised gratitude. "Hey, don't mind if I do. That's awful kind of you. You from out of town?"

Christabel shook her head and hung up the phone.

"You couldn't reach her?" Abigail asked, coming into the library.

"The desk clerk rang the room, but there was no answer."

"Well, she certainly is an enigma." Abigail took off one of her shoes and pulled her stocking away from her foot. "I told you, when I was talking to her at the hotel last night, I just couldn't get a handle on her. But, hey, I guess if you're that rich, you can afford to be eccentric. But to put all that money into the museum and then to walk off like that, that's really strange. You don't suppose it was anything I did, do you? I mean, the luncheon went off all right, didn't it?"

"Yes," Christabel assured her. "It went off extremely well. You're to be congratulated."

"The high point was when you read from Julia's diary. Oh, I wish it hadn't rained and they hadn't all stayed so long. I'm really bushed. Would you like anything to eat?"

"No thanks. If you don't mind, I think I'll go sit in the garden for a while."

"But it's all wet."

"Then I'll just look at it." Christabel walked to the French doors and looked out, putting her head against the glass. It was Kate's eyes that had bothered her from the beginning and all through the luncheon; whenever she'd looked at her, she'd had a strange feeling. Then, just twenty minutes ago, when she'd said good-bye to the last of the ladies and turned back into the hall, she'd caught a glimpse of herself in the mirror, and it had hit her. Kate's eyes hadn't bothered her just because of their expression: it was because they were the same shape and color as her own. It was too bizarre to imagine . . . but there was no denying it. They did look alike. The more she thought about it, the surer she was.

She turned abruptly and walked through the dining room and into the kitchen. Abigail sat, feet propped up on a chair, looking guilty because Christabel had caught her wiping frosting off a plate with her finger. "I'm going to call a taxi, Abigail. I'm going over to the hotel to see her."

"I'll come too."

"No. There's no need. You just stay and rest. It's the St. Charles, isn't it?"

"Yes. You sure you don't want—"

"No thanks, I'd just as soon go alone. I'll telephone if I get held up."

The bar had filled, and Doris, while glancing around, sizing up the prospects, told Kate her life story. She was twenty-one, "twenty-two next October, then I'll really be an old lady." She lived with her mother and two younger sisters and worked the swing shift at the crab-canning factory.

"Sure hope I don't smell like it," she whispered. In fact, she reeked of Evening in Paris. She came here almost every evening and danced until it was time for her to go to work at the factory at midnight. "Unless, well, sometimes . . ." she began.

"Yes, I understand," Kate said quickly. Poor little cow, she thought. No madam to protect her, picking up tricks and not even being sure she'll get paid.

"Would you and your friend like to dance?" There were two young men standing behind them.

"Why, sure," Doris said. "I mean, I would." She hopped off her stool and was led away.

"I'm sorry, but . . ." Kate began. Despite the difference in their ages, the young man looked genuinely disappointed. He was handsome, well built, and clean-cut in his navy uniform. "Well, all right."

"Name's James," he said as he took her arm. "I'm from Michigan."

"And I'm Kate."

"I'm not a very good dancer."

"It's all right, it's a slow one."

The band played "I'll Be Seeing You." She put up her arms. He smiled, and she felt his hand firm on her back. He wasn't much of a dancer, but he held her tight and she swayed with him, acutely aware of his touch and smell. A wave of longing as sweet and powerful as she'd felt at sixteen made her feel stiff and weak. She thought, This may be the last time I ever dance with a man.

The song ended, and the band swung into a boogie. "I'm not up for this," she told him.

He said, "Then let's sit it out." He held her hand as they walked back to the bar. Doris, gyrating, tossing up her hands, called, "Whoopee!" and waved at them.

"May I buy you a drink?" the young man asked. Whether out of desire, loneliness, or maybe just because the lights were so dim, he was looking at her that way.

"Thank you, but no. In fact, I have to catch a train. But thank you for asking." She opened her purse, found two one-hundred-dollar bills, and stuffed them into Doris's purse. "Please say good-bye to my friend for me. Tell her to get her tooth fixed. Good-bye."

"Sorry we have to wait, miss. I'll pull up soon's that old guy in front is finished loading up the luggage."

"It's all right," Christabel said.

They waited while the old taxi driver hoisted a suitcase into the trunk, set a hatbox on top of it, slammed the trunk closed, climbed into the driver's seat, and pulled away.

Minutes later the desk clerk shook his head at Christabel. "I'm terribly sorry, miss. Mrs. Cavanaugh just checked out. Not ten minutes ago."

"I want to go to the train station," Kate told the driver. "But first take me by . . ." She saw his face, wrinkled and brown as a walnut. She wouldn't have to give street names. He would know. "Go on over to where the District used to be. Just drive slow."

The cab crawled along the near-deserted streets. The waning light made everything look even more sorry. The buildings were dilapidated, balconies lopsided with age, shutters hanging loose,

paint faded, windows cracked. Here and there she saw places
that gave her a jolt of recognition—the long line of cribs on
Conti Street, boards nailed diagonally across their sagging doors,
signs that read "No Trespassing Under Penalty of Law, New
Orleans Housing Authority" hammered on the weatherbeaten
wood. Frank Early's saloon, where she'd heard Tony Jackson play
"I've Got the Elgin Movements in My Hips with a Twenty-Year
Guarantee," was still there, and so was the two-story brick building at the corner of Bienville where the *Blue Book* had been
published. Mahogany Hall was standing, though missing its cu-
pola, and the fanlight above the front door was so thick with dirt
you could hardly make out Lulu White's name in the leaded glass.

"Some jazz 'sociation be tryin' to save that," the driver supplied, "but the city got plans to bring it all down. Gonna get us
some kinda housin' projec'. Yes, ma'am, de-mo-lition." Eyeing
her in the rearview mirror, he began to sing,

> *"Gonna make it all nice an' neat,*
> *No mo' whores or dancin' feet,*
> *No mo' booze an' kickin' the gong,*
> *Re-form ev'body who wanna do wrong*
> *De-mo-lition, sad condition,*
> *De-mo-lition blues."*

She saw that her place, Mollie's place, had already been razed.
A little Negro boy pulled a wagon loaded with empty bottles
through the vacant lot past trash cans and an "All Day Parking
10¢" sign. She said, "You can take me to the station."

She got out of the taxi, paid the driver, and told him she was
leaving on track nine. As he started to unload her bags, another
driver came up to him.

"That woman," he said. "I had her yesterday. Sailed in here

like the queen of Sheba. Whole time I was drivin' her 'round I was tryin' to peg her. Then it hit me . . ."

"Yeah. She had me drive her where the District used to be, so I figured . . ."

"Yeah, that's what I figured."

"She's somethin', ain't she?"

"Yeah, she's somethin'. Look at the way she . . ." But she was already lost in the crowd.

It was a great relief to be alone in her compartment, free to sit and think about her beautiful, happy daughter. Soon the conductor would cry " 'Board!" the faces on the platform would disappear, she'd hear the clickety-clack of the wheels, she'd be still, yet in motion. She'd stop in Key West only long enough to pack another bag, then she'd go to Cuba. She knew she could find Lawrence's grave if she really tried. That was the best way now—to be still, yet in motion. The best way to, as Julia had said, commune with the souls of the people she'd loved.